The LIGHT of
ISHRAM

ॐ ◆ ॐ

Nancy K. Harmon

First Edition Printed and bound in USA
ISBN: 978-1-940222-11-0

Cover design by Adam Ritchey
Formatting by Kimberly Pennell

P

Pen-L Publishing
12 West Dickson #4455
Fayetteville, AR 72702
Pen-L.com

Dedication

This book is dedicated to my children, Jason and Brittany. They taught me perseverance, endurance, patience, and love.

Rakell Taznakie pounded on the elf's door loud enough to wake the dead and then ran off, blithering like the imbecile everyone knew him to be.

In fact, the racket *had* woken the dead. That damnable skeleton clan, the one Grig had taken such pains to tuck under the stairway, refused to go back into their closet no matter what he did. "I only keep you thieving blokes about to help with chores," he yelled. "So, do what you're told!"

About the time Grig thought he had the blighters rounded up, Taznakie came back, screeching more gibberish.

"Go away!" The elf launched a searing bolt of blue flame toward the village moron. "Just rewards to you." He shook his fist in the air.

But Grig's aim went astray and his skeleton clan ignited on the spot. They ran hither and yon like torches with legs. He managed to douse the whole lot of them with a shower of conjured rain, but not before they set his beautiful tree house on fire.

"You buggers are useless, no more than a mess of stinking ashes." With a sigh, Grig swept them away in a magical blast of hot air.

He spied Taznakie lurking by the well and shook his fist again. "Thanks to you, I must journey to Grecolix's bone yard straight away to find another clan. You know as well as I the skeletons are the only ones who can enter the Mutant Forest without losing their skins."

Neither did the corrosive vapors of the Nemrak trees affect their nonexistent brains. The long barbs that poisoned humans glanced off the skeletons without effect. "Lucky for them! And it's your fault, Taznakie," he shouted for good measure.

Taznakie blew a raspberry and ran into the woods.

Too irritated to wait for breakfast, Grig donned his leather jerkin with more zeal than necessary, drew his hair back and wrapped it with a thong, grabbed his staff and set out for the bone yard.

"Foul tempered, evil smelling, cantankerous old troll," he grumbled. "Wouldn't you know Grecolix has the only decent pickings within two day's walk?"

The last time Grig had the misfortune to conduct business with Grecolix, the coward had tried to steal the eyeballs right out of his head.

Grecolix specialized in performing thievery on his very own rock-stoop. Eyes were always high on the list of ingredients for the bone yard's patrons. If the supply ran short, the first body, dead or alive, to come along sufficed to replenish his supply.

It had taken all of Grig's stealth and cunning to escape the snare set by the double-crossing troll. A healthy dose of magic conjured at the last possible moment had laid the brute low with a giant headache. No doubt about it, Grecolix would be waiting for him with open arms and deviltry in his minuscule brain and even smaller heart.

❧ 2 ❧

Grig took no notice of the sun peeking over the treetops, nor the birds calling to him as he marched from the village. He'd seen the wall of flowers on his left and the sluggish stream on the right every day of his life, and they held no interest for him that fateful morning. Tallying the eccentricities he wanted in a good skeleton clan on one hand, he failed to see the dark, flapping blackbird of a druid square in his path until it was too late.

Grig had no use for druids, even if they were part of the human race. Nose and eyes smarting from the impact with solid flesh, the elf drew back ready to hurl an oath of disfiguring enchantment when he took stock of the situation.

To his reckoning, he stared the druid in the bellybutton, or maybe a fraction above. Either way, he didn't care for the odds. These men of the cloth were known to strike first and ask questions later, should it please their fancy.

Grig sketched an apology in the air and stepped to one side to allow the black-caped figure to pass. Like a great hulking bird of prey, the druid moved to block the way again. Worse yet, he stared holes right through Grig with strange copper eyes, sending shivers down the elf's spine.

"I beg your indulgence, good druid, but I must pass. I have much to do and the morning flies quickly. A freak accident has robbed me of my clan, and I journey to the nearest bone yard to replace them."

"You have no need of a clan," the druid replied with a soft brogue, never really looking at the elf.

Grig disliked the man on the spot. Temper held in check, he straightened to his full three-and-a-half feet. "Do you presume to tell me my business, you death knell of ruin?"

The druid gave a maddening half smile and a shrug, but said nothing.

A dark cloud formed above Grig's head. Wind whipped about his legs. He crossed himself in the sign of warding.

"Calm yourself, elf," the druid said. He waved his hand in the air and quiet returned. Then he gave that maddening half smile again.

"Where you hail from, I do not know, nor do I care," Grig said. "I ask only that you allow me to pass in peace, lest I be driven to violence we shall both regret. I warn you, you will not be pleased if you incur my wrath."

Those strange, copper eyes continued to stare through the elf. Again Grig squirmed, feeling like an errant child. "Out of my way," he commanded with less bluster. "Time is wasting, blackbird. I do not fancy standing here all day. Out of my way–"

"Theron Raurk," the Druid said.

Grig stared in surprise. "Wha . . . What?"

Taznakie burst upon the scene, yet again. "There he is. I found him and delivered your message."

Not to say that Grig understood a single word.

"Will you pay me?" Taznakie beseeched the druid with outstretched hands.

With a flick of the wrist, Raurk tossed a gold coin to the man. "You did well, Taznakie," the druid said. "Do not stray far. I may require your services another time."

Grig stared, mouth agape. "What did he say? No one, not even his very own mother, understands a word Rakell Taznakie utters."

"I understand him quite well," Raurk said.

The elf flapped his hands in dismissal. "Why in the world did you give him a coin? The village brats will only steal it from him."

Raurk eyed him with disdain. "Do you not pay your servants?"

"Servant?" Grig gawked from Taznakie to the druid.

"Servant," the druid confirmed. "He has performed a task for which I've paid him. I would have it no other way."

Grig shook his head in bewilderment. "I pay my servants, but Taznakie is a fool. He doesn't have the sense to pour piss from a boot with the instructions written on the bottom. Bah! You throw your money away. Better yet, you should toss it upon the fire."

Raurk's eyes crackled. "As would you, should you insist upon purchasing another skeleton clan."

"So you say, druid." Grig moved to turn his back on the man, and then thought better of it.

"You doubt me, but the wisdom of my words will soon become apparent. Our journey is to be long and arduous. Mark my words, Grig Andrious Dothrie, a clanking, gabbling clan of empty-headed cadavers will only be underfoot."

"Never pronounce my given name aloud!" Grig snarled. "Even a funereal specter such as yourself knows better. I would not have my soul besmirched in the mouth of yon fool. He hasn't the wit to keep it to himself."

"I see you are superstitious." Raurk gave an amused smile. "However, I assure you that your given name is safe upon my lips." Raurk bowed low. "Nor shall you suffer injury from the man you name village idiot."

Grig huffed. "Call it superstition if you will, but I call it good sense."

Raurk's eyes seemed to focus on something in the distance. "You, Grig Dothrie, have far more to worry about than yon fool. If you do not proceed upon your journey to Grecolix's bone yard posthaste, a howling pack of banshees will overtake your progress anon. I, for one do not intend to stand here quarrelling while danger approaches."

"I don't hear any banshees." Grig cast a wary glance over his shoulder.

Raurk wrapped his voluminous cape tighter. "Good day to you, sir. I do hope you take my advice and retire from the immediate vicinity at once."

The druid vanished, leaving behind the acrid smell of smoke and something else Grig couldn't identify. He gawked, open mouthed, at the spot where the infuriating stranger had accosted him.

"Bah! He speaks in riddles. First he says I don't need a new clan. Then he says I should hasten to the bone yard? The man's daft. I'd smell a banshee within a league."

❧ 3 ❧

Grig gathered his composure about him like a mantle and set foot upon the path. Before long, he spied Taznakie playing peek-a-boo in the forest. "Be gone with you." He shooed the man away. "Your tomfoolery will wake the dead." A wry laugh escaped his lips at the thought of his incinerated clan leaping and spinning about the tree house as they burned to cinders.

Taznakie startled him from his reverie by bounding onto the path and wind-milling his arms. Then the fool ran into the forest with a final jabbered word.

Grig shook his fist in the air. "If not for you, I wouldn't be making this journey in the first place. I should–"

The blood-curdling scream of a banshee shredded the calm morning air. All hopes of a peaceful pilgrimage fled with the final dying complaint of the she-demons.

"Damn, damn and double damn! That blasted blackbird has cursed me with his foretelling."

Grig jumped at a sharp tug upon his sleeve. "Get away from me."

Taznakie yanked all that much harder and pointed back up the trail. The elf swatted at his tormentor as if he were a giant gnat trying to fly up his nose. "Take your hands off me, rogue! No one lays hands upon my person without due retribution."

The nervous caterwauling of the banshees drifted closer with his every word. Grig's scalp crawled in direct proportion to their imminent arrival. The she-demons had a penchant for fresh meat. It mattered little whether it be man or elf, as long as it still quivered.

A quick glance over his shoulder persuaded Grig to settle his differences with Taznakie at a later date. "Out of my way, fool!"

Taznakie plucked at Grig's sleeve one last time, and then ran off the path into the deep woods.

"You'll get us both killed," Grig cried. "You can't outrun them that way."

A glimpse of the first banshee, wild white hair streaming behind her, stilled his protests. With a headlong leap, he followed the simpleton into the thicket of gnarled underbrush. Grig rolled to his feet and wasted no further time making his escape.

"Druid, this is all your doing," he muttered.

Brambles and thorns tore at his pants. A huge Jusong vine snaked from hiding to wrap around his ankle with bloodthirsty barbs. He pitched forward and sprawled flat upon his face.

At least three of the screaming creatures followed him off the path. They had the advantage of floating a hand span above the ground. The monsters experienced none of the hazards suffered by mortals. To make affairs worse, the blasted wenches wouldn't stop their infernal screaming.

Grig swore that banshees screamed in place of breathing. The Old Ones claimed banshees were women driven mad by the rejection of their lovers, thus all banshees screamed. They screamed about this and that and just about anything else a body could imagine. He'd never seen one yet whose mouth didn't extend in a terrible mockery of a human cry unless the creature had expired.

Not that death appeared to be an immediate option. The shrews breathed down his neck as he lay sprawled in the thicket. The warmth of the morning sun dwindled as they hovered above his defenseless back. Grig steeled himself for death as a she-demon sliced the bonds of the Jusong vine with three-inch long talons.

"On your feet, Grig Dothrie," Theron Raurk commanded. He yanked Grig up by the scruff of his neck. "It's most unwise to lie here while your life is in danger."

"Where'd you come from?" Grig's mouth hung open in shock. "You scared me half to death."

"Taznakie did his utmost to lead you to safety. Why did you not take heed of his directions? I have no time for this insanity. There are wars to wage, battles to be won."

"You fluttering blackbird of death!" yelled Grig. "This is your fault.

I was content to mind my own business until you came along."

"A necessary inconvenience," Raurk answered with a shrug.

"I can save myself as well as the next man." Grig cast about for the banshees. "They're gone. I don't need your help."

Raurk's words dripped with acid. "Those she-demons will not go far before they realize they've lost your succulent aroma. I give them little to no time before they return to pick up your trail. Perhaps this would be a good time to extricate yourself from this quandary."

"Damn," the elf groaned.

"Should you prefer, I shall return you to your former dilemma. For selfish reasons, I do not suggest it. It's not easy to find a hero such as yourself."

"I'm not a hero," Grig muttered, brushing debris from his jerkin.

An abrupt gesture from the druid cut him short. "They return. Go or stay? Make up your mind, Grig Dothrie. We have not a moment to waste."

The pack of shrieking banshees swept over the tangled undergrowth a mere stone's throw away and closed in. The elf managed a quick nod before Raurk swept him away in a thick cloud of reeking, phosphoric fumes. Hacking and coughing, Grig spat, "You miserable, son of a . . . son of a . . . I ought to stake you naked in the Mutant Forest. I'll grind your eyeballs to pulp. Smear Nemrak juice over your – over your – well, you know where. Don't ever lay a hand on me again, blackbird!"

❧ 4 ❧

"*Arise*, Master Grig," Raurk commanded with an amused smirk. "The day grows short while you take your leave. I can't believe you'd dawdle like a schoolgirl until the sun surrenders to night. Have I so misjudged you? Are you not worthy of this mission?"

"Where are we?" Grig fingered a nasty lump over his right eye. "I know nothing of this insane quest of yours. All I want is to return home in due haste." He swiveled about to locate the druid. His head threatened to explode were he not careful. "Was that necessary? Would not a less grandiose departure have sufficed?"

Raurk smiled at the elf's obvious discomfort. He shook his head with maddening deliberation.

"No. 'Tis imperative to leave a lasting impression upon one's enemies. Those she-devils will long remember the day they tangled with Theron Raurk of the Druid Council. I'm pleased to announce that more than one of their numbers should be nursing a mild injury or three. They are loathsome creatures at best. I can't abide their presence."

"You can't abide their presence," Grig mimicked. "You go flitting about the countryside wrecking havoc, and then have the gall to say you can't abide their presence. Why, I should—"

"Should what?" Raurk pinned him with an icy stare. "I do believe I'm the one who saved your miserable, complaining hide, and without a major mishap at that."

"That's easy for you to say, blackbird!" snarled Grig. "You're not the one courting a melon-sized headache. Until you came along, I enjoyed an orderly existence. I had my beautiful home in one of the oldest Burnet trees alive, a skeleton crew that wasn't incinerated, and best of all, *peace*."

"An unfortunate mishap," Raurk said.

"What's more, I don't need your assistance in acquiring a new clan, now or ever. It's your fault I'm forced to make this expedition in the first place. Be gone with you, blackbird, so I may continue my journey."

"Journey to where?" Theron Raurk gave an exaggerated shrug.

Grig couldn't believe his ears. "To the bone yard of Grecolix. You mentioned that very fact when we first did meet. Or does your memory fail you, druid?" This time Grig's words dripped with sarcasm.

"Nay, my memory is in perfect order," Raurk answered. "'Tis your mental capacity I doubt. We stand amidst the most fertile grounds on the troll's land. Where is it you would journey if not here?"

"To your very own funeral, were it a possibility," Grig said between clinched teeth. "Could you not simply tell me you had whisked me away on winged feet to my destination? You, druid, are a menace to humanity."

"And fortunate for you, Master Grig, my funeral is not an option." He gave the elf an inscrutable smile. "There's not another man in all the known worlds who could guide you through the next few weeks. Our quest will be more arduous than you can imagine."

"What quest?"

"Soon I'll explain all," Raurk answered. "For now, shall we address the business at hand? I do believe you will have fruitful pickings in this direction." He waved a shrouded arm toward the eastern horizon. "Somewhere in this vicinity, the air-pirate, Magried Whittlebottom, rests. He will serve our purposes quite well."

Grig stared mouth agape. "All I want is to replace my clan and return home. I have no need for a pirate, nor any other scalawag of the airwaves."

"Things have changed," Raurk said.

Grig shook his head. "I lead a quiet elf's existence and I like it that way. The village depends upon me to keep affairs running smoothly. I can't leave them. No, that is out of the question." In a huff, he turned his back to the druid.

Raurk enunciated every word with care. "Grig Dothrie, were the sky to fall upon your empty head, would you ignore it? Should the River Gandu change course to flow through your beloved tree house, would you turn a blind eye? Would you disappoint those same people of your village of whom you speak? There will be no village to which you may return unless we prevail in our mission."

"I refuse to believe such rubbish, blackbird."

Raurk appeared unruffled. "We have faced danger once today and escaped unharmed. You might as well get accustomed to it. We have only begun our adventure. I have spoken, elf."

"What if I refuse?"

The druid's eyes flashed. "It's for you to make up your mind. I can't do it for you. I must add that you should be quick about it. Our friend, Taznakie, grows impatient with waiting."

The elf turned to face Theron Raurk. Anger and bewilderment warred in his mind. For the first time, Grig allowed his eyes to stray past the tall, gloomy figure of the druid. To his wonder, he spied Taznakie dancing from foot to foot in an odd sort of jig. With one calloused hand, the man pointed at something in the distance, gibbering nonstop.

Grig, sighed under his breath. "Maker, what next?"

"Close your mouth, Master Grig," Raurk commanded. "You gather flies. 'Tis a most unpleasant habit."

Moving to stand nose to nose, or more like nose to belly button, the elf punctuated his words with a sharp jab of a finger to the other's chest. "Who you are and from whence you came, I do not know. Nor, do I care!"

"You've said that before."

"My life has been ordered and sane until you showed up. I much prefer it that way. With any luck, it will remain downright boring for the next thousand years. Take your simpleton and your riddles and be gone with you, druid."

Grig whirled about and tripped over a twisted hunk of steel. Definitely not the impression he wanted to make. "Who put that blasted thing there?" Although, he knew the answer before the words had escaped his lips.

Raurk sat himself upon a large boulder, leveling his gaze with the elf. "I confess, Master Grig. I can't allow you to leave. You're my only choice to rescue the stolen Light of Ishram. Even your magic and cunning may be insufficient to complete our labors."

"Then choose another."

"There are no others. I can count on one hand those with enough magic to fill a thimble." Raurk raised his hand with three fingers extended. "Sadly, three of them have already failed and gone to their next lives."

Grig eyed the other with cold anger. "You speak in riddles, man. Straight out, *who* are you?"

"I come from long ago. Or today. Or tomorrow as you would have it." Raurk's mind appeared to wander. "Some call me father, others simply Theron Raurk." He sighed again. "I fear you will name me far worse before we recover the treasure."

Grig gasped. "*You* are *the* Theron Raurk of the Druid Council? Why did you not tell me?"

Those strange, copper eyes misted momentarily. "I did. More than once. However, you refused to hear me. Come, let's find the pirate Whittlebottom. He has waited centuries for his release."

Grig slumped to the rock beside the druid. Staring at his toes, he asked in a soft voice, "Why should I require the services of said pirate? Would not an army of skeletons fulfill your purposes more fittingly? Why not a fleet of pirates and legions of soldiers? To where do we venture, blackbird? Tell me more of this stolen treasure. If I'm going to risk my neck, I would know why."

❧ 5 ❧

Raurk rubbed his short beard, seeming to stall. He delivered each word with grave care. "There's a far off land called Eden, ruled by the black witch, Urania Braith. It will take us long weeks to journey there under the best of circumstances."

"Why don't you just whisk us away from here as you did before? Or is that beyond your means?"

"Surely, my good elf, you know I can't do that. Your frail physique would never withstand the strain of another such escape.

"I guarantee Urania will do everything in her power to stop us. She is a jealous mistress and hoards the treasure for its magical powers. Though she can't use it, she will not relinquish the Light. For four thousand seven hundred thirty-one years she has crushed every army foolish enough to defy her."

Grig Dothrie squawked, "Four thousand . . ."

"Plus seven hundred thirty-one years and fourteen days, should you care to know," the druid added.

"Why not let it go if she can't use it?"

Raurk scanned the horizon. "The stakes are too high."

"What will you do with it when . . . if we succeed?" Grig asked.

"I will restore it to its proper place."

"What is this treasure?" Grig tried to stare into Raurk's eyes, but had to look away.

"The Light of Ishram is a book," Raurk said.

"A book?" Grig gawked in disbelief. "You'd risk our lives for a book? You're daft, man."

Raurk shook his head and looked away. "It's the last one in existence. Without it, mankind is doomed, as evidenced by the Thousand Years War."

"Bah! No book is that important."

Raurk rose to his feet. "Lord Hyperion Ishram fought his entire life to defend the Light. In turn, it endowed him with strength and wisdom. Urania would use it to destroy all the known worlds."

"Wait." Grig placed a hand on Raurk's sleeve, and then quickly withdrew it. "If three others have already failed, what makes you think I'll succeed?"

"The time is right." Raurk returned his gaze to the elf. Then, he deliberately turned his eyes toward Taznakie. "And the right combination of talent has at last presented itself."

The bored simpleton squatted upon his heels picking at a large wart upon his left thumb. When he realized the others watched him, he waved at the pair with a slobbery grin upon his face. Theron Raurk returned questioning eyes to Grig, waiting for the elf to speak.

Grig moaned, holding his head in his hands. "What does Taznakie have to do with this insane mission? I wouldn't give him the time of day for fear he'd lose it. I have yet to hear him utter a sane word and I have known him his entire life."

"Bah!" Raurk spat. "His words are as sane as yours or mine. He holds one of the keys to our predicament. History has slumbered until the proper circumstances aligned with the stars. Thirty-one years ago a spell of confusion blemished Taznakie's birth. To his misfortune, this curse renders him senseless to his peers."

"But you understand him."

"I do." Raurk nodded with a sigh. "Urania Braith vowed to destroy mankind the very day Taznakie graced this world. She will stop at nothing to destroy him because his soul is innocent enough to unlock the treasure while she can't. With his help, we will recover the Light of Ishram."

Grig shuddered. "Blackbird, you jest." He could imagine himself and an army of ten thousand marching against Urania. Or a cadre of skilled elves pitting their magical powers in battle, or . . . or just about anything else. For the three of them, one of those a simpleton, to confront a powerful witch . . . . What could he say?

"No, no, no!" Grig threw both hands in the air. "I won't do it! I have more respect for my miserable hide than that."

Raurk waved him to silence. "Keep your voice down, Grecolix

sleeps past yon hillock. Would you bring the troll down upon our heads? Our lives would be complicated tenfold should we find it necessary to explain our presence among his most prized pickings."

"Do you suggest we steal from Grecolix?" Grig's jaw dropped.

"Borrow," countered Raurk with a gleam in his eyes. "He would never sell the bones of Magried Whittlebottom. Why else do you think such a valuable skeleton hasn't been raised from the grave? It's best we avoid interference from the worrisome bore."

"I give up," Grig said. "A druid who is a thief, a skeleton pirate, and the village idiot, I name my partners. We are lost before we even start. Raven, you bring me naught but ill tidings."

For the first time, Raurk laughed. "It's about time you see it my way, Master Grig. I despaired you would ever come around. My maps tell me this is where we shall unearth the final partner in our quest." He gestured to a particularly grassy loam to the right of where they stood.

A loud groan of resignation escaped Grig's lips. "Should we succeed in this mission, I promise you, Theron Raurk, I'll haunt your dreams forever."

Almost jovial, at least for a druid, Raurk clapped him on the back. "*That* is the least of my worries, Master Grig. Will you say the spell of finding, or shall I? Better yet, let's ask Taznakie to do the honors."

Jumping to his feet, Grig turned his back to the gloomy druid. "You may do whatever you feel is necessary. Call me when you find your blasted pirate. With Taznakie garbling the spell, no telling whom we shall wind up with. Be it known this is not my idea of a replacement for my clan."

Unperturbed, Raurk approached the simpleton. With a few words and gestures, he explained the task at hand.

Taznakie beamed with pride and unbounded enthusiasm. Grig thought he might fracture his face with such a sappy grin. "Does he even know the words of finding?"

"That he does. Many a time I've witnessed Taznakie rouse a skeleton or two."

"I don't believe you."

"He keeps his secret well. He could not pay for a skeleton even if Grecolix understood what he wanted . . . and neither could you."

❧ 6 ❧

Feigning indifference, the elf watched Taznakie. "Damn that blackbird," he muttered. "He'll get us all killed, and for what? A book nobody has ever seen."

Grig's curiosity grew in spite of his acerbic mumblings. Taznakie had the brains of a rock, yet the man went through the motions of calling the dead without a hitch.

The words were inaudible, but Grig had an uncomfortable feeling that before long, the deceased pirate, Magried Whittlebottom, would stand before them.

"This is a fool's mission," he scoffed. Yet, he could not tear his gaze from Taznakie.

"What do you think?" Raurk asked, startling the elf out of another ten years.

"Damn you, blackbird! Don't sneak up on me like that. Next time, I might blast you to cinders before I realize who accosts me."

Raurk clucked. "Master Grig, I'll keep that in mind. Although I doubt you can do me harm of any consequence. Again, I ask, what do you think?"

Grig sneered. "No telling what he's saying. Can the dead understand him any better than the living? We may wind up with a pack of ill-tempered leprechauns for all you know."

"Listen carefully," Raurk said. "You understand more than you allow."

"Says you." Still, Grig couldn't help tuning his ears to the familiar words of calling.

One by one, they became intelligible as he truly listened.

"Servants of the nether world, hear my command.

I am the Master whom you must obey.

I search this day for the one, Magried Whittlebottom.
Present yourself for my inspection.
I would judge you worthy of resurrection."

When nothing happened, Grig turned a satisfied smirk to the druid. "Perhaps you should do it yourself. It appears the pirate doesn't understand gibberish."

Raurk wagged his head. "Give him time, elf. The man died more than ten thousand years ago. He has a far journey. Give him time."

Grig shrugged. "I don't have all the time in the world, blackbird. I'll give him the quarter of the hour and that's all. Then, you'll be obliged to get out of my way."

"A fair bargain," Raurk agreed.

"Your insanity has consumed most of the day as it is. Don't expect me to humor you further."

The druid smiled. "There's no need to humor me, Master Grig, for our Magried Whittlebottom approaches yonder." Arm extended, black cloak flapping in an eerie likeness to an enormous ravening blackbird, Theron Raurk directed the elf's attention to the brewing disturbance on the horizon. "What do you say to that?"

❧ 7 ❧

Grig stared mouth agape at the bizarre spectacle swooping down upon them. A wraithlike ship bobbed upon the airwaves, then light as a snowflake it settled to the uneven earth in front of them. The hull of the pirate ship never quite touched solid loam.

A mass of crackling, filthy sails snapped in an unfelt breeze, ripping the peace from the deteriorating afternoon. The last vestiges of the sun cast a lurid silhouette across the elf's face.

"Maker, preserve us," Grig intoned. A hair-raising premonition swept through his soul. "This will be the death of all of us. I want nothing to do with this foul specter. He's bad luck waiting to happen."

"Nay, 'tis a lie, goodly elf," a booming, rasping cry rose above the crackling of the sails. "My boys and I have waited long for the call of Rakell Taznakie. Fortunate is the day indeed. We are hale and hearty, and ready to serve you." He looked from one man to the next. "When do we start?"

Grig drew back as the pirate leapt nimbly to the ground at his feet. Sword in hand, the skeleton clanked and clattered about the small party. "Master Taznakie, a superb job of calling the dead." Whittlebottom swept the moldy, once plumed tri-corn from his head in a low, sweeping bow before the village idiot. "In ten thousand years I have never heard your match. And I have witnessed many a resurrection in my time."

Taznakie beamed at the compliment, resembling a radioactive torch in the gloaming of the late twilight sun. Scuffing a dirty toe at the ground, he mumbled something unintelligible.

Raurk said, "Taznakie thanks you, Magried Whittlebottom. He says he has practiced his entire life for this very moment. It's with the utmost pride he has summoned you from the grave to join our ranks.

"I am Theron Raurk and the elf is Grig Dothrie. We will be accompanying you upon our journey."

The pirate moved to stand in front of each man as he was introduced. Without warning, he stooped to peer into Grig's eyes. "You are a mite short even for an elf, are you not guv'nor? No disrespect intended, but I don't reckon you'd even come up to my bellybutton. That is, if I had a bellybutton."

Grig bristled at the insult, but held his tongue.

"Not that I'm any judge of you little people. In my time there weren't any of your kind. I've watched from my grave in hopes of some day coming face to face with one of your lofty breeding."

Angry, flashing eyes accentuated the calm of Grig's words. "Out of my face, you reeking scalawag. I'll teach you to respect the elves of this world. I'm but one of many with enough magic to blow your miserable carcass from here to eternity. Don't push me, or I shall do exactly that."

"Pardon me, guv'nor." Whittlebottom held up both hands. "I meant no disrespect."

"Your kind's fear and prejudice nearly brought our world to extinction. Do not rekindle the hatred once again."

"Nay, guv'nor." The pirate fended an imaginary blow. "I offer a thousand apologies, good elf. I but expressed my surprise. I have been indisposed for much too long. It's with a glad heart that I welcome this day."

"I'm happy somebody does," Grig muttered.

"Excuse me, guv'nor, I think we'd best move on. My mates tell me an extremely unattractive specimen of a troll approaches from the north. If I'm not mistaken, 'tis the unsavory proprietor of this bone yard. Not that he has any rights to my remains. My family buried me here long before that bumbling lout had the misfortune of gracing this world."

"Hush," commanded Raurk. "Take your ship and crew and meet us the day after tomorrow at the big rock slope facing Cranitaur Valley. Beware the dragon, Isis. She molts this time of year and does not take kindly to strangers. She expects us, but has little tolerance for the likes of you and your men."

"Away with us then," the pirate shouted, happy to be in the fresh air again after so long an abstinence. He leaped to the deck of his ship and shouted orders. At the last moment, he leaned over the balustrade. "I bid you adieu, gentlemen."

∂ 8 ∽

Cloe spied the intruders by chance as he soared over the troll's vast holdings. With his sharp crow eyes, he discerned that one of the men, in fact the only sane appearing one, wore the black garb of a druid. To his surprise, an elf stood at the druid's side. A piddling, sniveling elf.

Slightly apart from these two stood a third. And by the looks of him, he played with a few extra jokers in his deck. Anyone stupid enough to hop around Grecolix's bone yard on one foot while picking his nose deserved whatever the troll dealt him. "Grecolix will pulverize every one of them," he cawed.

The clincher came when the idiot waved his arms in petition and recited the words of calling. Cloe was not too bright, but he recognized an opportunity when he saw it. It would take very little to goad his master into impetuous, hopefully even fatal, action. The gods should so bless him.

Cloe hated the troll with a passion but, thanks to his mother's bungled spell, he must spend the remainder of his life as the oaf's familiar. She could have made him a hawk, an eagle or some other majestic denizen of the skies, but nooooo, not her.

Too stupid to acquire a familiar in the normal manner, Grecolix bought Cloe for the span of a thousand years. "Oh, the shame of it all," Cloe whispered for his own ears. "I shall never live it down. Never, ever," he wept. "I shall be dead in my grave long before I regain even the slightest shard of decency."

He screeched in anticipated triumph as he left the visitors behind and winged straight away to his master. Anyone stealing from Grecolix had damn well better be quick about it lest the troll make fertilizer of their bones. A little embellishing here and there should clinch the matter. To his good fortune, these three seemed in no hurry.

How he hated to call Grecolix master. This once, he could make an exception should it bring about the desired results. With any luck, the lout would meet his death in the druid. Cloe giggled in a very un-birdlike manner.

Giddy with the possibilities, he recounted his discovery to the stinking, blundering troll.

"Master," he mewled in a rather impressive resemblance of devotion. "Three men pilfer from your bone yard. Come, I'll show you the way. They've raised one of your treasured dead, Magried Whittle-bottom. You can't possibly allow them to get away with such disrespect." Chloe hoped this would goad Grecolix into a blind rage.

From past experience, Cloe knew the greedy Grecolix would see stars. Bright, blaring, beacons of red fury would consume the troll's tiny brain. Cloe laughed when Grecolix could barely utter the words of challenge.

Unfortunately, Grecolix grabbed the crow about its vermin-infested neck and all but shook the life from him. All before Cloe could divulge the whereabouts of the intruders.

"Trespassers," Grecolix roared to the heavens. "Raurk. Theron Raurk. It has to be Raurk," he deplored in a rock-gravel falsetto.

It seemed for once, Grecolix had put two and two together and not come up with five. In his heart, which was considerably smaller than his brain, he knew the druid had at last made good his threats. The blackguard had returned for Magried Whittlebottom. "We'll see about that," Grecolix bellowed.

The troll surged to his feet and stood over the ruined chaos of his evening meal. "I'm going . . ." He scratched his head in confusion. "Where was I going?"

"Raurk," Cloe gasped.

"Oh." Grecolix stormed from the bone and mud-wattle hovel he called home, murder written in his beady, coal-button eyes. "Fly," he told the breathless crow.

Cloe flapped and kicked at the gnarled, stumpy fingers still tight about his neck. As of yet, the urge to release him hadn't penetrated Grecolix's pea brain.

Thunderstruck, the monster stared at the wheezing, near lifeless bird dangling before his eyes. "Stupid crow," he barked. "Fly away." Still, he made no move to release his prisoner.

"Umph, umph." It took most of the precious air Cloe managed to inhale to utter that much. "Eck, eck," he tried, nearly swooning. Grecolix gaped at him with his mouth slack, spittle threatening to cascade down his multiple chins.

All at once, the tide must have come in. The troll looked at the disheveled bird, then at the sky, and back at Cloe. "Ugh," he muttered. "Fly," he commanded and flung the oxygen-starved crow into the air.

"Ayee!" Cloe screamed a very human exclamation. If he could have managed coherent thought in his oxygen starved haze, no doubt it would have been more colorful.

Cloe set his course for the intruders. He'd have preferred to go back and peck out Grecolix's eyes, but the troll moved too fast to risk getting within arm's reach again. So he had to satisfy his loathing from a distance. And Theron Raurk was just the one to put the hideous monster in his rightful place.

❧ 9 ❧

Grecolix had never learned the meaning of the word subtle. The moment he spied Grig and the others, he let out a blood-curdling yelp and dashed headlong across the jagged loam, oblivious of the danger.

The troll sprawled face first into a brambly thicket of stinging nettleworts. Seeing this, Cloe struggled to suppress a raucous caw at the sight of his owner spread-eagle in one of the nastiest predicaments imaginable.

Abrasive nettlewort could chew through a hide blanket in twenty minutes. Flesh melted like butter under the insidious burrowing effect of the corkscrew shaped burrs.

Though Grecolix's skin was more akin to granite, the burrs would do their job. Once embedded, they released a stringent toxin that caused itching, burning, and a great festering carbuncle. "And pain, pain, glorious pain," Cloe singsonged.

Grecolix surged upward like an enormous tsunami, clawing at the clinging barbs even as they disappeared beneath his tough, warty skin.

Screaming worse than a scorned banshee, the troll leapt and spun in a thundering jig. Trees, shrubs and an occasional rock escarpment fell to a violent death under the pounding feet of the stampeding behemoth. "Ayee! Ayee! Ayee!" Grecolix shrieked.

❧ ◆ ❧

At first sight of the maddened bone yard proprietor, Raurk urged his charges to put as much distance behind them as possible. But when the commotion of Grecolix's pain wafted to their ears, they couldn't resist the urge to stop and watch.

Taznakie jabbered something at the druid as if he wanted to go back the way they'd just come. Then he turned to point at the crow circling in wide, lazy loops overhead. He stooped and retrieved a hefty, fist sized stone and aimed at the bird with one eye closed, and then let fly.

At the last moment, with a flurry of midair backpedaling, Cloe managed to avoid a solid hit from the missile. Instead, it glanced painfully off the tip of his left wing sending him into a dangerous downward spiral.

"No," he groaned. His sheer drop arrowed toward none other than the rampaging troll.

The crow added his forlorn cry of despair to that of Grecolix. The troll, struck blind with pain, outweighed the bird by nine hundred and some odd pounds. It didn't take a fortuneteller or a genius to predict the outcome of such an encounter.

Cloe hoped it would be a quick death. There might be a messy splotch of feathers and sinew left, but little else to attest to his demise.

⋙ ◆ ⋘

"Fool," Grig spat. "No bird deserves that kind of death. Rather, it should be you." Disgust etched upon his tight features, he glared at Taznakie. "Ferndolay." He flung his slender hand in the direction of the tumbling fowl.

Out of nowhere a blast of frigid air sprang to life. Icy tendrils formed a protective mitt to halt Cloe's fall. In slow motion, the bird skimmed to safety upon a frozen rainbow of light.

"I suggest we leave this place at once," Grig snarled. "First we trespass. Then we rob. Then we deliver harm upon the innocent. This is a day to forget for all time. I want nothing more to do with you two, or your evil doings."

Theron Raurk failed to hide the annoying half smile playing upon his lips that Grig hated so much. "That bird is none other than Grecolix's familiar."

"I . . . No . . ." Grig stared in shock.

"I'm surprised you didn't decipher that fact for yourself," Raurk answered. "Your tendency toward softness," he said with great sarcasm, "will bring about more trouble than it's worth, Grig Dothrie."

"I didn't know."

"Yet, 'tis for this very reason that you'll serve my purposes well."

"Arrgin," Taznakie said and nodded.

"I agree," Raurk said. "Yon troll will not be delayed forever. Already he overcomes the pain of the nettleworts. Nor will it be long before his familiar is recovered adequately to follow us."

❧ 10 ❧

Grig mumbled under his breath, trying to follow the druid through the pouring rain. Untold hours had passed since their hasty escape from the infuriated Grecolix.

Fatigue sat heavy upon his shoulders. "Is there no end to this misery?" he wailed. Mud and slime caked his hide boots, threatening to suck them from his feet with every step. Still the druid made no sign of seeking shelter.

"Blackbird," Grig called above the storm. "I'm drowning. Would you have us travel all night in this torrential rain? Taznakie fell behind long ago, are we to abandon him?"

"Taznakie has gone ahead of us, good elf," Raurk shouted.

"How can that be?"

"I didn't think a modest bit of rain would delay you, Master Grig. A deserted cottage lays ahead no more than an hour's march. I would spend the night with a roof over our heads, should it suit you."

Grig heard the words, but they held no meaning. "How could Taznakie get ahead of us? What is this cottage you speak of?" He stared into the pounding rain.

Raurk peered from beneath his cowl. "We can continue on until we reach the next village should you like. I must say, that will surely be midmorning on the 'morrow."

"Cottage? Village? We're lost. There *is* no civilization so far north as this. I should have known better than to trust a flapping bloodsucker such as yourself, druid."

"I see I've earned a new name." Raurk smiled. "However, you are free to return to your village anytime you wish."

"You are free to return to your village anytime you wish," Grig sneered. "The only way back is through the bone yard. I'm sure Grecolix would be happy to pulverize my carcass the moment I step foot on his land. My life hasn't been the same since you came into it. I rue the moment we met."

Raurk stopped in his tracks. "It has only been since this morning, Grig Dothrie. We have yet to embark upon our journey and you are ready to call it quits. Why don't you resign yourself to your fate? Life is too short to grovel over every tiny detail."

"You call this a tiny detail? You and that imbecile have cost me my skeleton clan. A ravenous pack of banshees almost killed me, and Grecolix is after my hide. I stand here lost halfway between somewhere and nowhere, with no idea where we journey. This downpour robs me of my wits and I follow in the footsteps of a madman. I can't help but wonder what the morn' shall bring. I'm soaked to the bone and will surely catch pneumonia for all that you care."

The druid's eyes flashed in the gloaming, resembling those of a cat. In a rough whisper he said, "Grig Dothrie, let's come to an understanding once and for all. *You* are a participant in this expedition, like it or not.

"I don't like it."

"Fate cast our lots upon the wind long ago. The gods don't care whether you like it or not. When the witch stole the Light of Ishram, a chain of events ground into motion that we can neither deny nor stop."

"Why me?" He didn't want this. "I'm not a hero."

"Make your peace, Master Grig, so we may devote our full attention to the task at hand." Raurk glowered with beetled brows. "I have no more desire to stand here in the rain than you."

"I . . . I . . ."

The tall, black figure turned his back upon Grig with an elegant flourish and set his sights far in the distance, dismissing his companion.

❧ ◆ ❧

"You lousing, stinking purveyor of doom," Grig shouted at Theron Raurk's retreating back. "How am I supposed to get home?"

He sank to the ground in the middle of an oily puddle, elbows on his knees, and held his aching head in his hands. "Inhuman blackguard!" He shook one fist in the air. "I would rather die than follow you."

"Aye, and that could be accomplished with little ado," the pirate, Whittlebottom, agreed.

"Damn you!" Grig glared at the pirate.

Whittlebottom failed to notice that his abrupt arrival had sent Grig sprawling upon his back in the mud. "I say, old man. I got rather tired of waiting so I came looking for you. I brought a bumbershoot in case you'd like to use it."

Grig sat up and snatched the proffered object from the pirate and shoved it open. "What in hell is this?" The spiny, metal ribs flopped uselessly, as much a skeleton as Magried Whittlebottom.

"Sorry, guv'nor, I don't suppose it's of much use like that." He motioned toward the decayed umbrella.

"About as much use as you." Grig flopped back in the puddle. "Go away and leave me alone."

Whittlebottom studied his bony hands. "I could do that if you'd like, but I rather think your predicament fails to improve."

Grig restrained the urge to hurl lightening at the obnoxious air-pirate. "What do you want?" He groaned as wet, heavy flakes of snow mingled with the rain.

"You know, I had quite forgotten the delights of this world." He held his skeletal palm up to the sky.

"You're daft, man," Grig said.

Whittlebottom stared at him with empty eye-sockets. "Are you not enjoying yourself?"

"No."

"Odd, I must say this is just what the ship's doctor ordered. This is the life for me. Just smell the aroma of sodden heath. To sail the airwaves, unhindered by laws of man is my destiny. I can't express my pleasure enough." This time he raised his face heavenward.

From his prone position, Grig snarled, "I ought to wring your bony neck. That stench is you. Besides, what's the idea of scaring me half to death?"

"Oh, I say." The pirate appeared surprised. "Let me help you up, Master Grig. A sense of humor it is you have. Ha! Ha! Wring my bony neck. I haven't heard anything so funny since . . . well, since before I died."

Grig struggled to sit upright and wiped at his dripping face. "You can remember that long ago?"

"Why, of course. At the deathbed of my father, may the Maker rest his soul, my Great Aunt Hattie had the audacity to say I would always be her favorite nephew. Bah, she didn't fool me. That old biddy couldn't remember her own name most days."

"Shut up, you idiot. How did you get here? Did you see that flapping blackbird? He went off and left me."

The pirate rubbed a hand under his tri-corn with a scritching sound that drove Grig barmy. "I did say I had my crew bring me back, didn't I? I must be getting absent-minded in my old age. 'Tis a curse of our clan. My dear old Mum went completely dotty by the time she passed away."

In spite of his anger, Grig couldn't stop himself from asking. "And you're the only sane one in the family?"

"We were forced to hire an idiot girl to keep an eye on Mum so she didn't burn down the whole village," Whittlebottom said. "My older sister had not a better fate. It does appear the women of our family are harder hit than the men, so I should have another ten thousand years before I'm as empty headed as a prepubescent lass."

"Magried Whittlebottom," Grig said between chattering teeth. "If you don't stop blithering like a magpie, you shall lose your mind right here on the spot. Shut your mouth and listen without interrupting for the next ten seconds."

"Oh, I say. I'm sorry, guv'nor."

"I'm drowning! I need shelter. Do you understand?"

If the bony face of the pirate could have shown emotion, it would have been a cross between abject apology and utter dejection. "Why do you sit here on your bum in the middle of this puddle if you're so miserable? Even now your companions take their leave in front of a roaring fire. They have prepared a meal and await your arrival. Arise and we shall proceed."

Grig made no move.

"By chance, are your legs broken?" Whittlebottom cocked his head to one side. "The mutton will burn before long."

The elf rose from the muck and mire of the puddle with as much dignity as he could muster. He drew himself erect and brushed at his sodden clothing. "My legs are fine."

"Then what is the problem?" The pirate gave him a quick once over.

Grig fought to control his anger. "Did you not hear me the first time? I'm lost. That blackguard left me here to fend for myself. Bring your crew here and fly me to join my companions if you want to be of use."

Whittlebottom made a noise that resembled a chuckle. "Surely you jest. You must know a mortal can't ride the airwaves in my vessel. 'Tis a skeleton ship of the first class, not a passenger ship. A good joke, but very impractical."

"Is stupidity a curse of your clan as well?" Grig steamed. "I do not joke, you dim witted skeleton. If by chance you know the whereabouts of Raurk and Taznakie, take me to them. I couldn't care less whether it's afoot or in that accursed ship of yours, but get me out of this infernal downpour."

The pirate drew back in surprise. "I say old man, there's no need to shout. I can hear you perfectly well. Of course I'll take you to your friends. I mistakenly believed you were enjoying this glorious drizzle as much as I." He bowed low. "I offer my sincerest apologies, Grig Dothrie. I will take you to them straight away."

❧ 11 ❧

Hours later, Grig sloshed through another quagmire. "Whittle-bottom, is this your idea of straight away?" the elf bellowed. "I'd have been better off spending the night where Raurk abandoned me. At least I still had the possession of my boots and jerkin. Something I can't claim at this moment."

"Ah, yes, an unfortunate accident," Whittlebottom agreed. The pirate stopped to survey his companion. "You are a rather pathetic vision at this moment."

"Thanks to you. Did we have to go right through that last swamp? Can you tell me you couldn't find a way around it?"

"Master Grig, I thought you were in a hurry." Whittlebottom shrugged his shoulders. "The shortest distance between two points is a straight line. Or have the laws of physics changed over the last ten thousand years?"

Mud-spattered and reeking of swamp slime, Grig looked more like something a gerrub had tried to bury than an elf. "Just once, can you please answer a simple question with a yes or no?"

Whittlebottom cocked his head to one side, scritching his pate. "'Tis difficult, but for you, I shall try."

Grig wanted to yank his hair out. "For a disreputable scalawag of the airwaves, you're a puzzle. Your speech is far too refined. You're so syrupy polite it makes my teeth ache. I thought pirates swore and drank and caroused, all the while looking for poor gullible wenches to take advantage of."

Whittlebottom dropped his gaze. "If you must know, I worked as a schoolmaster before I took to the airwaves. A very good teacher at that, until I ran afoul of several adoring mothers."

Grig stuffed his fingers in both ears and shook them. "Surely, you're the one who jests."

"Nay, guv'nor. I've had my share of bawdy behavior in the past, but I pride myself upon always being respectful."

Grig peered at him through narrowed eyes. "I suppose you ask permission before chopping off heads in the heat of battle. Who are you trying to impress, you rogue?"

"Why you, of course," Whittlebottom answered. "'Tis my fondest desire to accompany you upon your mission. Though what use I'll be, I'm sure I don't know. The decision is yours when all is said and done."

Grig whirled to face the skeleton pirate. "You and that druid seem to think I have something to do with this . . . insanity." He waved at his surroundings.

The pirate placed a bony hand upon the elf's shoulder. "Of course you do, guv'nor. Without you, there's no hope."

"Never mind." Grig's shoulders slumped. "How much longer before we reach the others? My skin puckers and wrinkles like that of an old hag. And this is just the first day as that blackbird is fond of reminding me."

❧ 12 ❧

Grig's next cognizant thought came when he awoke to the delicious aroma of breakfast, and something else much less tempting. He covered his nose with one hand. "In the Maker's name what is that awful stench?"

Taznakie grinned and pointed at something just beyond, or near the elf's left ear. It never entered Grig's mind that the simpleton was pointing at him. Nothing so foul could emanate from a living body.

"Out of my way." He pushed Taznakie aside. "Where am I? Where's Raurk? Last thing I remember is arguing with that deranged pirate, but after that, my memory grows hazy."

Taznakie nodded and clapped his hands.

"You're all deranged."

Taznakie smiled again and pointed at the elf, while hopping around on one foot as if he'd waited too long to use the loo.

To Grig, Taznakie's words sounded more like a tribe of crazed banshees than something from a human throat. At last, the man darted from the dilapidated shack screaming at the top of his lungs.

"Good riddance." Grig sighed, no wiser than when he'd first awoken. And that nauseating stench seemed to grow worse. "What is that smell?" He searched for the source of the revolting odor with growing concern.

The elf looked up with hope as Taznakie clattered through the door. The simpleton babbled and once again pointed at something near or behind Grig.

For the first time, Grig noticed the brimming bucket of water in Taznakie's hand. "I do hope you've come to get rid of that loathsome stench."

Taznakie flung the contents full force at the unsuspecting elf. Next, he produced a coarse brush and a cake of soap and proceeded to scour the elf from head to toe, clothes and all, much to the elf's profound and vocal dismay.

The longer Taznakie rubbed, the more slippery Grig became. Soap blurred the elf's vision and flew every which way.

"Get off me, you fool!" Grig cried.

Taznakie refused to abandon his self-appointed task. At long last, the simpleton extricated himself from the writhing heap and stepped back to admire his handiwork.

Grig grabbed the soap and brush and attacked Taznakie with the vigor of well-earned vengeance. "I'll teach you to accost my person, you moron. What in hell do you think you're doing? I'd barely dried out from last night, now look at me."

"I'd say he eradicated the place of a rather pungent aroma," Raurk drawled. "I realize Whittlebottom blazed the trail for you, but I wish he hadn't insisted upon carrying you."

Grig paused to look up. "What did you say?"

"I but mentioned that the pirate carried you the last mile or so. The stench does have a tendency to wear off, but Taznakie has accelerated the process. Although you might want to rinse away the soap before it dries. I'm sure you understand my concern."

"Blackbird, I'm convinced your sole purpose in life is to drown me. I need not worry about this insane quest of yours, for I'll be dead long before we find your precious Light of Ishram."

❧ 13 ❧

"*Look* at me," Grig said. "That moron scrubbed me raw and ruined my clothes."

Raurk appeared to take a perverse pleasure in the elf's discomfort. "That is the least of our concerns at this moment."

Grig glanced up from his breakfast. "What do you mean?"

"The banshees have followed our progress. We must make haste before they discover our current whereabouts."

Grig slumped in his seat. First his altercation with Taznakie had nigh drowned him, now it seemed he must flee for his life yet again. And before he could sate his hunger. "Blackbird, if you don't drown me first, I'll surely starve to death."

He crammed his mouth full and rose to his feet. "I grow weary of this chase.

"What I shall do is summon Magried Whittlebottom and his crew to intercept the banshees. Their foul order should throw the she-demons off our trail for a short time."

Raurk stepped to the door of the rundown cottage. With two fingers to his lips, he emitted a shrill whistle loud enough to cause Grig considerable discomfort.

"Come, Master Grig, the day slips away from us," Raurk said. "If I'm not mistaken, we will run into more rain before long. Look yonder, already the storm clouds play hide and seek with the grieving sun.

"Maker, not more rain," Grig muttered. He'd had quite his fill of banshees, skeleton pirates, and rain. Enough rain to last him a lifetime. He glanced to the east just long enough to take in the darkening sky.

Resigned, Grig watched the retreating back of the druid. The sun had barely risen and already he ached with fatigue. He longed for a sound night's sleep in his soft down bed and the fragrant bloom of his tree house.

Grig returned to the cottage to gather the meager remains of his garments. He hitched, tugged, tied and adjusted them as best he could. Just the thought of his lost boots caused his tender feet to yammer in pain. But he needed to catch up to the druid.

❧ ◆ ❧

With ease to his long steps, Raurk set his sights in the distance, whistling a jaunty tune. "I for one would like to reach the next village before the noon hour passes," he called over his shoulder. He appeared to be in an exceptionally good mood.

"Wait," Grig said. "What did you mean by grieving sun? How can the sun be in mourning?"

Raurk hesitated for no more than a second. "All the known worlds will grieve should we fail in our task. Come. Whittlebottom can detain the she-demons for only so long. They are a determined lot, even for their likes."

Grig hastened to keep up. At the last moment he jogged to one side to avoid a lurking Jusong vine only to stub his toe on the backbone of an ancient, half-buried silo. He cursed at the top of his lungs and flailed at the air trying to forestall his headlong decent.

Arms and legs akimbo, he lay in a defeated heap. Dirty water from the previous day's rain ran in maddening rivulets through his hair and into his eyes.

"I'm sorely tempted to lie here forever. Let the world go to hell for all I care."

Then, Taznakie towered over him, jabbering and waving his arms. When Taznakie got no response, he scooped Grig into his arms and set off at a bone-jarring trot in pursuit of the druid. To Grig's dismay, not once did he stop his infernal diatribe.

Grig fought to free himself, but Taznakie was far stronger than the elf had suspected. "Put me down, you fool," he protested into the man's chest. "My legs aren't broken." But his objections carried no weight.

Taznakie increased his pace. In spite of Grig's blustering and jibes, he still appeared to love the elf.

Grig had often refused to taunt Taznakie, and now he reaped the rewards—Taznakie's unwavering "help" and unceasing gibberish. Grig resolved he'd ask to be set afoot as soon as they caught up with the druid.

To his amazement, the elf experienced an unexpected sense of security the moment he ceased his struggles against Taznakie. In fact, it almost felt like the cradling arms of his mother. Or what he could remember of her. For the moment, he allowed himself to doze.

❦ 14 ❧

"*Wake* up, Grig Dothrie," Raurk said. "I suggest you walk into this fine village upon your own two feet. People would not understand a grown man being carried."

"What?" Still half asleep, Grig blinked repeatedly, endeavouring to focus on the druid.

"We have a good prospect of filling our bellies and acquiring a new pair of boots should you so desire."

It wasn't until Raurk mentioned boots that he had Grig's full attention. "Put me down, you imbecile." He jabbed a finger into Taznakie's chest.

"Arlph?" Taznakie looked hurt.

Grig's tone softened. "I just meant that I'm capable of walking on my own. Uh . . . thank you for your assistance," Grig mumbled behind his hand.

Taznakie beamed.

Grig dusted at his breeches, making sure they covered him decently. "At this rate, we'll all end up in hell if this great, flapping blackbird has his way." He glared at Raurk.

Raurk countered with a smile. "Another ten minutes down the road and we'll be in town. We shall find an excellent cobbler who can meet your needs should you have the proper currency."

"And a tailor?" Grig perked up at the thought of new clothes.

"Aye, a tailor as well. The cobbler's wife runs the only hostel within a hundred leagues. A bit pricey, but we must make do. Come along, we don't want to be late." He sauntered down the middle of the lane, bold as a stray dog, still whistling his loathsome tune.

Grig wanted a new pair of boots in the worst way, but he didn't want to admit he hadn't the slightest inkling where they were. He'd never ventured much beyond the bone yard of Grecolix, and never in this direction.

He sidled up to Raurk, careful not to appear too eager. "Blackbird, where did you say we are? Not even your grieving sun belies the direction of our passing as it has taken refuge from sight. Have we wandered off the end of our world onto another?" That last thought sent black shivers of dread along his spine.

"My good elf, do you doubt me? I have visited this village often and know it to welcome strangers no matter how outlandish their appearance." This last was accompanied by a scornful once over of Grig from head to toe.

"Perhaps our first destination should be the tailor. Do you carry ample coin about your body, good elf, to replace your lost garments?"

Grig didn't know whether he should answer, or just hit the druid with a magical slap upside the head. That was the only way he could hit the man other than standing on a box and hoping Raurk would hold still long enough to get whacked.

"You're as daft as Taznakie, blackbird. Any coins I had were lost in yesterday's downpour. So you'll have to be humiliated by my appearance. Just rewards to you."

"Have you checked your pouch?" Raurk motioned toward Grig's being. "I do believe I hear the unmistakable clink of coins. Although, the need may not arise should fate smile upon us."

"We both know you dragged me bodily from my home." Even as he replied, Grig felt the weight of the purse against his skin. "I had no chance to prepare for a journey."

Taznakie muttered something unintelligible. "No," Raurk said. "He can't just conjure up new clothes. That's not the type of magic our friend possesses." He paused a moment to listen to Taznakie's garbled question. "When the time is appropriate, we shall all find out.

"Come, the lunch hour draws to an end and I'm nigh famished." He stepped up his pace, forcing Grig to trot alongside like a gimpy hostrich, that odd genetic cocktail between a horse and an ostrich.

"Where are we going? Do you even know where we are?" Grig hit a sharp stone. "Ouch!"

"You'll see," Raurk cast a smile over his shoulder.

By Grig's own admission, he was a tender-foot, and now he must scurry on bare feet to keep pace. Would the torture never end?

A tirade of obscenities accompanied his every step. Only when he spied the first cottage and a beautiful dark-haired woman standing within the yard, did it stop. His mouth hung open, collecting flies as Raurk oft commented.

Not only was this woman tall and graceful, but it seemed she knew the blackbird. She greeted them with the most beautiful voice Grig had ever heard. "Theron Raurk, I feared we'd seen the last of you. You still owe Father a game of Bones. He grumbles like a decrepit locomotive that no one plays as well as you."

"I'm happy to return." Raurk bowed low and kissed the woman's hand.

"Hold on a moment, and I'll go with you." She turned to call to someone within the house. Then she linked arms with Raurk and the pair strolled toward town, chattering like a couple of love struck school children.

To Grig's vexation, the druid introduced neither of his companions. To make matters worse, drops of cold rain pelted them, plastering Grig's meager garments against his flesh. Before long, a chill wracked him to the bone and his already injured pride urged him to act rashly.

"Stop, blackbird." He planted his feet and refused to move. "I'm sick and tired of this unspeakable mess you've gotten me into. I'm cold, hungry and . . . I don't know what. You prattle on with the most beautiful woman I've ever seen and you don't even introduce me—I mean us." He included Taznakie with a quick sweep of his hand.

Raurk turned to bring his peculiar copper eyes to bear full upon the elf. For a moment, Grig feared he'd overstepped his bounds. Teeth chattering, he mumbled, "I'm sorry. I just meant. Well, uh . . . . Who is this charming lady?"

The dark-haired woman, who appeared to have become blonde, turned her attention to Grig for the first time and smiled.

His damp garments made him feel naked. Grig wanted nothing more than to run and hide.

She smiled with a glint in her eyes. Her soft voice purred. "My name is Lillith." She reached with a graceful hand to greet the elf.

When their fingers touched, Grig felt himself turn ten shades of scarlet. "I'm pleased to meet you, Miss . . . ?"

"Lillith," she interjected. "We don't stand on formality, and a friend of my husband's is a friend of mine." She flashed the same dazzling smile.

He couldn't help gawking at this beautiful blonde . . . no, her hair had turned dark again. He shifted his gaze to the druid and back to Lillith. For a moment, he thought her jade green eyes mocked him, but then he realized it was naught but a twinkle of understanding.

She turned to Raurk. "My love, you didn't tell them? You keep me to yourself as if I were an expensive trinket. I'm not a bauble to wear about your neck."

Raurk shrugged with a sheepish smile. "It's not important to our journey, my wife."

"Not important?" Her eyebrows rose in question. "I suppose you haven't told them I complete this small troupe of wanderers? Though I think you simply want my company on this journey. If it were not you asking me to go, I'd refuse to step foot outside this village."

"Lillith, some things are better left unsaid. You know I don't always understand the portent of my dreams, but I do heed them. Had I not, I would be much lonelier without your charming presence."

"So one of your dreams brought you here?" She pouted with her head cocked to one side. "I hoped it was because you couldn't stay away from me."

"I must admit, it was both." Raurk sighed. "But Master Grig is fairly turning blue. Is the inn still open for lunch?"

Lillith sniffed with disdain. "I wouldn't allow that fat cow and her husband to feed the one I love. She would sooner poison you and your friends than allow you to walk away from her again. And 'tis your own fault it is for abandoning her at the altar."

Grig struggled to digest the thought that the blackbird was married to such a beautiful woman. The sight of her good looks upon the arm of that great, flapping specter was startling. Everything about the woman enchanted him, while Raurk was gaunt and skinny and maddening. His sharp features were scarred and sunken into his skull, while Lillith was all that a man might dream of.

Taznakie's eyes roved over her voluptuous figure as if he feared she might disappear. His mouth worked trying to form words that refused to come. He dropped to one knee in the middle of the road in an awkward resemblance of a bow. He mumbled something and grabbed her hand, then pressed it to his lips with a great smacking sound.

Lillith laughed and patted him on the top of the head. "'Tis I who am pleased to meet you, my good knight. I'm sure our journey will be much blessed by your presence."

With a glare from beneath unkempt eyebrows, Raurk looped his arm through Lillith's again and steered her away.

"Where do you suggest we eat, my darling, if not at the inn? And for your information, I did not desert that cow at the altar. You know damned well I can't stand her presence even in a very large room. All the better were it in the next world."

Taznakie remained with one knee planted in the mud, watching the couple move away. Grig hurried behind them as quickly as his outlandish garb and bare feet would allow.

He didn't care where they ate as long as it was soon. About to mention this, he realized Lillith had stopped. "Pardon me, ma'am. I see nothing here," he said.

"This is where we shall eat," Lillith said.

"I don't see a hostel."

Lillith laughed. "You are correct, and I do believe you could use a new set of clothes. What has this husband of mine put you through that you should be so disarrayed?"

Grig cast an "I told you so" glare at Raurk.

"Perhaps my brother will allow you a selection of his clothes. I assume it's your garments that reek so."

Taznakie agreed with a vigorous bobbing of his head.

"I see," Lillith answered looking Grig up and down. "Mother might have a pair of sturdy boots that will fit you."

Grig didn't see anything resembling a house, an inn, or even a barn. Several scrubby trees dotted the lot, but no dwelling. "This woman may be beautiful," he groused, "but she's as empty-headed as Magried Whittlebottom."

"Nay, elf," Raurk said. "Look again and you'll see the outlines of a house against the field."

Grig stared, but saw nothing. "One of us has lost his mind, and it's not me."

"The house is enchanted against the prying eyes of strangers," Lillith said. "Not that there are many people afoot these days."

"That makes them a lot smarter than any of us," Grig retorted.

Raurk clapped him on the back. "Don't be so gloomy, good elf. With any luck, we'll be welcome. Lillith, my love, does your father still smart from my abrupt departure last summer? I'm prepared to stay elsewhere if necessary."

Before Lillith could reply, a door burst open revealing a very large man outlined against the interior of a warm room. He gave a haughty sniff and looked directly at her. "Lillith, tell that blackguard I have not forgiven him for tearing out of here as if possessed. You and your mother were in a tizzy for months, and I'm the one who suffered for it." Not once did he turn to view the travelers.

"Yes, Father." She lowered her head to hide a smile.

"Hark! I smell an elf," the old man said. "Is this the likes of whom he brings to our table this time? Rakell Taznakie is that you? So then, you will be off on your foolhardy mission soon? Good riddance to the likes of all of you." Without warning, he slammed the door in their faces.

Taznakie pointed at his puffed out chest, and uttered an incoherent tirade.

"Yes," Lillith answered. "Of course Father knows you. He has long waited the day you passed our way. Don't let his gruffness disturb you. He's overjoyed to meet both of you."

Puzzled, Grig gawked at the two. "How could he smell us, Mrs. Rau . . . I mean, Lillith. Why didn't he just look at us?"

"'Tis easy to explain, but wait until we're inside. I believe the reason will become evident.

"Mother, Father," she called, pushing open the door. "I would bring our guests in should it meet your leave."

The room appeared enormous. The man sat in front of the yawning fireplace, rocking far faster than Grig thought possible, his back to the strangers.

"This is my father, Kevel Firth," Lillith said.

Kevel rose at once and turned to look them square in the face. "Don't gawp at me so, Grig Dothrie. My eyes are of no worldly use, but I can smell your curiosity as plain as that filth plastered upon your person. And where are your clothes? Does Raurk not allow you the basest comforts?"

He turned toward the simpleton. "Taznakie, your mother and I were long time acquaintances before her unfortunate death. I've always known you'd come to set right the atrocities of this world, as well as those around us."

Grig feared Taznakie would explode with pride at the mere thought this strange man should know who he was. Either that, or soil himself. The elf held his breath expecting the worst that could happen.

Strange was a fitting description for Kevel Firth. He stood taller than Theron Raurk, and twice as broad. A ruff of snow-white hair wreathed his otherwise bald pate causing him a weird and wonderfully angelic appearance.

Grig could see where Lillith's splendor and grace originated. Even in his old age, Kevel remained an imposing sight. All of this aside, his eyes were the most peculiar the elf had ever seen. They were a deep cerulean blue of unplumbed beauty. There was no white of the eyes, no lens, no pupil. Just that outlandish blue and totally useless.

Grig would have asked the man a million questions, but an energetic lad bounded across the room, launching himself at Raurk. His tousled, sandy-colored hair bobbed and danced with every movement.

"Raurk, I've worried myself sick wondering what happened to you," the boy said.

"I apologize." Raurk hugged him close. "Saving my miserable hide took precedence at the time."

The lad writhed in Raurk's embrace. "Three trolls and a gnome followed hot upon your heels the moment you were out the back door. I saw them from my window. Father confused them with a spell the best he could, but we all feared for your life. A shady lot, they were."

"Slow down, Dannel," Kevel barked. "These are our guests."

"Raurk's not a guest." Dannel paused for a deep breath. "Where have you been all this time? My birthday has come, and long gone. I thought you were going to help me celebrate. Are you staying long? Can I go with you when you leave? I'm ten, old enough to leave home if I want."

"Young man, stop your prattling," Kevel said. "And you, Raurk, put him down. I don't want you encouraging him in these wild schemes. He's a handful as it is."

"Yes, Father Kevel." Raurk placed the lad on his feet and winked. "Dannel, do as you're told."

The boy ducked behind Raurk's leg. "I'm sorry, Father."

"I don't want your mother worrying about you the way she frets over Raurk." Scowling, Kevel resumed his seat by the fire and rocked even faster than before.

The boy paid him no mind. "Master Elf, what are you wearing?"

Raurk intervened. "Dannel, take Grig to your room and find him something to wear."

Dannel grabbed Grig's hand and dragged him toward the stairs. "Master Grig, you may have the pick of all I own."

"Thank you."

"Be sure to step over the third riser. It's enchanted. You must promise to tell me everything that has happened so far.

"Raurk treats me like a child, and I'm not you know? Did you call Magried Whittlebottom from the dead? Is he as disreputable as I've heard? I can't wait to meet him."

"It wasn't me," Grig muttered.

"How soon will you be leaving? Mother would have you stay a month if possible. Father's health is not what it once was. Not that he's ill, but he envisions all sorts of disasters no one can explain . . ."

"Young man," Grig snapped. "If you don't stop your wild ranting, I shall leave this house immediately. This mess is Raurk's doing. Let him tell you what has transpired."

"He won't tell me anything." Dannel scuffed his toe at the floor.

"All I want are dry clothes, preferably without holes, and a hot meal. It seems days since I last ate, and would remedy that situation as soon as possible."

Lillith appeared at the door, saving Grig from another outburst. "Pardon my brother's enthusiasm. 'Tis difficult to keep a young lad housebound when he much prefers to be scouring the countryside for trouble."

Grig felt a blush creep to the roots of his bark colored hair. "My pardon, lady. I'm made irritable by my misfortune. But what are these disasters your father foresees?"

"All in good time." She turned to her brother. "Dannel will clothe you, and I've brought boots. Make sure you get several pairs of socks from this young scoundrel while you're at it. Come downstairs as soon as you're decent. Mother has lunch on the stove, and though Father appears gruff, he is concerned for all of you."

She turned and left. Grig longed to ask her more, but the lad piled numerous articles of clothing across his arms. "There's a basin over there where you can wash," he added. "Phew, no wonder Father smelled you."

❧ **15** ❦

The whole family sat at the table waiting for Grig to make his appearance. Dannel grilled Raurk for events since his last visit, punctuating his words with flying hands. For once, Taznakie remained silent, staring from Lillith to another equally beautiful, though older, woman.

Grig stared in mute imitation of the village idiot. He inched forward to take the lady's hand in his, stumbling over his own feet. "Madam, we have not met, but I assume you are the mother of this family. I'm Grig Dothrie, at your service." He raised her hand and planted a resounding kiss upon it.

"Restrain yourself," Kevel said. "Master Grig, your words may impress the ladies where you come from, but they're wasted here. This is my wife, Adelita. She is no more impressed with your prancing and posturing than I. Better you should sit in silence with your mouth hanging open, as our friend Taznakie, than spew such tripe."

The old man's sharpness confused Grig. "I beg your pardon."

"We've waited for you long enough. We shall delay no longer."

"Father, you're being rude," Dannel chided.

"Aye, Father, it's true," Lillith added. "You're out of sorts because of your dreams. Can't we eat in peace and then with our bellies full, discuss this in a civil manner?"

Raurk rose to his feet with a cup of cold milk in his hand. "Friends, we have a long road ahead of us. Let us enjoy this magnificent meal prepared by the tender hands of our loved ones." He set the cup to his lips and drained it. "That said and done, let's eat."

❧ ◆ ❦

Kevel's glare did not soften with the glad cheer of his family. But each time Taznakie spoke, he gave the man his full attention. Once, he even chuckled at something Taznakie said, but did not join the conversation.

He sat at the head of the table like a bleached specter of death. His face turned often toward the travelers in search of something . . . .

The meal drawing to a close, Kevel turned to sniff at Grig. "You reek of death. I can't tell if it's your own or another's, but the stench is overpowering. Why do you bring this stink to my table?"

Angry, Grig rose to meet his accuser. But Raurk waved him back to his seat. "Father Kevel, leave him be. 'Tis the stench of Magried Whittlebottom you perceive. The good pirate rescued Grig from a deluge yesterday, and the smell has yet to wear off in spite of Taznakie's efforts. You should have been there. Very entertaining, should you ask me. I'm not sure who got the better of it."

Taznakie tore his gaze from the two women at the sound of his name. He nodded in agreement and launched into an animated retelling of Grig's ignoble awakening that morning.

Everyone except the family patriarch and Grig Dothrie, derived pleasure from the story of the elf's thorough drenching. Finally, Kevel joined the laughter when Taznakie mimed the part when the tables turned on him.

Breathless at last, Taznakie sank into his chair with an enormous hiccup, almost unseating himself.

Dannel did fall out of his chair, laughing so hard tears streamed down his face. Abruptly, he grabbed Grig by one ankle and dragged him to the floor, tickling the elf with vengeance.

With a wild whoop of enthusiasm, Taznakie dove headfirst under the table, overjoyed to add his own efforts to the fracas.

"Stop," Grig gasped between guffaws. "I'm . . . I'm . . . get off me. I'm suffocating."

Taznakie took this as a cue to double his efforts. With one sturdy leg flung across Grig's chest, he produced a feather from an unknown pocket to torment his captive's ears and nose.

Dannel divested Grig's flailing feet of his new footwear. The lad could find no feather, so he enticed the family's pet gerrub, Malie, with a thick, creamy slab of butter, slathered across Grig's fragile pink toes.

Malie loved butter above all other foods as evidenced by her rotund, waddling appearance. Under any other circumstances, she remained a coward, but let butter be introduced and she turned into an aggressive, pushy, yowling imposter of her meek persona.

After the first few tentative swipes of her tongue against the sole of Grig's abused feet, Malie set about with a raspy, slobbery chirrup to clean away every speck of the mouthwatering treasure. She was in heaven and Grig Dothrie was in hell.

"Get off, please," Grig pleaded. But his tormentors were having too much fun to stop. Tears flooded his eyes as the feather wafted under his nose again and then trailed across his feet when Malie finished her feast.

Grig could endure almost anything, but not people touching his feet. He was beside himself wanting to end this mockery. But he was too small to unseat Taznakie by force. And should the truth be known, he had a certain soft spot in his heart for gerrubs. He refused to hurt Malie in any way, even if it did mean continued torture.

Short of magic, he was helpless. Already gasping for air, the added weight of Taznakie across his chest didn't help. "Gordiff hasnee biddlebux—" he gasped. "Hidenach biddlebiddle—"

"Stop!" Kevel Firth roared, exploding to his feet. "You'll bring every banshee in the neighborhood to our door. You know how they hate laughter. We've had more than our share of the she-demons of late."

Dannel and Taznakie giggled.

"Master Grig, you of all people are too old to engage in such childish shenanigans. These other two are no more than children." He stomped from the room with the contented Malie in his wake.

Dannel and Taznakie rolled away from their victim, still laughing too hard to get up. Free at last, Grig, jumped to his feet arranging his clothing. "It's your fault." He glared at the troublemakers. "I have half a mind to . . ."

"What? Blow them into the next world?" Raurk interrupted. "That's what you were about to do if you'd finished your spell. No wonder Kevel stopped you before you could bring about such evil."

"It was their fault," Grig mumbled.

Raurk glared at him. "Kevel was too kind to tell you what a fool you were acting. He's right. You're far too old to be rolling around on the floor with them." An expansive wave of his hand included the still sniggering culprits.

Grig couldn't believe his ears. "They started it. All I wanted to do was get them off me."

"Did you not hear your own words?" Raurk shook his head. "'Twas a spell of destruction for sure if I've ever heard one. Master Grig, you must be more careful with your incantations. At this rate, the slightest bungle of any spell and we shall all suffer the consequences. Would you have them go through life in a like manner to the unfortunate crow, Cloe?"

"It wasn't my fault," Grig repeated.

"I think you need apologize to our host."

"Raurk, leave him be." Lillith laid a gentle hand upon his shoulder. "That young rapscallion sidling under the table knows better." She pointed an accusatory finger toward Dannel. "He's the one who should apologize."

Adelita extricated her wayward son from his hiding place with only a minor bit of force. "I suggest you do as your sister says, young man. That is, unless you want a thrashing from me. Your father is already on edge without your tomfoolery."

"I'm sorry, Master Grig," Dannel apologized. He hung his head to hide the smile lurking on his lips.

"Mama, may I go outside this afternoon if I take Taznakie and Grig with me?" He cast a sly look at the simpleton. "It's been months since you and father have allowed me more than a tether's length from your side. I promise we'll only go as far as the stream. I bet we could find enough wild mushrooms for dinner tonight."

"I don't know . . ." Adelita pondered.

Taznakie hopped from one foot to the other and pointed to himself, the elf and then the boy. With a fierce imitation of a warrior, he made it clear he would protect all three of them.

"Please, Mama? Please? Just for a little while."

"What do you think, Raurk?"

"Why do you ask him? I'm the boy's father," Kevel barked from behind her. He had reentered the room unknown to the others. "I say let them go."

"I agree," the druid added. "Master Grig and Taznakie will look after him. I fear another such opportunity won't present itself for a long time."

Grig looked up in alarm. "After those two tried to suffocate me, why should I protect either one of them?" He added what he hoped was a dark scowl. He refused to admit that picking wild mushrooms and rock-hopping down the middle of a stream would be a fitting way to pass the afternoon.

"Oh, please, Master Grig?" Dannel wheedled.

"Only if you promise to behave." Grig folded his arms across his chest and glared in mock disgust. If they were lucky, they might see some of the forest people. It'd been forever since the tiny men had visited his tree house and he missed their tinkling laugh and bright spirits.

"Then it's settled," Kevel went on as if Grig had not spoken. "Be sure to get the bucket from the shed before you leave, and take this lazy gerrub with you. She's gotten fat these past couple of months."

"Thank you, Papa." Dannel threw his arms around his father. "I love you."

"Go on, get out of here." Kevel shooed the boy away. "I want a quiet game of Bones with Raurk before all hell breaks loose again. It never fails. Where Theron Raurk goes, trouble is sure to follow. Lillith, I fail to see what draws you to this man. We led quiet, orderly lives before he came along."

"Me, too," Grig muttered with a sigh.

His ire spent, the big man turned toward his daughter and hugged her. "Never mind. I prattle like a washerwoman. My dreams make me overwrought. Get the Bones and set up the table near the fireplace. My old carcass creaks and moans with this wet weather. Druid, prepare for a resounding defeat!"

❧ 16 ❧

Isis the dragon longed to sleep off the weariness that plagued her. Her new skin failed to stretch to accommodate such a large clutch of eggs, sending painful cracks along her protruding belly. Her constant, deep rumbling and sulfurous fumes hung over Cranitaur Valley in a heavy fog.

Her hide itched unmercifully. The previous morning she'd ripped loose a rag-tagged strip of dead skin that had gouged into the tender flesh below. Angry and in pain, Isis exploded like a cannonball from hell spewing flame and destruction in her wake. Miserable, she was tempted to wolf down everything in sight.

Terrified villagers ran blindly to escape her wrath. Man and beast alike huddled in dank root cellars, beneath rock overhangs and in deep wells to escape her unbridled fury.

That is, all but one dimwitted, popinjay noble with the ignoble name of McGeorge McGeorge, the 26th. More commonly known as Idiot, he took it upon himself to rid *his* lands of this flying nuisance once and for all.

Bernetta, his wench of the month, deemed the time ripe when Isis rocketed from her cave, bugling and burning. With a sharp jab in his ribs, she woke Idiot, who was snoring in a stentorian basso-profundo imitation of the grim reaper. "Wake up, Idiot, darling," she cooed. "Isis is on a rampage. I've saddled your hostrich, here's your sword. Get out there and do your duty to your kingdom—and me." She fluttered her eyes in a manner she knew Idiot couldn't resist.

Thus, our ignoble noble found himself mounted astride his hostrich with nothing but his sword and a drunken stupor to protect his dignity.

His mount, the sweet tempered Anthanon, hauled her feathered tail in Isis's burning wake. Not until the dragon suddenly reversed course and set down in her path did Anthanon realize she was about to die.

The hostrich applied the brakes and came to a screeching halt in the middle of the road. Petrified, she watched Idiot fly head over heels into the waiting jaws of Isis. The dragon eyed Anthanon menacingly, but made no further threat.

Communication of some sort passed between them before Isis heaved her awkward bulk into the air. Poor Anthanon rolled her enormous eyes and fainted dead away.

Disgusted, the dragon plunged headfirst into the deep soothing waters of Lake Cranitaur to sulk the remainder of the day. Far past midnight, she emerged from the chilling waters and made her way home.

The following morning brought the chirping of birds, buzzing of bees and the soughing of gentle winds. For the first time in weeks, she failed to spew malodorous fumes across the valley. She was at peace, even if still on a short fuse.

A deep nagging in her belly forewarned the imminent arrival of her clutch. Half asleep, she barely detected the filthy splotch bobbing like a drunken grasshopper upon the far horizon. She drifted into a light slumber.

~ ♦ 匥

Magried Whittlebottom, skeleton pirate of the airwaves, approached Cranitaur Valley with an eye peeled for trouble. He'd much rather be in the thick of battle, but he'd promised to follow Theron Raurk's orders to wait there, like it or not. Little did he realize that luck delivered them to Cranitaur Valley on one of Isis' rare good days.

Upon hearing they were headed to the dragon's lair, an old washerwoman in the last village warned them that dragons in molt are mean, cantankerous, rude, and downright irritable on the best of days. According to her, Isis was older than anyone could remember and suffered all the more for it. "To makes matters worse, she carries a heavy clutch of eggs," the old woman cackled.

The day dawned unbearably beautiful and the skeleton ship paid no allegiance to the laws of gravity. She executed donuts, loop-the-loops, whirly gigs, shooting the rapids, ding-dongs, wig-wags, and falling off cliffs.

It was only natural for the pirates to celebrate the occasion with song. They sang uproariously, inharmoniously to the virtues of Mother Earth, mothers, mothers-to-be, young women, fair lasses, maidens, little girls and even saucy grandmothers.

Cranitaur's citizens were used to the sight of dragons, but this apparition was unlike anything they'd ever witnessed. Frightened out of their wits, they dove for cover for the second straight morning.

As the ship neared Isis' cave, Whittlebottom bellowed, "Silence, you blighters. We don't want to annoy the dragon."

Isis turned her back, hoping the spectacle would vanish. It was no surprise she took offense to the strange apparition invading her domain that glorious, spring day. The cacophony of ill-tuned drinking songs blaring from the wooden bird's guts only increased her tetchiness.

"Ahoy, lady dragon," Whittlebottom shouted. "We bring you gifts and greetings from the Druid." With one bony hand, he held aloft a sparkling ruby as large as his head.

"Druid?" Wisps of cinders curled around her head. "You refer to Arvid Montplier?"

"Alas, lady, no. I refer to Theron Raurk," Magried denied.

"That young upstart?"

"Aye, I bring you greetings from that *young upstart*. He sent halloos—and treasure." An outright lie, but at least Isis was talking instead of burning them to ashes.

"Why?"

"My dear, Master Theron Raurk values your wisdom, your worldli . . ."

"My foot!" Isis snorted. "Raurk cares only for his absurd quest."

"Madam, please, that's not true."

"Why?" Isis repeated.

"You must take that up with Raurk," he replied. "But . . . I happen to know your true passion!"

The dragon groaned and shifted her bulk. "Is that so?"

"Aye, 'tis true, lady."

Isis rumbled, "Since you're so smart, tell me my true passion." She nibbled at a remnant of dead skin between her toes.

"That which we bring is far more valuable than gold and jewels."

"Pirate, you tread upon infirm ground. I grow weary of your prattle."

"A picture is worth a thousand words, but in this case, I bring you the real thing." Whittlebottom whisked a sapple from behind his back.

"You bring me a sapple?" Isis didn't bother to hide her disdain. "If I'm not mistaken, that's one from Cranitaur Valley."

Whittlebottom looked askance.

"I recognize the scent," she said with a sigh.

"Not that one, you fool," he hissed to his crewman. "Bring the other basket. You'll get us all incinerated."

"A thousand pardons, I offer you the real treasure." Whittlebottom held aloft an ashberry the size of a small melon and a sapple that rivaled a basketball.

"Are they any good?"

"Try them, please," he coaxed. "If they aren't the best fruit you've ever tasted, I shall remove myself from your presence straight away."

"More likely you'll burn in Golgotha, and I'll be happy to expedite your second demise. Now, give me that ashberry before I change my mind"

"My pleasure, but I bring much more than sapples and ashberries."

"More?" Isis exhaled, a dreamy glint in her eyes.. Glowing cinders threatened the pirate ship.

"We scavenged bushel baskets of paricots, crabbages, limons, spinapple, acquash, sumpkins, scorn and the one true fruit, pomegranates. Let me see." Whittlebottom scritched his bony pate. "I know there's more."

Isis's ears perked forward. "Did you say — pomegranates?"

Whittlebottom swept his moldy tri-corn low. "How many do you desire?"

"I would share with my daughters," she purred.

"Aye, lady dragon, we have oodles. Would you care for one?"

"Oh my, yes," she breathed.

❧ 17 ❧

Grig pulled a stern face. He didn't want to appear too delighted with their expedition and his new attire. Dannel had given him a pair of water-proof boots and soft leather breeches before they left the house. At the last minute, the lad had tossed him an even softer cap to cover his head.

The threesome strolled across the meadow separating the house from the forest. At least Grig and the boy strolled. The same could not be said for Taznakie.

The round face of Malie popped straight up over the weeds searching with her enormous, amber eyes to check their progress.

Grig hadn't believed the fat ball of fur with her stubby legs could keep up with them. Often as not, she outdistanced them and then raced back to see what the holdup was. It was obvious she enjoyed the fresh air and sunshine as much as the humans.

To everyone's delight, the brewing storm of that morning had blown over and left the day clear and crisp.

Dazzling arrays of winged insects darted from one tangle of wild flowers to another. Taznakie trailed in close pursuit, whooping and yodeling to outdo any banshee. Not only did he chase them, but he did his best to leap into the air to join the throngs.

What once was a choreographed rainbow of concentrated colors turned into a brightly colored muddle swirling in an ebb and flow that made no sense. Birds that depended on the array of nature to lead them to easy prey squawked in angry protest. The louder the birds called, the louder Taznakie bawled in reply.

Dannel yelled, "Taznakie, leave off. I haven't been out of the yard in months and I don't want to spend all our time chasing bugs."

The man planted both feet on the ground and scuffed his way across the meadow to join his companions. He pin-wheeled his arms and jabbered. From what Grig could make out, Taznakie had never seen such a breathtaking display of aerial proficiency by a living body and wanted to make sure everyone knew it.

No one noticed the first slender string of golden wings encircling the trio like luminescent pearls. They started at ground level and wound ever tighter around the three humans. Then, two threads of yellow, a single strand of palest pink, and ten different shades of green joined the living mass.

From that point on it was too fast and confusing to count. The humans could not move forward or back. The roaring buzz of so many small bodies packed together deafened them. Countless tiny balls of glowing fire with wings encased the whole maelstrom.

"What the devil?" Grig's feet lifted from the ground, his body supported by the whirling mass.

Grig glanced skyward just in time to see Malie tossed willy-nilly at the top of the spinning vortex. The gerrub's short legs paddled in search of solid purchase. Too frightened to even protest, her eyes consumed her face.

The nightmare went on as the ground below sped past in a blur of greens and browns. Grig thought he saw the silver glint of water between trees, but he could not be sure.

They were at the mercy of the spiraling throng.

∾ ◆ ∿

Grig lost equilibrium as the winged column swayed from side to side. Then solid ground rose to meet them with a resounding thump. The mass of insects departed as curiously as they'd appeared. A few scrub trees dotted their view, soft lichens crackled under foot, and they were hopelessly lost.

Dannel recovered first. "I've never seen anything so amazing. Where's Malie? Did they bring her, too?"

Grig silenced him with a slash of his hand. "I saw her once, but I have no clue where she's gotten to. We must find the poor darling. She must be frightened half to death. Then we'll figure out where we are."

"We're lost," Dannel announced.

"Dannel, you look over there," Grig said. "Taznakie go that way. I'll head in this direction. Don't leave the clearing or lose sight of each other. Yell if you find her."

It took the humans the best part of an hour to discover the missing gerrub. Grig heard her plaintive whimper before he pinpointed her hiding place. He shouted to the others for help. The slight trembling of the undergrowth gave her away and all three humans converged on the frightened animal.

"Come on, sweet darling, let's go home," Grig coaxed.

Taznakie pushed him aside. Earlier, he'd hidden a large leaf wrapped in several layers of cooling, wet leather in his pocket. Grig had wondered at the time about this, but now he knew.

On all fours, Taznakie stretched his arm as far as possible toward the gerrub. It didn't take long for her to smell the delicious butter, but caution stayed her for several more minutes.

At last, Malie inched forward, too frightened to claim the delicious tidbit at once. Taznakie drew the butter closer to himself with patience and gentle wooing. At last, she devoured her prize at the feet of her relieved rescuers.

"You're no worse for wear," Grig said and deposited the quaking gerrub inside his leather jerkin as much for his own comfort as for hers.

The warmth of his bare chest against the tiny animal appeared to calm her. Although he wouldn't admit it, he drank in the sensation of her furry little body nestled against his with the greatest of pleasure. It reminded him of his own departed Tanus, whom he still missed years after her demise.

He peered around, looking for landmarks. "Dannel, do you recognize anything?" He gestured to the surrounding forest. "Anything at all . . ."

The boy searched the small clearing. "Grig Dothrie, were I a crow, I might find my way home, but I must rely on my own two feet. Alas, they fail me." His voice quivered and tears gathered in his eyes.

"Don't worry," Grig answered. "We'll be all right."

Dannel's frown deepened. "Why did they bring us here? Do you think they wanted to show us something?" He took a deep breath and ducked his head. "Grig, I'm so afraid."

"I know, lad."

Taznakie tugged at Dannel's sleeve and pointed in the distance, but Dannel shrugged him away. Again, the simpleton repeated the process and pointed. "Stop, Taznakie," he scolded. "If we don't find our way home soon, we'll be lost out here all night. Father will be furious with me for not staying close to home."

This time, Taznakie yanked at the elf's sleeve and pointed. Grig swallowed hard. He was loath to admit they were in deep trouble and Taznakie's persistent jabbering irritated him. Grig brushed at the man's hand. "What is it, you fool?" His tone came out gruffer than he intended.

Malie popped her face out from hiding. Her gaze followed the outstretched finger of Taznakie toward something the elf and boy could not see.

With a mighty shove against Grig's flesh, she launched herself toward the horizon as fast as her legs could carry her. She'd almost disappeared from sight before anyone thought to follow her.

"Malie, come back!" Dannel wailed.

Grig sighed in exasperation. "Come on, before we lose her again. I'm going to skin that animal alive."

A few steps down the path, Taznakie sped past them. He jabbered over his shoulder with a satisfied smile as he followed the gerrub.

Taznakie and Malie disappeared into the forest. For the life of him, Grig couldn't fathom what would cause the timid gerrub to streak away from them in such a tizzy.

❧ 18 ❧

"**You've** fulfilled your promise admirably, pirate," Isis groaned. "But I fancy something less sharp. My tongue fair squeaks with the tartness of pomegranate juice."

"Perhaps a melon or three?" Whittlebottom fawned, tapping at his teeth with a long finger. "I believe we have several varieties."

"Of course." She searched the horizon. "Yet, I would ask more."

"I'll do anything within my power."

Isis sighed, dousing Whittlebottom with pomegranate scented ashes. "It has been long since I ventured from Cranitaur Valley. Tell me of your travels."

The pirate swatted at an ember of fire just blossoming on his jacket. "Alas, the wars took a heavy toll. Nothing will ever be the same. In my day, all the known worlds were aligned in a fair resemblance of order. Some, like Golgotha, have just begun healing."

"What do you know of Golgotha?" Isis' ears switched in agitation.

"Little, I fear." Whittlebottom shrugged. "Why do you ask?"

"Many of my brethren were sent to that despicable land for genetic engineering by the humans." She spewed a great blast of acrid fumes. "None of them returned."

"'Tis a dark mark against humankind." Seeing her distress, Whittlebottom hastened to change the subject. "Lady, I sense you are uncomfortable. What can I do to help?"

Isis snorted. "I'm miserable, my hide itches and cracks."

"Would you have me scratch somewhere?"

"No. Yes. Maybe. Beneath my chin." She sighed, and lifted her head to him.

With delicate care, he removed strips of dead skin hanging from her chin. "Lady, would a bit of oil help?"

Isis fastened her amber gaze on the pirate. "Where would you find oil? I thought all supplies were depleted. Isn't that what started all the fighting in the first place? Energy, I believe the Old Ones called it. Energy, such a strange word."

Whittlebottom hesitated. "We, uh, discovered a stash of ancient oils. Not the petroleum kind, but others more precious. One of these might prove soothing."

"Do you mean ancient as in before you died?"

"Could be," he answered, looking away. "I have no idea how they survived, nor how we managed to find them. Should they not be to your liking, at least most are edible." He called over his shoulder, "Mate, bring me the baskets from my cabin."

"They're right here, Captain," the man said.

"Good lad." He uncorked the first bottle of rare essence. "The label reads, 'Almond Oil'." He held the vial beneath the slit where his nose would have been. "Ah, a wonderful aroma. We also have lemon, orange, corn, flax, linseed, vegetable, and coconut oil." He moved to another basket. "Here we have palm oil, cashew butter, cocoa butter, peanut butter and a dozen more."

Isis clucked with her strange dragon tongue. "You were a very naughty pirate."

Unable to blush, Whittlebottom rubbed his chin and ducked his head. "Peanut butter is particularly tasty. The trick is how to spread it? My skeletal digits are of little use." He wagged his bony fingers in the air.

She nodded toward a dark corner. "Perhaps you shall find a butter knife that will suffice for peanut butter." She laughed uproariously. "Get it?" she jostled the pirate with her snout. "A butter knife for peanut butter! I've made a joke. Oh my, the first in centuries. Pirate, I declare you are good for this old dragon. Now, slap that peanut butter right here."

❧ 19 ❧

Theron Raurk studied his host with sharp eyes. He threw a double bone on the table. "What ails you, Kevel? I've never beaten you with such ease."

Kevel turned his eyes toward the sound of Raurk's voice. He appeared to age before the druid. "My eyes weren't always so useless to the everyday world. I would give my right arm for it not to be so."

Raurk nodded, and waited for him to continue, but finally gave up. "I know how it grieves you, but I sense there's more to this melancholia than the loss of your sight."

"Raurk, you toy with me!" Kevel threw his game pieces on the table. "You know damned well Dannel will want to go with you. I can't stop him, nor can his mother. You're the only one he'll listen to. My eyes may be useless in some ways, but they show me other certainties. He'll follow behind you if you don't agree to take him along."

"So, it's come to this already?" Raurk spread his hands on the table. "I fear we've foreseen the same vision. Is there no way you can restrain him when we leave on the 'morrow?"

Kevel rose from his chair and strode to the window, staring at nothing. "Can you restrain the wind? Can you deny the goldenfly wings to soar? Dannel can't be held. I ask only that you watch over him. Lillith will do her best to keep him from harm, but . . . ." He shrugged. "She possesses many qualities that even she doesn't know about and *he* is impulsive to a fault."

"Keep who from harm?" Adelita asked.

"Mother, I didn't hear you come in." He embraced his wife. "Raurk plans to leave in the morning. He must make haste in this insane mission."

"My concern is more immediate." Adelita ran her arm under his and placed her head on his shoulder. "Nightfall brushes the tree tops and our explorers have not returned. I fear something has happened."

"They're not back yet? I'll whip that boy's behind."

Adelita turned to Raurk. "Will you walk down to the stream and retrieve them? They probably just lost track of the time. Still, I'd have you look for them if you don't mind."

"Of course, I'll go." Raurk would gladly escape Kevel's suffocating presence. He'd known from the beginning that his young brother-in-law would do his utmost to follow them. Kevel's spoken fears had given validity to his own.

❧ 20 ❧

"**I** proclaim the kiwi butter the winner." Isis belched. "No more or I shall explode."

"Your belly grumbles like an old locomotive. Perhaps you'll be clucking like a brooding hen soon." Whittlebottom patted the dragon's flank with affection.

Isis giggled in a very undragon-like manner. "Aye, and this shall be my last clutch. She'll need her own court when she grows up."

"Excuse me, lady dragon, I do not follow."

"My daughter, Rilieann, shall be my successor." Isis avowed.

"No!" Whittlebottom gasped. "The Creator would not allow such a . . ."

"The Creator. That's what this whole insane quest is about. Not oil, or treasure, or energy, or whatever you men offer for excuses. I fear Raurk and the others will fail in their endeavors and all the known worlds will be plunged into war again."

"I don't understand," Whittlebottom said.

"What don't you understand? Surely you were not a stupid man."

The pirate shook his head, and then glanced toward his hovering ship and the darkening horizon. "Where has the time gone? I can't believe it's so late. I would rather broach this subject under the light of a new sun."

"Perhaps that is best, my friend. Send your men away and stay the night with me. My attendants have fled for safer ground, and rightfully so. By your leave, I would not be alone."

"Indeed, 'tis my pleasure to stay with you, my lady. We are much alike and I enjoy your company."

❧ 21 ❧

They were lost and separated. Taznakie and Malie had run off on their own. Dusk trailed a chilling hand down Grig's spine, and Dannel snuffled his fears into his sleeve. They called over and over, but heard no answer. Black clouds formed again in the south and bore down upon them.

"This is the blackbird's doing, and where is he?" Grig shook his fist in the air. "I'll wager he's holed up by the fireplace with Kevel Firth and a hot mug of ale. I didn't want to come out here in the first place, but *no*. Go along Grig Dothrie, they said. It'll do you good, they said. Well a fat lot of good it's doing me, lost out here in the middle of nowhere."

He sank onto a nearby stump. "Bah, to all of them. I'm going home tomorrow regardless of what Raurk says. He can't stop me."

"I'm sorry, Master Grig," Dannel mumbled. "I just wanted to get out of the house. Maybe we'll find Taznakie and Malie soon and then we can make our way home before it gets too late."

Grig sighed and patted the boy on the back. "I fear it's already too late, young man. I suppose there's nothing else to do but keep looking. Whatever you do, don't go running off like that fool, Taznakie."

❧ ◆ ❧

Raurk followed their footprints, but the trail stopped a hundred feet short of the woods. For all his skills as a necromancer, he could discern nothing more.

A curious array of dead and dying insects caught his attention. Their broken wings and battered bodies littered the ground where the trail ended. He knelt to sift the tiny corpses through his fingers. A chill swept through his being.

He spun and returned to the house at a run. Before he could utter a word, Kevel accosted him. "I smell the fear on you. Where are they? Where's my son?"

"I wish I knew," Raurk answered. "I followed their trail almost to the woods then it vanished. I found a carpet of dead goldenfly wings, but that was all."

Adelita and Lillith entered the room as the druid spoke.

Panic etched Kevel's face. "You must find them," he said. "They're in great danger. In my youth, such a horde whisked me away on the combined wings of millions and deposited me days from home. Untold numbers of their kind died in the process. Raurk, you must find them."

"But, Father, where should he look?" Lillith implored. "Perhaps it would be best if I go with him. I know the area better than my husband."

"No," Kevel shouted.

"Lillith, I shall not travel afoot." Raurk hugged his wife. "I would have you come to the meadow with me and point the right direction."

"But..."

"Then, you must return to the house. From then on, I travel alone. It's imperative that you stay here with Kevel and Adelita. Don't try to follow me. Should the others return in my absence, I beg of you, keep them here."

‽ ◆ ‽

Lillith and the druid crossed the meadow. "You didn't need my assistance, Raurk."

"Aye, 'tis true." He dropped his gaze to the ground.

She glared at him with hands on her hips. "For all I've told you, you could've gone on alone. What is it that bothers you? My brother and your friends are lost. Is that not enough?"

"'Tis more than enough, my darling," Raurk agreed. "I but wanted a moment alone with you. I love your parents, but my time with you is too short. A few moments delay before I depart will not matter. I can at least go in harmony knowing you still care for me."

Lillith gave him a quick hug. "Go in peace."

Raurk kissed her and then pushed her gently away. "Go up to the house and don't look back. I shall be out of sight before you're inside, and I would not have you witness my departure."

☙ ◆ ❧

Grig nearly tripped when Dannel came to an abrupt halt. "Damn you, boy. We'll never find them if you keep stopping every few feet."

"Shhh . . ." Dannel hissed. "I thought I heard something."

"Just like you did three hours ago?"

Dannel waved him to silence. "There it is again." The lad bounded into the forest off to their right.

"Stop," Grig called. There was nothing for him to do but keep up— or get left behind, again. "Blast you, boy. Slow down."

Dannel waved over his shoulder and shouted something Grig could not make out.

"Impudent brat," Grig panted, but he hastened his steps.

Dannel raced into the death-littered clearing with Grig Dothrie ten paces behind. The boy skidded to a halt. "Oh, my . . ."

"Don't run off like that again." Grig's gaze followed a strange sound and his jaw dropped. "Maker, preserve us."

Taznakie squatted on his haunches like a great wolf at rest with his arms between his legs. His head thrown back, he gave vent to an eerie wail of lament.

"What happened?" Dannel scrubbed at his eyes. "Are they all dead?"

Grig couldn't take his gaze from the petite gerrub squatting in the same pose as Taznakie. Her cries were all the more devastating as the piercing falsetto of her wails penetrated to the core of his being.

Dannel tugged at his sleeve and sank to the ground. "Who . . . ?" He sobbed his own grief.

A force of brutal strength had cleaved three griffins into bloody shreds. Several more lay dying. Too many dead or dying fauns to count were tossed about the meadow like broken toys. And one lone hippogriff.

With effort, Grig managed to tear his attention from Malie. Then his gaze settled on the hideously maimed hippogriff with its mutilated wings. He could say nothing as he stumbled over the blood-spattered, fly-specked corpses to reach the animal wrenching at his heart.

With eyes full of pain and shock, the creature silently begged Grig to end its misery. "I—I can't," he sighed, slumping to the gory loam next to the beast. He winced as he realized the animals' back legs pointed in the wrong direction, its spine broken.

"'Tis a mortal sin to slay such a wondrous beast," he defended himself when Dannel approached. "He'll die anyway, but I can't hasten the outcome." He swiped angrily at tears and then laid the giant, beaked head in his lap. "Go see if Taznakie and Malie are all right."

Grig sang a magical tune to ease the hippogriff's pain. The pitiful moans of the dying creature brought fresh tears to his eyes.

It took every ounce of his strength to finish his psalm. "I'm sorry, friend, I can do no more." With gentle words and kind hands, he smoothed the beast's passing into the next world.

Closing its eyes, the animal died in Grig's embrace. "My fabulous one . . ." he cried.

❧ ◆ ❧

Grig had no sense of time passing when he looked up to see Taznakie and the boy standing a respectful distance away.

"They're all dead," Dannel said. "When the hippogriff passed, so did the rest. Grig, why would anyone do this? These creatures have long been at peace with humans."

Grig disentangled himself from the crushing weight of the hippogriff's head and staggered toward his companions in a daze. "I don't know." Sobs choked his words. "But I swear I'll wreck revenge upon their heads before all is said and done." He allowed his friends to engulf him in their warm embrace.

❧ ◆ ❧

Raurk took to the air in the shape of a great, flapping blackbird before Lillith reached the house. If he'd witnessed the transformation, Grig would have taken satisfaction at the druid's resemblance to the bird.

A powerful beat of his dark wings sent Raurk soaring over the forest. His sharp eyes searched for a glint of light or a spot of color that might betray the whereabouts of his friends. He plied the sky on and on, hoping for a sign, no matter how insignificant.

Dread trod ever heavier on his hopes. More than once, Raurk turned toward home and Lillith, the one defect in his personal armor. Yet again, he resigned himself to the search. He could not return to Kevel, Adelita and Lillith and tell them he'd failed.

Raurk glided, conserving his energy. If he found them, he would need every ounce of his strength to bring Dannel and the others home. Looming black clouds raced from the south, increasing his dread. Raurk feared the worst should the storm reach them before he did.

He was about to retrace his path when a disturbance toward the western horizon caught his eyes. At first he dismissed it as too far for the humans to have traveled. But as he approached, the earsplitting death of thousand-year-old trees assaulted the air. The booming drum-roll of heavy feet echoing from the same direction settled on his ears like a death knell.

The earth trembled at the passing of a mighty force. Raurk's instincts and fear drew him ever closer to the raucous cacophony. But nothing could prepare him for the wide swath of forest laid waste under the giant feet of a three-headed rock-troll as tall as the loftiest trees. Even the air upon which he glided rippled at the passing of the colossal monster.

Grecolix, the bone yard keeper, was no more than a gnat compared to this behemoth troll, and probably twice as smart. A mutant of the worst kind plowed the forest before it. In each of the giant's three right hands, a massive club cleared a trail for its passing. In the three left hands, the beast carried enormous scimitars to cut down anything left in its path. Raurk wheeled to follow the giant's wake of destruction.

ȣ ♦ ȣ

At last, grief ran its course. Still sniffling, Grig looked up to find the clearing had grown dark. Millions of tiny winged fireballs covered the carnage. Their soft glow lit the meadow with a preternatural calm. With one hand extended, he motioned for the others to look.

Much to their surprise, the goldenflies herded them toward a broad path of destruction across the clearing. In their heads, each of them heard a disembodied voice saying, "Follow the troll. It will lead you to safety."

"Wait," Dannel wailed. "We'll meet our deaths in the dark. The troll might return, or we could fall or . . . Grig Dothrie, tell them!"

Not sure why, Grig searched the littered ground for a suitable branch. The voice in his head told him this was what he must do. At last, he found a broken limb about two feet long and quite bushy at one end. He held it over his head, waiting to see what would come next.

Thousands of tiny, glowing fireballs converged upon the bough, creating a wondrous torch. The light was faint, but with two more, they could see to walk. Grig motioned for the others to follow suit.

Taznakie held his torch aloft and then bounced in the air several times to see if the shimmering insects would dislodge. But, the creatures did not move, steadfastly shining their light upon the path.

"Stop, Taznakie," Dannel said. "We need to leave this place."

But Taznakie poked a finger into the ball of light to see what would happen, and then swirled the torch in the air. Before he was through, he had jiggled, prodded, smelled and even licked the living mass.

Malie arched her back with her plumed tail held high and hissed as the tiny creatures approached. Trembling all over, she hunkered to the ground, a quivering ball of fur when they attached themselves to her ears and tail. Even her whiskers glowed with shimmering light.

Taznakie scooped the gerrub from the ground and placed her upon his broad shoulders. The sight of Malie with her tail aglow rendered even him speechless. The others gawked, but then the voices inside their heads urged them forward again.

"This is pure madness to follow in the footsteps of a troll," Grig said. He glanced to Dannel and Taznakie for confirmation.

"What choice do we have?" Dannel followed the path with his gaze.

"None that I can see. We must leave the carnage behind." Grig had no idea what would happen to the bodies of the dead, and he didn't want to find out.

It might be hours before the jackals, coyowolves and other carnivores braved the ghostly setting, but they would come.

ꙮ **22** ꙮ

The mutant troll had one thing on its pea-sized brains, and that was to get from here to there. It made not the slightest bit of difference whether it knew where *here* or *there* lie. Neither did it matter should the monster need to mow down a whole forest, an isolated farmhouse, a rock escarpment, or innocent forest creatures.

The troll's inability to turn aside had caused the slaughter of the forest people. Those harmless creatures posed no more threat than a mosquito bite on the giant's broad behind. Something that must be scratched then ignored.

Yet this penchant proved to be the saving grace for Grig, Taznakie and Dannel. They could never match their human stride against that of the troll — and it could not turn back to ambush them.

Grig's nose burned at the acrid scent of death. Added to this, the putrid stench of the troll made him nauseous as they followed in the creature's footsteps.

More than once, he wished Raurk would drop from the sky and whisk them to safety. "Where's that blackbird when you need him?" he grumbled under his breath.

"What did you say?" Dannel turned to stare Grig in the face.

Grig shook his head. "Nothing, lad. Watch where you put your feet." He grabbed Dannel's shoulder to steady him.

Taznakie said, "Garpporoni."

"That's right," Grig answered. "We're going home come hell or high water."

ꙮ ♦ ꙮ

The travelers scrambled over, under and around fallen trees the best they could. "Damn that monster to hell," Grig said as he barked his shins for the umpteenth time.

Saplings bent under the assault of the monster troll slowly regained an upright position. Larger hardwood trees lay splintered across the path. As dark blanketed the forest, a shattered Burnet tree blocked progress in either direction.

"What are we supposed to do?" Dannel asked. "We can't climb over that in the dark." He swiped at a fat drop of rain. "Oh, great. Father will be furious if I get sick."

Grig sighed. He'd had his fill of rain the past two days. "We must seek shelter straightaway."

"Where?" Dannel turned in circles, scanning the forest.

"We'll find something." Grig's words lacked conviction. He didn't want to tell the boy about the eerie shapes flitting between dark shadows. Nor the feral eyes glimmering overhead. Worst of all was the peculiar slithering sound that caused the hackles on his neck to rise.

"What if the troll comes back?" Dannel shuddered with dread.

"Run like hell." Grig hid his fear behind anger. "I haven't seen a nook or cranny worth spitting at."

Taznakie flapped both arms and crowed, pointing to one end of the huge tree. When Grig didn't respond, he swept his hands in the same direction.

In a blink, he disappeared under a formidable bow of leaves with the frightened gerrub still clinging to his shoulder.

"Taznakie," Grig shouted.

"Gindess likt tunbe." Taznakie popped into view laughing as if he'd just played the world's greatest practical joke on his friends. Then he turned and winked out of sight again.

Grig opened his mouth to swear, but a terrifyingly close lightning bolt changed his mind. He dove behind Taznakie, slapping at his electrically charged hair. Thunder rolled across the forest upon his heels.

"Wow! Look at your hair, Grig," Dannel said, giving a nervous giggle. "That was really close. I thought you were a goner for sure. "

"Aye. So did I." Grig sighed and mouthed a silent prayer.

"What is this place?" Dannel scurried about the room. "It's dry and smells like home. Look." He gestured toward a low stool piled with brightly colored blankets.

Taznakie did his best to tell them about the enchanted shelter created hundreds of years ago when humans roamed the forests openly. It would keep them warm, dry and protected from hungry beasts.

"We're lucky Taznakie found it," Dannel said.

"They're plain to see for those with the sight for such things," Grig said, irritated that he'd not been the one to find it.

Dannel wrapped a blanket around his shoulders. "This feels so good. I wish we had something to eat."

Taznakie pointed to the small cupboard on the wall. It brimmed with the essentials to keep them alive as long as they didn't try to remove the contents to the outside world of mankind.

The glowing insects had entered the shelter with them, eliminating the need to cast a spell, or to light the many candles around the room. The tiny creatures aligned themselves along the ceiling, producing constellations of bright stars and moons. Intrigued, the travelers watched as the shapes merged and flowed into a new design adding another element of charm to the cozy interior.

⮞ ◆ ⮜

Exhausted and his belly full, Dannel yawned wide enough to crack his jaw. "I don't care what this place is," he mumbled. "If I have to spend the night in the woods, this is the way to do it. I can't wait to tell Papa all about it." The boy's face suddenly fell. "If we get back."

"It's all right, lad," Grig said. "We'll be home soon and you can tell him everything."

Dannel smiled and nodded. "Look, Taznakie and Malie are already asleep." He rolled into his blanket and snored softly before Grig could count to three.

Happy to be out of the night air and pelting rain, Grig still had misgivings. Worry about their sanctuary nagged at his subconscious. As a tree dweller in his own village, he knew of these havens. Unfortunately, they weren't always as safe as Taznakie seemed to believe. He wondered why this shelter appeared to them. "This is too easy." He startled himself and then looked around to see if he'd woken the boy.

Round and round his mind went, allowing him little respite. Had he uttered the magic words just before the lightning nearly singed him? In his garbled way, had Taznakie summoned it? Or could it have been the fairy-like creatures that provided a soft glow from the ceiling? Did it even matter? They had a dry place to sleep, food to eat, and safety from prowling night creatures.

That thought brought his hackles to full attention. He'd seen those skulking shadows dogging their footsteps. What might've happened had they not found the shelter? Once or twice, he'd spied the flash of glistening, wet fangs in the tight packed web of darkness. He didn't want to think about what was behind those dagger-like incisors. Surely, they'd be dinner for some unspeakable beast if the shelter hadn't appeared.

He'd nearly drifted to sleep when he remembered. These shelters had a penchant for appearing in one place and then moving during the night. Where would they awake in the morning and at what price?

Grig had witnessed unwary travelers exiting in the morning into the jaws of wild beasts. He'd even heard a rumor about a group of men who'd plunged to their deaths high above a raging waterfall.

At last, exhaustion won out, and the elf fell into a deep slumber. The last thing he remembered was Malie insinuating herself into the crook of his left arm. And he dreamed of the night the forest little people brought another gerrub to his tree house for healing.

Near starved and mortally wounded, blood and filth had caked her tiny body. His first thought was to sing the same psalm he'd crooned to the hippogriff. But the lifeblood and a fierce will to live still flowed in her veins.

He fell in love the moment he'd cradled the poor darling in his arms. With a basin of hot water and a rag steeped in an infusion of stinging nettleworts, he'd sponged away filth and blood. Only then did he discover she was a beautiful white gerrub with apricot tipped hair. Resolution grew in his heart. He vowed to do everything in his power to heal her.

❧ ◆ ❧

Incessant rain weighed Raurk's wings with fatigue. He saw no reason to return to his human shape, so he sheltered under the relative safety of a giant tree. He'd traveled much further than the hikers could have walked, but turning back never entered his mind.

He'd passed the sleeping three-headed troll several hours ago. The monster had fallen asleep on its feet and keeled over in mid-stride. The morning would bring another day of senseless rampaging through the forest, but for now, it slept like a newborn.

The thought of the mutant troll sent shivers through Raurk's body. If Dannel, Grig and Taznakie ran into this monster, he'd be taking home three broken bodies. Malie would make no more than a bloody footprint ground into the forest floor.

Raurk slipped into a light doze, aware of his surroundings and his failure to find his friends. He was still a mortal who must rest at times. As soon as it was light, he would be airborne.

Grig bolted upright. His labored breath seared his lungs. Heart thundering in his ears and sweat blurring his vision, he searched for his companions. To his relief he found them sound asleep. The only one missing was Malie, and he discovered her cowering under the blankets at Dannel's feet.

Didn't they hear the cry that had awoken him—or had he dreamt it? Had he cried out in his sleep? Grig sank back on his pallet. Why had he dreamed of Tanus? It'd been ever so long since she had passed, yet he still missed her. He let his mind wander again to the night she'd been brought to him. Before long, he slipped back into the world of dreams.

The gerrub's left ear had dangled by a small thread of flesh and a great slash extended across her eye. Her poor tail had been broken in numerous places giving it an odd question mark shape, but this injury had already healed. A poisonous Nemrak thorn pierced her left front paw.

He didn't know where to start, so he fed the injured animal slivers of butter to win her trust—and to bolster his own spirit.

Mending her ear and cheek with a bit of magical webbing proved the easy part, though only time would tell whether she would lose the sight in her left eye. Then he could no longer put off the issue of the poisonous thorn. If anything killed her, it would be this. Had she been stronger, he would have removed it first. Nemrak worked slowly, so he had bolstered her strength as best he could before subjecting her to more pain.

The cruel rear-facing barbs on the Nemrak spike prevented extraction from the point of entry. Of necessity, he needed to push or pull the hook through to the other side. He prayed it would not leave a path of destroyed nerve and flesh behind.

Every time he tried to examine her foot, she jerked it away in painful protest. As a last resort, he steeped pieces of tanus root in strong nettlewort tea. The brew would draw the poison from the wound and numb the pain.

He managed to clip away the underside of the thorn from her paw after a soothing soak in this potion. If the gerrub had been a larger animal, Grig would have been licking his own wounds about then. Again he immersed her infected foot in the numbing liquid and prayed it would be enough.

The gerrub bordered on sleep by the time Grig deemed the mixture had done all it could. He gripped the tip of the thorn with strong pincers and pulled with all his might. If he didn't get it the first time, there would be no second chance. Tanus (he wondered when he'd named her after the root) could not withstand the searing pain again.

Putrid ribbons of sinew clung to the barbs as he forced it through her flesh. But he wasn't prepared for her reaction. Even to this day, he could never forget it. The little thing had screamed in pain and fainted, ripping Grig's heart to shreds.

Grig jerked awake for the second time. "Enough of that," he muttered and lifted Malie from Dannel's side, crooning at the quaking animal. "I'm sorry I frightened you, little one.

"I had a terrible nightmare. I dreamt of my beloved Tanus, but then she turned into a giant troll chasing us. It had three heads and six arms. I can still feel its teeth peeling the flesh from my bones. Yon simpleton tried to cast a spell to save me, but it went awry. Dear Malie, what shall we do?" The gerrub purred and nestled against him. In return, Grig nuzzled his face against her head.

Malie calmed at his soft words, but his voice had woken Dannel. The boy mumbled, "I had the most awful dream. The sooner we quit this place, the better. Malie kept me awake most the night shivering and moaning under my blanket. I think she's had enough excitement for the rest of her life."

"That makes two of us," Grig said. "Wake Taznakie while I see what's left to eat. This place smells worse every minute we delay."

⤎ ◆ ⤏

Poking his head like a turtle from its shell, Grig did a double take. They were in virgin, unscathed woods. Where was the destruction inflicted by the rampaging troll? More importantly, where were they?

The steady drizzle cast a forlorn, sad pall over the travelers. Tendrils of fog twining in and out of nowhere added a ghostly presence. If not for the solid earth beneath his feet, Grig would have had nothing to be thankful for.

Taznakie burst past him into the dense undergrowth. For one brief moment, Grig almost thought he understood the man's babbling. Then reason took over to reassure him that he had not gone insane.

"Stop your prattling! And get over here before you get lost." He laughed at his own words. "We're already lost."

"Tradidi," Taznakie answered.

"This safe shelter of yours moved during the night," Grig said. "We're surrounded by dense forest. So don't go wandering off by yourself."

"Yowlf."

"You, too." He glared at Dannel just emerging into the world of daylight. "And where's that damn gerrub of yours? We'll not be wasting our time hunting her down if she wanders off again."

Dannel handed the gerrub to Grig. "Don't worry, I shan't go far. Not that there seems to be anywhere to go."

"That's right," Grig said, crossing his arms over his chest. "And don't you forget it."

The boy parked his behind on a large rock and studied their surroundings. "Even if we could see the sun, we still don't know which way to go." The moisture upon his young cheeks mixed with the drizzling rain.

⤎ ◆ ⤏

Raurk took to wing hours before the weary trio arose. He approached the scene of slaughter with a heavy heart, dreading what he'd find. Long tendrils of greasy smoke rose in spite of, or perhaps because of the drizzle, but it could not mask the smell of charred flesh.

Circling high above, his sharp eyes spied a measured procession of forest people paying homage to their brethren. They had set the funeral pyre rather than leave the dead for predators to scavenge and squabble over, though there seemed little reason to fight with such obvious abundance.

Making sure the men saw his approach, Raurk dropped to the ground and prepared to resume his human shape. The nearest forest dweller said, "No, remain as you are Theron Raurk. Allow us to honor our fallen as befits them."

"Aye, Rando, I'll do as bid. I ask only to know what has passed and whether you have seen three travelers, a boy, an elf and a man. They're my charges, and I fear no good has come to them."

Rando turned grief-filled eyes upon the druid. "You came from yon direction." He motioned with his head. "That should be explanation enough. The troll destroys everything in its path, including your friends should they be foolish enough to put themselves in its way. Although I do not believe that event has transpired as of yet."

"What are you telling me?"

Forest people seldom answered a direct question, and not at all if they should so deem, but Raurk must take that risk. Without their help he might never find his friends. This forest was one of the few unsullied sanctuaries left and infuriatingly dense. The only consolation being there were none of the poisonous, man-eating fauna of the mutant woods. Although he could think of a dozen other reasons to fear for their lives.

Rando turned his full attention to the man in bird disguise. "That hideous creature killed a hippogriff. There are few enough left in this forest and that . . . that monster murdered one." Tears streamed un-heeded down his weathered cheeks.

"Where are my friends?"

"The forest pixies brought your friends here. Now they lead the men and boy to safety. If it'd been up to me . . ." He shrugged. "That's better left unsaid." The little man turned to leave.

Raurk called, "Wait, which way did they go?"

"For all the good it will do, they followed the troll," Rando called without slowing his steps.

ॐ ◆ ॐ

Rakell Taznakie yanked at Grig's sleeve for the third or fourth time. But before Grig could reply, the simpleton lifted him from the ground, tucked him under one arm, and trotted into the deep forest yodeling like a madman. Dannel followed with Malie tucked under his arm.

Struggle as he might, Grig couldn't escape. Taznakie dumped the squirming elf on the ground a good hundred yards down a path no one else could see. He pointed to the forest floor while doing his usual dancing from one foot to the other, but Grig could decipher nothing. Let alone anything to get so excited about.

Then the elf saw the ghostly path imprinted in the earth and nearly did a jig himself. Whether it was an animal track, or made by the feet of the forest people, it was a path. And a path meant they were going somewhere—anywhere. "Praise the maker."

Grig had a sudden flashback at the thought of the forest dwellers and the injured gerrub. He didn't know an animal could faint, but he was thankful when Tanus' yellow eyes closed and she went as limp as an old rag.

While she slept, he secured a poultice about her paw with another of his magical webs. At last he allowed himself hope that the little gerrub would heal. Loath to lay her down, he engulfed her in a warm blanket and settled in front of the fire with his precious bundle to pass the long night.

"Grig. Grig Dothrie. Master Grig!" a faraway voice called. "You look like you've seen a ghost. Are you ill?"

Grig shook himself roughly. "I . . ."

"Good elf, what is it?" Dannel tugged at Grig's sleeve. "Which way should we go?

Grig focused on the slender impression of faded trail before them. "I . . . ." He looked both ways. "I don't know." But he did. Even as the words left his mouth, he spied the question mark shape of Tanus' tail disappearing downhill to their right. Maybe the delusions of his longings deceived him, or truly a specter beckoned, but he would follow Tanus anywhere.

"This way," he whispered. "It's a path, and it has to lead some-where.

❧ 23 ❧

To say the giant troll had three tiny brains is not entirely correct. It seems the great Maker took one miniscule brain and divided it into pieces and then portioned them between three heads, known as Borg, Brog and Boog.

Saying this troll only moved dead ahead is also misleading. They might never backtrack, but depending on which entity gained control for the day determined their actual course.

Borg, residing in the left cranium, always veered to his left. Boog, on the right, pulled to the right. And of course Brog, in the middle, traveled straight as a banshee's attack. Given sufficient time and space, the giant might complete a circle if Borg or Boog were in control.

The morning following the massacre, Borg awoke first, and though playing with a short deck, he did not lack for other, less appealing attributes. By far, he excelled at being the slyest, craftiest, meanest and most covetous of the three entities. He proceeded to bash his siblings senseless with his great club. This would be his day, and he balked at nothing to achieve it. For the very first time, he acted as the sole captain of his hulking ship of ruin.

❧ ◆ ❧

"Can't we stop for a while?" Dannel asked. "I thought you said this would lead us to water. It seems like forever since we ate breakfast."

Their meal from the safe shelter had held them through the morning, but now Grig's stomach growled. The boy and Taznakie looked flushed to his eyes.

The elf surveyed the path, stalling. "I believe it will. We've been going downhill for a long time, and that's a good sign. Water always runs to the lowest point." Every time he'd doubted their path, Tanus turned to him as if asking what took them so long. She might be a specter, but he placed all his hope in her.

To his relief, Grig had seen signs leading him to believe they neared one of the little people's villages. But they were old, as if civilization had come for a short stay and then moved on.

He did not mention this to the young lad tagging along in his footsteps. Even a deserted village held promise of water and the bounty of long neglected gardens. Yet, were it not for his frequent visions of Tanus, he might have turned back.

Grig realized Taznakie hadn't added his two cents' worth in ages. He whirled about, afraid the simpleton had wandered off on his own. But Taznakie stood there grinning and waving in his guileless manner. Grig hid a sigh of relief. "You were so quiet I thought you'd fallen off a cliff."

"Grumph," Taznakie said.

"Master Grig," Dannel interrupted. "Who's Tanus? You've been talking to her for hours, but it's just us three. Have you gone dotty with hunger?"

"I have no idea what you're talking about." Grig didn't want to share his vision of the spectral gerrub. "'Tis no one. You're imagination runs wild." He turned away to avoid further questioning from the boy.

Before he could take a step, Taznakie grabbed him by the sleeve, turning the elf in his tracks. Confusion marred his face as he pointed to Malie, then at the trail behind Grig. Malie chirruped with excitement, but she made no move to leave the safety of Taznakie's shoulder.

Dannel glanced from one to the other. "What is it? There's nothing there. This may be a path, but even I can tell no human foot has passed this way in ages."

Taznakie shook his head. Again he jabbered and pointed to Malie, then at the trail ahead. He didn't wait for the others, but bolted down the path they had been following.

"Damn," Grig spat. "Come on, boy, he's chasing bugs again."

Grig and Dannel skidded to a halt as they rounded the next bend in the trail. Taznakie had found water. On his hands and knees, he slurped from the stream. Malie perched daintily on a rock in the middle of the small brook slaking her thirst. The others ran to the stream and drank their fill.

Grig's tender feet hurt and they were still hungry, but at least they had all the delicious, cold water they could drink.

෫ ◆ ෬

The elf lay upon his back under the canopy of a large tree, his attention focused on the ghostly gerrub climbing the branches overhead. Rakell Taznakie and Dannel Firth snored a few feet away. "Well, Tanus, I knew you'd lead us to water. This is as good a place as any to stop for the night."

After drinking his fill, Grig scoured the immediate area hoping to find something to eat. His efforts were rewarded with numerous toadstools they feared to eat. So he lay awake, his belly complaining, his feet throbbing, endless possibilities of disaster running through his head, and questions . . . . So many questions.

The following day, they must press on. But where was the path taking them? Could Taznakie see Tanus just as he did? Why would the vision of *his* beloved gerrub appear to that oaf, and maybe Malie, too?

How had they gotten into this mess in the first place, and where was that blackbird, Theron Raurk? Had the druid abandoned them for lost? Did he lounge by a roaring fire with Lillith, Kevel, and Adelita, spouting nonsense about how he'd done everything possible to rescue them? Those thoughts lulled him into an uneasy sleep.

෫ ◆ ෬

Raurk had followed Rando's suggestion to follow the rampaging rock-troll to find his friends. He'd sensed their essence at the huge tree that blocked their progress the previous night, detected the presence, or maybe the absence of the safe shelter, but found nothing of the travelers. With the shelter moved, he had no way of knowing whether they had entered or not.

Frustrated, the druid took to the air again searching for a telltale sign the humans had passed this way. He came upon the troll just in time to witness Borg bashing his Siamese twins senseless.

Raurk resisted the urge to blast the miserable lot of them to hell, but Rando's order to follow the troll had been explicit. The three-headed monster remained his only chance of finding his friends.

Occasionally he varied his flight in random directions to no avail. It was no mean feat to find his way back. He couldn't miss the squeal of splintering wood, the shriek of glee constantly issuing from Borg's mouth, and the heavy thudding of giant feet, punctuated by the thwack of a huge club meeting with rock-flesh as Borg sent one or the other brothers back to dreamland.

Raurk soared on a sudden updraft, pondering whether he might chance returning to Lillith and her parents long enough to let them know what had happened. Just as quickly, he rejected the idea knowing it was the worst thing he could do. Anything could happen in his absence, and he might never find the men and boy.

At one point he thought he'd spied a bit of color that might belie the whereabouts of Grig and the others, but upon closer inspection it proved to be a decimated tree stump festooned in colored lichens.

In this manner, the day passed in a slow crawl for Theron Raurk. Nightfall brought him a short reprieve, but no peace of mind. As sleep enveloped him, he vowed to continue his search until he either found his friends well and hale, or could take their body's home for burial.

☙ ◆ ❧

Taznakie awoke hours before his companions. He'd recognized the signs that foretold of a village nearby. More than anything, he longed to find food to surprise Grig and the lad. Luck drew him to a slight hollow on the opposite side of the brook.

Malie played in the soft grass chasing goldenflies in the first sunshine they'd seen in two days, and when he went to join her, he'd seen the tiny door at the base of a massive tree. Upon further inspection, he discovered ten more, and even better, a wiry bladder vine. The tough skins made excellent vessels once gutted and rinsed. If he found something to eat, he'd have a means of transport.

Berry vines of every imaginable sort trailed along the ground and in the trees. He'd never imagined such a bonanza. For every berry he placed in his gourd, three went into his mouth. There were so many, he went back to clean two more gourds to hold his bounty.

The look on Grig's and Dannel's faces when they awoke proved sufficient reward for all his hard work. Berry stains covered his own face and even Malie had missed a few dribbles on her furry chin.

Taznakie watched his friends eat for several minutes and then ran to the stream to refill an empty gourd with water. He'd left the opening on one small so the water would not slosh out when he walked.

If their situation had not been so desperate, Grig might have considered staying the remainder of the day to rest. He came very close to surrendering to temptation, but the need to find home won out. He watched his friends, still debating. "I think it wisest to keep going. There's nothing to be accomplished here. What say you?"

The lad stared at the ground for the longest time before answering. "Grig, you know so much more than I, but I have to agree. If we run into the troll that killed the forest creatures . . . . We may die before long anyway, but I don't want to just sit here and wait for it to happen."

Taznakie jabbered something, and it was clear from the vigorous nodding of his head that he agreed. Before anyone could move, he jumped up, grabbed all four gourds and headed across the stream to pick more berries.

"Wait, I'll help you," Dannel called.

"Me, too." Grig followed.

They spent the next hour cleaning gourds and filling them with berries. Grig imitated Taznakie's small opening in three of them to hold water. They might not come across another stream pure enough to drink. Food they could manage without, but not water.

At last, Grig surveyed their bounty and sighed. "As much as I'd like to stay, we can't delay any longer."

Tanus appeared at the edge of the clearing with her crooked tail held high in the muggy breeze. With a pang of guilt, Grig wondered who was watching after his two large male gerrubs at home.

Taznakie pointed and motioned for the others to follow.

"Wait," Grig said. "Are you telling me *you* can see her?"

Taznakie bobbed his head and bounced up and down with excitement.

"Who is she, Master Grig?" Dannel stared in wonder. "I thought I saw a strange gerrub yesterday, but I wasn't sure. She's much clearer today. Where did she come from? What happened to her tail?"

Somewhat miffed that the specter of his beloved pet should appear to these two, Grig glowered at Malie, perched on Taznakie's shoulder. "I suppose you see her, too? Why is it everybody in the world can see Tanus when she was *my* beautiful darling?"

Malie jumped to the ground and went to greet the newcomer, chirruping an invitation. Tanus ran to rub faces and do all the other silly things gerrubs do in greeting.

Much to the surprise of both animals, they passed cleanly through each other. Malie wheeled about to scrutinize this oddity only to discover the other gerrub protruding from her own side.

Tanus didn't seem to understand that *she* was the apparition. Playfully, she batted at Malie's nose only to see her paw pass through solid flesh. With a yowl of alarm, Malie scaled Taznakie's leg to rest on his shoulder again. Not to be outdone, Tanus followed suit.

Beside himself, Taznakie couldn't decide what to do. Jabbering nonstop, he twirled trying to catch a glimpse of the gerrub on each shoulder. Then he jumped up and down on one foot while flinging both arms skyward for what reason, no one knew.

Malie held on for her life. At last, Taznakie grabbed the corporeal animal and held her gently on the ground, allowing Tanus to sniff her from head to tail.

Whatever transpired in those few moments convinced the timid little Malie this stranger posed no threat. Immediately she darted off with Tanus close behind. When she reversed course, Tanus kept going and ran straight through her.

Back and forth they played, until Grig put a stop to their shenanigans with a loud whistle. "Will you two imbeciles kindly forestall your antics? I don't want to spend another night wandering through the forest."

24

Grig soon got over his hurt feelings that Tanus would make herself known to anyone but himself. He hid a grin behind his hand, loath to let his companions know he enjoyed himself.

In spite of this, he heard—or felt—something in the back of his mind that cast a cold chill of foreboding in his heart. He had no idea what the dull booming and rhythmic pounding meant, but it rested uneasily on his senses.

◆

The morning after Borg's rampage brought giant headaches to his siblings. Boog and Brog were none too pleased with his insurrection. They'd always bickered between themselves, but such insurrection was unheard of. Before he could blink awake, Brog and Boog lambasted Borg with a resounding clout of their clubs. They took charge in no uncertain terms, and would go where *they* pleased.

The brothers quarreled and groused without pause. Now and then one or the other took a wild swing with the giant club within its control in hopes of landing a crippling blow. At one point, Boog tried to slice off Brog's ear, inciting an outright brawl.

Arms flailing, clubs whistling, and machetes coming dangerously close, Brog retaliated. If Boog had not landed a lucky blow, Brog might have succeeded in decapitating his sibling. With bloodlust in his tiny brain, the next victim would have been Borg. It never entered Brog's pea-brain that his victory might also be his death.

Unlike himself, the straight as an arrow Brog, made an unprecedented right turn. Throughout the day, he made several more random turns that ultimately put them on a collision course with the humans.

≈ ♦ ⋞

As the day wore on, Raurk grew weary of the constant bickering and sought food and water. He couldn't lose track of the rampaging monster if he'd tried.

To his delight, he found a clear lake nestled in the unspoiled woods. As man, there was little here for him except water. As the great blackbird, he dove into the frigid water, catching fingerlings skimming below the surface. Time and again he dipped into the water to satiate his hunger.

At last, he sunned himself on a massive boulder in the middle of the lake. He could still hear Borg, Brog and Boog as they squabbled their way through the forest. He sought only a moment's respite to regain his strength before resuming his search.

Unbidden, his eyes drifted shut and he tucked his head under one wing. Weary to the bone, he fell asleep.

While he slept, the troll traveled much faster than usual, narrowing the gap between Grig, Dannel and Taznakie.

≈ ♦ ⋞

Late afternoon found the humans surveying an immense grassland pitched downward at a sharp angle. Dannel got the giggles and threw himself to the ground and rolled as fast as he could down the incline. Taznakie joined the lad. Whooping and hollering, they left a fuming Grig behind.

"Stop," he bellowed. "You'll break your necks, or wind up in nettles or . . ." Grig ran for all his worth. He'd heard the strange booming again that had haunted him earlier. This time, it was much closer.

He stopped where his friends rested in the grass, his breath short and his hands shaking, and stared straight ahead. "Get up!" His words could not convey his terror. "We have to go back." The racket from behind had become unimportant.

Dannel rose first. "What's wr . . ." But the words died upon his lips. Following Grig's gaze, he blanched.

The slope upon which they stood faded into rough scree, that accumulation of broken rock fragments at the base of mountain cliffs, not twenty yards away, then disappeared into nothingness. But that was not what bothered Dannel. In all his youth, he had no way of understanding the panic robbing him of reason. "Grig? Do? We?"

"The River of Lost Souls," Grig whispered. "We can't cross it. Turn back. There's no way around. I don't know what Tanus was thinking . . ."

"I don't understand," Dannel said.

Grig grasped him by the arm and shook. "They'll leach us dry. We'll be lost forever." Try as he might he couldn't shut out the tormented wailing overwhelming them.

Taznakie stood and plucked at the elf's sleeve. "Grumph! Grumph!" He pointed back the way they'd just come. The source of all the commotion remained out of sight, but by the looks of the flying debris and the din that assaulted their ears, there was no escape in that direction.

The troll's heads appeared over the trees as they watched. The leagues separating them would vanish quickly under the assault of the monster.

"We're trapped," Grig cried.

"A bridge," Dannel screamed, pointing. "If we can just get to it, we'll be safe. The troll's too heavy. It'll crash to the bottom."

Grig dashed forward with the hope of rescue. Their footing turned to a mass of slipping, sliding flat stones. He fell and barked his shins, but shot to his feet again. Dannel raced ahead scrabbling and sliding over the loose rocks.

Grig stopped at the bridge, staring. He'd rather take his chances with the mutant troll closing the distance between them.

To his horror, the opposite end of the suspension bridge lay in darkness like no other he'd ever witnessed. Intermittent flickers of lightning pierced the blackness. Muffled thunder drowned out the lament of the lost souls.

Behind them, the monster approached too close for comfort. Grig scanned the bridge again and then turned away. With luck, they might run along the edge of the deep chasm to safety. He sighed. "There's no escape."

"What?" Dannel gaped in horror.

"We're going to die. It's that blackbird's fault. We're going to die!"

He'd never wanted to be a hero. But he'd be a dead hero if they didn't do something soon.

He didn't notice the boy tugging him toward the bridge. He couldn't digest the thought of facing death on that flimsy contraption poised between solid earth and hell, or going back toward the three-headed monster just coming into sight. His foot caught on a rock and he grappled for Dannel. "What are you doing?"

"Look." Dannel pointed with a trembling hand. Shock etched the boy's face. Taznakie stood frozen halfway up the slope, staring at the approaching monster and certain death.

"What's he doing?" Grig demanded.

"Hurry," Dannel pleaded. "The bridge."

"No, we have to go back. He'll be killed." Grig couldn't tear his gaze from the troll. It resembled nothing he'd ever seen.

Taznakie called to his companions, "Grah! Grah!" and waved them away as the troll drew near.

Resigned, Grig set foot upon the loose, splintered planks of the suspension bridge. He gulped air and closed his eyes to keep from swooning . . . and froze.

"Don't stop," Dannel urged.

The lost souls' voracious hunger threatened to suck Grig's psyche from his mortal body. He felt like toxic ants crawled all over him. His scalp tingled and his head felt like a sponge wrung out to dry. He jerked his foot back as the plank split under his weight.

"We have to go back," he pleaded.

"We can't." Dannel tugged at his hand.

It seemed an eternity before they reached the arid soil of Golgotha. The other side of hell as far as Grig was concerned. He turned back just in time to see Taznakie taunt the troll with garbled insults, wave his arms and bellow obscenities. "Run!" Grig yelled.

Instead of retreating, Taznakie crept as close to the behemoth as he dared. "Yaargh!" He lobbed a stone at the giant's nearest head. For good luck, he sent three more in quick succession.

The rock hit the target with a resounding thwack. Pleased with himself, Taznakie jumped up and down, cavorted and even turned cartwheels.

Brog managed to make an unprecedented second right turn in less than three minutes, like a huge gallion at sea. He was on a rampage surpassing even Borg's mutiny of the day before. Blood suffused his tiny brain. His eye throbbed and all he wanted was revenge—sweet, bloody revenge.

Brog roared at the tiny, capering monkey. He took six giant steps and lunged toward his tormentor.

Taznakie watched long enough to ensure the troll followed, and then shot down the hill at breakneck speed.

Brog hesitated as they neared the river of souls, but another well-aimed stone spurred the monster forward.

Taznakie reached the bridge and sprinted across. Halfway there, the flimsy structure bucked and swayed when the troll landed a huge foot square in the middle of the rotted slats.

In slow motion, the troll tumbled into the fathomless gulf. Three screams of pure agony escaped their thick, rock-like lips as untold hordes of tormented spirits extended ethereal tendrils to wrap the giant in a frigid embrace.

Stunned, Grig and Dannel watched the bridge splinter into a multitude of fragments. Taznakie dangled from a frayed rope. "Yaarg," he screamed.

The lost souls finished with the troll and came for the human. Gray faces floated with frightening speed toward Taznakie. Smoky tendrils licked at the man's feet, inching ever upward. Tasting and digesting as they went. The human's tender soul proved to be more delectable than the rock monster. It would take mere moments to snuff out the mortal body and bring the man into their fold.

Grig's hands shot into the air. "Raldux rendalix servitious german cleetus." Pure instinct drove him to conjure one of the magical healing webs. With a muttered prayer, he flung it toward his struggling friend.

The net stretched until it was large enough to engulf Taznakie. Grig retained a strong filament within his grasp. "Dannel, help me," he shrieked.

Dannel added his weight to the line, his hands burning as it slipped. "He's going to die," the boy cried.

Taznakie's weight pitched to one side and then the other. "I can't hold it," Dannel wailed.

"You have to," Grig answered.

"I can't."

"Yes, you can. Now, pull," Grig roared. "Again!"

Dannel whimpered, but he put all his strength into the battle.

Little by little, they gained ground. Taznakie reached one hand over the rim to cling to scruffy weeds bordering the lip of the canyon.

"Pull!" Grig admonished. With a superhuman effort, they hoisted Taznakie onto parched earth.

Taznakie sported a bloody nose and minor scrapes and bruises, but he lived. His bruised soul suffered far more than his mortal body.

Tears flooded Taznakie's eyes as he untangled himself from the webbing and collapsed into a heap upon the ground. The elf and boy could offer him no comfort other than their presence, so they curled up as close to Taznakie as possible.

Sometime during the night, Dannel complained about the cold and Grig covered them all with the healing web and they slept like the dead. Only Malie remained awake to witness the arrival of the large blackbird in the predawn hours of the morning.

➶ ◆ ➷

The air scalded Grig's lungs. His head clanged like a cymbal. Shards of lightning stabbed through his closed eyelids, and the thunder never seemed to stop. With dread, he rolled over to find his arm pinned under Dannel. He shook himself awake.

That's when he spied Theron Raurk sitting on a blackened stump with a slight smirk upon his lips. To look at the man, no one would know he had a care in the world as he scratched Malie under the chin.

The druid's presence didn't surprise Grig. Annoyed, but not surprised. Mustering all his ire, he bolted upright. "Where have *you* been? We were nearly overrun by a three-headed troll and a lot you care. What do you have to say for yourself?"

"What would you have me say?" Raurk said with a shrug.

"I suppose you've been out pretending to look for us." Grig stomped back and forth. "If Dannel hadn't been along, you'd be sitting by the fire playing Bones and drinking ale with Kevel Firth, waiting for us to find our own way home."

"I'm here now," Raurk said.

"We could have died." Grig folded his arms over his chest and glared. "Taznakie fell into the chasm and we nearly lost him while you did nothing."

"For your information, my good elf," Raurk said. "I've been following the same troll to which you refer. It was the only clue I had."

"So what took you so long?"

"The troll developed a sudden penchant to wander." Raurk neglected to say he'd fallen asleep by the enchanted lake and slept through their final encounter with Borg, Brog and Boog. He still didn't know what had woken him from his charmed sleep, but it took long into the night before he picked up the troll's passing.

To his dismay, all signs pointed toward the condemned world of Golgotha. One of Urania Braith's cherished creations.

❧ 25 ❧

The black witch, Urania Braith, cocked her head to one side to listen. The soft down on her neck stirred at the touch of an unseen hand. She'd sensed a ripple in time and it felt like Raurk.

The druid had entered Golgotha again. "Damn." She'd oft wondered how long it would take him to break the ban imposed by the council. It'd taken all her feminine machinations with the old fools to convince them she was right. With Raurk in Golgotha, he would try to right her wrongs in that forsaken land.

"What is it, my lady?" Lorca, the Eunuch Watcher, wrung his hands. Urania's closest companion and sometime confidant shied from her reach.

"Come here, my love." Urania crooked her finger at Lorca.

"What do you want?" He edged closer.

"You saw this coming, didn't you?" Her lips curled into a patronizing smile and she toyed with his long hair. "Don't even think about lying to me."

"I wasn't sure." He looked away. "I wanted to wait until I knew it was true."

Urania smiled again, then turned to stare out the window. "As one of those rare men who anticipate the future, how could you not be sure?"

"I'll do better next time."

"Yes, you will . . ." She paced from the fireplace to the table, snatched up a glass of wine. Then set it down again, sloshing the blood-red liquid over her fingers. "Raurk will ruin everything. The meddling busybody hasn't the good sense he was born with."

She turned to glare at Lorca. "No good can come of this."

Lorca gave a sly wink. "By no good," he said, taking another step away from his mistress, "you mean no evil?"

Her lavender eyes deepened to over-ripe plum. Pale face flushed, she ran both hands through her dark hair in a gesture of annoyance. In two steps, she closed the distance and slapped the eunuch with all her strength. Her long nails dug into his tender flesh, leaving rivulets of blood across his cheek. "You go too far, you insolent, sniveling jackanapes."

Lorca staunched the blood with a small handkerchief. He lowered his gaze to the cold, stone floor. "Sorry, my lady. I shouldn't have made light of the situation."

"It's well that you're sorry. Raurk will be the death of us all, and that includes you." She gathered the fur-trimmed cloak about her neck and stared hard at the man. "Get out!"

Urania waited until Lorca was half out the door. "Have the kitchen send more wine, and tell them I want roasted gerrub for lunch. I grow hungry." She licked her lips in a slow, obscene gesture.

He hesitated, then sighed and turned to face her. "Yes, mum." He dropped his gaze and backed from her presence, muttering to himself.

The door closed with a soft thump before she moved. For the moment, she chose to ignore the hate and rebellion smoldering in his eyes. "Aravis," she said, and the deadbolt slid into place. She remained motionless for several minutes more, listening.

Satisfied she was alone, she glided into her private chamber. She placed her hand in the middle of the carved heart on the wall next to her bed. A small door slid open, revealing her favorite room in the castle.

"Bless you, King Faris, for your paranoia," she whispered. Urania had wrested possession of the castle from the former king and occupied it as her own. The memory of him huddled in this secret room, quaking like a child brought her immense pleasure. "You squandered your claim to Eden, now it's mine." She brushed a stray lock of hair from her eyes.

She'd taken delight in torturing him, savoring the moment when he'd begged for death. In the end, his heart failed before she could deliver the final, satisfying sword-stroke across the quivering wattle of his neck.

Soft light flooded the space, highlighting the ornately carved dais in the middle of the room. The Light of Ishram lay closed in the center.

Urania approached, but did not touch the fragile cover.

A spell of preservation lay upon the book. The one time she'd attempted to touch it, she'd felt the Light's ravening power bleeding through her defenses. Excruciating pain had torn through her body, leaving her crippled for days.

"One of these days, I'll own you."

❧ 26 ❧

Dannel launched himself into the strong arms of his brother-in-law. Tears streamed down his innocent face. "Raurk, they kidnapped us and we couldn't find our way home. A monster killed the fawns and griffins. There was one hippogriff and Master Grig couldn't save him, so he sang it to sleep. Are you angry with me? Will father punish me for getting lost?" With a sigh, he murmured, "Can we go home?"

Grig would swear on his mother's grave that the druid didn't have it in him, but here the tall craggy bird of doom sat rocking to and fro with Dannel in his arms.

"Hush, little one," Raurk crooned. "You know very well your father loves you with all his heart. He'll be overjoyed you're safe."

Dannel buried his face against Raurk's shoulder. "Will he punish me?"

For once, Raurk laughed. "Nay, I can say with certainty he'll not punish you." The druid kept his voice calm. "You must be strong, young man. This promises to be a long journey, and we will not return home this day. Maybe not for many more to come."

Dannel stared around him for the first time since awakening. "What is this place? I hate it. Does anyone live here? Is it so awful because of the River of Lost Souls?"

"I see you're feeling better, my brother," Raurk said.

Dannel's bottom lip quivered. "All I want is to go home."

Raurk smoothed the boy's hair with a gentle hand. "All right. Let me see if I can answer your questions. This world is called Golgotha, the Place of the Skull."

Grig watched from their makeshift bed on the ground. "The place of the skull? Is this land dead?"

Raurk looked around. "At one time, you couldn't have told

Golgotha from any other world, but men performed many evil acts here. The Thousand Years War left it as you see it, and Urania would keep it thus." He averted his eyes. "But one dreadful act marred this land long before that."

"Tell me more," Grig said.

"A shameful act of murder, and the skies rained down fire, and earthquakes shook the land. I've been told this took place so long ago that Golgotha is as old as time."

"Older than you?" Dannel stared at him with huge eyes.

"As hard as it is to believe, yes. Golgotha is a world unto itself where the sun never shines and wicked creatures roam unchecked. The River of Lost Souls used to be a good and peaceful place where the dead rested, but its proximity to Golgotha has tainted it forever."

Taznakie mumbled, "Farrago?" He'd been unresponsive upon awakening. Instead of bounding about, waving his arms and chattering, he sat watching the druid rock Dannel in his arms.

Raurk shifted his gaze to the man. "What's that you say?"

"Farrago?"

"Yes, they're poison and I fear you have been infected. 'Tis a blessing you are strong and will recover soon. A lesser man would not have survived."

For the slightest of moments, Taznakie beamed at the compliment, but it was a shadow of his normal fervor. With sad eyes, he gazed toward the river, and then turned to gesture toward Tanus. "Frag uf uf?"

"What's he babbling?" Grig demanded. The spectral Tanus had reappeared while the men talked. Grig had never seen her look more beautiful. Even the numerous breaks in her tail did not detract from the magnificence of that plumed appendage.

"Our friend asks why the lost souls did not swallow Tanus," Raurk translated.

"Well, what's your answer to that one, blackbird?"

Raurk took his time. "Every once in a while, a pure and gentle soul is born into this world that nothing can destroy."

Dannel sat up straight. "Will the lost souls suck the life from the troll? Will it be able to climb from the river and come after us?"

"I don't know," Raurk answered, but he did not look the boy in the eye. "I can only give my word that Tanus will always be a tiny angel who has blessed us with her presence. If I'm not mistaken, you'd still be wandering around in the woods if not for her."

Dannel nodded. "At first, only Master Grig could see her, but by the next day even Malie knew she was there."

"Humph. She came to see me." Grig hid his feelings behind his usual gruffness. "I don't suppose either of you still has anything to eat. I lost my gourds crossing that atrocity you call a bridge."

Taznakie pulled a flattened gourd from beneath his shirt and inspected it. The tough, leathery skin had saved it from total obliteration. The berries inside were mush, but they tasted like ambrosia.

"I'm not hungry," Raurk refused his share.

"How did you manage to save it?" Dannel asked.

Taznakie gave an elaborate shrug.

༄ ◆ ༄

Ink-black clouds roiled and scudded across the bruised sky in a harbinger of catastrophe. Green streaks of lightning cast a sickly pall over the landscape. Fat slugs of contaminated raindrops dashed against the travelers but did little to relieve the dusty torture of their trek.

"When was the last time this hellhole saw rain?" Grig muttered. "I mean real rain, not this . . . filth." Gnarled, leafless trees cast misshapen shadows with each blinding flash. Gouts of fine dust marked the passage of their feet and choked the breath from their lungs. Even the rocks suffered from incessant pounding of the elements.

"Too many years to count," Raurk said. "Hurry, we must make haste while it's still light. The sooner we leave Golgotha, the better." He'd felt the prickles of time shift during the night. He could only wonder whether it was due to his entering the forbidden land again, or another of Urania's spells.

"Raurk, I'm so tired," Dannel said. "Can we stop for a while?"

Raurk shook his head. "Not yet, lad. It's not safe here." He'd spied the glistening, green body of a lone praying-man just before noon lurking at the edge of his vision.

These creatures were genetic rejects from man's insanity. Tall insect bodies supported the heads of what had once been humans. He'd never seen a real praying-mantis, but doubted the insect could have been as frightening as these man-sized mutants.

In true irony, the faces of the atrocities were angelic. Rosy cheeks and a permanent smile hid the viciousness of their crippled mentality. Sorrowful eyes captured the attention of their victims just before the final attack. Raurk didn't dare risk an encounter.

In their arrogance, the scientists had bred these parodies of human-kind to be the ultimate weapons of destruction. Years of evolution and isolation turned them into icons of death.

A staggering rate of reproduction and constant inbreeding ensured their survival—and subsequent loss of all humanity. Where one or two might die, six more hatched. Within hours of birth, the monsters repro-duced. All that kept them from overwhelming Golgotha was their ravening penchant for cannibalism.

☙ ◆ ❧

Dannel rode on the shoulders of Taznakie, too tired to walk. Covered in dirt and dust, Malie nestled inside Grig's jerkin, her feet nigh flayed to the bone by the coarse pumice.

At Raurk's suggestion, the elf had taken time to cast a tiny webbing to cover each soft pad and stop the bleeding. Although he didn't voice his concerns, Raurk feared the smell of fresh blood would attract attention. The inhabitants of this wasteland would greedily lap up any moisture, no matter how trivial.

"Will we never stop?" Grig mumbled under his breath.

"I'm thirsty too," Raurk said. "But I shan't waste precious breath on such grousing. We'll stop as soon as possible." A lesser necromancer might have succumbed to the desire to fly away and leave the others on their own.

"Raurk . . ." Grig said.

"Yes?"

"Why not go back the way we came?"

"There are many ways into Golgotha, but only one way out. Even if the bridge remained intact, we can't use it to leave. I want to be gone from this place every bit as much as you, but . . ."

"So, why don't you just whisk us away like before?" Grig mumbled, not bothering to hide his ire.

Raurk turned a blistering gaze on the elf. "The laws of magic do not apply here." He held up both hands. "Before you say more, yes your spell for the healing web works, however that is pure chance. Should I try to whisk you away, as you say, we might wind up in worse circumstances than this."

"I don't see how anything could be worse."

"Hush, save your breath," Raurk said. "We still have hours to travel before we find water. Pray that the well has not been defiled during my absence. The arachnoids were barely hanging on last time I visited. By now they may have gone the way of the dinosaur."

"You mean someone lives in this awful place?" Dannel gestured to the windswept land. Barren trees chattered like insects in the constant wind. An eerie whine whistled from the distant hills. He gave a violent shudder. "You can put me down now."

Taznakie lowered him to his feet.

"There's more life here than you can imagine." Raurk's gaze never settled in one place.

"Where is this well?" Dannel asked. "Do you think the arachnoids will give us water?"

"I certainly hope so." Raurk sighed with a faraway look in his eyes. "We're doomed otherwise, and Urania will have won."

❧ 27 ❧

"**Wait** here while I see if it's safe," Raurk rasped through parched lips. Not that it would matter. Without water, they'd all be dead before the day was put to rest.

Dannel stumbled and nearly fell. Were it not for the strong hand of Taznakie, the lad would have sprawled face first into the pumice-like dust.

In spite of the constant blowing of the cold air, sweat dripped from their faces. Sand penetrated every crease and rubbed tender skin raw. Malie, still tucked within Grig's jerkin, refused to even poke her head out.

Raurk placed one foot upon the furrowed road and waited. When nothing happened, he advanced toward the well. From the corner of his eye, he caught sight of two gangling arachnoids.

They were at the top of the food chain when it came to the genetic mutants roaming the plains of Golgotha. For whatever reason, these beings retained much of their human intelligence and values. Still, it remained to be seen whether the creatures would allow the druid and his charges access to the life-giving water.

"Halt!" The shout rang across the barren plains, seeming to roll on forever.

The eight-legged, knobby-kneed cross between arachnids and humans could move at lightning speed without a sound. For all Raurk knew, one or more of the hideous beings might be standing between him and the well, but he'd never know unless they chose to reveal themselves. To make another move without consent would be suicide.

"What do you want?" This time the creature sounded much closer. Years of dehydrated, arid conditions made the voice hoarse. "Come stranger, you are perilously close to death. What do you want?"

Taznakie leapt into full view beside the druid. With his usual zeal, he pantomimed their need, punctuating his words with strange gyrating gestures of his hands and the guttural squawking of a madman.

"Now you've done it," Grig moaned.

To their surprise, he *had* done it. "Drink your fill, humans," that same rusty voice intoned. And with nothing more than a whisper, the path opened for them.

Aware of the hairy creatures lurking just out of sight, Raurk moved with care. The arachnoids would present themselves when they were ready.

❧ ◆ ❦

The humans huddled in the lee of the well, seeking refuge from the incessant wind. Dannel leaned in close to the druid. "Are they going to eat us?"

Raurk had wondered the same thing but did not voice his concerns. Determined to find out, he rose to his full height and spoke into the nothingness. "We mean you no harm. Please allow us passage to the Fortress of Masada, where the Zealots perished. We would quit this land as soon as possible."

"We allow you passage, but you must seek shelter," the unseen arachnoid hissed. "We have witnessed signs of impending unrest tonight. The moon grows full. Blood will flow unrestrained. We can't protect you."

"Is that right?" Grig made a scoffing noise. "And where do you suggest we spend the night? I haven't seen a single hostel in this forsaken hellhole."

"Mind your tongue, Master Grig." Raurk scowled. "Lest you have it cut out for your troubles. These creatures are the last friendly beings in Golgotha. Surely they'll know of a safe refuge for the night."

"The Voice told us to expect you," the arachnoid confirmed.

"How do you know this voice was talking about us?" Grig asked.

"It said we would know," the arachnoid answered.

"So, you just *know* we're the right travelers?"

"That is correct, master elf. We have searched many years for the right haven to meet your needs. Only in the past few days have we uncovered such a shelter, hidden beneath the rubble and refuse of the Thousand Years War. There will be much bloodshed this night. Come, the moon sets and danger is not far behind.

❧ 28 ❧

"**This** is your idea of a safe refuge?" Grig stared in disbelief at the opening carved into solid rock. "I'd rather take my chances out here. At least we could run should the need arise."

"You must enter," the arachnoid urged. "Already I hear the cries of our brethren as the lunacy overtakes them. I'll position this stone across the entrance. No creatures of immorality may enter without risking immediate destruction. Even we aren't permitted. The bloodlust will be upon us as well."

"Is there no other recourse?" Grig had a terrible fear the spider-men would forget them. They would suffocate beneath the scorched sand and rock of the wasteland.

"I fear not, my friend," Raurk said. "Better to be buried alive, than torn limb from limb and eaten."

Taznakie stooped and scuttled crab-like into the awaiting haven, followed by Dannel and Raurk. Grig acquiesced with bad grace. Peering back at their host, he sighed. "How will we know when it's safe to come out?"

"Someone will come for you," the arachnoid said. "Hurry. Arachnoids aren't exempt from this madness. I cannot guarantee your safety should the bloodlust descend upon me . . ."

❧ ◆ ❧

Grig paced the cramped interior. The oil torches provided by the arachnoids gave off an acrid smoke. All attempts to light the chamber by means of magic had failed. He found himself wishing for the glowing, fairy creatures that had lit their safe shelter in the woods. He sunk to the low bench cut into the stone and then jumped to his feet again. "What the devil is this place, a tomb?"

Raurk nodded. "Once, it was the tomb of a rich man, but they buried another in his place—if only for three days. That event took place long before the wars decimated Golgotha."

"Why didn't they just blow it to hell?" Grig slid to the floor with his back to the wall.

"Be of good cheer, elf," Raurk said. "At least we're safe from the elements. The arachnoids have provided water and a place to sleep. You could still be wandering around lost, or pursued by the mutant troll."

Taznakie interrupted, "Frigo?"

Raurk peered into the dark. "Yes, Tanus is here. Even our little Malie has another of her kind to keep her company."

"Humph!" Grig snorted.

The boy stretched out on the stone bench with his head in Raurk's lap and soon dozed. Raurk and Taznakie weren't far behind. Even the dull booming of thunder and faint howling of the ever present wind could not keep them from long overdue rest.

Grig lay upon his side with his back to the others. In spite of his fears, he soon snored, exhausted from the day's trek. To his dismay, nightmares invaded his peace. Try as he might, he could not wake himself. The rhythmic throbbing of the thunder plunged him ever deeper into his nightmare.

An angry crowd surrounded him. People dressed in strange garb shouted in an even stranger tongue and milled about. Fear and anger burned in their eyes. He couldn't discern the object of their fury, but shouts in the distance heralded the arrival of an important person.

On impulse, Grig climbed a bedraggled, wind-burned tree, to get a better look. But as the crowd drew nearer, he slipped and plummeted into the path of half-a-dozen soldiers. Behind them, a beaten, exhausted man dragged a strange cross-shaped tree upon his shoulders.

Grig shrank back to fade into the crowd. For a moment, he celebrated his good fortune at his well-timed flight, but a hairy, rough hand lifted him to his feet. "You, what is your name? You shall carry the cross."

The words were as unintelligible as those of Rakell Taznakie. Grig shrugged with hands outstretched, endeavoring to demonstrate his ignorance, but the soldier thrust him like a child toward the staggering man. Two soldiers lifted the cross and placed it upon Grig's shoulders. The heavy weight sent him to his knees.

A sharp spear in his side prodded him to his feet. Hot tears of frustration, hate and pain coursed down Grig's face. He staggered under his burden, and someone jammed a wreath fashioned of thorny vine upon his bowed head.

"Stop," Grig called, but the soldier nearest him cuffed him across the mouth.

At last, no one prodded, spat on or cursed him, and Grig dropped the cross to the ground. For the first time, he raised his eyes from the earth, only to be confronted with a long line of crosses identical to the one he'd struggled to carry.

On each cross a man hung, nailed in place. Several moaned, barely clinging to life. Others rotted in varying stages of decomposition. Grotesque ravens squabbled over the most delectable morsels of putrid flesh. Without being told, Grig knew this was the Place of the Skull—and *this* was the horrible deed of which Raurk had spoken.

"You have the wrong man," Grig cried. "I'm not the one you want."

Two sweating, well-muscled soldiers flung him atop the cross and bound him with ragged strips of hide. Much to his horror, they produced hammers and crude spikes. He would share the same fate as those unfortunate men already nailed to the wooden crosses. Grig screamed as the spike ripped into his flesh.

He awoke with his own screams ringing in his ears. A huge blackbird hovered over him. A skeletal hand protruded toward him from the flapping robes. Grig scuttled backward, but there was nowhere to go.

His rasping breath, coming hot and rancid, seared his lungs. The vision disappeared, but in his ears, he still heard the ringing of the hammers. The brutal tearing of flesh as the iron bit into his palms. Without knowing what he did, he wrung his hands, soothing wounds that were not there.

"Why didn't you tell me?" he accused the thin air where he'd sat moments before. He searched for the druid, only to discover that Raurk still rested on the stone bench. But now, Dannel sat upright next to him, confused and terrified.

Raurk glared at the elf, a bitter smile upon his lips. "What could I have said to prepare you for the full horror of this place? Still, you doubt that which you witnessed."

As much as Grig longed to deny the truth, he couldn't. A shudder wracked his body. "Who was he?"

"Raurk—" Dannel interrupted.

The druid did not take his eyes from Grig. He weighed each word. "Do you remember I said a dreadful thing happened in Golgotha?"

"Raurk . . ." Dannel insisted. "Listen, don't you hear it?"

"Hear what?" Grig snapped. "Young man, didn't anyone teach you not to interrupt?"

Raurk cut him off with a curt gesture. "The thunder has ceased."

"Not that," Dannel shrieked. "Listen. There's something at the door."

The guttural snuffling outside their sanctuary drove terror into Grig's heart. He knew that sound all too well. The wild boars were a holdover from the days before the Thousand Years War. But in this tainted land, would they be unchanged?

He'd healed too many men gored by the mighty yellow tusks. He feared a boar could roll away the stone from the opening. They would be trapped in this ancient rock coffin staring into the face of death.

Seconds later, the stone wobbled with an unnerving grate and rolled an inch or so. Grig stared in wide-eyed terror. "Maker, preserve us," he whispered.

He glanced toward Raurk only to see the druid mouthing strange incantations. "Damn this place," the druid said. "My spells are useless."

The stone budged bit by bit as the boar smelled the humans inside. The opening grew as wide as Grig's body, but the animal still could not enter.

It stood outside, panting and slobbering. What the arachnoid had moved with ease, this creature struggled to dislodge. The laws of magic and brute strength didn't always hold true in Golgotha.

To Grig's relief, the monster made no move to peer into their shadowed haven. The huge stump of a boar leg loomed in the narrow opening. The creature's labored wheezing blasted plumes of fetid breath over the travelers.

"Raurk . . ." Dannel gagged, but there was nothing in his stomach to bring up.

Then the monster returned to its labor. The rasping of rock against rock terrified Grig. "Come on, you bugger," he hissed. "Let's get it over with." He jumped to his feet in anticipation of an attack.

With a final shove of its brawny shoulder, the half-man/half-boar cleared the portal. It threw ham-sized fists into the air with a bellow of victory. The spoils of its labor were within reach and it would enjoy every delectable crumb of its human quarry, morsel by bloody morsel.

In no hurry, the creature lowered its bulk upon fat haunches to peer into the deep recess. Its keen olfactory senses deciphered the presence of four tangy life forces wafting from the humans. The stink of terror overrode each of them. And how the creature loved the sharp flavor of that particular stench.

One at a time, he decoded the aromas. Most delectable was the rich, earthy smell of a young human. He would save that one for last, a fitting dessert.

Two were about the same age, but one was not completely human. Then a light came on in its brain. The smaller one was an elf, even more succulent than the average human.

The last life smell was all human, but he didn't like it. It was both young and old at the same time. This odor held the essence of a human of ancient origins. It was unlike any he'd savored before. Nonetheless, it was human and ripe for the picking.

The creature delayed no longer. Snorting, it dropped to all fours to enter the den.

A huge clap of thunder drowned out Dannel's frightened screams. Clinging to Raurk, he buried his face in the druid's scrawny shoulder. The lad missed the barrage of lightning hitting the mutant creature. There were no cries of alarm or pain. No running about as a flaming torch of bacon. The creature died where it stood, blackened to an unrecognizable stump of charred flesh.

The boar had violated the threshold of the sacred chamber. Just as the arachnoid had predicted, no creature of such depravity could enter.

A terrible wind and dust storm followed the death of the boar. Barrages of lightning sent the men to the deepest reaches of the ancient tomb. Thunder rocked the earth beneath their feet. They clung together in fear for their lives.

Hours later, the humans still sat stunned as the first drops of sweet, refreshing rain pattered the parched earth. A soft swish of fragrant air trickled into their safe haven. It was still too dark to see more than a few feet past the entrance, but each of them recognized that Golgotha had changed.

"You might as well sleep while you can," Raurk said as he cradled the sobbing boy in his arms. Dannel's wild screams had at last subsided to a mere hiccough or two. "We can go nowhere until the arachnoids come to release us. We must all be rested for the morrow."

❧ 29 ❧

Kevel Firth gnawed on his bottom lip as he stared into the fire. What he saw there was not with his human eyes, but with the eye of a coyowolf. It was a strange inner sight of animal cunning and wisdom that few ever possessed.

He'd ceased fretting days ago about his young son, Dannel. Raurk had found them and they were alive. That's all he needed to know. Raurk loved Dannel as his own. If anyone could bring the lad home safely, it would be the druid.

If Kevel's visions had shown him that Dannel and the others ventured deep within the world of Golgotha, he'd have been less calm. The Thousand Years War had taken a toll in more ways than one. Horror stories flourished regarding the genetic experiments abandoned to die in that world of eternal drought, constantly blowing wind, and unceasing thunder and lightning. Not to mention garish tales of cannibalism.

"Father," Lillith interrupted his thoughts. "Making yourself ill with worry won't bring them back sooner."

"Leave me be."

"At least let me bring you something to eat."

Kevel turned his opaque eyes to bear upon his daughter. "Do you believe they'll return home safely?"

"Of course, Father." Lillith's words carried no conviction. "It was you who told me Raurk had caught up with them. I'm positive Dannel and the others will be fine."

"You were never a good liar, my daughter." Kevel turned to the fire again. "I pray they'll return soon. I worry about your mother." He couldn't admit his own fears. "Will they return simply to leave again?"

"I don't know, Father." Lillith bowed her head. "It's not my decision."

Kevel turned on her with an angry frown. "Is there no way you can stop Dannel from joining you on this fool's errand? I fear he's determined to tag along regardless of my pleas. Raurk agrees."

"What are you saying?" Adelita demanded. She carried a tray of food for Kevel. "Kevel Firth, he is but a boy. You must stop him. I'll lock him in his room. Take all his clothes away until he's quit of this silly notion . . ." She set down the tray and drifted from the room like a wraith.

❧ 30 ❧

The healing balm of rain signaled a new dawn for Golgotha. Perhaps it was fitting that the change was brought about by the death of the wild boar. No sane mind could bring such a creature to life. But then, Grig remembered sanity was not a major factor in the Thousand Years War.

The elf didn't think he'd ever sleep again, but the gentle rhythm of the shower did its work. Before he knew it, he was snoring in a dreamless sleep, propped on his left side. Malie curled against his belly as he lay passed out on the stone floor.

In his slumber, he heard the gentle soughing of huge limbs swaying in the breeze. The aroma of his cook stove lured him ever deeper. It was the best sleep he'd had since leaving his home in the giant Burnet tree.

He could have gone on sleeping for the next day and a half if it hadn't been for Malie and Dannel.

Grig hadn't taken his shoes off, but the mischievous Dannel remedied that problem. The elf was sleeping deeply and it took little coaxing to interest the gerrub in the soft down atop Grig's toes.

Grig jerked awake searching for—what was it he was looking for? There was a lump of charred flesh scraped to one side of the opening, but Malie scampered to safety, out of his reach.

"Master Grig, you would sleep the day away," Dannel said with a giggle. "The spider people brought us food, and you have yet to look outside. There are flowers, and leaves on the trees, and a stream, and birds and ... you missed the most glorious rainbow I've ever seen. Now the sun is just breaking through."

"Go away," Grig mumbled. Even at home, he was a slow riser. Golgotha didn't improve his morning demeanor.

"This is too good to miss." Dannel bolted like a colt into the fresh air.

"Raurk, do something about that young scoundrel before I blister his breeches." With a great show of annoyance, he slid his feet into the leather boots.

Raurk laughed. "Master Grig, if you can catch him, I commend you. The lad is fleet of foot. Besides, he speaks true. Come witness the first sunrise in Golgotha in millennia. There'll not be another one such as this in all the known worlds."

"Leave me be." However, it wasn't long before Grig's curiosity got the better of him. Could a forsaken place such as Golgotha change in such short order? He peered through the low opening only to come face to face with Taznakie.

Startled, Grig lost his balance and landed in the remains of the boar. He leapt to his feet, shaking both hands and cursing. He'd fallen into what appeared to be the monster's skull.

"Yuck! Why didn't someone move *that*?" He shivered as bits of jawbone, teeth and something less definable flew in all directions. "Thanks to you, Taznakie, I'll reek from now until doomsday."

Taznakie shrugged and danced out of reach. Nothing could diminish his elation at finding Golgotha changed. "Gre rere," he shouted and ran about nearly colliding with one of the arachnoids. "Gre rere," he said again and jigged clear of the spider-man.

"Pardon me," the mutant said to Grig. "I bring you Purification berries. Crush them between your hands and rub the pulp into your skin. They will be sticky for a short time. When the smell is gone, wash your hands in the stream. Do not try to eat them as they will cause extreme discomfort to your person."

Grig stared, mouth agog. "If Golgotha has been a barren wasteland for as long as anyone can remember, why should I believe these berries will take away the smell? Have you made up this story for some unknown reason?"

The spider-man shrugged. "We were told to bring you the fruit of yon plant to rid your person of the stench. Should you choose to disregard this advice, I can do nothing more." The arachnoid turned to leave.

"You were told?" Grig demanded. "By whom? The same voice that told of our coming."

The eight-legged man nodded. "Yes, of course. The Voice has

spoken to us for as long as any of us can remember. We would not think of disobeying. Please, take the berries. You will see. They will work."

"Grig, don't be rude," Dannel said. "These beings are our friends. They gave us shelter and now they've brought us food. The sooner you wash your hands, the sooner you can eat."

"The sooner you wash your hands, the sooner you can eat," Grig mimicked. Still skeptical, he crushed the fruit between his hands. The resulting delicious aroma made his stomach rumble. Before he could stop himself, he lifted the back of one hand to his lips and tasted the juice.

Fortunate for him, it was no more than a small swipe of his tongue across the slick pulp. He frothed at the mouth, doubled over with excruciating stomach cramps and fell to the ground. He could not catch his breath or stop thrashing from side to side.

Black spittle erupted from his mouth and spewed down the front of his jerkin. About the time he thought it had stopped, the whole process started anew.

The last thing he remembered was hearing the arachnoid say, "I warned him."

☙ ◆ ❧

When Grig awoke, he lay stretched upon the stone bench in the cave-like sanctuary. His limbs refused to move. With any luck he was dead. Never in his life had he experienced such pain. His entire body ached and his gut threatened to spasm again. He would drown in his own vomit if he couldn't roll to one side.

Strong arms cradled him, rolling him to his left, and then he did throw up. This time it was clear, and he didn't feel like his toenails were being dragged through his nose.

A damp cloth wiped his mouth and someone urged him to drink from the cup pressed to his lips. Those same strong arms rearranged his limbs on the chilly bench so he'd be more comfortable.

This scene was reenacted numerous times over the next day and a half. By the end of the second day, the sun shining through the opening burned his light-sensitive eyes. "Argh," he croaked with a painfully blistered throat.

"Drink this." It was the arachnoid. "It will help ease the pain. Now that you are awake, it will be safe to treat your discomfort."

"*This* is what you call discomfort?"

The spider-man gave a strange shrug. "I warned you not to eat the fruit. The results might have been fatal."

"You should have let me die. How long . . . ?"

"The best part of two days," Raurk answered. "Golgotha has changed, but our presence here attracts too much attention. The arachnoids have already fought off several bands of intruders. It's not fair to burden them further. I pray you'll feel better in the morning. We must continue our journey."

❧ ◆ ❧

The arachnoids signaled danger with a high-pitched whistle. Without words, they moved into position to defend the cave. Raurk, Taznakie and Dannel huddled beside Grig's stone bed waiting for another battle, but this time it never came.

At long last another whistle pierced the fuzz in Grig's brain and he sat up on his own for the first time. "What was that all about?" he rasped through parched lips.

Raurk gestured toward the entrance. "That last whistle means it's safe to come out. We were just about to eat breakfast when they spotted a band of wild boars. The spider-men are anxious for us to leave."

❧ ◆ ❧

Their hosts waylaid Grig in the middle of breakfast and divested him of his stained clothing. His repeated protests fell on deaf ears. They left him to shiver in the damp air in all his glory.

Taznakie reached into the front of his jerkin and withdrew the healing web Grig had cast to halt his fall into the River of Lost Souls. "Grumph." He draped it across Grig's shoulders with tender care.

It might not be much, but at least it protected his bruised body from the chilly morning. "I had no idea you'd kept this," Grig mumbled. It was as close to a thank you as he could muster.

Finally, he could eat with a degree of dignity, but his peace did not last long. Taznakie gibbered and pointed toward the elf's scraped and battered midsection.

"What?" Grig sighed, half expecting to see his guts leaking down his front. Instead, the purple and black bruises disappeared as he watched.

The healing web performed exactly as it should. No one, especially Grig, expected it since the laws of magic seldom behaved as expected in Golgotha. But the results were undeniable.

Grig wound the shawl around his body, face and head. It was even better than the food resting in his belly. In all his years of casting the spell for the healing webs, he'd never used one on himself. He stood there and let it mend every scratch, scrape, bruise or hangnail, allowing the sensation of well-being to lure him into complacence.

"Master Grig, look," Dannel intruded into his thoughts. "The arachnoids brought you new clothes. They're just like your old ones."

Grig poked his nose out just enough to see what the boy prattled about. Much to his delight, the eight-legged creature offered him a new pair of breeches and a soft jerkin. "Where did those come from?" He didn't want to let the healing web go, but walking around wrapped in this manner wasn't practical.

"We made them," the arachnoid said. "The wild boars make excellent leather, and we had more than enough carcasses to fill our needs. We used your soiled garments as a pattern."

Distaste roiled in Grig's gut. "I'd rather go naked. The boars are part human." He shook his head. "Return my old clothes to me, they'll be fine."

"Grig Dothrie, stop your foolishness," Raurk commanded. "Don't ascribe human traits to the boars because they walk upright. They've long ceased to be human. Dress yourself. We have overstayed our welcome."

Grig handed the healing web to the nearest spider-man. Nose wrinkled in distaste, he donned the garments. "They smell," he whined. "My old clothes fit better. Malie won't come near me with this stench. I . . ."

Taznakie blew a raspberry in the air and walked away. "Jonda juse, rathie borie-bon," he called over his shoulder.

"What'd he say?" Grig asked.

Raurk chuckled. "He says he has no problem thinking of the boars as animals. Apparently the memory of that drooling beast salivating at us through the doorway is all the conviction he needs. He doesn't care how they die, as long as they die . . . . As in bone yard dead."

"Quit whining like a little girl, Grig," Dannel pleaded. "I want to go home."

"All right, all right," Grig said. "I'll put these on, but how do you propose we get out of Golgotha? Even Raurk can't fly away with the aid of magic. It appears we must travel by foot."

"True," Raurk agreed with a sad smile.

❧ 31 ❧

"Follow this road, it will take you to Masada," the arachnoid said. "It's the only way out of Golgotha. There's still grave danger, so stay alert. When you reach the fortress, don't enter after dark. It's safer to camp in the open."

The spider-man turned to leave, but hesitated. "Here is your cloak." Instead of handing it to Taznakie, he stroked it with loving fingers as if it were the finest fabric ever known. "I . . . no, it's yours and I must return it."

"What is it?" Raurk asked.

"I could not help but notice the effect it had upon Master Grig when he donned it. What manner of cloak is this? Even now, your animal wears a smaller version on each foot."

"It's nothing special," Grig answered.

The spider-man seemed surprised. "Could you teach me to make one? Many of our people have suffered injury. I would offer them the comfort of such powerful healing."

At the look upon Grig's face, the mutant made haste to apologize. "I'm sorry if I offended you. Here take it." This time, he handed Grig the fine webbing, and turned away.

"Wait," Grig called. "Take it, I can make another. It just surprised me you should want it."

"No," the arachnoid said. "It was wrong of me to ask. It's far too precious to waste on mutants such as ourselves." He waved one leg to indicate his brothers lurking just out of sight. "There's a reason the genetic engineers discarded our kind."

"It's all right," Grig said. "Take it."

The druid cut him short. "We must be on our way. However, should you and your brothers venture this way in a short time and happen to stumble upon such a fine cloak as this, well then, 'tis yours for the taking. Goodbye, our friends."

"I understand." The arachnoid bowed low to show his respect and skittered from sight.

"What was that all about?" Grig demanded. "I'd have given it to him. They're simple enough to conjure."

"The arachnoids are embarrassed to ask for such a gift. History, and Urania, have convinced them they are unworthy of even simple comforts."

"Why didn't you tell them I could make more?"

"I did. Now, get on with it. Dannel and I'll blaze the trail while Taznakie stays here with you."

Raurk turned to the boy. "Dannel, I'll race you to that first tree. The one bent over like an old washerwoman."

Grig couldn't help laughing at the sight of the scrawny druid charging down the road at full tilt with Dannel hot upon his heels. At the last moment, the lad raced ahead to slap the tree with joy. More than ever, Grig was reminded of a great flapping blackbird.

Taznakie tugged at his sleeve. "Oh, all right," Grig said. "Hold this while I invoke the spell."

Taznakie pointed to the healing web and then to himself with a large hand. "Oblik inore agami."

"What are you saying?"

"Oblik inore agami." Taznakie tried again with much pantomiming.

"Yes, yes, this one is yours. Give me a few moments and I'll make more."

Taznakie nodded and pointed to his chest again. "Frap." His hands sketched a web in the air.

"Are you insane?" Grig stared. "No. Absolutely not. Get out of my way and let a man work."

Taznakie moved to one side, but he watched every move and mouthed the same words the elf uttered.

Grig turned his back on Taznakie's distracting antics. With each spell uttered, he added to the pile of large, small and in-between sized healing webs growing in the middle of the roadway.

At last he felt satisfied. "Let's go, Taznakie," he snapped without looking around. "Raurk will be halfway to Masada before we catch up."

A dozen paces down the road, the elf sighed. Taznakie was too quiet. This could only mean trouble. Fearing what he'd discover, he turned back.

It was worse than he'd imagined, Taznakie had managed to bind himself from head to toe in a strange, misshapen cloak. It was a nightmare of uneven, lopsided slapdash strands.

"You blasted idiot! I should leave you here. It'd serve you right for not listening."

"Umph . . ." Taznakie whimpered.

Grig walked around the man, eyeing the results of his bungled spell. "I'm going to regret this." He plucked one of the cords, testing its strength. "Maybe next time . . ."

༄ ♦ ༄

It seemed like hours had passed and Grig was no closer to freeing Taznakie. He rubbed his sleeve across his brow. "When I loosen this one, that one gets tighter."

"Umph."

"Maybe if I cast my web over yours, it might heal it, so to speak. Be still while I work."

Taznakie nodded. "Biddlewif."

Grig stepped back, raised his arms in the air. "Raldux rendalix servitious german cleetus," he said. He watched in anticipation as several strands popped and sizzled, and then reset themselves even tighter.

"Damn!" Grig wiped sweat from his eyes. "Tell me every word and nuance you uttered. One word at a time mind you."

Taznakie mumbled under his breath, "Raldoix."

The elf could not help smirking at the obvious butchering of his words. "You fool, that's raldux. Close doesn't cut the butter with magic spells."

"Unumph," Taznakie said.

"Here goes nothing." Grig took a deep breath and closed his eyes. "Raldoix redow."

"Umph, umph."

"I know nothing happened, you idiot." Grig scratched his head. "All right, what's next?"

Taznakie whispered, "Rendaulix."

"Rendaulix redow," Grig shouted with no better results. "Okay, let me try, raldux rendaulix redow." He jumped away from the hogtied Taznakie as if he expected violent results. "Double damn!"

He circled Taznakie again, touching and testing the iron-hard filaments. Then he heard a low snigger. "What was that?" He turned in a slow circle searching for the sound. His scalp crawled as an eerie silence settled over them.

"Where in hell is Raurk?"

"Umph . . ."

"Never mind," Grig said with a sigh. "Give it all to me at once. Make sure you pronounce each word with care."

Taznakie looked frightened, but he did as told. "Raldoix . . . rendaulix . . . swervitious . . . germanon . . ."

Snake-like cords whipped out of nowhere, binding the elf tighter than his companion. "Not another word!"

"Cleetious . . ." Taznakie finished.

Grig should have known better than to have Taznakie repeat the spell word for word, no matter how slow. A spell is no more than a string of commands uttered in the proper sequence. The real magic lay in the sorcerer.

A clap of thunder deafened Grig and the unbreakable filaments jerked him against the hard chest of Taznakie with an ever increasing number of cords binding them into a suffocating cocoon. "Village idiot is far too kind for you, Taznakie. Don't utter another word. Do you hear me?"

"Unumph."

The sniggering came again, much closer this time. "Blast it, Taznakie. What have you done?" Panicked, he couldn't turn his head to see where the sound came from. "If you ever open your mouth again, I'll rip your tongue out," he said between clinched teeth.

The tough strands convulsed into a death grip. If the slightest peephole remained, it was wasted. Grig's nose pressed against Taznakie's solid chest. "Whoof dere?

No answer.

Blind to the nature of the danger, he dismissed one spell after another. It was a miracle any magic worked in this forsaken land, so why had Taznakie's botched spell been so amazing? How could the simpleton do magic in Golgotha when a druid such as Raurk couldn't?

The soothing effect of the healing web lulled him. Before long, Grig's eyes slid shut and he drifted into a numbed doze, only to jerk awake at the sound of scurrying feet.

The cocoon tilted in slow motion, hitting the ground with a bone-jarring thud. "Gef off me youf ifiot. I'mf stuffocating," Grig lisped.

Taznakie managed to shift his considerable weight to one side. Then they flipped end over end down the embankment. The web's iron strands tightened with each impact. At last, they came to rest against a boulder sturdy enough to halt their descent.

Before Grig could catch his breath, the snuffling of fetid air whispered against his ear.

"Hep! Hep!" Grig gasped. His heart stalled as one pair of feet, and then another tested the footing. Four distinct weights rested upon his back and a slobbering, chawing sound raised the hackles on his neck.

Grig prayed they were being rescued. "If weef gef looth, beef reafy to runf!"

"Umph?"

It didn't take the creatures long to hack through the first, tough filaments. From the corner of one eye, Grig saw huge, yellow canines. Every fiber of his being screamed this was the end.

Four sets of incisors worked to expose the meat hidden within. Red, feral eyes set in pointed snouts paused to scan the horizon for danger. Serrated whiskers contrasted with greasy, slicked-back hair covering the teardrop shaped bodies. Short front arms with misshapen hands that might have once been human pawed at the opening, testing the strength of the remaining coils.

Rising on their haunches, the monstrosities wouldn't reach Grig's waist, but they were strong. Ounce for ounce, pound for pound, they were the strongest, the most evil depraved dregs discarded by the genetic engineers.

Grig's hope plummeted as they came nearer to being liberated. The close proximity and rank odor of the mutants told him more than he wanted to know. He realized the whimpering he heard was his own.

The creatures' palatable wickedness clouded Grig's mind. His eyes smarted from the stench, his limbs grew heavier with every passing moment and his brain refused to work.

Then, a wet snout thrust into the opening next to his ear with a slurping sound. He gagged at the chilling snuffles and rank odor. But when sharp teeth snapped at his flesh, strange words of enchantment erupted unbidden from his lips.

The cords binding them whipped away faster than they had come. The closest creature was struck across the cheek and eye. It howled in pain and sliced at its own face with dagger-like claws.

Black blood dripped from the mutant's hanging eyeball, rotten teeth grinned through a gaping hole in its lacerated cheek. Blinded with pain, it leapt to tear at the elf's exposed neck.

The smell of blood drove the remaining attackers into a rabid frenzy, tearing and gouging the fleshy tissue from their injured companion.

Sickened, Grig tried to turn away. Then he caught sight of Raurk charging toward them. His staff in one hand, the druid skidded down the embankment on the slick, new grass.

"Yaaarg!" Raurk lambasted the closest rodent-like creature in the head with a mighty swing of his walking stick. Brains, blood, sinew and oily slime exploded over the two downed men. A moment later, the druid dispatched the remaining assailants to wherever such fiends go after death. Brute strength was a way of life — and death in Golgotha.

"It's about time you showed up." Grig rose on one knee. "What took you so long?" He waved a hand toward the bloody carcasses. "I thought we were going to die."

Raurk wiped his staff on the grass as best he could before answering. "We waited at the tree ten minutes, no more. One of the arachnoids came to say you were in trouble and we returned. Pray tell, how did you get yourself in this predicament in such a short time?"

"Ten minutes? That's not possible." Grig glared daggers at the druid. "Thanks to this moron, we've been trussed up here for hours."

"Nay, good elf." Dannel joined them. "We waited only a short time.

The Light of Ishram

When the arachnoids came for us, we hastened back. That's when we saw you fall over and those things follow you over the embankment."

The lad took a good look at the mutilated corpses for the first time. Fist-sized vermin scuttled over the smashed brains, tearing at each other for a share of the meal. Dannel turned pale and gagged.

"Are you okay, lad?" Raurk patted him on the back.

Dannel wiped his mouth with the back of his sleeve. "It just surprised me. Wow, look at those teeth! Can we take a couple back to Papa? I've never seen anything like them. Even the boars weren't so hideous. What are they?"

"Sewer rats," Raurk answered. "At least that's what they started out to be. The geneticist inbred them for their rabid quality, and then crossed them with myriad other creatures for size and disposition."

"That's depraved." Grig scowled.

"They didn't let that stand in their way. The results were successful beyond their wildest dreams, if you call *that* success." Raurk pointed with his staff. "I'm surprised to see so many of them in one place. With any luck, we wiped out the entire remaining population."

"That's disgusting." Dannel peered closer. "I want to take a tooth home to father." He reached a hand to touch the nearest monster.

"Stop!" Raurk bellowed. "You can't take their teeth home. Even the smallest nick could prove fatal."

"Aw, gee," Dannel said.

"Go back up to the road and watch," Raurk said. Then he turned his full attention to Taznakie and Grig. "Are you able to walk?"

They nodded in unison.

The druid looked them up and down, hiding a grin behind his hand. "I fail to understand how you two got wrapped up together."

"Ask Taznakie." Grig stood and staggered slightly. "Whatever you do, don't ask him to repeat his spell or we'll all end up as dinner for whatever atrocity that happens to wander along next."

"Why would I do something so foolish?" Dawning washed over the druid's face. He grinned in an uncharacteristic manner.

Grig refused to meet his eyes.

"You didn't."

"I'm leaving, and I suggest you do the same." Grig scrambled up the steep embankment.

"Wait," Raurk called.

At the top, Grig eyed the spot from where his healing webs had disappeared. "At least someone benefited from this fiasco." He set his sights on the distant tree where Raurk and the boy claimed to have waited. "Ten minutes, my behind."

❦ 32 ❦

Grig set a ruthless pace, angry at himself for letting Taznakie bind him like a roast and at Raurk for leaving him to fend for himself.

"Stay, Master Grig," Dannel cried. "I can't keep up."

Grig hadn't spent his ire and charged forward.

"Good elf, halt this moment or I shall be forced to use my staff upon you," Raurk commanded. "It will serve you no purpose to outdistance us. You've had ill luck on your own today as it is."

Grig whirled in his tracks, giving Raurk a withering stare. "You're the one who left me with this blithering idiot to defend myself against those *sewer rats*. I could have gone my entire lifetime without being trussed up with that—Taznakie, and been more than happy. If it hadn't been for you, I'd be home in my own bed at nights, not wondering if I'll make it *through* the night."

Raurk nodded, but said nothing.

"I was content in my life before you came along, you great flapping blackbird of doom. I intend to quit this craziness the moment we escape Golgotha."

"You'd be dead by now," Raurk said.

"I don't believe you. Who would want to murder me?"

"Your village is abandoned, the well fouled. Nothing grows where once abundance flourished. The witch Urania dispatched her despicable minions to destroy all life in your village the moment she divined your roll in rescuing The Light of Ishram. You're fortunate to have escaped with your life."

Grig's shoulders slumped. "They're all gone? The children and elderly, too? What about the animals, the livestock?"

"Nemrak trees have overgrown everything." Raurk nodded with a wan smile. "Jusong vines strangle the life from your once beautiful tree house. Banshees play their appalling games of sacrifice on the village green. No one is safe."

"But . . . Why?" Grig couldn't believe his splendid home had vanished. "I've lived in that tree forever and my father before me, and his father before him."

"I don't think you grasp the gravity of our situation, good elf," Raurk snapped. "Urania knows that you have a real chance to rescue the treasure. Until now, no one has posed sufficient threat to concern her. You, my friend, are a different matter."

"I don't want her treasure." Grig stood with hands planted on his hips. "All I want is to go home."

"Did you not hear me, Grig Dothrie? You have no home to go to. Only when The Light of Ishram is returned to its rightful place can any of us return to our former lives."

"All this . . . for a book?" Grig turned in a slow circle, surveying their surroundings.

"A very powerful book. 'Tis the last of its kind."

"You've said that before. I refuse to believe a book could be worth so much." Grig turned his back to the druid. "How do I know you're telling the truth?"

"You don't."

Grig allowed his gaze to travel the distant horizon. "Why me?"

"I don't know." Raurk sighed and wrapped his cloak about his lanky body. "The wind grows chill. Since we've come to a resting place, this will suffice to spend the night. Even should we continue forth this day, we'll not reach the fortress before nightfall. I'd much prefer to enter Masada while the morning sun smiles upon us."

"Bathie traserra?" Taznakie questioned.

Raurk scanned the horizon much as Grig had done moments before. "Yes, we stay here unless you have a better idea. If I'm not mistaken, we'll find water at the base of this cliff." He strode from the road toward a giant outcropping of shale, leaving his companions behind.

To Grig's surprise, they discovered water and much more. Trees with pendulous fruit surrounded them. Golgotha had become a land of plenty, although still deadly.

Malie, who had been inconspicuous all afternoon, sprawled upon the sun-warmed rocks long after the great orb dipped below the horizon. When Grig tried to hug the gerrub, she protested and swiped at his hand to show her irritation.

"Leave her be," Raurk said. "It's time we discuss your misfortune this morning."

Grig refused to look at the druid. "Can't we put it behind us?"

"Not yet, Master Grig. First, I would know how you came to be trussed like a pig to Taznakie. Second, what was the spell you uttered to free yourself?"

"I told you, it was Taznakie's fault."

Raurk shrugged. "It was you who uttered the spell of release. It appears you're able to work magic when I can't."

Grig stared at the druid. "Are you having a good laugh at my expense? I don't understand."

Raurk sighed. "Neither do I, but please explain your actions. Perhaps then I'll understand."

"I told Taznakie to stay out of my way, but he didn't listen. When I tried to free him, he managed to bind us together."

Taznakie mumbled something in his defense, and gestured like a deranged windmill. Grig huffed in disgust, but Raurk listened until the man's last utterance. Now and then, he muttered, "I see. I see."

"What'd he say?" Grig demanded.

"Why did you ask him to repeat his spell?" Raurk seemed to ponder. "What did you expect to happen?"

Red faced, Grig scowled. "I hoped to reverse his mangled curse. I thought I could undo it one word at a time, but that didn't work. So I had him repeat the whole thing." He averted his burning face from the sharp gaze of the druid.

Raurk stifled a chuckle. "As I drew near, you voiced a spell I'd never heard before. The cords binding you didn't just go away, they exploded."

"I said nothing. Surely, you were the one who uttered the spell."

"Nay, good elf," Dannel interjected.

Grig gawked at the boy. "You must have imagined it. I tried everything I know, but nothing worked."

"My magic doesn't succeed here," Raurk seemed to choose his

words with care. "Some of your spells work, and Taznakie's go astray with surprising effects. I wonder why only certain spells work. How is it you conjure a spell and don't remember it?"

Grig shook his head. "I said nothing."

"I heard you," Dannel said. "It was randitkin rotherdam exaabolta re-ecoc. It sounded very musical and wonderful. You should have seen the sewer rats when the healing web exploded."

"I said no such thing. That's just a bunch of gibberish. Taznakie there might as well shout such tomfoolery."

When Taznakie screwed up his face to repeat the strange words, Raurk clapped his hand across his mouth. "No. I've seen the results of this spell. Never utter it except in a life or death situation."

He turned copper eyes toward Grig. "How is it you come by this spell, Master Grig?"

"Bah! Nothing happened when Dannel said it."

"It just goes to show our young friend hasn't a magical bone in his body. I don't want to take the chance of Taznakie being misunderstood. What might happen should he repeat it is . . . well, let's just say unimaginable." Raurk gave a violent shudder.

"Enough of this," Grig said. "Do we follow the same road tomorrow? It appears a bit too convenient to my mind."

"Who built the road if Golgotha has always been a wasteland?" Dannel interrupted. "Was it the arachnoids, or maybe those other creatures we've seen? Who would go to all that trouble in the first place?"

Raurk laughed. "Be still my young brother. None of these creatures could build such a high-quality road. The Romans built roads wherever their empire extended millennia ago. This road we follow leads to Masada. It's one of the few that survived the Thousand Years War."

"Who were the Romans?"

"That's a question no one can answer with certainty. So much of history has been lost." Raurk shook his head. "What little I know is the Roman Empire stretched to all corners of the known world of their time."

"Wow! They must have been great warriors."

Raurk laughed again. "They were exceptional warriors, but they produced nothing of their own, so they conquered their rich neighbors to feed their greed. They levied taxes on top of taxes. Once in awhile a wise emperor would try to set things right, but in the end, corruption from within did what no enemy could. They were conquered by their own greed, lust, and avarice."

"What else is new?" Grig mumbled and wandered away, not waiting for a response.

"It sounds like you were there," Dannel said.

"Not until many years after the Empire fell. The little I know I've pieced together over the years. The road to Masada has been preserved for practical reasons, since it's the only way out of Golgotha."

Raurk looked down and realized he'd been talking to himself. Dannel snuggled against his side, a pout upon his childish lips. With gentle hands, Raurk lowered the lad to the soft grass where he might sleep undisturbed.

"We must decide who will take the first watch," Raurk muttered. "We can't assume we'll be safe even if we have allies in Golgotha now."

"Unhumph," Taznakie agreed.

"Grig," Raurk called to the elf. "Return to our small circle where we might watch over each other."

Grig mumbled under his breath, but made no move to rejoin them. His attention remained riveted on the far horizon. Raurk followed his gaze. "What draws your attention, good elf? We must stay close for the night."

"One minute," Grig said with a nod.

"I think it best we post a guard. We can't do so if you insist on remaining aloof from our company."

"You babble like yon boy," Grig retorted. "Look there and you'll see that which I watch." Hand extended, he pointed to the heavens where great swaths of stars winked from view and then reappeared moments later.

"There are three of them," he said. "I've watched for nigh on an hour while you prattle your history lesson. Whatever they are, they're huge. Whole sections of the sky disappear at their passing. Just the sight of them chills me."

He whirled to face the druid. "Are they a part of this land? No, I think not."

"They aren't of Golgotha or the Thousand Years War." For once, Raurk's voice belied his concern. "I fear Urania has sent her wicked pets to find us."

"What are we to do?" Grig did not take his eyes from the approaching menace.

"With any luck, we'll be quit of Golgotha before they discover us. We'd make a tasty morsel for such beings."

Grig scowled at the behemoths. "They move quickly."

"It's less than a day's march to Masada," Raurk answered. "Pray that it's enough."

"Prayers won't make *them* go away," Grig couldn't keep the despair from his voice.

"We must arise before first light." Raurk rubbed a hand over his tired eyes. "Which watch would you stand?"

"The first is mine. I'll wake Taznakie, and then he can wake you. I trust he has sense enough to sound an alarm should the need arise."

Raurk stooped to drape his cloak over Dannel. "I implore you, do not stray so far from our sides again."

"As you wish. Now, where has that blasted gerrub gotten to? She slept most the day and can damn well keep me company. And Tanus too, if she shows herself again."

છ ♦ ๗

"Wake up, Grig Dothrie." Raurk shook him by the shoulder. "Our winged opponents approach. I'll carry the boy. You wake Taznakie. Then gather whatever fruit you can carry to take with us."

The three men collected their meager rations and headed toward Masada with few words. Malie nestled against the warmth of Grig's bare chest. All of them shivered in the unexpected predawn chill. Yet the menace from overhead did more to freeze the blood in their veins than the weather.

Merciful dark masked details of the flying behemoths other than their size, larger than the elf had first suspected. With each wheeling arc across the horizon, they closed the gap between them and the men. The creatures blasted gouts of fire into the still morning leaving swaths of new growth smoldering in ashes.

"Faster," Raurk urged.

Awake now, Dannel couldn't keep up with their loping strides. Taznakie scooped the lad up and placed him upon his broad back. Still, they lost ground against the approaching danger.

"What're they waiting for?" Grig felt as if his lungs might burst. "Surely they could have overtaken us long ago." He cast a glance over his shoulder.

"They . . . play . . . with . . . us . . ." Raurk panted. "Either that . . . or they await the arrival . . . of their mistress. I pray that . . . is not the case. We aren't ready for an encounter with Urania."

Taznakie shrieked, "Gratanalk!" He pointed at the approaching beasts. The rising sun struck sparks from the monsters' scaly hides. Blue, green, turquoise twinkled in the icy heavens.

"Dragons," Grig wailed. "They're huge."

"Gratanalk," Taznakie said again.

"There's something strange about them." Grig stared at the flying monsters. "Blackbird, are you sure they're not products of the Thousand Years War?"

"I'm positive. Urania has sent the most bizarre dragons I've ever seen to be our nemesis."

"Then we die here," Grig said.

The druid increased his pace. "I refuse to give that witch the satisfaction of our demise!"

ᘒ ◆ ᘑ

The dragons did nothing to close the gap. There was nothing to hold them back, yet as the fortress of Masada came into view, the creatures abandoned the sky.

Graceful as they might appear on the wing, the flying reptiles were heavy and awkward on the ground. Each thundering jolt of the dragons' feet threatened to knock the men to the ground. It took a stern command from Raurk to keep Grig and Taznakie from bolting in panic.

Long tails whipped from side to side clearing the land like great scythes. Nothing could escape their razor like, marauding appendages. Glassy green eyes rolled on each side of long prickled snouts. And strangest of all, awkward, bulbous heads gimbaled atop long vulture like necks. Their wattle jigged and bobbed in an undulating mass of scales.

In slow motion, first one monster rose into the sky with an enormous blast of sulfurous dragon fire. Then the second and third dragons climbed the airwaves circling far over Masada and back again to torment the men. Every pass brought them closer to the road and their prey, seeming to mock the men.

✄ 33 ✄

The final ascent to the fortress loomed on the horizon. Raurk shouted, "Run!"

The dragons increased their hazing. One close encounter left Taznakie's hair smoldering and Dannel screaming in terror. "Yaark!" Taznakie bellowed, thrusting the lad toward Raurk. He motioned his companions to go on, and then planted his feet in the middle of the road.

"Yahnuo nuo nuo," he crooned, beckoning the fiends closer.

"Not again," Grig moaned.

"No, Taznakie," Dannel screamed and darted toward his friend. Raurk grabbed the boy and ran for the safety of the fort.

The elf started to follow, but something in Taznakie's words struck a deep chord within his heart. Twenty yards down the road, he turned back just in time to witness the first direct assault upon the simpleton. The scene unfolded in slow motion in front of Grig's eyes, but he couldn't move a muscle.

The three dragons formed a huge vee and dove at Taznakie, belching blistering brimstone fumes.

Taznakie made no move toward safety, not that an escape route existed for him. Instead, he gestured over and over for the dragons to come get him. At the last, he opened his arms wide as if to accept their embrace.

Even if Raurk had not been burdened with the lad's safety, he could do nothing to help. Golgotha had rendered his magic unpredictable, if not fatal. Should he attempt a normal spell of protection they might all be maimed or killed.

A last look over his shoulder convinced Raurk to flee even faster toward the sturdy walls of the fortress. At least the threat from the dragons would be diminished if they could reach the ruined city.

He must surrender this fight to Taznakie whether he liked it or not. Raurk could not allow Dannel to die. Resigned, he ran for his life and that of his young brother-in-law.

Perhaps the monsters had expected Taznakie to fall on his face and grovel, but the man held his ground. In fact, he didn't flinch when the marauders swooped within arm's reach, burning a swath of destruction along each side of the road.

"You fool," Grig roared, racing back toward Taznakie. He tugged at the man's sleeve. "You'll get us all killed."

"Rrragh!" Taznakie snarled at their tormentors. With his feet braced and both fists raised, he waited for just the right instant.

Closer and closer the menace approached, still belching flames. Then Taznakie made his move. Arms to the heavens, slowly and deliberately he bellowed, "Raldoix rendaulix swervitious germanon cleetious!"

It was the same spell that had bound him and the elf together in a suffocating cocoon. Cables hard as steel whistled through the air to wrap the first dragon in a death embrace.

Grig could not believe his eyes. The dragon hurtled toward them like a runaway locomotive. He'd never seen anything like it. Mouth agape, he stood transfixed waiting for the inevitable.

Taznakie tackled him around the waist, carrying them both over the side of the road and to relative safety. The trussed monster hit the packed road once and bounced into the air knocking its right hand companion into a spiral.

The first dragon came to earth again and slid to a devastating halt. Grig shuddered at the sound of breaking bones. He wanted to vomit, but could not pry his eyes from the fallen monster.

At a shout from Taznakie, he turned to watch the other careening dragon dive head first into a towering outcropping of unyielding rock. It squawked and flopped around, then keeled over dead in a tremendous spray of water, the bulk of the dragon still visible.

ॐ ◆ ॐ

There remained just one attacker and it whirled in ever tighter circles above the men, not sure what to do. Urania had said to kill the men any way they wanted. Instead, the monster's two clutch mates lay in broken pieces. Killed by the human the witch had declared stupid.

Urania would be furious. Keening its grief, the lone dragon dropped to the road next to its sibling. Confused and frightened for the first time in its life, it nudged at the broken body of its sister bound in this strange egg.

৯ ◆ ৯

Seizing the moment, Taznakie jumped to his feet ready to hurl another spell, but Grig beat him to it. With every ounce of his concentration, he spat, "Randitkin rotherdam exaabolta re-ecoc, you bastard. Come and get us." The same spell he had claimed not to have uttered the previous morning. He might deny it, but he spoke it anyway.

Arm thick cords exploded away from the dead creature. Cords stronger than anything he'd ever seen before sliced the air. He wasn't sure what he intended when he shoved Taznakie out of the way and shouted the words of release, but it was more than spectacular.

A mutilated wing lay next to the standing dragon as it screamed in agony. Dragons are much like Grig Dothrie and his feet when it comes to their wings. Attempting to rise into the sky, it never saw the oversized, whip-like wire that broke both back legs. Suddenly, its grotesque head lay in the blood and dirt of the Roman road staring back at its still writhing body.

"Taznakie, Grig," Dannel screamed. Raurk could no longer hold the boy as he fought his way free of the druid's restraining arms.

"Get back!" Grig shrieked at the boy. Panic gripped his gut as he watched Dannel slip in a puddle of congealing, vitriolic dragon blood.

The three men converged on the boy at once, careful to avoid the dragon's blood. Raurk snatched Dannel up and carried him over the side of the road as far from the dead dragon as possible. With the utmost care he laid the boy upon the new grass to survey the extent of his injuries. Dannel beseeched each of them with pain hazed eyes before passing out.

Grig pushed the druid out of the way. "Raurk, get his clothes off. I need to check the extent of his burns. Taznakie, find water and bring it here if you still have that bladder gourd. If not, we'll carry Dannel to the water. We have to stop the poison before it eats him alive."

The elf sat upon his haunches watching Raurk strip the boy with trembling hands. "It could be worse. It could be worse," he chanted. "His upper arm is not too bad, but his face will bear a scar."

Then the druid rolled Dannel to his right, exposing the bubbling flesh of his entire left side and back.

"No . . . I can't. I can't. There's nothing I can do," Grig averred. "Dannel Firth will die."

"Naorgh retuth andulith," Taznakie spat at the elf dangling in his fisted hands. The words might be nonsense, but his meaning was clear. Taznakie ordered him to save the boy.

Flushed from the exertion, tears streaming down his dirty face, he shook Grig and pointed at the pile of berries he'd dropped at the elf's feet.

"Put him down, Taznakie," Raurk ordered. "We have nothing with which to treat Dannel's burns."

But Taznakie gestured again at the berries with one hand and rattled Grig's entire being with the other. Then he plopped the elf to the ground with the unspoken threat of breaking Grig's neck should he fail to heal the boy.

"I told you to bring water," Grig moaned. But Taznakie didn't budge. He shoved an armful of fruit toward the elf. "What do you expect me to do with these?" Grig stared in disbelief.

Raurk whispered, "The arachnoids . . ."

"No, it won't work," Grig shook his head. "Take these away, you fool." But still he did not let go. Deep in thought, he crushed three or four berries and watched the sweet-smelling juice drip to the ground.

In his mind, he saw himself lick the sticky liquid from his fingers, but his stomach remembered the last time he'd tried it even if his brain was on automatic pilot. He gagged and his brain cleared of the mind-fog threatening to incapacitate him.

He grabbed the succulent fruit from Taznakie, and squashed double handfuls between his strong fingers. Then, he smeared the pulp over Dannel's seared flesh.

The dragon blood eating into the boy's slight body could not withstand the powerful healing of Golgotha's Purification berries. The pulp sucked the poison from Dannel's body and exhaled it into the air.

Raurk reached to help, but Grig pushed him away. "Hold him upright so I can get to his back and sides.

"Taznakie, do you or don't you still have the gourd?"

Taznakie reached inside his jerkin and produced the flattened vessel. Holding it up in triumph, he smiled like an angel.

The elf nodded. "I should've known. Go find water and make sure it's clean. We must rinse his wounds once the berries have done their work. I don't care how far you have to go, just find water."

He turned back to his patient. "Hold him up off the ground," he told the druid again. "Don't get dirt into the burns."

ޫ◆œ

At first, Taznakie refused to go anywhere near the dead dragon even though he'd seen the splash of water when the monster collapsed. But as his search for clean water failed, he gritted his teeth and turned his attention toward the sister with the broken neck. It had come to rest in a copse of young saplings. He knew water existed there, if only he could get to it.

He refused to admit his fear the dragon merely feigned death. What if it had just been stunned? It might leap to its feet at any moment. Then his heart sank as he realized the beast had fallen into the pool of water.

He smacked himself in the forehead with a broad fist and cursed. Shoulders drooping, he turned in defeat. Should he go back and tell Grig he'd failed or continue looking? If the dragon had died in the pool, it would be as poisoned as the blood eating at Dannel's flesh.

With a huge sigh and a last baleful glare at the massive corpse, he resigned himself to failure. He could not help his young friend even though he'd threatened Grig's life for giving up. It was a bitter pill to swallow.

Nothing could prepare him for the hissing, spitting missile that launched toward him. He'd never seen Malie so agitated.

Finally, he managed to dislodge her from his broad chest. But the gerrub didn't give up. Tail plumed to its fullest, she batted at the man with ferocious swipes of her tiny paws.

"Whadnut? Whadnut?" He tried to soothe the furious gerrub.

She smacked Taznakie's cheek again causing him to whirl around to escape her fury. As fast as her stubby legs could carry her, she raced back to the dragon, perched atop the giant and dove headfirst into the chilling water.

Taznakie howled in outrage. Malie would die, too. Gerrubs couldn't swim and the water was deep. What should he do? There was no one else to save the flailing Malie and the dragon carcass poisoned the water. They would both die. Who would take care of the others?

"Grargh," he shrieked. Maybe they would all die before they escaped Golgotha, but he refused to allow Malie to drown. He dove into the pond expecting to writhe in pain just as Dannel had done. When he got nothing but a mouthful of clean, pure water, relief washed over him.

Breaking the surface with an exultant whoop, he laughed like a madman. Malie had risked her life to save Dannel. He would save the gerrub. Not only that, he could return with his gourd filled with the precious liquid. Fortune had smiled upon them.

ॐ ◆ ॐ

Grig and Raurk heard the ruckus, but had no idea why Taznakie carried on so. At the sight of the brimming gourd, they couldn't care less even if Taznakie did carry a dripping wet Malie draped across the back of his neck.

"Give me that," Grig demanded. "Hold the lad while I bathe his wounds."

Pink, healthy flesh emerged from beneath the berry pulp as Grig washed each burn. To his delight, droplets of fresh blood oozed from the gaping holes left by the dragon poison. But the venom in the boy's system no longer held any threat.

Dannel moaned and shivered from the cold water, but didn't return to wakefulness. Taznakie dug in his pocket for the treasured healing web he'd harbored for so long. It still retained that enticing warmth and silky feeling he loved so much.

Yet Grig Dothrie refused the proffered gift. Something told him it wasn't up to the task. He must conjure the most powerful mantle of healing possible. This was no light task to be given to hand-me-downs.

With loving care, he cast one of his finest spells, producing a thick, soft healing web to engulf the shivering boy. It took only moments to wrap Dannel from head to toe and nestle him in the strong arms of the druid.

Shaken, they strode toward the fortress of Masada. Two men and one elf carrying a sneezing gerrub and a battered boy allowed themselves the luxury of hope.

❧ 34 ❧

Huge wooden gates, preserved by an unknown magic hung askew. Once-proud walls of stone lay in random heaps of rubble. Untold years of lightning and corrosive windstorms had taken their toll on the mighty structure. "Take the boy," Raurk said. "I'll go first." His usual calm seemed to falter.

Exasperated, Grig sighed. "Don't tell me we have to face more of Urania's freaks. I thought you said we'd be safe once we reached Masada."

Raurk could not hide a small chuckle. "And I believe we shall be, but I can't allow you to pass through these gates on blind faith. Masada holds its own assortment of terrors though not always of living flesh.

"That's why the arachnoids warned us not to enter after dark. Not all spirits depart once the living flesh has rotted away, and dark is the time of their sovereignty. Wait for me here. I'll whistle twice when I deem it safe to enter."

❧ ◆ ❧

It seemed like Raurk had just departed when two shrill whistles broke the late afternoon stillness. Grig nodded to his companions. "Let's go, we can't be free of this place soon enough."

The dark inside the fortress walls wrapped around the travelers. Grig thought for a moment he spied fleeting shadows of black on black in the dark streets and windows.

He couldn't tell whether his mind played tricks on him, or if they were real. Afraid of what he might see should he look too closely. What little he did make out would cause him nightmares for months.

The place was thick with dust and devoid of human traces except for the tracks left behind by Raurk. Here and there, the druid's long black cloak had nearly obliterated his footsteps.

To their relief, he stood not twenty yards past the walls, waiting for them. He waited next to what appeared to be the base of a crumpled well. Like everything else in this world of shadows, Grig would not swear to it. He had learned long ago not to trust appearances.

A wispy shape flicked between them and Raurk, causing the fine hair on Grig's neck to stand on end. Dannel moaned, but remained in his dream world of healing. Raurk motioned for them to proceed.

Grig and Taznakie hurried as fast as they could toward the beckoning druid. Yet, as they closed the gap, the druid moved away, beckoning for them to follow.

"Damn, what kind of game does he play?" Grig muttered.

"Why didn't you wait for my signal?" The words came from behind them nigh scaring Grig to death. Raurk stood there solid as a rock, his cloak flapping in a nonexistent breeze.

Confused, Taznakie gawked between the man and the apparition beckoning them. Several times he opened his mouth to speak, but nothing came out. Pale as a sheet, he poked at the druid's arm.

"Yes, it's me," Raurk said. "The hour grows late. Stay close at hand so something like this doesn't come to pass again. It's imperative you do as I say. We have only one chance to escape Golgotha."

The three humans jogged the ancient passageways of the fort, sometimes doubling back for no apparent reason. "Where in hell are we going?" Grig looked back the way they'd just come.

"There's no time to explain." Raurk said. "Just stay with me."

Before long they were too tired to ask, let alone care. Daylight faded. Soon, it would be gone altogether and then they would be fair game for the shadowy residents of this eerie stronghold.

At last the druid stopped, searching their surroundings. Wraithlike shapes followed their every move, waiting for them to stumble. Almost out of breath, Raurk wheezed, "Take my hands and whatever you do, don't let go. Run for your lives."

Raurk guided the small party toward a wide breach in the wall that lay directly ahead. "Don't let go," he repeated.

To Grig's distress, there was nothing on the other side of the wall except a broad view of the green land below — far below. Digging in his heels, he shrieked, "No!"

The druid's momentum carried them forward and over the brink. They were doomed. Only scavengers would find their broken bodies on the jagged rocks below. Raurk had finally killed them.

Grig closed his eyes and let his feet carry him to what he knew to be certain death. A scream of terror escaped his lips as he stepped into space only to be absorbed by the cottony softness of unadulterated dark and cold.

❧ 35 ❦

Grig landed in a shallow stream. Sputtering water from his mouth and nose, he broke the surface. "Damn you, Raurk. If you aren't already dead, I'll kill you myself." A quick check revealed no broken bones, but he shivered violently with chattering teeth.

Malie scrambled up the far embankment, her short legs plowing a groove in the soft mud. She was every bit as wet and bedraggled as he.

She chirruped her displeasure at Grig. Twice in the same day she'd been drenched, and she sneezed repeatedly. Like their ancient ancestors, the cat, gerrubs hated water with a passion and Malie voiced her complaints loud enough for the whole countryside to hear.

"Grig," Dannel called. "Malie, where are you?"

Malie shot off in the direction of her young master's voice leaving Grig to struggle from the water on his own. "What kind of escape do you call that?" Grig shook his fist in the air.

Finally he decided since he was still alive, he should rejoin his companions. If Taznakie was with them, it'd be an easy task to find them. The man was as graceful as a rampaging troll with a blinding toothache.

"Grig," Raurk bellowed.

"Here." He scrambled up the embankment. To his delight, Raurk, Taznakie and Dannel stood by while Malie flitted from one to another. All three laughed at her antics, just as happy to see her.

Raurk laughed and clapped him on the back. "I told you not to let go. No telling where you might have ended up." His gruffness did not belie his happy smile.

Grig shook water from his hair in imitation of Malie. "Where are we?"

This proved a moot question as he spied Lillith streaking across the meadow toward them. In her wake, Adelita and Kevel followed only slightly slower.

Sobbing and laughing all at once, Dannel ran to meet them, naked. In their escape from Masada, he'd lost Grig's thick healing blanket.

Kevel reached them first. Even his blind eyes could not hold him back. "My son, I thought I'd lost you." He hugged the boy to him. "Where are your clothes, Dannel Firth? You're shivering. Adelita, get this child something to wear. He's far too old to scamper about the meadow like this."

"Papa, it doesn't matter," Dannel said. "I wish you could have been with us. First, we were carried away by a swarm of insects. Then we discovered the slaughter of the forest creatures. Grig sang a hippogriff to sleep. All the others died when it passed."

"You're safe. That's what counts." Kevel hugged the boy even tighter.

"Papa, you're squashing me." Dannel escaped Kevel's embrace. "After that, a three-headed troll chased us into a place called Golgotha, the place of the skull. We had to cross the River of Souls to get there and I was really scared. That's where Raurk found us. Grig ate poison berries and almost died. Taznakie saved us from the dragons and . . ."

Kevel's face clouded in anger. "You took my son into Golgotha?" He glared first at Grig and then Raurk.

"Father, not now," Lillith soothed. "I'm sure Raurk will tell us the whole story when we get back to the house. And by the looks of them, I think a hot meal is in order. Look at poor, Malie. I'll bet that's the first, last and only time she's ever been swimming in her entire life."

Taznakie shook his head and launched into the telling of how the gerrub dove into the pond using the dragon as a springboard, but to no avail. As usual, it seemed he was not understood. He was left standing alone while the others retreated to the house. Kevel had scooped his young son into his arms and insisted on carrying him.

❧ ◆ ❧

Wrapped in a warm blanket, Dannel snuggled in his father's lap. "Not another word, young man," Kevel scolded. "You can tell us all about your adventures tomorrow."

"Yes, Papa." Dannel stifled a yawn. Before long he drifted off to sleep.

The druid lifted Dannel in his arms. "I'll put him to bed, and then we can talk," he whispered. "First I'd like something strong to drink, not to mention a hot bath. I would wash the stench of Golgotha from my pores. I can only declare these clothes ruined."

Kevel nodded. "I'll burn them tomorrow."

"And don't interrogate these two while I'm upstairs," Raurk said, although the effort was wasted. Grig snored in his chair and Taznakie curled in his treasured healing web on the broad hearth. Raurk had no doubt Malie holed up in the kitchen as near to the stove as possible without getting singed, sleeping off the effects of their fortunate escape.

Kevel stared through the other man with his strange coyowolf eyes. "Does Dannel speak true? I never know with that boy. His imagination oft runs away with him."

"He speaks true." Raurk had hoped this moment wouldn't come so soon.

"He's an inventive soul to say the least." Kevel seemed to wither in his chair. "Not that he means to lie, but sometimes his enthusiasm gets the better of him. If I know you, Raurk, there's more to the tale than Dannel has told."

"Father, Raurk's tired," Lillith interrupted. "Can't this wait until morning? Let him rest while he can. At least they're safe. The retelling will change nothing."

Raurk shrugged and smiled as his wife led him to the stairs. In truth, he would postpone his encounter with Kevel as long as possible.

He had discovered many certainties while in Golgotha that he'd told no one. They were truths he'd denied even to himself until now. He needed time to sort through his troubled visions.

❧ 36 ❧

Lorca laid the rolled parchment aside on the cluttered table that served as his desk. He raised a glass to his lips and took a long drink of sweet wine. Should he take the missive to Urania now, or wait until after dinner? "Why couldn't the messenger have waited until morning?" he muttered.

Chances were she'd take out her ire on him. The welts upon his back stung at the remembered disgrace from the previous evening when she'd cast him bodily from her chamber. "Best to wait, I think."

As a Watcher, he was a slave to Urania's every whim. Even so, he'd learned long ago how to avoid her attention, and now this. She'd been in a foul mood all day, even surpassing her usual cryptic insults and barbs. This latest news would only serve to infuriate her. "Maker, preserve us," he sighed. "Is there no end to her insanity?"

The missive from Urania's spy reported her pet dragons murdered by Raurk and the elf. In spite of all her scheming, the druid and his lackeys had escaped Golgotha without injury. "No doubt, she'll blame me. That'll teach you to ignore your Watcher, Urania Braith." His flash of ire died as quickly as it'd come. "I told you not to send the sisters. And serves you right, too."

A ray of sunlight glinted across the table, causing him to look up. Urania stood at the French window, a perplexed look marring her perfect, dark beauty. "You talk to yourself, my pet?"

"No . . . uh . . . 'tis nothing," Lorca said. "I didn't see you come in." He stood and bowed in the witch's direction.

"It's cold in here, stir the fire you useless slug," Urania said.

He could never predict whether to keep the room warm, or frigid. "Yes, mistress." Lorca moved to the fireplace and rearranged the smoldering logs. Flames leaped upward and he added two more pieces of wood. "Is that better?"

"Bring me the velvet throw from my bedchamber. I've been outside, and the wind cuts to the bone."

This time Lorca did not answer, but retrieved the coverlet as told. "Where would you like it?"

"Around my shoulders, imbecile." Urania sat in the overstuffed chair facing the fireplace. "I've always liked this room. What about you, my pet?"

Her low, seductive voice sent shivers through him. Should he answer truthfully or attempt to appease her? She played a new game and he had no idea which way to turn.

"Come, Lorca, I asked your opinion."

He glanced at the high ceilings, ornate wallpaper and lavish tapestries. He thought it pretentious and ugly with its gilt mirrors, shining black candelabras, and intricately woven rugs. "It suits you." He moved to the sideboard to refill his goblet, putting more distance between them.

"Pour me a glass." She used that same honeysweet tone.

"You don't like the summer wines. Shall I send for the dark red you prefer?"

Urania half rose, and then sank back. "Never mind, come sit at my feet." The smile she gave promised many things. No doubt, all of them unpleasant.

Lorca let his eyes drift toward the scroll on his desk. Did she already know? His heart trip-hammered in his chest and the air turned sour in his lungs. Should he give it to her now?

She followed his gaze and gave a condescending smirk. "What are you waiting for, Lorca?"

"I'm comfortable here, mistress." He edged toward the open windows.

Urania raised her hand in the air, palm upward and curled her fingers one at a time into a fist. "My little gerrub, come here." She pointed to the floor next to her. "Warm my feet."

Enchantment wrapped around Lorca's legs and dragged him toward the witch. He could not resist. With a look, she forced him to his knees and then into a sitting position. "That's much better. Don't you think?"

"What do you want?" Lorca hated being manhandled by her tainted spells. He sat with mere inches between them. Even if he could escape, there was nowhere to hide.

"Lean against me, my pet." She ran her fingers through his shoulder-length hair and along his jaw line. "I've always thought you were too pretty to be a man, even a eunuch."

Terror struck at Lorca's heart like a sword. He fought to control his breathing. The witch thrived on fear. "I . . . I don't know what you mean."

"Don't you?" She pulled at his hair, exposing his neck. "The messenger brought the sad news of the sisters' demise directly to me— and then to you. And yet, you have said nothing. I can't help but wonder where your loyalty lies."

"I was just on my way to find you." He'd gone cold with fear. Drops of sweat ran down his neck and inside his collar. The thunder of his heart roared in his ears.

"You know how much the sisters meant to me." She brushed crocodile tears from her long lashes. "I can never replace them."

"I'm sorry," Lorca whispered. "Shall I send for the dragon master? I hear there's a new clutch about to hatch. Maybe you'll find suitable replacements."

"Lorca . . . Lorca . . ." Something sharp pressed against his neck as the witch wrenched his head backward. "You, of all people, know how I deal with traitors."

❧ 37 ❧

Rather than the exhausted sleep he craved, Raurk lay awake beside his beautiful wife, his mind twisted in confusion. How could he tell Kevel and Adelita that Dannel must accompany them in their pursuit of the Light of Ishram? How many more must he place in jeopardy before they defeated Urania Braith?

Most of all, how could he explain that Dannel was a key factor in defeating Urania when he didn't even know himself what role the boy would play?

Afraid he'd wake Lillith with his tossing and turning, Raurk slipped from her side. He couldn't help gazing back at the striking, intelligent woman who'd promised to always be his. "I love you," he mouthed and closed the door softly as he went out.

She'd vowed to follow him anywhere. But he wished he could spare her this particular journey. The events of the past couple of days crushed any such hope. Besides, she would prove invaluable in the care of her young brother.

He took the steps two at a time, making sure to skip the third riser from the bottom. Should he step on that one, the whole household would be awake the rest of the night.

To his good fortune, Kevel often renewed the spell that warned of intruders. On his last visit, Raurk had escaped with his life because of this simple charm.

Not only did this step squeak loud enough to wake the dead, but it screamed, it howled and it thumped maniacally. "Thank you, Kevel," he whispered.

"It's about time you decided to come back down," Kevel accused. "I was about to come up and get you, but I didn't want to wake Lillith. I'm glad you saw where your duty lies."

Raurk answered with a wry grin. "I assumed you'd still be awake. Has everyone else gone to bed?"

"All but Taznakie," Kevel agreed. "He's in the kitchen nursing Malie. Seems she got wet and has taken a cold. Gerrubs should never be soaked the way she was."

"Aye, but I don't think she had much choice when Grig fell in the stream with her."

"Hah, that's not what I refer to." Kevel barked a harsh laugh. "Taznakie says she dove into the spring of her own free will. He assumed the dragon carcass had poisoned the water, but Malie knew better. She risked her life to save my son. Are you blind? Did you not notice the poor dear was nigh drowned?"

Raurk chuckled. "I had other things on my mind. I seem to remember she appeared to be wet, but gave it no further notice. Dannel's life was at stake. I couldn't afford to worry about a wet gerrub."

"She's a brave little soul."

"Does she need a healing spell? It won't take but a moment," Raurk answered.

"Taznakie wrapped her in a strange contraption he claims Grig Dothrie used to save his life. He brewed tanus leaves for her to inhale. Last time I checked, she was breathing much easier."

"I'm glad she's better." Raurk would have liked to check on the gerrub, but Kevel's presence forestalled him. "Dannel would miss her if she were to die."

Kevel rocked in silence for several minutes. "For the life of me, I don't know where the other gerrub came from. Pretty little thing, but it's a shame about her broken tail."

Raurk never understood how Kevel *saw* so much when his earthly eyes were useless. "That's Tanus. Actually, I should say that's the specter of Tanus. She was Grig's pet, but she's since passed into the next world. Thanks to her, they found their way out of the woods. Otherwise, I'd have never found them. She does seem to come and go whenever it suits her."

For the first time, Kevel turned his face toward his son-in-law. "You've stalled long enough. When did you know for sure Dannel would accompany you on this fool's errand? Or, have you known from the first?"

"Now I know why Dannel always asks so many questions," Raurk said. "He learned from the best."

"Humph!" Kevel rocked faster. "Your useless flattery won't work on me, Theron Raurk."

The druid felt the hackles on his neck rise. "If I'd realized his involvement from the beginning, I'd have refused this burden. It's bad enough subjecting Lillith, a grown woman, to such danger. I'd not ask permission to take Dannel with us if an alternative existed."

"Would it make any difference . . ." Kevel's voice broke. "Would it make any difference if I said no?"

Raurk pondered for a moment. Should he tell the truth?

"Never mind," Kevel said. "I won't force you to lie. When do you leave?"

"We daren't leave later than the noon hour tomorrow. That should give you plenty of time to tell Adelita."

"I've already told her." Kevel groaned and covered his eyes. "She's not happy about it, but at least she's — resigned. It'll be easier for the lad to go if his mother . . . . Well, at least she won't fight you."

"I appreciate that." Raurk bowed his head toward the other man. "I can't ask for more."

"Be warned though, Adelita will burden you with a ton of things you'll never use. Please have the good manners to accept without a fuss. You can discard the surplus as you see fit."

"I wouldn't think of offending Adelita."

"See that you don't."

Raurk rose from his chair and bowed low. "I have a few matters I must attend to." He turned with a heavy sigh to go, but at the last minute stopped. "You don't much like me, do you?"

Kevel's chuckle held little humor. "Liking you has nothing to do with it. You're taking my children from me. No one, not even you, can foretell the extent of danger you'll face. But if you value your own life, you had better return with both of them."

"I would have it no other way."

"I'll make your life a living hell should you fail," Kevel said. "I'll curse you and spit on your grave, for that is where you'll be when I'm through with you. Have I made myself clear?"

Raurk nodded. "Perfectly clear."

"Then go, take care of your *errands*. Should you fail to return before morning, I'll make your explanations to Lillith and the boy." He dismissed the druid with a wave of his hand and huddled deeper into the huge rocking chair. "I knew this time of parting must come, although I hadn't thought it would be quite so soon."

"Neither did I."

❧ 38 ❧

Only another druid could have followed Raurk when he left the house as a small goldenfly, and he preferred it that way. Even his beautiful Lillith was not privy to the rituals of the Druid Council.

He trusted her more than most but, by nature, the druids were not wont to divulge their inner workings to prying eyes. From the very beginning of time, they'd been dedicated to preserving life and sanity. But, due to persecution, they'd reverted to being a secret society. During the dark ages throughout history, too many of their brethren had been burned at the stake as witches.

At the bottom of the meadow, he assumed the shape of a great blackbird. He almost wished Grig could see him. He circled the treetops and then set his sights for the west. There he would meet with his peers and plead his cause.

He hoped the council would set aside their differences with him. Short of that, all he could ask was that they wouldn't interfere. Though he expected little, he must make one last petition before embarking on the next leg of their journey.

Urania had long ceased to be a harmless eccentric as several members claimed, but could he convince them? Because she'd once been part of the ruling body, most ignored her ravings. They much preferred to turn a blind eye to the truth than admit her evil spirit.

Couldn't they see what it'd already gained them? The Thousand Years War was in part a result of her scheming and her need for power-- and their blind loyalty to the witch. How could he prove his point?

Without missing a beat, Raurk morphed into the shape of an eagle riding the airwaves on oversize wings. He wanted no accidental sightings of his midnight expedition and would change several more times before reaching his destination.

In the end, he became the wind itself being tossed hither and yon in what appeared a haphazard route. To the casual observer, he was no more than a quick disturbance of the passing air. In truth, his path remained swift and direct toward the craggy mountains of Canada.

He landed on a rock ledge in human form. Before entering, he turned to admire the world spread out before him thousands of feet below. As always, the view took his breath away, but he could take no pleasure from it that night.

How many times had he stood on that very shelf and allowed himself to fall into empty space? As gravity pulled him to sure death, he had transformed into one of his many airborne entities.

There was no other access into the council chambers. That single factor had defended the sacred refuge against intruders for thousands of years. "Aye, and will continue to do so," he mouthed.

He anticipated his fellow council members would be waiting for him. Just as he always knew their whereabouts, they knew his. More often than not it was a nuisance, but tonight, a blessing. He need waste no time waiting for them to assemble from all corners of the aligned worlds.

The cavernous room cut into solid rock chilled him as he entered. He smiled at this small indication of the council's displeasure with him. They remained such petty, narrow minded fools.

"Theron Raurk, why have you come before us this night?" Tall and thin, Arvid Montplier dressed in sliver robes. His long, blond hair hung down his back in a single plait secured by a gold clasp. "We have more important business to attend to. Someone has upset the balance of Golgotha."

Raurk covered a laugh with a sharp cough. "Who would do something so foolish? Last time I visited, it was exactly as Urania had left it."

"Ahem," Montplier cleared his throat. "As shameful as Golgotha is, at least we knew what to expect. The River of Souls has wandered into a new path. Be quick about your affairs, so we may get on with ours."

From anyone else, Raurk would have taken offense, but he knew Montplier did no more than what the council expected. As head of this body, he must remain outwardly neutral.

More importantly, Montplier held the tie-breaking vote should it come to that. There were eight council members including Raurk and Urania. Montplier made nine. The man was his staunchest ally in the battle against the witch.

Raurk allowed a twisted grin to settle upon his lips as he addressed the council. "What do you fear? Are you frightened the lost souls will at last find peace?"

"What do you know of the matter?" a gruff voice called.

Raurk shrugged and pulled a chair from the table to sit. "Very little."

"Don't play your games with us, Raurk," the same man said.

"If you must know, I was present when the recent changes in Golgotha took place." Raurk leaned forward to place both elbows on the stone table. Finally, the poor beings that inhabit Golgotha have a chance at life as it should be."

"I don't trust your judgment," another man said. "They are naught but mutant rejects."

"That is your loss." Raurk did not flinch at the man's biting tone. He leaned back and removed a small knife from a hidden pocket to clean his nails. "With time, Golgotha should take its rightful place among the aligned worlds. That is, if the council doesn't interfere again."

"Enough," the council's oldest and most conservative member blustered. He often lobbied to study and reflect upon a matter for a good half-century before taking action, regardless of how simple the issue might be.

Roused from sleep, he wore a parsimonious, self-righteous smile. He found fault with everything Raurk did. "What makes you think you can undertake such drastic changes on your own—without our advice? No one gave you permission to enter this forbidden world again."

Raurk rose to his feet to pace. "I didn't enter Golgotha of my own accord. Innocent lives were at stake."

The aged man cleared his throat. "You know full well the council, at Urania's urgings, outlawed your presence in Golgotha years ago for just such indiscretions."

"Hear, hear," rang around the table.

Emboldened, the old man rose to his feet, back stiff and head trembling. "I, for one, am tired of your lack of respect for this learned group. It's my recommendation that you be stripped of all power. In addition, I vote that you be ejected from this governing body once and for all." He vanished in a huff and a swooshing of air falling in upon itself.

"A thousand pardons," Raurk bowed low. "I didn't come here to offend, but to beg your assistance. Can't we put aside our differences, if for only a moment?"

A young man, dressed in ruffles and high heels, sniffed in distaste. He already displayed the obdurate tenacity of his elders. "You refer to the issue of Urania Braith, I presume." He sneered through painted lips too perfect for a man.

"I do." Much to Raurk's regret, he feared this young popinjay would become a mirror image of the eldest councilman before long.

"What would you have us do? I thought we settled this subject once and for all. The witch has left our learned assemblage of her own will, much to our loss. Too bad you haven't followed suit."

Raurk stared, aghast. "Have you never wondered why the witch deserted the council?"

The lord fluttered a hand toward Raurk. "Why do you insist on wasting our time? Just because she chose to leave the council doesn't mean she's our enemy."

"How can you be so naïve?" Raurk seethed.

"Ah, I see you haven't changed. I refuse to stay here and be insulted. I'll be in my library. Call me should a sane voice be needed in the event of a vote." He strode from the chamber, slamming the door behind him.

Two down and four to go. Raurk turned to address the remaining council. "Since you seem to think I'm a threat, perhaps I should leave. Arvid Montplier, I apologize for imposing on you and my fellow members."

"As an associate of the tribune, you are always welcome," Montplier said. He glared at the men still seated at the table. "Finish your business."

Raurk nodded first toward Montplier and then the remaining members. "Thank you. I fear Urania grows stronger with each passing day."

"What makes you say that?" another councilman asked. "I had no idea you were privileged to that fine lady's plans. At least, not since you broke her heart."

"I did no such thing." Raurk could no longer check his anger. "Are you so blind that you can't see the obvious? Or perhaps you're in league with her to tear apart the worlds again?" Raurk moved to stand in front of the man. He fought the urge to shake his fellow councilman like a rag doll.

"Montplier, arrest this man," the councilman shouted.

"I can't." The tall druid shrugged. "He has every right to be heard. Leave, if you're offended by his presence."

"I'll stay." The man sank into his chair and sulked like a petulant child.

Raurk turned slowly to face each man in turn. "Urania thrives on chaos and is intent upon destroying all remaining druids, as few as we are. With our demise, the conventional order of nature will be destroyed."

"You sound more interested in saving your own hide," someone drawled. "Still, I would hear your plan before passing judgment."

"I but come to warn you," Raurk countered with a touch of sarcasm.

"What do you suggest?" another asked.

Raurk splayed his fingers toward the remaining members. "My visions tell me that Rakell Taznakie and Grig Dothrie are key to our mission. With their help, perhaps we will be successful in destroying Urania."

Shouts of anger rang out from around the council table. "Silence, gentlemen." Montplier held up a hand. "I propose we move to my chambers. It's damn cold in here. Anyone who wishes may join us."

❧ ◆ ❦

Raurk stood in front of the blazing fire, warming himself against the chill settling in his bones. "Don't those idiots understand?" He raised his gaze to Montplier and the councilman with the drawl, Dorn. The three other men said nothing.

"They understand," Dorn said. "But they don't want to admit we were wrong. It's not but stubborn pride. Can you foil her plans without annihilating the lady?"

Raurk shook his head. "That is not possible. We must afford Urania the same quarter she gives us . . . none. She is ruthless and dedicated to her cause."

"Do we know what her cause is?" Dorn crossed his arms over his chest.

"You've seen her work already," Raurk answered. "Need you ask?"

"Not really." Montplier smiled with a slight nod of his head. "Your point is taken, my brother. I propose those of you who don't agree, leave. This is an issue we can't resolve in one short night. However, Theron Raurk and I have much to discuss."

The three silent councilmen stood to leave.

"Goodnight, gentlemen. Thank you for your time," Raurk said. Montplier and Dorn remained.

"For the record, Master Raurk," Montplier said. "We're behind you all the way. If we don't stop Urania, she'll destroy everything we have worked so hard to regain. I still believe she had a hand in prolonging the Thousand Years War."

"You are more correct than you know." Raurk returned to sit at the table.

"I'm willing to learn," Montplier said. "If the council thinks the events at Golgotha are earth shattering, they have a rude awaking in store for them. This is nothing compared to what Urania has planned for us."

"I sense you're in a hurry," Dorn said. "However, I must ask why you need include Dannel Firth in this affair. He's naught but a child. What possible reason can you have for dragging him along?"

At last, Raurk relaxed. He leaned back in his chair and sighed. "I wish I knew Dannel's part, but it eludes me. Not until he slipped in the dragon's blood and came close to death did I know for sure that he must accompany us. Until then, I had only a vague precognition that he'd take it upon himself to follow us."

"What do you mean?" Dorn shook his head. "Forbid the boy from going. That should put a stop to it."

"It's not that easy. This incident somehow transformed Dannel. A young man with no magical power whatsoever suddenly became a force to reckon with. And his power may not even lie within the realm of enchantment."

Montplier shook his head. "I don't understand."

"He's the link for which we have searched all these years. Urania doesn't know it yet, but between the three of them, she is doomed."

Dorn laughed. "The world is doomed if we don't stop her. Do you have a plan, Raurk?"

"If I can persuade the council to help us, all the better. I fear the most I can hope for is they won't interfere. If I must fight them every step of the way as well as Urania, we shall waste valuable time. Against such odds, we *will* fail."

Montplier sighed. "There's little chance of swaying the most pig-headed council members to your cause. Nothing short of Urania showing up in the council room wielding death and destruction would move them to take immediate action."

"Nothing has changed," Raurk said with a sigh. He rose from his seat and paced about the room.

"Even should we convince them, they'd debate it for a day or two just to be sure," Montplier said. "Urania came highly recommended for the council and the fools still refuse to believe she's evil. They've grown complacent over the years."

"Then, will you help?" Raurk looked ecpectantly toward his colleagues.

Montplier nodded in thought. "I fear the day she sets foot in this chamber again and will do my utmost to prevent it. Perhaps we can't move this pack of dunderheads to action, but we *can* keep them out of your hair."

"What can I do to help?" Dorn asked.

"The transformation of Golgotha should occupy them for months," Raurk answered. "If they had your insight, they'd know these events are for the better."

"We might arrange to distract them," Montplier said. "Will that help?"

"I can ask little else. Dawn is near and I must take my leave. I have far to travel. Grace and peace be with you, my brothers." Raurk made a formal bow before turning to leave.

❧ 39 ❧

Raurk took to wing again, and raced against time. He feared Dannel might awake early and miss him. The lad was just impulsive enough to go looking for Raurk when he discovered his absence.

But fortune smiled upon him this morning. Lillith greeted him at the door. "Shh, everyone's still asleep." From long experience, she felt no alarm to find her husband gone. "Come in this house. I swear you're chilled to the bone. Warm your feet by the fire while I get you a cup of hot tea. I'll make breakfast as soon as the others are up."

Raurk settled by the fire as instructed and lifted the still wheezing Malie in his arms. "Well, little one," he said. "You're the real hero of the day and we didn't even know it. It was very brave of you to jump into the spring with a dead dragon. You might have been poisoned or drowned."

Malie squirmed until she was comfortable in Raurk's bony lap. She nuzzled his hand, begging him to scratch the delicate spot right between her eyes. "Do you like that?" He moved his hand to the gerrub's ear.

Raurk had little time to get comfortable when Dannel made his usual explosive entrance into the room. In a flash he had dislodged Malie and taken her place. "I'm ready to go. I have a pack and a blanket and a bladder gourd just like Taznakie's. I even remembered to put in an extra pair of boots, pants and a shirt. That'll keep me for months."

"Is that so?" Raurk ruffled the boy's hair.

Dannel nodded. "Tanus came to see me last night. Malie has a cold and Taznakie wrapped her in the healing web, so she's much better. Can we take Malie with us? Grig really likes her even though he complains a lot. I found out Grig has two gerrubs at home. He calls them Was-he and Was-nt because they're so different even though they're littermates. And Taznakie has fashioned a way for Malie to ride on his back in the web, and . . ."

"Hold on one minute, young man." Lillith didn't hide her alarm. "Where do you think you're going? This isn't a picnic or hunting for mushrooms."

"Lillith," Dannel wailed. "You're just a girl. If you can go, so can I."

A stern-faced Kevel entered the kitchen, wiping sleep from his eyes. "I'm afraid he's right. He's going along whether we like it or not. I spoke to Raurk last night, and it's necessary."

"And you agreed?" Lillith stared at her father.

Kevel splayed his fingers and shrugged. "Who am I to argue with a druid? Besides, your mother has packed enough food for an army. Would you argue with your own mother?"

"Raurk, tell them this is insane," Lillith implored.

He couldn't look his wife in the face. He'd expected and dreaded her protests. He smiled sheepishly. "I can't disagree with Adelita on such an important matter. Have you packed a bag yet? As soon as everyone has eaten, we must take our leave."

෮ ◆ ෯

A pall settled over the breakfasters until Malie raced under the table in hot pursuit of the spectral Tanus and knocked herself senseless trying to pass through Kevel's stout leg.

"What's this?" he shouted, jumping to his feet. "You silly little fool, you'll break your neck." Scooping the gerrub up in his large hands, he nuzzled her under the chin. "Dannel, you must take this incorrigible creature with you. I don't want her wandering around the house moping and whining because she can't find you."

He turned to leave the room, but stopped at the last moment. "Get your things together. The sooner you leave the better. It'll give me time alone with my wife for a change."

Dannel rose to follow his father, but with a slight shake of her head, Adelita deterred him. "You and Lillith, help me with the dishes while these men do whatever it is they do."

෮ ◆ ෯

Kevel gave them each a rough hug. "I won't ask which way you're going. If I don't know, I can't betray you. Besides you wouldn't tell me anyway. Lillith, you take care of your brother. I have no idea why either of you need go in the first place."

Lillith watched as her father turned his back to them. The time for them to depart had come, and she was as ready as she'd ever be. She'd dressed like the men, except for her beautiful long hair which she couldn't disguise. As a last resort, she braided the thick mass and wound it around her head, then jammed a soft hat down over her ears. When she looked in the mirror, the effect was that of a rather fetching waif. On her back, she carried a blanket and pack loaded with her share of the supplies. She hugged her father roughly and turned to Adelita. "Mother, please don't cry. We'll be back soon."

"I know you will, my daughter, but I can't help but worry." Adelita brushed tears from her eyes and hugged each of the travelers in turn.

❧ **40** ❧

"**Dannel**, slow down," Raurk said. The lad danced ahead with energy to burn. No one could tell he'd been grievously injured just the day before. "I fear we must change direction soon."

The poisonous Nemrak trees towering over the dense woods of Burnet and evergreens brought sorrow to his heart. More proof that nothing remained safe from the invading mutant forest.

Dannel retreated and reached for the druid's hand. "Raurk, I think I saw someone in the forest."

"I doubt that," Grig said. "We haven't come across another living soul in hours. Why would anyone in their right mind be wandering around out here?"

"Hush, Grig," Raurk cautioned. "I saw them as well. There are three of them . . ."

"Three? What's with three?" Grig squawked. "First we're nearly run over by a three headed troll. Then it was three dragons, now you say there are three unknown beings skulking through the woods. I for one am fed up with three. Give me ten or a hundred or a thousand, but I never want to see three of anything again! It's a sign of bad luck."

"Alas, I hate to be the one to tell you," Raurk said.

Grig folded his arms across his chest and glared. "Tell me what?"

"Three is Urania's number. 'Tis a sure sign of bad luck, as you say."

Taznakie bobbed his head up and down, but not in agreement. He grinned unabashedly at the three small figures that had appeared in front of them.

"We're here as you requested." The first man spoke in a raspy falsetto voice. "The path ahead is clear, but it's best if we guide you through the forest. It's our sworn duty to see that you remain safe."

The druid bent to shake hands with each of the diminutive men.

"This is Wraith, Wrath and Wrue. They're wood-elves. I'd like you to meet Grig Dothrie, Rakell Taznakie, Dannel Firth and my wife, Lillith. These gentlemen are here to insure safe passage through the forest they call home."

"Wraith? Wrath? Wrue?" Grig echoed. The wood-elves didn't come to his waist, but there was no denying they were every bit as human as he. Even the soft green shimmer of their skin resembling the bark of a willow tree couldn't belie this truth.

Wraith nodded with a grin. "'Twas Mother Oak's idea of a joke. It's our pleasure that you have asked us to help in your great journey. We are too small to do much else. The Nemrak trees have taken root throughout our forest. You must exercise extreme caution."

Taznakie lifted Wrue from his feet and held him at eye level. Then he poked the tiny man in his round potbelly. Next he played with Wrue's pointed ears and miniature feet. When he rubbed the elf's moss like hair and eyebrows, he laughed until tears streamed down his face.

At last he planted a loud slurping kiss on each of Wrue's bristled cheeks and returned him to solid ground. In succession, he subjected Wraith and Wrath to the same scrutiny. This was his very own seal of approval. Elves were not new to him, but he'd never known any such as these.

❧ ◆ ❧

Most of their lives the wood-elves had spent avoiding men. Taznakie was a new experience for the wood-elves. In fact, he was a unique experience for anyone meeting him for the first time.

They were so small, and most men so big that should trouble arise, avoidance was by far the most prudent course of action. They were also among the forest's shyest inhabitants, but they fell in love with this big oaf with the inquiring mind. The warmth and sincerity of his voice gave meaning to his garbled words. And anyone who carried a bedraggled, furry creature on his back couldn't be all bad.

Wraith grabbed Taznakie's immense left hand. "This way. Although the mutant forest invades our beautiful home, there are still many safe trails. It's our pleasure to point them out to you." Clearly he meant Taznakie.

Not to be outdone, Wrath took Grig's hand and Wrue seized Dannel as his charge. Somehow they couldn't bring themselves to be so familiar with the tall, gaunt druid. And if the woman was his wife, all the more reason to be respectful no matter how beautiful she might be. Though they believed Raurk their ally, he still frightened the sap out of them.

Grig refused to admit the small wood-elves helped allay his fears of this forest. This place, so different from his charming home, gave him the creeps. There were too many things he didn't understand. The longer they traveled, the more impenetrable the forest became, and far less light pierced the overhead canopy. "How does anything grow in this gloom?" Grig motioned toward the overgrown forest.

"I never gave it any thought," Wrath answered. "I suppose we're used to the gloom."

Raurk, with Lillith at his side, brought up the rear of the procession, and he couldn't put to rest his concerns. Under normal circumstances he would have relished the unexpected moment to spend with his wife, but he sensed they were being stalked.

He looked toward Wraith, Wrath and Wrue but could detect no signs of concern. Were they so busy entertaining their new found friends with bird calls that they failed to hear what he did? Or did he imagine it? If he were to ask, would it cause panic?

Casting about with his mind, he searched for other living creatures, but came up with only a few stray birds attracted by the elves excellent imitations.

The relative quiet concerned him. An hour before, the place had teemed with life, even if it wasn't familiar. He'd also noticed Grig probing the woods with his senses. Now he focused his gaze on Taznakie's back and the undersized elf leading him.

For a moment, Raurk wondered whether an unseen spell diverted their attention. And what was that shushing rustle that teased his ears?

Lillith whispered, "Something's bothering you. And don't trouble to deny it. I know you too well."

Raurk shook his head. "I'm not sure. Perhaps I'm getting dotty in my old age. Nobody else appears to be concerned."

He halted in his tracks. "Do you hear that?"

Lillith closed her eyes and listened. "I don't hear anything."

"Aye and that's part of what vexes me. Where are the birds and insects, the curious woodland animals? And why is Malie cowering in the sling Taznakie made her? Normally, she wants to know everything that's going on."

His wife shrugged, but a glint of fear shown in her eyes. "Shouldn't you say something?"

"My instincts tell me there's nothing there, but my gut tells me different. Which should I trust?" He tilted his chin toward the wood-elves. "Wraith, Wrath and Wrue don't seem concerned. Since this is their home, I assume they'll know if something is amiss." Still the druid worried.

Dannel intruded upon his thoughts. "Raurk, I'm hungry."

"Then we shall stop if our hosts agree." If something followed them, he'd have a better chance to detect the source while they rested. This would also give them a chance to sort through the many odds and ends Adelita had stuffed into their packs.

Wraith sniffed the air and nodded. "Yes, this place suits as well as any. I'll build a fire to warm you." He managed to produce a small fire for the travelers in spite of the dampness, then stood back to survey his work. "Dry your hands. I have observed that you do not soak up the moisture of the forest as we do."

The clearing allowed only two bodies at a time to huddle close together for the warmth. The overhanging branches dripped fat beads of moisture into the weak flames. Hissing and sputtering, it provided welcome comfort to the men even as it threatened to die out at any moment.

Wrue stretched to his full, slightly less than two-feet-something height and scanned the dense forest around them. "We have traveled much longer than planned. With your permission, we will call in the sentries and prepare for the night. It's not safe to travel after dark."

"What sentries?" Grig glanced nervously around him.

"You'll see. It grows late. Do we have your permission to call them?"

"This place is so murky, how do you know what time it is?" Grig asked. "It looks like twilight to me and has from the moment we set foot in this forest." He gestured to his surroundings. "Where do you expect us to sleep? There isn't enough ground for even one of us to stretch out. Unless of course you think we can sleep in the trees."

"You are very wise," Wrath agreed. "The trees are the safest place for the evening."

Grig scratched his head and peered upward into the dark. "How are we supposed to get up there? Besides, what's to keep us from falling out on our heads in the middle of the night—even if we did manage to scale one of these monsters in the first place?"

"That'll be no problem," Wrue said as if this was all in a day's work. "But, we must call in the sentries before they grow restless."

"Do as you must," Raurk replied. "I'm curious to meet these sentries."

In turn, each of the wood-elves whistled three times and waited. "The sentries return soon," Wrue said.

Three sets of feral, jewel-like eyes approached from downwind, several feet above the forest floor. Dannel leapt to his feet and screamed, "Look out!" The warning came too late.

Three gargantuan serpents, slithering and hissing encircled the elves. Grig and Raurk raised both hands to cast a spell of protection, but before they could get a word out, Wrue reached his small hand to the nearest monster with amazing results.

What had just been a writhing, coiling mass of muscle became no more than a walking stick. In turn, Wraith and Wrath retrieved their staffs.

"Why did you not tell me of your sentries?" Raurk chuckled. "I thought we were being followed."

Wide eyed, Wrath turned to him. "We thought you knew. You carry a staff of your own, is it not a guardian?"

"I fear not."

"May I look at your walking stick?" Wrue held out both hands. Running them over the silky smooth surface, he examined it from every angle. "Your staff is not wood. In fact it appears to be more akin to stone than a tree. No wonder there's no life left in it. How sad." He returned the heavy staff to Raurk.

"The staff of a druid is shaped from a petrified tree, so I suppose you are correct in saying it's stone. But why could I not detect the presence of your three vipers? Are they illusions or real?"

"I do not understand the meaning of your question," Wrath said. "Every wood-elf carries a staff presented to them by their mother. My staff, Thane, is as solid as that great dead thing you carry around. In that sense, they are real. I suppose the creature they become is an illusion. But are they alive like you or I, I don't know. When I die, Thane will be buried with me because it will no longer be anything but a staff of wood."

"If you have no objections," Wrue said. "We must prepare a shelter for the night. It won't take long, but if this drizzle increases, I'm sure you'll want a roof over your heads."

"This I have to see," Grig whispered to Dannel. "If Taznakie can sleep in a tree without falling out, I'll be surprised."

"Master Grig," Wraith said. "You're an elf, do you not sleep in a tree?"

Grig's hackles rose. "Of course I do, but inside with both feet planted on a solid floor. I see no such dwelling hereabouts."

Wraith's face registered horror. "Inside the tree? Not in the branches above your head? How can that be?"

"Perhaps I should ask you the same question," Grig huffed.

"Grig Dothrie," Dannel interrupted. "If you insist upon quarreling about every little thing, we shall never get any rest. I'm tired and wet. My skin puckers like a wrinkled old hag. Can't you please just let them show us what they mean?"

"Well if that's the way you feel about it, I'll just get out of everybody's way. I know when I'm not wanted." Grig would have expected a reprimand more from the druid than Dannel and it galled his britches that a child should speak to him so.

Doing a quick about face, Grig attempted to stalk back the way they had just come. Fortunate for him, he had no idea which direction that might be. The thick forest would have swallowed him without a trace.

❧ ◆ ☙

By the time the wood-elves completed their task, the slow drizzle had increased to monsoon proportions. Not a soul remained dry enough to brag about it should the thought have crossed their minds.

No one bothered to question how several conveniently placed limbs just happened to form a sturdy ladder for them to climb to the aerial heights of their shelter. By then they couldn't have cared less as long as there was a possibility of comfort for the night.

Lillith ascended first to their forest shelter at the urging of all three tiny wood-elves. Dannel, Grig and Rakell followed in turn. Bringing up the rear, the druid mounted the ladder more than a little resembling a drenched raven.

"Wow, look at that," Dannel turned in a circle. "This is so . . ."

"Step aside boy and let the rest of us in," Grig said. He took no more than a moment to survey their shelter. "This murkiness is oppressing. Not the least bit of light. There's not room for all of us." He sniffed the air. "Besides, it reeks of wet bodies. Better we should spend the night on solid ground."

Taznakie grumbled an oath from the dark. With a large hand, he edged Grig toward the brink of the platform.

Raurk motioned Taznakie away. "Grig Dothrie, I suggest you close your mouth before our large friend dumps you over the side. If you don't like the dark, then fix it. I know you to be quite capable of remedying that particular discomfort. Have you lost your powers, or perhaps forgotten them?"

Grig unleashed a very picturesque expletive. He felt rather annoyed (or perhaps stupid would be more accurate) with this scolding. He spat several words of enchantment, and numerous fairy lamps blinked into existence to light their temporary home. "I hope that meets your requirements. Someone else will have to do something about these wet clothes." He plucked at his soggy garments.

"Are you ill, Master Grig?" Lillith's concern shown in her voice.

"It's just that I'm chilled and . . . I'm sorry." All his bravado deserted him.

"Do you need something?" She stooped to peer into his eyes.

"Yes. No. I don't know." Grig hesitated. "My feet are like ice and my brain feels likes it's burning up. I've been soaked to the skin more often than not these past few days. I'm beginning to hate water as much as Malie. Perhaps we have acquired the same malady."

Lillith placed a slender hand on the elf's forehead. "I'm afraid you're running a fever. Take off those wet clothes while I find a dry blanket to wrap you in. I'm sure Raurk can do something to dry us all out."

"I beg your pardon," Grig blustered, his face burning. "I can't take my clothes off in front of a woman."

"My lady, you give me too much credit," Raurk denied. "I can warm our small shelter, but I'm not a washerwoman to be drying clothes with magic."

Digging in her pack, Lillith produced a blanket that was at least somewhat dry. She tossed it one-handed to Grig. "I'll turn my back while you undress, although you worry overmuch about your modesty. After all, I do have a young brother for whom I care for upon occasion.

"In the meantime, Raurk, I insist you do what you can to provide us with warmth before we all get sick. Poor Malie hasn't been out of that pack in hours. We'll wrap her up with Grig, she'll like that a lot."

With a wave of his hand, Raurk transformed several of the fairy lamps to emit heat. "I pray, dear wife, that is sufficient to satisfy you," he acknowledged with a slight bow.

A warm glow radiated through the shelter. Wraith, Wrath and Wrue watched mesmerized as the heat soaked through their diminutive frames. "In all our years we've never beheld the likes of such," Wraith said. "As we grow older, the chill air often adds to our discomfort. As you witnessed, fire is nigh impossible to build. Should we succeed, it's haphazard at best."

Grig turned his back to divest himself of his sodden garments, and then wrapped the blanket around his body. As he turned back to the others with his clothes, Taznakie snatched them from his grip. He hung them from the overhead boughs and spoke in quick, singsong words. "Iadou dolomadou."

'Twas the simple spell of a washerwoman, but in his mouth, the results produced awe-inspiring results. The forest lit up like a torch, wind buffeted them and everything in sight dried instantly.

Taznakie beamed as he returned Grig's garments to him. The wood-elves examined their own dried clothing and exclaimed, "Well done." Like small children, they clapped and cheered for their hero.

"Well done, all right," Grig snapped. "I can't believe he didn't incinerate everything within sight. I keep telling you, never let that man utter the simplest of spells. He'll kill all of us before this insane journey is through."

"I hate to intrude upon your rejoicing," Raurk said. "But at this late hour we must fill our stomachs and rest. Since we didn't get around to it today, we should divest ourselves of anything we can't use. Adelita's intentions were good, but we can't burden ourselves with so many extras." He motioned toward the laden packs tossed to one side.

"Late tomorrow or early the next day, I hope to reunite with the pirate, Magried Whittlebottom. It's been far too long since we've heard from him. Although, under the circumstances, there was little any of us could do about it."

"Whittlebottom?" Grig echoed. "I'd forgotten about him. He's probably up to no good."

Raurk sighed. "I hope he's waiting at Cranitaur Valley without getting into trouble. By now he and Isis have probably done each other in. She's just plain cranky with molting and he — well, let's just say he's a bit of a rogue when it comes to getting into mischief. We shall be lucky if the entire valley is not reduced to shambles."

"Let them burn each other to cinders for all I care," Grig scoffed. "Then maybe we could all go home and forget this ridiculous farce."

Dannel's eyes glowed in the fairy lamps. "Magried Whittlebottom, the pirate? Will I get to meet him? I've heard ever so much about him and his ship and how he plundered the skies. Wow, I can't wait."

"Yes, you'll meet him," Raurk answered. "But we need attend to more immediate concerns. I'm famished."

Somehow the food Adelita packed had remained dry in the downpour. Even the wood-elves ceased nibbling on their green leaves and accepted several stalks of celo-melon, something they'd never seen before. "This is excellent." Wrue smacked his lips, enjoying the succulent fruit. "Does it grow wild in your world? Could we cultivate it?"

"I'm afraid not," Raurk denied. "The constant shade and rain aren't favorable. However, if you were to visit the home of Kevel Firth and take them our greetings, I'm sure he'd allow you the pick of their garden. This is just a minor sample of what they grow."

"And they would share with us?" Wraith stared in wonder.

Lillith handed each of the little men a slice of sapple. "Father loves to share. Besides, you'd be welcome company for him and Mother."

"That's as it should be," Raurk said. "Shall we set a watch for the night?"

Wrath shook his head. "Lightning will watch overhead, Quake will protect us from below and Thane will remain on the platform near me. Nothing can threaten us while they act as guardians. As you mentioned, this is the time for a good night's sleep."

Before long, Grig's psyche sank into frightening nightmares, but they paled when he awoke to find Thane staring him in the face. Like so many, he had a natural abhorrence for serpents and these giants measured as big around as his waist.

He attempted to extricate himself from the creature's hypnotic gaze, but every time he moved his head, Thane followed with unblinking eyes. As a last resort, he shooed the sentry with fluttery hands to make it leave. Still it did not retreat. The serpent continued to match his every move.

"Thane likes you." Wrath chuckled. "He's been stretched out next to you most the night."

"No wonder I had such horrible dreams. I thought it something I ate."

Wrath gave a merry laugh. "It wasn't until you started thrashing about that Thane settled by your side. Only then did you calm. I fear your dreams trouble you overmuch."

"My dreams were fine before Raurk entered my life. Now, get this thing off me."

"If you stroke him between the eyes, he'll stop staring at you," Wrath said.

"Stoke him between the eyes? It'd be just my luck your sentry will swallow me whole just as he's probably done to Malie."

"Nonsense," Raurk joined them. "Don't insult our hosts when presented with such an honor."

Grig shook his head. "I don't like snakes." But he couldn't stop himself from reaching for the large serpent with a tentative finger. With teeth gritted in a death-lock, and as much bravado as he could muster, Grig slid his thumb down the wide expanse between glowing eyes and received quite a shock. "Thane's skin is warm and velvety. I—I thought he'd be cold and clammy."

"Are you cold and clammy?" Wrath crossed his arms and huffed.

Dannel woke at the sound of voices and inched forward so he could see. "Can I touch him, too? Where can I get a sentry like Thane? Would your Mother Oak allow me such a staff?"

Dannel had woken Lillith and Taznakie with his exuberance. "Dannel," she scolded. "You can't go around asking people for gifts. You know better than that."

Dannel dropped his gaze, only slightly cowed. "I'm sorry, but the guardians are wonderful. Just think of how they might protect us. No one would have to remain awake at night to make sure we're safe. No wild animals could sneak up on us, or . . ."

"Aye, 'tis true," Raurk agreed. "However I do not see that as an immediate possibility."

"Dannel is correct." Wrue pulled at his beard. "I've never heard of Mother Oak presenting a staff to any but her children. I suppose we could ask her," he pondered. "There might be a way, but it's not my decision."

"Please," Dannel pleaded.

"Hush," Raurk said. "Since we're all awake, we should start the day with full bellies. Then we must sort through this mountain of things your mother would have us carry to our graves."

☙ ◆ ❧

Hours later, Wraith held up a miniature hand as a signal to stop. The wood-elf appeared agitated. "We can't proceed in this direction. The mutant forest has invaded farther north than we anticipated. The sentries must find a safe path and lead us. While we wait . . ."

A great blur descended from the trees, startling the travelers. Hissing and posturing, one of the huge snake sentries circled the travelers. Grig batted at the monster. "I thought these things were supposed to protect us." He wasn't brave enough to touch the serpent even though the thought flitted through his mind.

Much calmer than Grig thought the situation warranted, Wrue cautioned, "Don't touch it! It's not *our* sentry. In fact, it's not a sentry at all. It appears we have encroached upon this creature's territory, and it's not wont to let us pass.

"Don't move a muscle," Wraith said. "Perhaps it'll leave us once it discovers we mean no harm. Where is your small animal? She would make a quick snack if the serpent spies her."

Taznakie mouthed a few words and pointed to his pack. Malie hated snakes almost as much as she hated water and quaked at the deepest recesses of her safe haven. It might take weeks to coax the gerrub from her hiding place. Although the spectral Tanus stood on his shoulder, watching every move the serpent made.

"What do you propose?" Raurk whispered. "I'm reluctant to kill this creature if we can avoid so doing."

"We could let Taznakie bind it up," Dannel volunteered.

"No," Grig and Raurk chorused.

"I smell only fear on its skin," Wrue said. "If we do nothing, we should be safe."

"Do nothing. Do nothing?" Grig couldn't believe his ears. "You mean this behemoth will slither away in a few minutes of its own accord?"

"Exactly," Wrath agreed with a nod.

In the meantime, the snake made its way up Grig's left leg, stopping every inch or so as it tasted him with its flickering, forked tongue. In his opinion, this problem would not just go away.

Soon, the serpent wound itself around his waist and crept upward, stopping only when it stared him in the eye.

"Don't move," Wrath whispered.

"Get it off me." More than anything, Grig wanted to blast it into a million pieces, but somehow, he felt this was a test. If he could pass it, he wasn't sure what would happen. Besides, he couldn't remember which spell to utter.

An eternity later, or maybe only minutes, a shrill whistle broke the silence. The snake swung its massive head in the direction of the sound, sniffing the air with that evil-looking tongue. Then it turned back to peer into Grig's frightened face.

The whistle sounded again, this time more insistent. The snake could no longer ignore it. Much to the elf's relief, it lowered its ponderous weight to the ground and glided away as quickly as it had come.

Everyone babbled at once. "Are you all right? Did it hurt you? What did it want? Could you talk to it?"

The weight removed from his body, Grig's eyes rolled up into his head, and he passed out, adding to the confusion of the moment.

Raurk bellowed, "Stop! All of you stop. Let me examine him before you pronounce Grig Dothrie dead. I wager he's unhurt, just badly frightened."

෩ ◆ ෨

Grig awoke to the sound of his own name shouted in his face, accompanied by a rude slap across one cheek. "Am I dead?" he mumbled. "Where am I? Where did it go? Did it bite me?"

"None of the above," Lillith assured him. "Wraith, Wrath and Wrue think the forest gnomes called it away. They're known to cull the cooperation of certain wild animals. It seems this was one such being. We must have frightened it."

"We frightened it?" Grig squawked. "What about me? I'm the one it wanted to swallow whole."

"Nonsense," Raurk said. "Are you able to travel?"

Grig inspected himself with his hands. At last he nodded. "I think so."

"Excellent, it's probably best we move on as soon as possible."

Grig braced himself. "Why didn't you stop it?"

"It meant no harm," Wrue said.

Grig huffed. "Why didn't the guardians warn us?"

Wrath answered, "We'd sent them away only moments before, if you will remember. They would've come if they'd sensed true danger. Thane has just returned and will show us the path. Please, can we move on?"

"Just point me in the right direction." Grig said. "The sooner we get away from the snake's territory, the better."

❧ *41* ❧

Precious little light penetrated beyond the dense canopy and the usual slow drizzle had commenced some time earlier, making everyone miserable and short tempered. To make matters worse, cloying mud tugged at their every step.

Head down, Grig ran smack into the back of Raurk. "What in hell are you doing?"

"We're stopping for the night." The druid waved at the three wood-elves as they disappeared into the forest covering.

"It's about time," Grig said. "Another hour and I'd be sorely tempted to turn tail and run. Rain, or mud, or giant snakes, or impenetrable forest couldn't stop me. All I want is my beautiful tree house where one lives inside, not in the branches."

Lillith placed her hand on Grig's arm. "Hush, you'll offend our hosts. It's not their fault we're stuck out here."

"I know." Grig hung his head.

Before long, the elves completed the sleeping platform, identical to that of the night before. Much of the food Adelita packed had begun to spoil from the constant dampness. If not for the accompanying chill, none of it would have survived even this long.

"Well, I guess tomorrow we'll have to forage for our supper." Lillith gave a wan smile. "If only we could eat the leaves like the wood-elves."

"Yuck." Dannel groaned. "I'd rather go hungry."

"The way thing's are going, we may have to resort to eating leaves," Grig said.

"Hush, Master Grig," Lillith admonished. "Things could always be worse."

"Humph." He stared into the pitch black forest. "I don't know how."

"Will you light our shelter again, good elf?" she asked. "Raurk, will you provide the heat?"

"I'll do it myself," Grig snapped. "There's no need to bother the great and powerful Theron Raurk for such basic chores."

Grig waved his hand and fairy lamps appeared to light their small corner of the woods. Another swish and half of them emitted delicious warmth. "If you want to get dry, you'll have to ask Taznakie, but that may prove more dangerous than staying wet all night."

Taznakie's expectant face fell at the insult, but he said the words of drying without complaint. This time, he managed to curb his enthusiasm, or perhaps fatigue won out. The results, however, were excellent. Once again, the travelers enjoyed the sensation of being warm and dry all at the same time, minus the brilliant display of the previous evening.

"We've sent the guardians to their posts," Wraith said. "All is safe for the night. Tomorrow we'll reach the Tongalooa River and you can be on the next leg of your journey."

Nestled like giant birds on the leafy platform, the humans rested well, considering the clatter put up by the forest inhabitants. Grig wondered if this meant the sentries weren't doing their job or . . . . He fell asleep in mid thought.

Wraith, Wrath and Wrue waited until their guest slept soundly before holding a consultation between themselves. They were unaware that Raurk remained awake, listening until he assured himself the wood-elves plotted nothing of evil intent. Or worse yet, abandoned them to their own means.

At last even the druid drifted upon the wings of peaceful sleep. No one woke to witness the silent departure of the tiny wood-elf, Wrue.

☙ ◆ ❧

Grig felt like he'd just closed his eyes when Dannel pounced on him. "Wake up, Grig Dothrie. The sooner you get up, the sooner we can be on our way to the river and find food and we're going to take a boat downstream and Malie is even out of the sling for a change and it's all downhill from here."

"Young man, remove yourself from my being," Grig spat. "Or I shall be forced to flay your backside. There's no reason to act like a heathen just because we may be living like heathens. First thing I want to do is get these boots off. The mud has made them as hard as stone. Look, I shall be unable to even walk."

"But Grig, the rest of us cleaned our shoes last night. Why didn't you?"

"Get out of my way, urchin!" the elf barked, and then fell out of their lofty aerie. In his anger, he'd forgotten they rested high above the forest floor. Fortunate for him, the tree branches broke the worst of his fall.

"Aargh," Grig bellowed. "Raurk, why couldn't you just leave me alone, you great flapping harbinger of doom? I was content . . . nay, happy in my ignorance of you and your ridiculous Light of Ishram. Whether you like it or not, I'm leaving."

Since Grig had protested every step of the journey, no one paid the least bit of attention to his ravings. Taznakie blew a raspberry at his last words. No one bothered to watch when he stomped away from the base of the tree. They knew he might venture a step or two into the dense woods, but there remained nowhere for him to go.

"Shouldn't someone stop Master Grig?" Wrath followed Grig's progress with his eyes.

"If you must," Raurk said. "However, I think he'll return soon."

The wood-elves sidled down the tree with grace born of a lifetime of practice. They were much more aware of the dangers of the dark forest than the others. "Grig? Grig Dothrie, where are you?" they called, heading in the same direction the elf had departed.

Grig heard them, but still angry, refused to heed their calls. Stubborn pride forbade him to make even the slightest sound. As an elf of the forest, he too could move undetected through the low hanging branches. He'd had a bellyful of this insanity and intended to return home. His mind told him this path lay in the right direction. All he had to do was backtrack.

∾ ◆ ∿

Fifteen minutes later, alarm arose among the travelers. On the ground, Raurk probed the forest with his keen eyes in search of the disgruntled elf. Angry at himself, he called, "Grig Dothrie, don't be a fool. Come back before you get lost." Silence greeted him.

Raurk turned his face upward to the tree where they'd slept. "Lillith, keep Dannel with you. No use putting anyone else in danger. Taznakie, come down and help us look." But the *us* in this case proved rhetorical. Wraith, Wrath and Wrue had disappeared.

"Blast! This is not a good start to the morning, Grig Dothrie," he bellowed in frustration. The forest remained silent.

Taznakie gestured at a large shadow moving quickly toward them. Thane had come to retrieve them. With no other choices, they followed. Bending double and even crawling upon hands and knees at times, they labored behind the guardian much farther than seemed possible.

What seemed like hours passed before they spied the wood-elves staring at a rather strange looking, pillar-like figure. Raurk did a double take when he realized the muddy stump frozen in place appeared to be none other than Grig Dothrie.

Taznakie poked a tentative finger toward the elf, but before he could touch Grig, Quake interjected his massive body.

"Don't touch him," Wrue said with a forlorn look. "The mud-slobber has imprisoned Master Grig. If you touch him, the same thing will happen to you. 'Tis no wonder he failed to answer."

"How did he get so far from camp?" Raurk inspected the bundled Grig from a distance.

"The mud-slobber dragged him here. They're immensely strong." Wraith gestured to a slimy path. "There's the trail of his arrival. We must go back as soon as possible before the creature returns. Master Grig is lost to us."

"There's got to be something we can do," Raurk said.

"I fear not," Wrue answered. "There's no cure for what the mud-slobber has done."

Incensed, Taznakie fought the giant snake to reach his friend. He refused to leave Grig behind. Had he known what a mud-slobber was and their propensity for sucking their victims dry, he might have had second thoughts, but in his ignorance he enjoyed bliss — and an undying loyalty. Stomping his feet and pin-wheeling his arms, Taznakie threatened the three elves with total annihilation if they didn't help.

"Talk to him, druid." Wrue cowered behind Raurk. "No one can touch Grig Dothrie without suffering a like fate. We'll all die an agonizing death if we don't leave soon. The mud-slobber returns, do you not hear it?"

"Aye, that I do," Raurk agreed. But he'd never heard the likes of it before. It resembled a bastardized cross between a slithering reptile and the galumphing of an injured troll. A nauseously sweet smacking of stringy mucous breaking contact with the earth turned his stomach. If the events weren't so dire, Raurk might have stayed to witness the arrival of such a creature. "Taznakie, bind Grig so we can tow him."

Taznakie wasn't always the brightest glow in the sunset, but he understood without further instructions. With both arms raised, he roared, "Raldoix rendaulix swervitious germanon cleetious . . . Laithos." A looped strand affixed itself to the bundle from head to toe. Pleased, he looked toward the druid for approval and was rewarded with a grimace.

Raurk rammed his walking stick through the loop and the sheathed elf tottered to the ground. "Grab the other end," he told Taznakie. "You and I shall carry Grig, while the others distract the mud-slobber."

Wraith, Wrath and Wrue were nigh petrified at the sound of the approaching monster. At Raurk's words they bolted toward camp. The druid and Taznakie were left on their own.

Grig's weight proved of little consequence, and Taznakie motioned Raurk aside before hoisting the elf upon his shoulders. But with the dense undergrowth, he dropped his bundle to the ground before long. Taznakie wound up pushing and pulling the slimed elf through the most difficult spots.

Raurk brought up the rear and fretted at the imminent arrival of the enraged mud-slobber. Just as Taznakie was about to sling his pack to the ground again, the druid called a halt. "Wait, we'll never reach safety like this. Move out of the way." With arms raised and a few spoken words of enchantment, Raurk parted the forest, just as Moses parted the waters of the Red Sea. A direct line to their tree-nest lay before them.

If it had been anyone else, and the mud-slobber hadn't been hot on their heels, Taznakie might have taken time to ask why the druid waited so long. The monster loomed into sight, crashing its way toward them.

"Ayah!" Taznakie bawled and loped as fast as his legs would carry him to sanctuary.

Between Raurk and Taznakie, they managed to carry Grig to the tree platform. "Lillith, where are the wood-elves?" Irritation made his words harsh.

Lillith shook her head. She and Dannel watched with horrified eyes as the mud-slobber galumphed its way to the base of their tree and attacked the knurled trunk. "It's a giant garden slug," she screeched. "Dannel, where's the salt Mother packed? Find it, quick!"

The boy tore at everything in his pack then started on his sister's without finding the sack of salt. "I can't find it," he wailed. "We must have thrown it away."

"Unh, unh," Taznakie held out the bag.

"Hurry, Lillith," Dannel screamed. "It's halfway up the tree."

She untied the sack and tipped it to dump the contents on the mud-slobber, but at the last moment, rammed her hand into its recesses and drew out a large fistful of the white mineral. "Here goes." She rained salt over the oversized mutant.

The giant slug let out with a guttural bugle that raised the short hairs on Raurk's neck. The salt ate through its tough hide like acid, melting the creature from without. Lillith flung two more handfuls at the monster, hastening its demise.

With a dangerous glint in her eyes, she eyed her husband. "Why didn't you just kill it?" She glared at Raurk with her hands planted on her hips.

"What, and rob you of all the fun? If I go around killing every living thing that poses a threat, I'd leave a wide swath of destruction in my wake. Besides, what would you have done if I hadn't been here?"

"Are you planning on going somewhere?"

Raurk shook his head. "No, of course not, but you never know what might happen."

Although still angry, his words made her think. "I suppose we'd learn to rely upon our own resources if you were . . . unavailable."

Raurk tipped his head.

Lillith gave a wry smile. "Well, next time, at least try to find something smaller to pick on. And what is that thing?" She pointed toward the bundled elf.

"*That,* my dear, is our friend, Grig Dothrie. The mud-slobber wrapped him in a cocoon of slime. The wood-elves say to touch someone in this condition results in like consequences."

"Then how did you carry him?"

"I had Taznakie bind him before we carried him back. The question is how to restore Grig. My repertoire of magic spells doesn't come with instructions for de-sliming elves."

Taznakie, pointed to the ground and then to Grig Dothrie.

"Yes, my friend, 'tis safer to move him to solid earth before attempting anything." Raurk agreed. "Can you handle the task by yourself?"

Taznakie beamed and nodded. With great care, he avoided the puddle of slime at the base of the tree and moved several feet away before laying Grig on the ground with a soft thud. He was much gentler now that danger had passed. Drawing himself erect and taking several deep breaths, Taznakie cleared his throat to utter the spell of release.

"Wait, let me," Raurk intervened. He'd seen the unbridled results of this spell when Grig used it to release the dragon in Golgotha, and could not allow Taznakie free will in such close quarters. "Randitkin rotherdam exaabolta re-ecociana," he intoned, revising the last word to tailor it to his purposes.

The iron-like cords melted away from Grig's icy countenance right about the time Wraith, Wrath and Wrue decided to reappear.

Wrue studied the elf and shook his head. "It would be best if we left him here and moved on. The stench of the mud-slobber on him will attract others."

"We're sorry for leaving you alone to face the beast," Wrath said. "But, where has it gone? And what happened to the forest?" He nodded toward the trees only now returning to their proper alignment.

Wraith appeared skeptical, glancing over his shoulder. "Is it safe to assume the mud-slobber is dead since you're standing here un-worried?" The wood-elf couldn't help casting another glance over his shoulder.

"Lillith killed it," Dannel said. "She says it was just an overgrown garden slug. At home, she drowns them in ale, but we didn't have any so she threw salt on it. The salt melted it. That's what's left." He gestured toward the pool of drying mucous.

The elves inspected the creature's remains. Wraith shuddered and made an intricate sign with his fingers. "What's salt? Where could we find this thing? Is it magic?"

"You guys don't know what salt is?" Dannel looked askance at the elves. "Don't you put it on your food? Mother packed a bag of it for us. We almost threw it away yesterday, but I guess Taznakie put it in his pack when nobody was looking. We buy it at the village mercantile. I don't know where they get it, but it's not magic."

"The lad speaks true," Raurk said. "But all this talk does nothing to restore Master Grig to us. Is he frozen through and through, or is it simply the slime encasing him?"

For the response he got, the druid might as well have asked the wind the same question. The wood-elves remained in shock. No one, let alone a woman, had ever killed a mud-slobber. The only woman in their lives was Mother Oak. "We—well," Wrue stammered. "There is no cure."

"I refuse to believe that," Lillith said. "Raurk, could we sprinkle a bit of salt on Grig and see what happens? I almost dumped the entire bag on that awful slug, but something stopped me at the last moment. It might have been my frugal nature, but I don't think so."

"Try it. What do we have to lose?" the druid pondered. "We'll start with a small amount on his toes and see what happens. I doubt we'll cause him further harm."

"We have to try. Dannel, will you go back up and get it?"

"I brought it with me." Dannel handed the bag to his sister.

"Will you do the honors, my dear?" Raurk turned to Lillith. "Remember, just a little to start with."

Everyone held their breath as Lillith removed a pinch of grainy salt from the bag and scattered it across the tips of Grig's toes. The slime covering the elf's foot melted upon contact. Encouraged by a slight wiggle of toes, Lillith sifted a handful across his legs and torso.

"Do his whole body," Dannel cried. "He's starting to move. Hurry, Lillith, he might suffocate."

She flung a handful of salt over Grig, watching the filthy glop slump away from his being. His eyes opened and he blinked in bewilderment. "What happened?" His words came out a raspy whisper. "I'm freezing to death."

Taznakie shouted, "Iadou dolomadou!" All the while making wide, sweeping gestures. The elf glowed like a radioactive torch. His hair whipped in a breeze only he could feel and the toes of his soggy boots curled with the sudden drying spell. Much to Grig's chagrin, his leather pants and jerkin shrank in an alarming manner. But he was undeniably dry to the bone, and warm.

"Enough!" he shrieked, as his dwindling clothing cut him in several rather delicate areas. "Call this idiot off before I start to shrink, too." He tugged at the offending garments hoping to stop their distressing contractions. If he didn't get out of them soon, he'd be in dire straits. Grig leapt to his feet pulling and prying at the leather.

With his usual zeal, Taznakie ripped the jerkin over the elf's head, nigh tearing Grig's nose from his face. Tears ran down Grig's face at the affront, and his breeches still shrank. Without being told, he knew what was coming next. "Get away from me, Taznakie, before you do any more damage. "I'll do it myself," he screamed and scuttled backwards.

Taznakie pinned Grig to the forest floor, attempting to rip his breeches off.

Wraith, Wrath and Wrue watched horrified, not knowing what to do. Malie was nowhere to be seen and the humans had the audacity to laugh until their sides ached. At last, Raurk took pity on the elf. "Taznakie, cease your labors before you emasculate Master Grig. Those pants aren't coming off like that."

Taznakie stopped, but disappointment showed on his face. He jumped to his feet and with a powerful tug pulled Grig with him. Grig went flying into the air only to butt heads with the trunk of the nearest forest giant.

"Ooh . . ." Grig slumped to the ground unconscious.

"Stop it, before someone really gets hurt," Lillith commanded. Reaching into the small pouch she wore at her waist, she extracted a delicately engraved pair of garden shears. "I knew these would come in handy sooner or later. Raurk, help me cut his breeches before his circulation is completely cut off."

The wood-elves took one look at Lillith's shears and hightailed it into the forest in need of peace and solitude. Malie and Tanus trailed behind at a discreet distance sensing their distress.

"Malie. Tanus, come back," Dannel called.

"Let them go, son," Raurk advised. They'll come back when the elves do."

⤛ ◆ ⤜

Grig regained consciousness wrapped in Taznakie's healing web and tucked away on the tree platform. He suffered more with the knot upon his head than from his encounter with the giant slug.

With a gentle finger, he probed the lump for signs of permanent damage. "I hope you're happy," he snarled at Taznakie. "I have nothing to wear, and my head feels like a frigging klaxon. Don't ever try to help me again, you imbecile."

"Ah, I see you're awake at last." Raurk was far too jovial for Grig's liking. "As soon as you're ready, we'll be on our way. Wraith says we can still reach the river this afternoon, but we must hurry. I fear the elves grow weary of our presence."

"What am I supposed to wear?" Grig wanted very much to rain on the druid's parade. "I'm not about to go traipsing through the woods in my current attire."

"Dannel has left you his extra set of clothing." Raurk indicated a small pile of garments. "Taznakie and I'll wait below with the others."

⤛ ◆ ⤜

Grig nursed his headache with poor grace. "Dannel, if you tell me it's all downhill from here one more time, I vow I'll dump you in this creek, clothes and all."

The boy snickered and danced ahead. "I promise, not to say that ever again, Master Grig. But it *is* all downhill from here. Look."

"Aargh," Grig growled, grabbing for the boy.

"Heal yourself, Grig Dothrie—or quit being so irascible," Raurk said.

Grig glared at the druid, but said nothing.

Wrath looked uneasily from Raurk to the elf. "We must return to

Mother Oak before long."

"What's your point?" Grig asked.

"You'll come to a meeting of two streams and that's where we leave you."

"You can't leave us now," Dannel said. "How will we find our way?"

"Follow the brook downhill and it'll take you to Mecca, the water gnome village." Wrue said. "The main thoroughfare through town leads to the Tongalooa River."

"The gnomes will provide you with lodging for as long as you choose to stay," Wraith said. "A riverboat travels downstream from there. I understand it's quite comfortable if you like that kind of thing."

"Humph," Grig mumbled.

"What's wrong?" Wrue searched Grig's face.

"I don't like the idea of water gnomes leading us anywhere. Every experience I've had with those round-shouldered scoundrels has lead to no good. You expect me to entrust my life to a gnome?"

"Put your qualms aside, good elf," Raurk said. "If we want to sail downriver, we have no choice but to trust them."

"Treacherous heathens if you ask me." Grig's heart sank to his toes.

Wrue held up his hand to halt. "It's not safe for us to venture further. Remember to turn left where the two streams meet. You can't miss the gnome village. You'll smell it long before it comes into view."

With a sly grin, he looked at his brothers. "Now?"

Wraith and Wrath nodded in unanimous consent. "We, uh, have a — uh something to present to you. Dannel asked if Mother Oak would give him a guardian. It—we thought it was a good idea, so we petitioned her."

"Did she agree?" Dannel nigh jumped up and down with excitement. "I can't believe you took me seriously."

"Dannel," Lillith scolded. "Don't leap to conclusions. Listen to what they have to say."

Wraith blushed. "Well, yes. As a matter of fact, Mother Oak liked the idea very much. She conferred with Father Redwood and they have sent staffs for all of you . . . except Theron Raurk."

"I hope you aren't offended," Wrue apologized. "But you carry your own staff and . . . well, what use would you have for one of ours?"

"Did they agree?" Dannel interrupted. "Where are they? When do we get them?"

"If you don't cease your prattling, I'll stuff you in that sling with Malie," Raurk said. "Master Wrue, do not worry about me. As much as I would love such a magnificent creation as your guardians, I have little use for one. You were correct not to request a staff for me."

The three wood-elves breathed a collective sigh of relief. "I'll call them," Wraith answered. "But, there's one condition before we present the guardians. Mother Oak and Father Redwood said it's the only way . . . otherwise they'll be nothing but dead wood," he added hastily.

"Condition," Dannel wailed. In his mind, he saw his wonderful dream slipping away because he couldn't fulfill their condition. "I'm just a boy. What can I give?"

"A small matter, only." Wrath held up his hands. "You must become blood brothers with us, including the druid and his wife." He looked frightened at his own words. "It's the only way."

Raurk laughed. "Then let's proceed with this ceremony so young Dannel will come down to earth. We can't have him floating off into space."

"Oh, yes," Dannel breathed.

Raurk ruffled the boy's hair. "What would you have us do?"

Wrue sighed with relief. "First we must make small cuts across the palm of each of you, then ourselves. Then we mingle our blood with yours so that you will become part wood-elf and you will be part of us."

"Now it's my blood I must give? What will be next?" Grig muttered crossly.

"Oh." Dannel didn't sound convinced, but then he thought about the guardians again and raised his hand to Wrue. "I'll go first," he said, clenching his teeth.

As each wood-elf pressed his palm to that of the travelers, he pronounced, "Brother, you are mine." Then they gave a sharp whistle for the guardians to greet their new masters, although master didn't explain the true relationship.

Sprite greeted Dannel first and then Lillith met Rainbow. Next came Grig's introduction to Tsunami and last came Blunder for the reverent Taznakie.

Nancy K. Harmon

At the touch of the silky staff, Taznakie nigh went into raptures and then guffawed at something only he could hear. Gesturing toward his chest, then the wood-elves, he laughed even harder. With a huge embrace, he gathered the baffled trio into his arms and crowed his mirth for the world to hear.

At last, Taznakie released the worried elves. Turning to Raurk, he gesticulated and gibbered something. "Ah, I see," the druid replied amused. "He says that at last he understands the joke."

Grig, retorted, "Joke? What joke?"

Comprehension dawned in Wrath's eyes. "He means Mother Oak's joke at naming us Wraith, Wrath and Wrue. She'll be pleased. We were but saplings during the Thousand Years War, but she chose our names to remind her of the foolishness of the old ones."

"It's time for you to go, and for us to return to our homes. You should reach the gnome village before nightfall. I bid you safe journey."

Wraith nodded. "Whistle when you want the sentries to return to you. As you reach a hand for them, they'll assume the shape of a staff. I also bid you safe journey."

Wrue eyed them with sorrow. "My brothers have said it all. At the least, this has been a new experience for us. May your search be successful, and a safe journey."

In turn they shook hands with each of the travelers and turned to depart. It was only when they were almost out of sight that Taznakie remembered something that must have been very important. Digging in his pack like a man demented, he extracted the bag of salt and said something to the druid.

"Of course," Raurk replied. "But you'd better hurry before they're gone."

"What a wonderful idea," Lillith murmured as she watched the gangling figure of Taznakie race after the wood-elves.

❧ **42** ❧

"**When** will we get there?" Dannel danced around them, too eager to be still. "Will the pirate, Whittlebottom, be waiting for us?"

"All in good time," Raurk replied. "In regard to the pirate, I don't know. He's a bit of a free spirit and wont to do as he pleases."

"Then why did you bother to raise him from the dead?" Lillith asked.

"We each have our role to play in this quest." Raurk sighed. "Even if I don't always understand what that role is."

"The wood-elves spoke true," Grig interjected. "I can smell the city even from this far away." Grig found himself looking forward to reaching the river town in spite of his dislike of gnomes. "What I wouldn't do for a real meal and better yet, a dry bed with sheets."

"Aye, we all could use a decent meal," Raurk agreed. "But we shan't have it tonight if we keep lollygagging."

"And a bath . . ." Lillith peered longingly toward the city and the silver ribbon of the Tongalooa River showing between the trees.

❧ ◆ ❧

The feel of the walking staff in Grig's hand provided a comfort he'd not expected. Oft times, he rubbed the smooth surface marveling at the silkiness and warmth of the burled wood. The animal feel of it in his small hand, pleased him. It felt like it'd been made just for him.

At first, Grig thought all he need do was throw the staff to the ground and it would assume the shape of a sentry. But after several near disasters, he learned to envision the desired creature in his mind. He'd discovered there were several forms it might assume, but the simplest to achieve being that of a giant serpent. Once, by accident, he transformed Tsunami into a brightly colored, miniature dragon.

Nancy K. Harmon

Dannel, Lillith and Taznakie also experimented with their new prizes. Taznakie reveled in the power of his sentry. After placing the staff on the ground numerous times for it to transform and then retrieving it almost at once, he crowed with delight.

Raurk laughed. "Taznakie, you're going to wear out your gift from the wood-elves if you're not careful. Besides, we'll never get to Mecca what with having to stop every few paces for you."

"Gee, Raurk, don't be so grumpy," Dannel said. "We're still trying to figure out how the guardians work."

"Very admiral," Raurk replied. "But do it while we continue to walk."

"I want to let Sprite ramble by himself but when I put him down, I feel like . . . I don't know," Dannel wailed. "I feel like I've lost a hand. You don't know what it's like. Your staff is just a dead old stick."

"Aye, 'tis true. But such a wondrous gift would be wasted on me. Let Sprite do his job while we walk. I'll wager he stays close at hand. We can't afford to tarry. The sun already lowers over yon treetops. I prefer not to enter a strange city after dark."

~ ◆ ~

Grig spied the first lofty spires of Mecca long before the town came into view. Either the wood-elves idea of a village differed from his, or they'd never been close enough to comprehend its true nature.

"This doesn't look like any village I've ever seen," Grig said. "I have nothing in my experience to compare it to." It consisted of shacks, hovels, nice homes and even a few towering structures. "I've never seen such tall buildings in my life. Raurk, what is this place?"

"Mecca," Raurk answered over his shoulder, never missing a step. "One of mans' largest cities. Few have rebuilt after the Thousand Years War, but this one sprang out of nowhere. Several worlds converge upon this site and people from all over have settled here to take advantage of the river and the transportation it offers."

"You mean the riverboat?" Dannel bounded forward to get a better look at the city.

"That's exactly what I refer to. Now as I was saying, the land of the wood-elves is the Congo. Over that way is China and downriver where we shall travel on the morrow is Texas. These worlds didn't always exist in this order, but strange things happened when Earth broke apart."

Dannel and Taznakie couldn't crane their necks far enough to get a good look at the community far below. Beside himself with excitement, the lad leapt to the top of a large boulder. "I never knew more than one world existed. Why are the buildings all so different? Are we staying in one of them tonight? Is this where we go to find the water gnomes to take us down river? How will we ever find the right ones? Father says gnomes aren't always trustworthy."

"Cease your prattle, young man," Raurk growled in fair imitation of Kevel Firth. "You make my brain tired with so many questions." For added measure, he swept Dannel from his feet and hoisted the lad over his shoulder.

"All in good time," he drawled. "We still have an hour to go before we reach the city proper. I trust we'll find adequate lodging and a hot bath in one of the many hostels."

"And food?" Dannel interrupted. "Can I have my own room? Are the gnomes friendly? Are there elves and men here, too?"

"That and many more," agreed Raurk. "Mecca lives up to the name, a true crossroads. As for your own room, I make no promises."

$$\approx \quad \blacklozenge \quad \ll$$

Every step drew them closer to the strange city and even stranger wonders they had never known. To their amazement, streetlights twinkled on as late afternoon dwindled into dusk creating a fairylike luminescence that boggled their minds. Dannel called Sprite to his side. The staff grasped in his hand provided a buffer against this outlandish new place.

A rumble of steel wheels on cobbled streets added to the travelers intrigue. The carts they saw pulled by men appeared small. Only when they approached closer would they realize just how large the rolling conveyances were. The largest was pulled by several four legged-animals they did not recognize.

Still some distance away, Raurk held up a hand. "I want everyone to stay close to me. Master Grig, please reserve your normal acerbic remarks until we're safe behind locked doors. Your aversion to gnomes will do nothing to further our cause."

"My what?" The elf harrumphed. "I haven't said a word regarding our hosts. Nor do I intend to." He crossed his arms over his chest and looked away.

Lillith caught one hand in the druid's and with the other concealed her smile. "My husband," she crooned. "You are too hard on Grig Dothrie. I'm sure he'll behave in a fitting manner. After all, he didn't fall out of a tree yesterday." She giggled. "Well, maybe he did. Nevertheless, the sound of a hot bath and a real bed arouses my interest."

As impossible as it seemed, Dannel grew more jubilant as they passed from wilderness into the great city. The colors and smells overwhelmed him. Electric lights twinkled from most street corners and from windows lined along the thoroughfare. People of all shapes and sizes meandered about the streets intent on going nowhere and everywhere.

"Raurk," the boy whispered. "How do they know where they're going? How will we ever find a place to stay?"

"This way. Soon we shall reach a fork in the road. According to Wraith, Wrath and Wrue, we must bear to our right. That boulevard will take us as far as the waterfront and to Loudou's Inn. I believe he's expecting us.

"By the way, young man, while we're at it, you exude a certain gullibility with your constant questions and gawking. I suggest you close your mouth before you step on your bottom lip. There are always unsavory characters willing to take advantage of strangers."

Taznakie waved his hand toward the road ahead. He'd caught sight of the split the druid mentioned. With visible effort, he restrained himself from running ahead.

Lillith gasped in horror as two misshapen dwarves reeled drunkenly toward them. The Thousand Years War had stamped a horrific birthmark upon their beings. The one somewhat in the lead swung about to intercept the travelers. His left eye, bulging from his head, scanned the ground, while the right peered over his shoulder at something nobody else could see.

"Come on, brother," he drawled. "I 'spect we have visitors to our fair city. 'Tis our duty to make them welcome."

"Just let them pass," Lillith whispered.

The dwarves planted themselves in their path. "For a gold piece, my brother and me can show you aroun' town." He motioned to his companion. This first man stood almost a head taller than his brother, and appeared every bit as drunk. His reeking breath made Grig gag before he managed to cover his nose with his sleeve.

The second dwarf's ugly face looked like raw meat around the edges of his black, scraggly beard. Grig stared at the two until he realized something crawled in their whiskers. He stifled a violent shudder and looked away.

The second brother's right shoulder hunched nigh to his ear and the left sloped off into a nonexistent arm. Both dwarves' heads looked as if their mother might have slammed them repeatedly against a convenient wall during their infancy.

Raurk shook his head. "That shall not be necessary, my good man. We have directions already."

The first brother replied in a slur, "Ah, come on, I insist. We can show you a good time for no more than a single copper." His words grew more incoherent with every utterance. It seemed the brothers had been on the town for many days—if not months.

Brother number two stumbled forward, colliding with Lillith, dislodging her hat and loosening the waves of beautiful hair. She bit her tongue to keep from screaming, as the dwarf reached to caress her cheek. "You're sure a purty laidy," he mumbled, unaware of impending danger.

It wasn't so much what he said as the maggots feeding hungrily upon the pus-encrusted sores on the back of his hand that alarmed Lillith.

"Enough!" Raurk warned in a rough whisper. "Remove yourself at once."

"Or what?" Brother number one countered with stupid guile. If he'd known who commanded him, he might have tucked his tail and run. As it was, he hadn't sense to know the seriousness of the tall gaunt figure, nor that the beautiful woman was his wife. Instead, he blundered on. "Don't be selfish little darlin'. Your cust'mer will never know the difference if we takes a little sport with his new laidy. We can all share . . ."

Like lightning striking, Raurk uttered, "Ricktos arrestios." The dwarves turned to stone. "Let's go." Raurk grasped his wife by the elbow and steered her around the offending statues without a backward glance.

"Raurk, you're just going to leave them there?" Lillith strained to see over her shoulder as the druid hurried her away.

"Aye, that I am. The street sweepers might wonder where the garbage came from, but I doubt it. 'Tis far safer to haul it away and keep their mouths shut. All the better should it fall over and shatter into a million pieces." Raucous laughing and a loud crash followed their progress.

"That's inhuman," Lillith accused. "Won't they come looking for you?"

"No one will gainsay a chap who turns men into stone. I say good riddance to the vermin."

Lillith dragged her feet. "I've never seen this side of you, Raurk. Don't you care that you just killed two humans?"

"They ceased to be human when they threatened you, my love. Do you have any idea what those two had in mind for you?"

"No." She shook her head. "I don't suppose I do."

⮎ ◆ ⮌

Malie popped her head from the confines of Taznakie's sling. Her natural curiosity got the better of her and she had to see what was going on. The new smells and sounds piqued her interest beyond the limits of her feline heritage to resist. She perched with claws dug into the broad shoulder of her human friend and chirruped her pleasure at all the new sights.

That all changed when another gerrub intercepted their path. Big even for a male, and proud, he dared them to pass. It didn't take a scorecard to know they dealt with an alpha male. Anyone trying to verify this boy's credentials would have his lights put out for the effort.

The swaggering, posturing, orange striped creature was magnificent. He was a street savvy, arrogant throw back to his jungle ancestors. The six, no, eight smaller females following him reinforced his already inflated ego.

Malie took one look and slid back into the safety of her carrier.

Taznakie winced as her violent shuddering betrayed her fear. He bent to inspect the newcomer, but the male rewarded him with a painful swipe of long claws. "Aarck!" he exclaimed, drawing his hand out of range. With one eye still on the tom, he said, "Ragitoo oria mortia."

"Protective I'd say," Raurk answered. "I imagine he's had a pretty tough life. The gnomes around here have a fancy for gerrub stew. These girls are his and he intends to protect them at all cost."

"Balagwa?" Taznakie asked.

"I imagine he's attracted by the possibility of adding another female to his harem," Raurk answered. "Otherwise, he wouldn't risk an encounter."

He eyed the tom in thought. "Lillith, do we have anything left in our packs for them to eat? No telling when we might need a friend."

Dannel answered, "I have a bit of dried meat Mama packed for us. I put it right here on top." He lowered his satchel to the ground and extracted a greasy bag. "I'll feed it to them."

"Not like that." Grig held out his hand to stop the lad. "He'll shred you to pieces before you can move. Give it to me and I'll show you."

The elf ripped the meat into nine pieces, the exact number to match the tom and his harem. With a flick of his wrist, Grig tossed it to the orange tabby, making sure he received the largest offering. Then, as the chap allowed his alpha female to come forward, Grig placed the next largest piece on the ground for her inspection. Ears flattened against her head and poised to bolt for safety, the tortoise shell gerrub daintily retrieved her prize.

After that, it took only a few minutes for the others to claim their morsel and disappear into the dark of night. The male didn't slink away like his charges. Instead he strutted like a proud ship at sea with his tail held high and nary a glimpse back until he disappeared from sight. It seemed Malie remained strong in his nostrils, but his ladies called him into nocturnal safety.

"Whew," Lillith whispered. "That's a proud one. I bet he keeps his girls in line. Poor Malie would never make it in his world."

"Agaoth!" Taznakie seemed to agree.

"Well, now that we've passed his majesty's inspection, shall we find our inn?" Raurk motioned for them to proceed. "I've enjoyed the clan, but we're drawing far too much attention."

❧ 43 ❧

Urania Braith jerked upright in bed, the thick furs falling away from her bare breast. She stretched and rubbed sleep from her eyes. Faint rays of sun played around the edges of the window tapestries. The room was icy cold, just the way she liked it. One glance showed her Lorca, curled into a tight ball at the foot of her bed, trying to stay warm. "As befits him," she mused.

In her dream she'd heard the words to the poem she'd loved so many years ago when she foolishly believed Raurk cared for her. The thought of the druid angered her. "Lorca, wakeup." She kicked at the sleeping Watcher.

"Yes, mistress?" Long years with the witch had taught him the need to wake alert and ready. His hand went involuntarily to the ragged cut beneath his right ear and then to his short, slashed off hair.

"Ah, I see you remember our agreement," she said. "Perhaps you'll think twice before disappointing me again."

Lorca glared at her through half closed eyes. "How could I forget? I'm scarred for life."

"Ah, my pet. Is that any way to speak to me, your mistress? Your hair will grow back, and that tiny cut is nothing compared to what I could have done." She'd never admit she loved tormenting the man. She leaned over to brush at his hair, making sure her nakedness was well exposed.

Lorca jerked from her touch. "Obviously you had something on your mind, Urania. What do you want?"

She didn't like his insolent tone, but she had other things on her mind. "Do you remember the book I told you to destroy?"

"I've destroyed many things for you. Why would I remember a book?" He avoided looking her in the eyes.

"Is that the way it's going to be today?" She playfully slapped his cheek. "Never mind, I have much to do." She threw the furs to the floor. "Drag your lazy ass off my bed and ring for breakfast. And open the windows. I would enjoy the scent of the fruit trees. They're especially delicious this time of year. Eden was aptly named by the Old Ones . . . . And now, I shall destroy it just as I will you." She pinched his cheek hard enough to leave a bruise.

❧ **44** ❧

The thoroughfare Raurk and his companions followed seemed to wander about at random, but always led them toward the Tongalooa River. The streets grew dirtier as they progressed through the dingy industrial area. The few remaining lights were grimy and outshone by the moon overhead. Shadowy figures slipped from one dark stain on the cobbled street to another.

Unseen footsteps in the gloom raised goosebumps along Grig's spine. They couldn't reach the inn soon enough to suit him. Every so often, he caught an unexpected glimpse of the big orange tom and his ladies shadowing their path. "I thought we'd seen the last of that one when he sauntered off." Grig nodded toward the gerrub just slipping from sight.

"Aye," Lillith glanced in the direction indicated. "I don't suppose it's wise for wild gerrubs to be too trusting in a town that craves their flesh in the stew pot."

"And not wise for us to dally, either." Raurk herded his flock of innocents toward the light shining at the end of the lane. "'Tis Loudou's Inn," he said. "It blazes like a lone beacon in the distance, and none too soon at that."

Across the front of the dilapidated building, bold letters flashed. "Loudou's Motor Lodge & Inn," Raurk read for his charges. "A bit rundown, but 'tis a welcome sight."

The ramshackle white building had seen better days, but retained its elegance in its own disheveled glory. The low, one story structure nestled against the cliff overlooking the great river, beckoning to weary travelers. In its heyday, the inn had bustled with activity and remained far busier than any of their competitors.

Around three sides, a wide veranda perched on stilts waiting for the next rainy season and the inevitable flooding that followed. For many months, the dark waters might lap at the structure, but the inn always managed to stay in business. During these times of monsoons, the hotel staff ferried their guests back and forth in rowboats kept on hand for that very reason.

Loudou's Inn served as the last stop on the line for many travelers before embarking upstream, or down as Raurk and his charges would do on the morrow. It was the epicenter of Mecca. Fortunes were often made and lost at the gaming tables. The inn belonged to a long line of Loudou men and would one day belong to the current proprietor's sons and grandsons.

The innkeeper himself perched atop the veranda's railing, watching the latest group of travelers headed his way. "Come right up," he greeted them with a smile. "From the looks of you, you'd be Theron Raurk. We've been expecting you. A skeleton chap by the name of Magried Whittlebottom came through here day before last, said you'd be along any time."

Loudou appeared to be a jovial man, and from the look of him, he liked to eat. In fact, his girth rivaled his height. White mutton-chop sideburns framed his quivering jowls and accented his rotund face. Bushy eyebrows waggled up and down as he spoke. His bald pate shone in the twilight.

"Dinner's just finishing up, but I'm sure Cookie will have something left. She likes to keep a reserve for late arrivals. She's a good woman," he mused. "If not for her, most of my guests would find lodging elsewhere. Many another innkeeper has tried to steal her from me, so I up and married my darling last spring. Smartest thing I ever did."

"We could use a good meal," Raurk agreed, while Taznakie nodded and smacked his lips with unbridled enthusiasm.

"Well, then, come right this way," Loudou boomed, holding open the wide double doors. "I've reserved two rooms down that hallway for you, but let me serve you supper first.

"Oh, by the way. That skeleton fella, the pirate, I mean, left you a message."

"I'm all ears," Raurk said.

"No, you don't understand." The innkeeper shook his head. "Wait,

I'll get it while you find a table. It's handwritten. I told him you might not be able to read it, but he insisted."

"Not a problem," Raurk said. He led the way across the broad dining room to a table tucked away in the corner. It was a beautiful room with soft rose-colored walls, plush carpet, sparkling chandeliers and a raised bandstand where a desultory musician tapped at a large table with white and black lines on it.

Dannel couldn't wait for everyone to settle into their seats before he raced across the room to see the strange instrument. "Hey, mister," he called. "What do you call that thing?"

"Beat it, kid. Can't you see I'm working here?" the old man snapped.

"Yeah, and if you want to get paid, play that thing the way I know you can," Loudou barked from the doorway. "We got some new guests here ain't never seen a piano before. How about giving them a little Mozart or Beethoven? On second thought, I got a hankering to hear Chopin.

"Go off with you lad and let the man work," Loudou advised. "He really is quite good when he's not in his cups."

"Dannel, our dinner is here," Lillith called. "I don't know about you, but I'm starved."

She didn't have to call her brother twice. He was a growing boy, and from the looks of the mountain of food on Taznakie's plate, so was he.

Right about then Malie decided she'd had enough isolation in her carrier. It might also have had something to do with the large bowl of butter making the rounds of the table. She shot up and over Taznakie's shoulder before anyone could stop her. With a few short hops, she reached the cherished treat.

"Loudou, bring us another plate," Raurk instructed.

"My word, how did that awful creature get in here?" the innkeeper almost shrieked, dropping the dish with a nerve-shattering clash. "Shoo! Shoo!" he waved at the gerrub. "Who let you in? I'll have their hide for this."

Frightened, Malie bolted straight into Taznakie's laden platter. Her short legs churned for purchase. Meat, potatoes, greens and a wide assortment of other delicacies flew willy-nilly forcing the onlookers to flee the table.

"No," Loudou shrieked.

Taznakie bellowed, "Aargh."

Dannel grabbed for the floundering Gerrub. "Stop, she's mine," he wailed.

"Cease!" Raurk bellowed.

But not until a very ugly gnome approached with a heavy ax and hefted it through the middle of the table did true pandemonium erupt. To make things worse, the gnome lunged for Malie over the remains of the ruined table as she scrambled just out of reach.

Loudou fainted, his portly figure slumping in the middle of the dining room.

"Come back here, you little varmint," growled the gnome. "I'll see you skinned and simmering in a stew pot."

Over the uproar, the pianist hammered out Chopin's "Minute Waltz" with maniacal vengeance.

Terrified, Malie caterwauled while backing under the nearest table. Lillith laughed until she cried. Taznakie thought this was great fun and threw himself bodily atop the scrabbling gnome. Grig couldn't believe his eyes. Unable to decide which way to run, he stood paralyzed, gawking in horror at the melee.

"Enough," the druid roared loud enough to shake the roof. He jerked the gnome to his feet with one hand, and Taznakie with the other. "Cease your struggles."

Loudou awoke long enough to see nine round, fuzzy faces pressed against the window, and passed out again.

Taznakie subsided, but the gnome continued to thrash about until Raurk gave him a rough shake. "Enough, I say, or I shall be forced to restrain you by other means."

The druid's tone carried more weight than his actual words. "The gerrub is a pet. You shall not harm one hair upon her head or you will answer to me. I suggest you go back to your table and sit down."

The gnome eyed him with hate, but retrieved his ax and skulked back to his table. Turning his back, he mumbled something unintelligible, but did not stop.

In the ensuing quiet, Dannel scuttled under the table to retrieve Malie. If not for the large bowl brimming with butter, he would have never succeeded.

"Look at this mess," Lillith moaned. "How will we ever pay for the damage?"

"No need," Raurk muttered. "I want all of you to stand over there out of the way." Then for the first time, Lillith truly understood the magnitude of her husband's power. Spreading his arms with the cloak over them, the scene of chaos was hidden from them. Under his breath he uttered a few words and dropped his arms to reveal that all was exactly as it should be. "Sit down while I attend to Master Loudou."

"Whew, I must have passed out," Loudou wheezed. "Sorry, I don't know what came over me." He turned to survey the dining room. "Did any of you by chance see the gerrubs at the window? There were at least, what? Six of them." His gaze wandered from one traveler to the next. "No, I suppose not. I'll get you that plate," he said. "I must be imagining things in my old age."

With an air of nonchalance, Raurk rejoined his friends. "Grig, hold on to Malie. We can't have this happening again."

This time the innkeeper brought the dish and Raurk introduced Malie as a beloved pet, all without undue incidence.

And the piano player banged out a strange rendition of "The Band Played On," never missing a beat.

❧ ◆ ☙

Near the end of the meal, Taznakie excused himself, taking along a large platter of leftovers and the dish of butter. He left by the French doors closest to their table. After a few minutes, he returned without the plate and appeared pleased with himself.

As they left the room, the piano player pssted at Raurk. "If I were you, I'd watch my back. Yon gnome didn't take kindly to the scolding you gave him. He seems to be taking an inordinate interest in your affairs."

"Thanks for the warning," Raurk said. "I'll keep that in mind." He caught up to his companions.

"What was that all about?" Lillith whispered.

"A bit of fatherly advice," Raurk whispered back. "Ah, here's our host," he boomed for everybody's ears.

Loudou waited to escort them to their rooms. "I'm assuming you don't want to enjoy the gaming tables tonight. Though I don't suppose it'd be fair to gamble against a druid, would it?"

"Aye, 'tis true." Raurk nodded. "The odds would tend to be stacked in my favor."

"Well—yes." The innkeeper smiled, perplexed. "Right this way. I've reserved the two best rooms in the inn for you." He bustled ahead to throw open the doors. "There's a connecting door between them should you wish to open it.

"Throw your gear in here, and I'll show you the spa. It's right across the hall as you can see. The pool is fed by an underground hot spring and is incredible for relaxing after a hard day's journey. I've left plenty of clean towels and robes for your use. Shampoo and soap are all around the edge of the pool, help yourselves."

Loudou turned to leave and then stopped. "I almost forgot. Here's the note from the pirate. What else?" He paused to think. "Oh, yes. You can leave your dirty clothes in the hall next to your door. My staff will clean them and have them back by morning. I bid you adieu."

"Wow," exclaimed Dannel. "Look at that, and the water's really hot. Me first," he yelled. Handing Malie to the nearest pair of hands, he tugged at his clothing while on the run. At the edge of the concrete, he leapt feet first into the luxuriant waters.

Taznakie shed his garments and cannon-balled into the hot pool. His entrance managed to shower everyone, including Malie.

"You imbecile!" Grig growled as he lost hold on the cringing gerrub. "I'll pay the devil to find her."

Raurk chuckled. "Not to worry, Master Grig. Unless I miss my guess, she's hiding safely under the bed."

"Although, if I were you," with a cock of his head, he indicated Taznakie and Dannel at the far end of the pool, "I'd be more concerned about what those two miscreants are plotting than where Malie is hiding. You might want to consider immersing yourself under you own steam rather than waiting for their coercion."

"I shall do no such thing," Grig spat.

"Suit yourself. Lillith and I shall retire to our room until you boys are through with your fun. Call us when you're done. I'm looking forward to a hot soak."

Taznakie and Dannel took it upon themselves to introduce Grig Dothrie to the pleasures of the warm, spring fed water. Taznakie grabbed the elf from behind while Dannel tugged at his trousers.

"Don't touch me, you fool. Get away, boy. I'll have your hides for this."

"Make me," Dannel retorted, dancing around with his thumbs in his ears, waggling his fingers. "You stink. Why don't you take a bath?" He pinched his nose with two fingers. "What's the matter, Grig? Malie got your tongue?"

Taznakie divested the elf of most of his remaining garments. With a mighty heave, he hoisted Grig overhead and lobbed him into the pool.

Grig panicked. "Help. Help. I can't swim. I'm drowning." He flailed his arms beating at the water and once or twice sank below the surface.

Dannel couldn't help laughing. "Put your feet down, Master Grig. The water's not that deep."

"What?" Grig sputtered.

"Put your feet down. The water's shallow."

"Oh!" Grig replied as he followed instructions. In fact the water reached his armpits. "Why didn't you tell me?"

Taznakie launched himself at the unsuspecting elf. "Grolf, grolf, grolf."

Dannel dove under the water and seized Grig's legs, trying to upend him.

"No, no," Grig screamed. "Get away from me!" But he might as well have been talking to the wind. His feeble protests couldn't deter the youngest members of the party.

In spite of his continued complaints, Grig enjoyed the rough-housing. He discovered with little effort he could hold his own in a water fight. Soon, the heat of the natural hot spring soaked away his aches and pains, making him glad Taznakie and Dannel had won out over his protests.

చు ◆ ⋖

"If you three are through making a mess, there are others of us still waiting," Raurk said, frightening Grig out of his good mood. "That's assuming you've left any water. This place is afloat. I don't think even a natural spring can keep up with your antics."

"Aw, Raurk," Dannel said. "We were just having fun."

"Our host sent in more towels and robes for you." Raurk motioned to a heap of dry clothes in his arms. "He assumed with all the commotion you'd need them. I'll hang them over here. It appears to be the only dry place left."

"Don't be mad," Dannel said.

"I'm not angry." Raurk grinned mischievously and peeled off his robe. "I've come to join you."

❧ 45 ❧

"*So,* what's this message?" Mellow as a gerrub, Grig felt better at this very moment than he had since leaving home. The thick, luxurious robes provided by Loudou added to his feeling of well being. His stomach was full, and he was warm and dry all at the same time. There were no mutant trolls, dragons, mud-slobbers or other monsters chasing him. But most of all, he anticipated crawling into a real bed with clean sheets.

Raurk removed a crumpled, stained piece of paper from his pouch and read, "Isis is clutching and needs me. I'll meet you in Amarillo with supplies for the remainder of the trip. I remain at your service, Magried Whittlebottom."

Grig scratched his head. "What's that supposed to mean?"

"I'd say the dragon is about to lay a clutch of eggs," the druid surmised. "What I don't understand is why she'd want the likes of Whittlebottom anywhere in the vicinity."

"Let him go, for all I care," Grig said. "He's a nuisance at best."

"Like it or not, that's not possible."

"Whatever you say." Grig yawned. "I don't know about you, but I'm going to bed. I can't remember the last time I slept indoors with a roof over my head."

"Raurk, where's Amarillo?" Dannel asked between yawns. "Is it another world? How did it ever get such a strange name?"

❧ ◆ ❧

Grig awoke to the sound of Malie at the window, hissing and chirruping at something outside. He leapt from bed realizing someone outside their window at this time of night meant no good.

Maybe it was the disgruntled gnome from the dining room. On

second thought, maybe it was just the orange tom and his ladies. More than anything, Grig wanted to sink back into the warmth of his bed.

"Grig, what was that?" Dannel whispered. "I thought I heard voices."

"Aarumph," agreed Taznakie.

"Quiet," the elf hissed. "Be still while I take a look." On tiptoes, he slipped to the left of the window. With a slight twitch of a finger, he moved aside the curtain just enough to peek through the opening.

The dim moonlight outlined two figures creeping toward the window. What came next was too fast to be sure. First, Grig's beloved Tanus flew from the roof to land atop one hunched figure. She passed right through the interloper, causing him and his partner to look up in wonder.

Then, a streak of orange, hissing gerrub plummeted like a rock from the eve, raking with long claws at vital parts. Twenty pounds of pure fury seemed to be everywhere at once. If that wasn't enough, a tortoise shell and then a calico female hurtled toward the other man.

In rapid fire, six more fur balls launched themselves at the swearing, writhing peeping toms. The girls weighed only a fraction of the tom, but they hung on for dear life with sharp claws. The calico seemed especially ferocious, attacking the intruders' ears and noses. She doubled her efforts when the miscreants rewarded her with a loud howl of pain.

"What the devil?" Grig muttered. He'd never witnessed such a bizarre spectacle in his life. He still couldn't make out details, but the cursing, angry shouting revealed the rough guttural voices of dwarves, or perhaps gnomes. The hunched, short-necked outlines pointed toward the latter. The longer he watched, the more sure he became. Nasty creatures, in his opinion.

"'Tis the gnome with the ax and his friend, come to even the score I assume," Raurk said.

Grig jumped. "Don't go sneaking up on a body like that, blackbird."

Raurk laughed. "My pardons, good elf. The tom and his ladies ran the troublemakers off. I told you we might need a friend. I think it's safe to say those two won't be bothering us again tonight."

"What about tomorrow?" Grig glanced toward the window.

"We'll deal with that then should the need arise. Go back to bed."

"Who were they?" Dannel's voice shook in spite of his attempts to be brave. "Why didn't the sentries warn us?"

The druid nodded toward the corner where three staffs leaned. "Did you set them to watch?"

"Oh," mouthed Dannel. "I forgot. I guess we all did."

"They can only do what you allow them to," Raurk answered. "It might be wise for one of you to set his guardian to work. I'll have Lillith do the same in our room."

"But who were they?" Dannel persisted.

Raurk didn't answer at once. "That's not important, young man. Perhaps the 'morrow will tell." He stifled a yawn. "I, for one, intend to get a few more hours sleep and so should you. Good night, all."

෨ ◆ ෴

Grig had just drifted off again when he sensed someone standing by his bed. "Wha . . .?" he mumbled, cobwebs clouding his brain.

"Can I move my bed next to yours?" Dannel said.

"I . . . well . . . uh . . . ." Grig stared at the boy, not comprehending. "What?"

"I'm scared. Can I move my bed next to yours?" Dannel pleaded.

"Oh, all right, but make it quick."

Again, Grig wafted upon the velvet wings of sleep. Dannel said, "Where's Malie? You don't suppose she somehow got out do you?"

"No, of course not. She's over there with Taznakie. Who, by the way, is sound asleep, just as you should be."

"I can't sleep," the boy whined. "Grig, talk to me for a little while. Please? I don't understand why so many people . . . Well, why were they spying on us? What did Raurk mean about different worlds coming together in Mecca? Why did the wood-elves help us when they didn't even know us? Grig?"

"Yes, lad," he answered with more affection than he intended. All at once, the fears and uncertainty of the ten-year-old boy tugged at his heartstrings. When he'd been just about the same age, Grig had gotten lost in the forest. All too well, he remembered his own panic and the relief when his mother found him. It'd only been for a short time, but the panic still lived in his heart.

Dannel hiccoughed, stifling a sob. "It's all so different. I thought we'd have fun and go home in a few days. And I—I miss my mother."

Grig sat up and patted the boy's shoulder. "I know, lad. I don't understand any more than you, but we have to go on."

Dannel sighed. "Maybe we can go back tomorrow."

"Hush lad, and I'll sing you to sleep."

"Not the song you sang to the hippogriff!"

Grig chuckled at the sudden flash of terror in the boy's eyes. "'Tis naught but a lullaby my mother used to sing to me when I was a lad."

It took less than five minutes and Dannel Firth snored ever so softly, while Malie tiptoed from Taznakie's pillow to the boy's. "Good night, young man," Grig sighed. "I wish you pleasant dreams."

᷆ ◆ ᷆

The first rays of dawn stabbed through the fog in Grig's brain. He'd lain awake for hours listening to Malie purr in contentment. It was a soothing sound, always to be enjoyed, and those hours were no exception. Alas, it also reminded him of how much he missed his two males back home.

That blackguard, Raurk, was secretive about this whole mess to the point of obsession. He wondered again if it'd been necessary to wrest him from his beloved home. And with this thought came the certainty that his tree house had perished, swallowed by the mutant forest. His village, no longer inhabited, and most of the neighbors he'd known and loved had perished.

Until this very moment, he'd been able to deny the druid's terrible news . . . accusations . . . predictions. He wasn't sure what to call them. All he knew for sure was that he could never return to his village. In that horrible moment, reality came crashing down around his ears. He longed to sob his sorrows just as Dannel had done. "Malie," he whispered. "Come humor an old elf."

At long last, he'd slipped into a deep, dreamless sleep, one arm cradling the gerrub.

He couldn't believe it was time to drag his weary behind out of bed again. Where would it all end? Would any of them survive to tell of their journey? If they did manage to rescue the Light of Ishram, what then?

Without warning, Taznakie threw open the curtains and crowed his pleasure at the new day. He was already dressed and out the door before Grig could think about moving.

The elf called, "Wait, where are you going?"

"Look," Dannel exclaimed from the window. "The gerrubs are back. Tanus is with them. I'm going outside, too."

"Tanus?" Grig whispered. "She's here? Wait for me young man. I want to see Tanus before someone scares her away." He donned the nearest article of clothing and made his way to the veranda where Taznakie and Dannel played with their new friends.

Soon, Raurk and Lillith joined the festivities. The druid seemed less mordant than usual. "Our host indicates our boat will be along an hour or so after lunch. I've purchased tickets for all of us. We're all set. I'm looking forward to the journey downriver."

"And a right pleasant trip it should be," Loudou boomed as he maneuvered a laden tray through the door.

"Be a good lad and scoot one of those tables over here. That's a good boy. We couldn't ask for a more beautiful morning to eat breakfast on the veranda. Couldn't have done better if I'd ordered it myself."

Suddenly, he stopped, mouth dangling open. "My word, where did all these gerrubs come from? They must be the same lot I saw at the window last night. I believed I'd imagined them. Shoo, shoo," he waved his arms and stomped his feet. "What are they doing here?"

The tom backed up a step or two, but then held his ground. With hackles raised and ears laid back, he hissed at the innkeeper.

"Hold on, my good man," Raurk interjected, perhaps saving a repeat of the fiasco from the night before. "The gerrubs followed us. They were drawn by the scent of our female. They're doing no harm."

"That's easy for you to say," Loudou blustered. "You'll be going off this afternoon and what am I supposed to do if they decide to hang around? They're dirty, beggarly creatures at best."

"That's not true, Mr. Loudou," Dannel protested. "Gerrubs are very clean and they catch all sorts of rodents. Malie keeps our house free of such pests all by herself. I'll bet with nine of them you wouldn't have to worry at all."

"The boy has a point, Loudou," Raurk added. "You have a big place here and right on the waterfront. I'll bet when it floods every scurvy, four-footed critter in Mecca seeks refuge on your doorstep. For a few leftovers, the tom and his girls would keep every one of them away."

"What if they don't cooperate?" The proprietor eyed them with a skeptic gaze.

The question was answered for them as the little tortoise shell emerged from beneath the porch with a fat mouse in her jaws. "That should be proof enough." Raurk pointed. "You might have to make clear to your customers that the gerrubs aren't dinner on the hoof. Well, what do you think?"

"I don't know," the innkeeper pondered. "I just might give it a try. I could call the male Rajah. Yes, that suits the fella well. The others I'm not so sure about. As I get to know them, I'll think of names. Yes, indeed, Rajah it is."

➣ ◆ ❧

Grig, Taznakie and the boy whiled away the remainder of the morning immersed in the hot spring-fed pool, playing and relaxing. Not until Lillith stuck her head through the door to say lunch was ready did they leave the water. Just as at breakfast, they enjoyed the view from the wide verandah. Thus it was they caught their first glimpse of the boat that was to take them downriver.

Taznakie leapt to his feet, spraying his food and gibbering like a deranged baboon. He acted as if he'd never seen a boat in his life. At least not one like the paddle-wheeler chugging around the bend to dock at Loudou's jetty. A loud hiss of steam and soot escaped the stack as the captain tamped down the engines.

"That's our boat?" Dannel couldn't believe his own eyes. "It's big enough to transport everyone in our village. Are we the only passengers? When can we get on? I wish Papa could be here with us. How long will it take us to get to Texas?"

Raurk chuckled. "Yes, young man. That's our boat, the Tongalooa Tanniger. I doubt she'd be making the trip downriver if we were her sole passengers. The sooner you finish your lunch, the sooner we'll go aboard."

The next fifteen minutes were pure agony for Dannel, and Taznakie wasn't much better. At last, the druid told them, "Go get your packs and head down to the wharf. I'll meet you by that red and blue vendor's cart right over there as soon as I settle with Loudou."

❧ 46 ❦

His business done with the garrulous innkeeper, Raurk stepped into the street to search out his companions. He was pleased to find them all headed in the right direction. Another moment and they would reach the prearranged meeting place. A second look showed him all nine of the feral gerrubs followed close upon the heels of Taznakie. Malie watched from her vantage point in the sling, chirruping loudly.

Lengthening his stride, the druid hurried to overtake his companions. "Wait, Taznakie." The gerrubs halted too, but made no move to skitter for shelter. Noonday should have seen them holed up in a safe out-of-the-way refuge.

"What can we do?" Lillith asked.

"Can they come with us?" Dannel beseeched.

"No, of course they can't," Grig said.

"Yanikie olaffo," Rakell piped up.

"Hush, all of you," Raurk said. "As much as I'd like to have them along, it's out of the question."

"Why not?" Dannel whined. "I'd help take care of them."

Grig started a smart retort, but the druid stayed him. "Dannel, I know you've good intentions, but Mecca is their home. They belong here."

"A voice of reason for a change. I must be hearing things," Grig mumbled.

"Grig Dothrie, do you think Tanus could convince Rajah to go home?" Raurk eyed the gerrubs.

"I'm not sure."

"There are more dangers ahead of us than behind. I fear these little ones would fall prey to much worse than a hungry gnome where we shall venture. Besides, I wouldn't be the least surprised to discover a whole passel of babies squirreled away somewhere for safekeeping. At least they know how to stay out of danger on their home ground."

Raurk did not look at the elf while he spoke. Instead, he followed the progress of an odd looking pair of travelers climbing the gangplank. The first walked with a pronounced limp and the other had one eye and an ear swaddled in bandages.

At the top, they bullied their way ahead of the other passengers. When reprimanded by the deckhand taking tickets, the gnome caressed a large ax with loving fingers. There was no threat spoken, but the implication was clear.

Without further ado, the pair brushed past the crewman and hobbled toward the rear of the large, flat-bottomed boat.

"Sorry, what were you saying?" He drew his attention back to Grig. There was no question in Raurk's mind these were the peeping toms from the night before.

"I said Tanus isn't at my beck and call," Grig answered. "I have no idea whether she can communicate with living gerrubs or not. I don't even know if I can communicate with her."

"Grig." Dannel tugged at his sleeve.

"What is it boy?"

"Look." Dannel extended a finger toward a large pile of netting. "Tanus is behind that barrel. I saw her run behind it when you weren't looking."

"Where?" Grig demanded, not seeing the spectral gerrub.

"She's right over there." Dannel pointed. "Look, here she comes. Rajah's going to meet her."

"Aye, and I'd love to know what they're talking about." Raurk watched as the gerrubs held palaver. The tom glanced at the humans more than once, surveying one anxious face after another. At last he turned soulful green eyes back to Tanus.

From then on, the gerrubs chirruped back and forth for several minutes with nary a glance toward the waiting travelers. An expectant hush enfolded them as Rajah made his final decision.

He herded his girls together and sent them across the square toward Loudou's Motor Lodge and Inn. Before taking his departure, he presented himself to each human in an arrogant ritual of farewell.

As he approached the druid, his entire demeanor underwent a miraculous change. His posture was one of subservience. "Well, old man, I'll miss you too," Raurk said. "You take good care of those ladies, and be sure to watch over the innkeeper's property. I know you can do it." Raurk scratched the proffered chin. "Off with you and be safe," he added.

Tanus raced the big male back to the inn while Malie chirruped goodbye from the safety of Taznakie's shoulder. It was difficult to tell who longed to return home the most, Grig Dothrie or Malie the gerrub.

"Out of my way," Grig said. "We're wasting time standing around here with a bunch of scurvy varmints." He pushed his way toward the gangplank, unsettling numerous travelers. Scowls and grumblings erupted in deep guttural dialects, but Grig was too distressed to hear them.

"Master Grig." Lillith caught up to him. "Won't you tread a little softer before we're forced to defend our honor? I'm sure Tanus will return as soon as Rajah and his ladies are safe."

The elf stopped with a heavy sigh. "Aye, I know, but I do miss her so. She was always such company to me. I still miss her no matter how many years since her passing."

Lillith slipped her arm through Grig's. "And she'll always be there when you need her."

"Do you think so?" The elf cast a baleful glance over his shoulder.

"I know so." Lillith offered a brilliant smile. "Shall we explore this marvelous boat? I want to inspect every inch of her."

Raurk smiled as he watched Grig Dothrie and Lillith glide up the gangplank in front of him. If only their air of nonchalance rang true. His joy faded as he spied the battered gnome who'd smashed the table the night before. Strangely enough, this fellow sported a dirty bandage wrapped about his head.

❧ 47 ❧

Grig took in the sights with wondering eyes. Like a gaudy granddame, the Tongalooa Tanniger trekked the length of the river festooned in her finest. Brass gleamed and twinkled in the cool sun, dazzling the travelers.

"What are these? And look over there." He pointed to gilded gingerbread fretwork hung from the roofline.

Dannel ran his hands over mahogany balustrades and columns. Their beauty belied the practical nature of their true purposes.

"I believe that helps cut the strong glare of the afternoon sun," Raurk said. Twin stacks chuffed thick steam onto the midday breeze, only to float away in wispy tendrils of imagination. "Aye, the Tanniger is a work of dreams."

Dannel surveyed the open, lower deck with its numerous pens crammed with livestock and children alike. "Can we go down there?" He eyed several youngsters chasing hither and thither at the annoyance of the other passengers, but little was done to curb their enthusiasm. The poorer passengers (or perhaps those aboard for only a short distance) lounged about on whatever means of relaxation they had brought with them. Others simmered meals over makeshift grills and got on with life. One more stop, even if it was Mecca, did not interest them.

"Not yet," Raurk answered. "We shall lodge in a cabin on the upper deck. It'll offer a bit of privacy not afforded to the other passengers." More to his liking, it provided them with security, no matter how meager it might be. From the looks of the two gnomes casting furtive glances in their direction, they would need it.

Prickles of dread tiptoed down the back of Raurk's neck. A strong foreboding laid a brutal hand upon his heart.

Amused, he wondered how they would explain the heavy bandages swaddling their ugly faces. How he'd love to hear *that* accounting. Perhaps he should make an effort to confront them later on.

Unbidden, a snippet of a strange poem flashed through his mind. *On the land of forgotten snore . . .* He'd wondered for years at the meaning of this odd work to no avail. Maybe fate would reveal what no amount of studying could accomplish. He made a mental note to reread the entire work at his earliest opportunity.

Those ancient lines might, or might not, mean anything, but he'd not let it be said he missed an opportunity, or a warning, by ignoring an omen. Long ago, his life as a druid had taught him to trust his insights. And if it turned out to be of no consequence, so be it. If nothing else, he would have revisited a familiar friend.

He patted the small volume of poetry tucked inside the folds of his cloak. The ancient book predated even the Thousand Years War, and was treasured as all books should be in this time. He'd cast a spell of preservation upon this volume just as the previous owner had done. Now, he carried it with him at all times. It was one of the few possessions he called his own.

Shaking himself from this reverie, Raurk followed the others up the gangplank. He was content to allow them to go ahead and take in the sights and smells of the grand riverboat.

Lillith hesitated, searching right and left. "Where do we go?"

"Upstairs." Raurk motioned toward the narrow passageways at each side of the deck. "There'll be a crewman at the top to direct us to our cabin."

Dannel and Taznakie reached the next landing. "Raurk, he wants to see our tickets," the lad called.

"All in good time, young man. These old bones don't move as quickly as they once did. I have everyone's ticket right here." His formerly empty hand now held the proper identification. "Here you go, good man. Is there anything else you'll be requiring?"

"No, sir." The river-man inspected the tickets with a bit of awe. "We've made sleeping arrangements for all of you. Other than the Captain's quarters, you have the best accommodations on the Tanniger. It'll be a bit tight, but it beats sleeping on the open deck. The mist off the river eats right through a body in the mornings."

"Thank you," Lillith said.

"You're welcome, ma'am. Once you've settled in, take a tour of the upper deck for yourself. There's a small dining room aft for those who choose to stay aboard when we dock. Unless you have business in town, I'd recommend it. Wandering around in an unknown port can be dangerous.

"Captain Ardle will be happy to show you around as soon as we get under way. I imagine the lad would enjoy that." He nodded toward Dannel. "Until then, it might be wisest to remain in your cabin." He saluted and turned to leave.

"Why?" blurted Dannel. "I want to see everything."

"I just meant it would be safer until everyone has claimed their two square feet of deck before you go downstairs. Tempers tend to run short if the boat is crowded as it is today.

"I'll tell you what." The crewman's face brightened. "Give me about an hour and I'll give you the grand tour myself. I'm off duty then and won't need to rush. I'm First Lieutenant on the Tanniger, just call if you need anything. I'm stationed at the top of the stairs until we depart."

"We shall take your advice," Raurk agreed. Already the ruckus of a noisy altercation floated upward from the river level. Sheeple bleated in their pens with a trace of panic at their unfamiliar surroundings. The scraping and scuffling of several large bodies appeared to do nothing to ease their qualms.

The Lieutenant executed an about face, but then reversed again. "Sir, be sure to keep your door locked." Just as quickly, he'd returned to his post, leaving the travelers gawking at his back.

Dannel pushed open the door. "Top bunk is mine." He launched himself like a heat seeking missile toward his target.

"Garumphil!" Taznakie concurred claiming the opposite, unfortunate perch.

Grig eyed the remaining bunks. "Well, I suppose that leaves me the floor since there're only two cots left."

"Why, not at all," Lillith soothed. "I'll share with my husband, leaving the remaining bunk for you. Although by the lumpy appearance of them, the floor might be more comfortable." She prodded the nearest bed to confirm her words.

"What shall we do to pass the time until this young scoundrel can escape the confines of our humble prison? Dannel, at this rate, you'll fair explode before the hour passes."

Raurk declared, "I, for one, claim the chair by the window, and a moment of quiet to reflect. I'd also suggest the rest of you might want a short nap. It won't be long before we're under way and the time will appear to pass quicker." He gave Dannel a stern look.

The druid sank into the rope chair by the window, closed his eyes and took deep cleansing breaths to clear the dust from his mind. With his nerves calmed, he reached inside his cloak for the treasured volume of poetry. The book fell open to the poem that so often intruded into his conscious thoughts. "Dreamscapes," he whispered. Again he closed his eyes allowing a mental image to form as it may. This verse never ceased to spark his imagination.

"What are you looking at?" Dannel interrupted.

"This, my young man, is a book of poetry," Raurk answered. "It helps to soothe my mind when I'm troubled."

"Does it have pictures?" Dannel leapt from the top bunk.

Raurk wagged his head in amusement. "Sorry, words must suffice."

Dannel peered over the druids shoulder. "Words? I don't understand. How can those be words? Let me see. What does it say?"

"'Tis a shame you never learned to read," Raurk said. "The world would be a much quieter place without your constant chatter. And you would be far wiser for your curiosity."

"Tell me what it says, please," Dannel pleaded. "How do you know what all those little marks mean?"

"Harrumph." Grig rolled over in his bunk. "I thought you were going to take a nap."

Dannel laughed. "I promise to be quiet if Raurk will read to me."

"So read to him, already." Grig was growing irritated. "Maybe then he'll shut up. The boy kept me awake most of the night and I'm tired."

"If I must," Raurk sighed. "This is called Dreamscapes." And he began to recite:

> "I went to the Library of Congress on Saturday,
>   though I was hungry on Wednesday.
> Being too short to reach the top shelf,

I grabbed a rainbow instead.
When to my surprise,
out pops a hotdog all slathered in diamonds,
and strutting a snuffy little tutu.
Gingerly, I smooched the pooch—"

"That doesn't make sense," Dannel interrupted.

"I never said it did." Then Raurk continued to read:

"but bitter drops of sweet wine rained in my
brain, blurring my vision of the train
as it chug-a-lugged down the ascending stairs.
Grazing raptly into the seafood depths of your mind,
I dreamt that I was not there."

"What's a train?" Dannel bounced from one cot to the other.

"Hush up, boy!" Grig snapped. "Let him finish this fool nonsense. Go on blackbird." In spite of his cross words, the poem stirred a deep memory.

"All right," Raurk acquiesced. "But any more interruptions and I shall put the book away."

"I promise to be quiet." Dannel squatted on the floor next to Raurk. "I'm ready."

"Here goes, then:

"So, I went to the Library of Congress on Saturday,
though I was hungry on Wednesday.
The cop said, "Pull over, madam.
You can't tip toe through these two lips
without a license."
Being only violently mild,
I held out the pooch for him to smooch,
but the pooch turned to chocolate,
and absconded with his frothy hair.
The very same pooch,
who gave up his life to peddle bon-bons
to skirling hoards of wayward Girl Scouts,
still dressed in his snuffy little tutu."

"What's a . . ." Dannel clapped both hands over his mouth. "Sorry."

Raurk eyed him over the top of the volume.

"So, I went to the Library of Congress on Saturday,

though I was hungry on Wednesday.
The dictionary cracked open,
and I spied your beautiful face,
artfully etched upon a pilaster of frozen rain.
My heart flip-flopped at the sight of your smile.
Brazen blue lips of the god leapt from the page,
searing my breast with a rosebud kiss.
Savior me, I cried, as
I dreamt that we snuggled on the thorns
of a land of forgotten snore.
All because I smooched the pooch, when . . .
I went to the Library of Congress on Saturday,
though I was hungry on Wednesday."

Raurk closed the book and returned it to his pocket. "Are you happy now?" Any hope of deciphering its meaning had evaporated with Dannel's constant interruptions.

Grig snapped, "In the name of good, what is all *that* supposed to mean? I've never heard so much gibberish in my entire life. What, pray tell, is a library? You fill this boy's head with nonsense."

"I wish I knew," murmured Raurk. "I've done my best to unravel the meaning for years. Several lines came to me unbidden as we boarded the Tanniger, so I thought I'd reread the poem just to be sure I hadn't missed something."

Taznakie babbled something for several seconds. The druid shook his head. "No, I don't believe so."

"I think it's a curse," Dannel chortled with far too much enthusiasm. "It's a curse. It's a curse." He sang and danced about the small cabin.

"Bah, it doesn't mean a damn thing," Grig spat. "Go to sleep. 'Tis no more than the demented ravings of a lunatic mind. The results of radiation sickness is my guess."

"*You* go to sleep," Dannel scoffed. "The lieutenant is back. I'm going to meet Captain Ardle." He yanked open the door.

"Huh?" the river-man grunted in surprise. "Master Raurk, the Captain has time to show you and your friends around, should it please you."

Dannel nigh flew from the cabin. "Come on, Raurk! I want to see the control house."

"It's called the wheelhouse," the lieutenant said.

"Okay, I'm going to the wheelhouse," Dannel chortled. He stopped momentarily, looking around. "Lieutenant, which way do we go? Is that where the captain steers the boat? What makes it run? How many crewmen are there? Have you been aboard long? Are there always so many people traveling the river?"

"This way, young man."

Dannel bolted toward the prow of the boat, followed by Taznakie and belatedly by the lieutenant.

Raurk turned to the others. "Is anyone else coming along?"

Lillith shook her head. "I think I'll stay here. I'd like a few moments of peace, if you don't mind."

"I'll not leave your wife alone, even if you will," Grig huffed. With a sullen glance, he turned his face to the wall.

"As you will, then," Raurk agreed. "But *do* lock the door behind me. I must hurry to catch up with Dannel before he wears out our welcome."

☙ ◆ ❧

The lieutenant introduced each guest to Captain Ardle and the boat's pilot. "But you're not a gnome!" Dannel wailed. "I thought gnomes owned all the riverboats. They were supposed to take us downriver."

"Well, young lad," Captain Ardle said. "At one time, all the river boats *were* owned by gnomes. But much to the misfortune of the former holder, gambling hit him like a drug. My grand pappy won the Tongalooa Tanniger in a poker game. First my grandfather, then my father, and now me; I'm the proud owner and captain of this mighty boat. We ply the waterway every day of the year. So, may I show you about?"

"What makes it go?" Dannel interrupted, peering out the window.

The Captain's sunburned face split into a broad grin. "Why, the paddlewheel of course, Dannel. We have several men who act as pilots. They steer with this big helm." He touched the polished mahogany with affection and pride. "The paddlewheel, of which you see the top most part out this window, does all the work churning against the water down below."

"But what makes the paddlewheel go? If you're headed up river, won't the current just push you backward?"

"Aye, youngster, but the paddle takes a bite out of the water, so to speak," the Captain answered. "Even headed downriver, we can't just float. There are far too many snags and bottom-rakers to allow that."

"So what makes the paddle turn?" Dannel persisted.

The Captain cocked his head to one side. "You're a smart lad. When I tell most people the paddlewheel makes the Tanniger go, they accept that as an answer and don't think any more about it."

Raurk smiled at his young charge. "Captain, I have to warn you, Dannel will ask a million questions if you allow it. If you prefer not to answer, please say so."

"Not at all. I'm happy to enlighten this youngster. We don't often get someone so interested in the workings of my beautiful boat." The river captain laughed and turned to the boy. "Dannel, step up here on this box and look out the window at the stacks. See the steam drifting out the top? In a moment, when we leave the dock, you're going to see a good deal more, but don't be fooled. It's all a sham."

"What's a sham?"

"That means it's fake. There hasn't been a true steamboat in fifty centuries. The Tanniger is nuclear powered. All the controls are right here on this panel."

"Wow!" Dannel said. "Can I drive it?"

"Sorry, I can't let you do that, but reach up there and give a good long blast on the whistle, and we'll be under way."

 every ◆ ಳ

Lillith breathed a sigh of relief as the boat edged away from the dock. "I'm glad to be away from that place," she said. "Something just didn't feel right. Where's Malie? I haven't seen hide nor hair of her since we came aboard."

Grig answered without turning over. "She's here with me. I don't want her wandering around with those filthy gnomes all over the place. Before you know it, she'd be somebody's dinner."

Silence ensued, broken only by the rhythmic churning of the paddlewheel slicing through the water. Lillith was almost lulled to sleep in her chair when Grig sat bolt upright. "What do you think it meant?"

"I'm sorry. What?"

"The poem. I think there's more to it than meets the hearing."

Lillith nodded with a gentle smile upon her lips. "That's what Raurk has said for years, but he still has no clue what it means, or whether it's important. The book came to him in a most strange manner many years ago, but you'll have to ask him about it."

"Do you read?" the elf asked.

"No." Lillith shook her head.

"I'd hear the poem again. Do you think Raurk would read it to me?" Grig appeared troubled.

"I'm sure he would, but I don't see what difference that'll make. Raurk has studied it for years and fails to understand the meaning."

"I suppose it's nothing. Still, something about the poem haunts my memory. I feel as if I've heard it before. I have no earthly idea where or when."

"You're not the only one." Lillith chuckled. "But if you should decipher the true meaning, please tell Raurk. When all is said and done, he throws up his hands in frustration. I've tried to convince him it's no more than the wanderings of a troubled soul, but he can't let it go."

Grig shuddered. "A specter has crossed my grave. I grow as restless as young Dannel. Would you mind if I joined the others, madam?"

"No, of course not. I'll lock the door once you leave."

❧ ◆ ❧

Grig had no problem following the sound of Dannel's chatter to the forward wheelhouse. "Excuse me, gentlemen, might I join you?"

"You must be Grig Dothrie," the captain said. "I've heard many good things about you. We're just about to go aft to the machine room to inspect the paddlewheel. Would you like to accompany us?"

It still bothered Grig to hear his name in the mouth of strangers, but it seemed no one else gave it a second thought. Resigned, he nodded his head. "I'd enjoy the tour. You must be Captain Ardle. Sorry to be late. I was going to rest, but found myself wide awake."

He turned his attention to the druid. "Raurk, that blasted poem of yours allows me no peace."

Captain Ardle brightened. "Master Raurk, you're an enthusiast of the written word? I have quite a collection in my cabin. In my trade, I meet many people from all parts of the aligned worlds. I've begged, borrowed and practically stolen some of the finest volumes still available. I'd be honored if you'd visit me this evening to share my passion in life."

"Captain, you're needed on the bridge." The lieutenant skidded to a halt. The man breathed heavily. He'd raced aft to catch up with the travelers. "The pilot says there's a huge river eddy dead ahead. It's the biggest he's ever seen. It's forcing us into shore."

"I'm on my way. Make an announcement to the passengers they shouldn't try to leave. I pray this won't take long."

"What's a river eddy?" Dannel peered over the bulistrade with wide eyes.

"Go up front and you'll see," the lieutenant replied. He glanced over the side at the churning river. "I've got to get back downstairs. "There's a couple of fellas been causing trouble ever since they came on board."

"These two wouldn't be a couple of gnomes with bandages wrapped around their heads, would they?" Raurk gave a knowing grin. "We had a run in with them in Mecca. I'd be careful if I were you. The one is a little too free with his ax for my liking."

"Yes, sir, I'll be careful. I really must leave. Go up front to see the river eddy if you'd like."

⤸ ◆ ⤹

"Is it alive?" Dannel whispered. He stared with blank eyes at the swirling, oily-looking water. Smaller, green and blue phosphorescent eddies gyrated within the larger black mass.

"It'd be a lot easier to deal with if it *was* alive," Captain Ardle answered. He watched the dark, roiling water as it devoured everything in its path, sucking plant, animal and debris to the bottom of the deep channel like so much kindling wood. "I've not seen such an enormous one in many a year. Why, it'd drag the Tanniger down in a second. Don't let that slow, slick surface fool you. There's hell brewing in the lower depths."

"Are we at risk?" Grig didn't like the looks of this monster.

"Not as long as we stay out of the deep water. We'll let it get well past us before we shove off again."

"So beautiful . . ." Dannel's eyes focused on something the others couldn't see. "And it's hungry. That's why it sucks down everything within reach." Mesmerized, the lad placed first one uncertain hand upon the rail, and then the other, ready to hoist his weight onto the bottom rung.

"I say, young man, what are you doing?" Captain Ardle asked with a frown etched upon his face.

"It's calling my name. Don't you hear it?"

"Dannel, stop!" Raurk commanded.

Taznakie's reaction was more to the point. "Yechtell," he ordered as he grabbed the boy around the waist with strong arms.

Dannel fought with all his might. "Don't you hear it? It's hungry. It wants me."

"What the hell?" Captain Ardle shook his head. "It's just a river eddy, boy. There's nothing alive about it. Stay out of the way and it won't hurt a thing."

"You're wrong. It *is* alive," Dannel mumbled, still struggling. "I have to go to it."

"Hush, Dannel," Raurk brushed his hand across the boy's eyes. The lad slumped against Taznakie's chest.

"Take him back to the cabin," Raurk said. "Captain, I do believe this is not your ordinary river eddy. I've witnessed such phenomenon before, and this one is different. It radiates a sense of malevolence. Perhaps the eddy itself is not alive, but the spirit within harbors evil intent."

Ardle eyed the churning mass of black water stagnated off the Tanager's port bow. "I've never seen one stall like this. It's huge. How will we ever get past it?"

Grig wrinkled his nose. "It stinks. Do they all smell like that?"

The captain scratched under his cap. "Most of the time, they harbor a rather musty odor, but nothing like this. I can't remember such a large eddy ever appearing in broad daylight. Something about the cooling evenings bring them to the surface. This one is acting in a very peculiar manner. I can't fathom why it doesn't move on."

Taznakie raced back to join the men at the rail. He related something to the druid. "He says the lad is sleeping, but he thinks we should move along as soon as possible. I have to agree with him."

The river man looked perplexed. "What would you suggest? There's no way around it." He gestured at the eddy with his head.

"How deep is the river at this point, Captain?" Grig stared at the oily water.

"I don't rightly know. Is it important? The Tongalooa changes course as often as it floods. I believe this stretch is pretty deep."

"Do you have an idea?" Raurk asked.

"Maybe. Do you feel the heart of it? Perhaps it's one of Urania's creatures?"

"I believe it is," Raurk agreed with a sigh. "It carries her stench."

"I don't understand," Captain Ardle glanced from the elf to the druid and back. "Are you telling me this isn't really a river eddy?"

"Aye," Grig Dothrie agreed.

"Greyflex," Taznakie nodded.

"Oh great," the captain groaned. "I'll never meet my deadline at this rate."

Raurk rubbed his chin. "Perhaps I might be able to solve our predicament, Captain. If you'd like to go ahead with your other duties, it'll give me time to think. I fear this vile spirit has been sent by our enemy. There's no need for you to waste time on such an obstacle."

"Yes . . . Yes, of course," Ardle agreed. "Now that you mention it, it does sound as if things might be getting out of hand on the lower deck. I'll report back as soon as I find out what's going on."

"By all means, don't rush," Raurk urged. "This may take quite some time."

$$\rightadorn \quad \blacklozenge \quad \leftadorn$$

Grig paced along the rail, allowing his hand to trail the length of the silky banister. Now and again he stopped to peer into the depths of the slowly spinning monster. "Well, have you figured it out yet? We've been sitting idle for nigh on two hours."

The druid sighed and shook his head. "I fear it'll be necessary to ask Dannel to return to our presence. I can't discern the nature of this spirit. Perhaps with his help . . ."

"Gropple?" Taznakie interrupted.

"No, of course it's not safe, but we must take the risk."

"That's easy for you to say," Grig scoffed. "How do you propose to keep the lad from throwing himself into the maw of that thing?"

"Taznakie, please fetch the young master along with his guardian and my wife. Whatever you do, *do not* allow him to gaze into the heart of the eddy.

"While he's gone, Master Grig, this is what I have in mind."

∾ ◆ ∿

"What, pray tell, are you up to?" Lillith demanded. "Why did you send for us? Dannel was sound asleep."

"Raurk, I brought Sprite like you wanted," Dannel said. "Should I set him to watch? Why can't I look at the river? Why haven't we moved on yet? Is the river eddy still there? It's alive, you know? It spoke to me, called me by name."

"Hush, Dannel," Raurk admonished. "I want you to face Grig Dothrie. Don't take your eyes off him. Hold Sprite in both hands, because he'll lend all his strength to you. Then you'll call this spirit just as it called to you. Above all, you can't go to it. Grig and Lillith will help you fight the being's allure."

"Me?" Lillith said. "I know nothing of this thing."

"You need only know your brother's spirit," Raurk answered.

"But, how can I call it?" Dannel cried. "I don't know its name."

"Listen and it will tell you. The rest is up to me and Taznakie. I want you to face Grig with Lillith right behind you. Lean against her if you must. Allow your mind to wander. Before long the creature will find you." His words were soothing, hypnotic. "Don't fight it. You're safe with us."

Satisfied at last, Raurk returned his full attention to the roiling water. Behind him, he heard Dannel mutter, but he daren't look away. If this being was sent by Urania Braith, it would take all his concentration to dispose of it.

"Yes . . . Yes . . ." Dannel whispered. "I'm here. I'm coming." He tried to turn toward the water.

"No!" Grig hissed. "Look at *me*, lad. Call its name, but don't look at it. Make it come to you."

"I can't."

"Yes, you can," Lillith urged.

"I told you. I don't know its name." Tears streamed down Dannel's face. "I must go to it. Raurk, don't you understand? It loves me."

Lillith dropped to her knees and hugged the boy close. "It doesn't love you. We're your family. We're the ones who love you. This monster will destroy you and all of us as well. You must call its name."

"Grenfell." Dannel's blank eyes remained on Grig, but it was doubtful he saw the elf. "Its name is Grenfell. The witch sent it to find me. I have to go to it."

Taznakie shook his fist at the oily river. "Harifirtu fredgen," he spat, glaring at the eddy.

Theron Raurk silenced him with a chop of the hand. "Wait."

"Grenfell?" The simpleton raised clinched fists over his head. "Harifirtu fredgen," he said again.

Grenfell was the first intelligible word Grig had ever heard come from Taznakie's mouth. Under other circumstances, he might have liked the results a lot better. A dark green, hooked tentacle churned across the surface of the eddy sending spumes of stinking froth against the side of the paddle wheeler. The boat rocked in the wake and screams rang out from the lower deck.

"Don't," Dannel mouthed. "Don't hurt it."

Raurk and Taznakie pitched against the guard rail. More screams from below and the splashing of heavy bodies hitting the murky water. The Tanniger tilted to port at a steep angle. A second tentacle raked the boat and then disappeared beneath the water. A moment later, the Tanniger canted toward the stern as the huge appendage lifted upward.

"What in hell is going on here?" Captain Ardle fought his way up the deck hand over hand. "Do something!"

Raurk untangled himself from the tangle of thrashing limbs. The pitching of the deck threatened to send him sprawling in the opposite direction. "Airleon," he shouted and raised his staff.

The monster boiled from the depths and hung over him, showering them all with fetid river waste. Raurk caromed backward on a wave of slime and filth coming to rest against the cabin wall. A single yellow eye stared at him from thick folds of slimy flesh.

Dannel dug his teeth into Grig's hand and ran for the railing. He had one leg flung over the top before anyone could react. A high keening sound came unbidden from his lips.

"Stop!" Lillith screamed. The slick deck tilted under her feet and she slid with frightening speed toward the stairwell. "Dannel, stop!"

"I can't." He launched into thin air, plummeting toward the brackish water.

Two giant tentacles swept toward the boy in what seemed like slow motion to Grig Dothrie. "Randitkin rotherdam exaabolta re-ecoc." The words leapt from his mouth of their own accord.

Grig couldn't move. His world came to an abrupt halt. Even the spray hung in midair and the giant creature stared at him with hate in its one eye. The elf was only vaguely aware of what followed.

Theron Raurk bellowed, "Aristiano accordi!" He swung his staff at the monster's nearest limb. Molten blood gushed from the severed flesh, but the creature had captured Dannel with the other tentacle and fought to sink into the river's depths.

Taznakie pushed the druid aside. "Grumphilla ascondorta!"

The eddy exploded in mid air. Dannel fell like a rock into the river's depths. Taznakie leapt to the top of the rail and dove into the water, following the boy below the surface.

"Help them," Lillith screamed. She fought her way to the rail and attempted to cast herself after the pair.

"Stop," Raurk commanded, but she tore at him with adrenalin-stoked fear. "Stop it, I say." He held her to his chest to cease her struggles.

Coming to his senses, Grig Dothrie cast his arms in the air with a bellow. Lightning shot from the tip of Tsunami, his guardian staff. Sturdy lines knit into a healing web and descended into the murky water. Grig pulled the seine tight with a magic touch. "Airleon," he whispered and it rose to the surface with the limp bodies of his friends.

"Let me go," Lillith whimpered. "Dannel's dead."

"Out of the way," Grig said. He hoisted the net to the deck with the aid of his guardian. The contraption dissolved of its own accord and Dannel flopped to his back.

Taznakie coughed up filth and then spied Dannel sprawled next to him. He jerked upright and rolled the boy to his side, slapping him on the back. Dirty water seeped from Dannel's nose and mouth, but he didn't move.

Captain Ardle pushed Taznakie away. With a practiced hand he rolled Dannel to his stomach and straddled the lad. "One, two, three, push," he counted under his breath and leaned with his weight against Dannel's ribcage. More water gushed from Dannel's mouth. "One, two, three, push," he repeated.

"What's he doing?" Lillith couldn't drag her eyes away from her ashen faced brother.

"One, two, three, push." Ardle flipped the boy over and listened for a heartbeat. Next he pinched Dannel's nostrils closed and blew into his mouth.

Dannel gagged. Ardle pulled him to his right side and the lad vomited up the muck and filth of the Tongalooa. "That's a good boy," Ardle said. "Get it all out."

➯ ◆ ➮

Raurk and Lillith strolled the upper deck, hand in hand. "Dannel will be all right," Raurk said. "We couldn't ask for a better healer than Grig Dothrie."

"I know." She stopped to lean on the railing, surveying the placid waters of the river. "What *was* that thing?"

Raurk shrugged and settled his back against the handrail. "No doubt another of Urania's pets."

"She's a foul woman." Her words carried the stress of the day.

"Lillith, I'm shocked to hear such words from your beautiful mouth."

She glared at him, her lips set in defiance. "I don't care. It's true."

"I don't gainsay you, my love. Nevertheless, we shall reach Amarillo day after tomorrow. Magried Whittlebottom will be there to meet us. I fear Urania will increase her efforts as we draw nearer to her home."

"Do you even know where we're going?" Lillith asked. "Or do we follow a willy-nilly path set by that—witch?"

Raurk stroked his wife's cheek with his fingertips. "I know this is difficult for you, my love, but it can't be helped. If we don't stop Urania, the worlds will return to war. She thrives on chaos. There'll be no hope for humankind."

"You're avoiding my question." She leaned forward to kiss him softly on the lips.

He sighed. "I can only say, yes and no. She has wrested the Garden of Eden from its rightful owner. My guess is she harbors the Light of Ishram with her. Getting there is the problem."

"If you don't know how to get there, how will you know when we reach it?"

Raurk shook his head. "I can't tell you exactly what will happen, but there'll be no doubt in anybody's mind when we arrive."

Lillith nestled closer to lay her head upon his shoulder. "Raurk?"

"Yes, my love? What is it? You seem over troubled tonight."

"You told Grig the Light of Ishram is a book. The last of its kind in existence."

"Aye, 'tis true."

She pulled away to look into his eyes. "Why do they call it that?"

"There aren't enough hours in the day to tell the whole story." He sighed, staring into the dark. "Where shall I start?"

Lillith laughed. "I won't say at the beginning because I'd like to be able to rest tonight."

"The short version, then . . ." But he said no more.

"Are you all right?"

He paused to gather his thoughts. "Long before the Thousand Years War, a very brave man, from the House of Ishram, used the Light to wage war on evil. He was killed, but only after defeating the foul hordes descending upon his land. The Light has remained in his family until Urania stole it."

"Why did you think of her poem when we boarded the Tanniger?"

"What are you getting at?" He peered into her eyes.

"Nothing, I was just curious." She snuggled under Raurk's arm, watching his face.

"The poem intrudes into my consciousness when I least expect it." Raurk felt Lillith's gaze boring into him. He was grateful for the darkness to hide his embarrassment. "I've no idea why. Perhaps mere intuition."

"She loved you at one time."

"Nay, Urania's not capable of love. She longed to gain power over the Light and thought I could give it to her. She's not a lover scorned if that's what you're thinking." He took Lillith in his arms, felt her body melting into his. "How could I care for anyone else when I have you?"

❧ **48** ❧

Raurk struggled to restrain Dannel with an outstretched arm. "Hold on, young man, you'll get yourself trampled." He'd barely stopped the youngster from dashing out in front of a string of loaded wagons, each pulled by matched sets of four animals.

"But, what are they?" Dannel strained against Raurk's grip.

"Those are hostrichs," Captain Ardle said from behind them. "Useful animals, but dumb as a post." He flapped a hand at the dust kicked up by the wagons.

"Look." Dannel pointed at two men bringing up the rear of the wagon train. "They're riding the hostrichs. We don't have hostrichs at home. Can I ride one?"

"Around here, riding them is an everyday occurrence," Ardle answered. "But I doubt you'll get a chance to ride one. These cowboys are a might tetchy about their animals."

"Why do they call them cowboys? What are those four legged animals?"

"I never gave it any thought young man, but those other critters are beefra. I must leave you now. I need to supervise the cargo coming onboard."

Raurk made a slight bow. "Thank you, Captain, for your hospitality. In spite of the river eddy, the trip was . . . pleasant."

Ardle saluted and turned to go. Halfway up the gangway, he stopped and turned back. "Raurk, Amarillo is a dangerous place. The summer heat sets in and tempers run short." He nodded toward Lillith. "A beautiful woman like your wife . . ." He shrugged. "What can I say?"

"Thank you, Captain. I'll be vigilant."

"Aye, then. Good luck to you." Ardle saluted again and hurried away.

"What was that all about?" Lillith nodded toward the river captain.

Raurk steered them away from the gangplank before answering. "Amarillo has a thriving slave trade. If you fell into the wrong hands, it'd be better to kill yourself than suffer the horror of such a life."

A shrill whistle split the air. "Over here, guv'nor."

Raurk turned at the sound of Whittlebottom's voice.

"I say, it's about time you showed up." Perched atop a crate, Whittlebottom waved a colorful bandanna to get their attention. "I've been waiting days for you. And this strange gerrub appeared day before yesterday and she won't leave me alone." He swatted at Tanus as she tried to rub against his leg.

"Don't hit her," Grig said. "She's mine."

"Not now, Grig," Raurk said. "I'm sure Tanus is safe without our interference."

"She's your pet? But how did she get here?" Whittlebottom asked.

"Get on with what you were saying." Raurk gave him a stern glare.

"Yes, well . . . . The people around here are right friendly, but we should move on soon. I sent my crew back to guard Isis. Seeing as how we're getting close, I don't want them or her in danger."

"Are you sure that was wise?" Raurk asked.

"Uh—well, yes in light of the stir my men caused around here. It's been a long time since they've been around women."

Raurk groaned and covered his eyes.

"I say, old man, nothing to worry about. I paid for all the damage before they left. Besides, I'd forgotten what an unruly bunch they were. The buggers never did like taking orders." He retied the bandanna around his neck. "That's better. I thought you'd be here yesterday. What took you so long?"

"We were delayed."

"A shame, it was," Whittlebottom answered. "The law around here is about ready to . . . . Well, anyway, it was all I could do to convince the blokes I'd leave as soon as you showed up."

"Are you Magried Whittlebottom?" Dannel interrupted. "I've waited ever so long to meet you." He offered his hand to shake, then jerked it back tucking it in a pocket.

"That I am, young man." Whittlebottom's face with its empty eye sockets shifted to the woman at Raurk's side. "Who may this lovely creature be?" He swept a new ten gallon cowboy hat from his head and bowed.

"This is my wife, Lillith," Raurk said.

"I'm pleased to meet you, ma'am."

Lillith raised an eyebrow at the pirate. "My pleasure, I'm sure."

Raurk took Lillith by the elbow. "I think it best we not dally. It appears the law to which Whittlebottom refers has found us." He nodded toward two hungry-looking men headed in their direction.

Whittlebottom shrunk behind the druid. "Did they see me?" he hissed.

"Gentlemen, can I help you?" Raurk moved to stand in front of his charges.

The taller of the two tipped his hat to Lillith. "Afternoon, ma'am." His attention shifted to the pirate cowering behind Raurk. "Do you know this man?"

A loud shout rang out from a storefront down the street, drawing their notice. "Is there a problem?" Raurk asked.

The stranger shook his head. "Now that you're here, maybe not. I'm the sheriff and this is my deputy. Sorry to say, the pirate stepped on a few toes."

Raurk's hackles went up, but he said nothing.

"He promised to leave as soon as you arrived," the sheriff said. "I thought for sure he was lying, but it appears I was wrong."

The sheriff's head jerked toward shrill cursing and the sound of a fistfight. A scruffy looking man careened into the street and landed in the dust. A cheer went up from the bystanders as a second man launched himself toward his victim. Dust swirled around the fighters and two more men joined the scuffle.

"Fight! Fight! Fight!" the crowd jeered.

"Damn," the sheriff swore. "Let's go, deputy." He jogged toward the escalating fracas and waded in.

"Well, that was most timely," Whittlebottom said. "I suggest we take advantage of the distraction before the sheriff comes back."

Raurk turned to look at him. "I don't suppose you had anything to do with it?

"Me, guv'nor? I'd never stoop so low. This way. I have supplies waiting for us at the livery. Sorry I couldn't acquire any hostrichs for our use. It seems the blighters don't like skeletons." He led them down a back alley, away from the waterfront and the law.

❧ **49** ❧

The ghostly moon rode high in the night sky as it shown on the flat, nearly featureless plain. The hint of a shadow cast strange misshapen darkness across the landscape.

Shivers of dread crawled down Grig's spine. These were not the normal, delicate premonitions of alarm prickling at his psyche, but gut wrenching, heart pounding, convulsive shudders robbing him of the air in his lungs, slapping him rudely in the face to get his attention.

He mopped at the sweat rolling down his face, nauseous and disoriented. Then he swiped his eyes to clear the dust. He'd just stepped away from camp to take care of personal business out of sight of Lillith. Now he was lost.

How could things have gone so wrong in such a short time? Raurk, Taznakie, Lillith and the boy were gone as if they'd fallen off the face of the earth. Not even Tanus showed her face. Or maybe he was the one who'd plunged into oblivion. This thought frightened him more than he thought possible. With each passing moment, his feeling of dread mushroomed.

Had he been in deep forest he could understand turning in the wrong direction. But this place was flat. Completely, totally, disgustingly flat.

Grig hated the stunted, wind-blown mockeries of trees Raurk called cactus. He'd learned the hard way these atrocities packed a mean set of thorns. Some, like the Nemrak thorns, had backward facing barbs making them nigh impossible to extract. He turned to view the distant horizon. "Where is everyone?" The sound of his own voice was better than none.

There had to be an explanation, but damned if he could figure it out. "Fifty paces. That's all I took. Fifty paces and it might as well be a million." He turned in a circle. The hard packed ground gave no trace of human passage in the last millennium. "You'd think I'd sprouted wings and flew away."

The soughing wind echoed his words as it swept across the prairie. "Hello!" he called, hoping to attract attention. "Raurk, Taznakie, where are you?" Still no answer. He'd even be happy to see the specter of Tanus, but like the others, she was nowhere to be seen.

"Where's that imbecile when you need him? At this rate, I'll perish before anyone comes looking. And with my luck, it'll be a slow, painful death."

Breathing deeply, he made a complete circle scouring the land, yet nothing new marred the perfect emptiness. Afraid of becoming even more confused, he sank to his haunches and battled with abject terror.

"Damn you, Raurk!" he shouted at the empty desert. A lone beast in the distance howled a plaintive response. He shivered and wrapped his jerkin tighter around his torso. There was naught to do but wait for the druid to find him.

He glanced toward his left. "If I can't see them, can they see me? They'll have to send someone . . . . Won't they?"

Maybe his guardian, Tsunami, could find him. He leapt to his feet again and whistled, but he was so disoriented he had no idea which direction to watch.

Not that he really expected the guardian to come slithering to his rescue, but he would have liked *something* to happen. Dejected, he dropped back to the ground, toying with the dusty pebbles scattered about.

A low howl answered by another startled him. "What was that?" He searched the moonlit prairie. Nothing moved. More howls rolled across the landscape, but now they moved away from him.

He started to light a fire, but somehow that just didn't seem right. Afraid to fall asleep, he shivered and fidgeted, fidgeted and shivered. And prayed the howling animals would continue to move away.

❧ 50 ❧

Raurk sat up straight from a deep sleep with the surety that something had gone amiss. A quick check of his companions reinforced his misgivings. The bitter, dry cold forced Grig and Dannel to share their warmth, but Dannel huddled beneath their blankets — alone.

Taking in his surroundings in a wide sweeping arc, he was just in time to see the back of Grig Dothrie disappear as the boundary between two worlds shifted. Captain Ardle had warned that Texas still had places not quite *settled* in since reuniting with the known worlds. Until this moment, he'd not witnessed this phenomenon.

Raurk prayed Grig would remember his admonishments to stay put should something such as this happen. He might be a druid and master of many strange powers, but they didn't include moving worlds.

Eventually Texas would resume proper alignment and Grig would be returned to their midst. All the better should it be before trouble or starvation paid a visit. In the meantime, Raurk must wait, no matter how impatiently.

For once, the druid wished he owned one of the wood-elves' guardians. Perhaps such a creature, neither flesh nor blood, could cross between the misaligned worlds. "You ninny. 'Tis naught but wishful thinking," he mouthed.

Seated cross-legged on the ground, Raurk watched with an unblinking stare at the point where Grig had walked from this world into the next. When East Texas and the Rio Grand realigned, he'd be there to snatch the elf to safety. There could be no room for delay.

Hours later, Lillith found her husband still watching and waiting as dawn assaulted the early morning sky. "What is it?" she whispered, slipping her arms around his gaunt shoulders. "I got cold and couldn't find you."

"Grig went through there." He tilted his head toward the immediate horizon.

"I don't see anything," Lillith said.

"There's nothing to see right now, but I swear that's where he went."

Lillith laughed softly. "Please stop speaking in riddles. Why are you sitting here staring at the barren landscape while poor Tanus is prowling around the camp looking for Grig Dothrie?"

Raurk didn't take his gaze form the horizon. "Sorry, my love, I daren't risk the chance I'll miss the opening between this world and the one where Grig Dothrie went. It may be very brief."

"How did he get lost?"

Raurk sighed. "He walked away from camp during the night and became trapped. It's up to me to ensure his safety."

"You're only human," she said.

"None of them would be here if not for me."

"Theron Raurk, stop berating yourself."

"I should have been more careful."

"What will you do if the opening doesn't appear again? It looks exactly like it did last night when we went to sleep. How will you even know if it does come back?"

Raurk shook his head. "That's why I must remain vigilant. I can't risk missing my only opportunity."

"Can I watch while you rest?"

"Please sit down if you wish to keep me company, but I must remain alert until the time to act presents itself."

Another hour passed, and another as flies the size of fists buzzed annoyingly about Raurk's head. Lillith sat with him until first Dannel came to take her place, and then Taznakie replaced the boy. Each in turn grew bored and went about their morning routine.

At last, a slight ripple in the fabric of the day set Raurk's senses on alert. A glint of sunlight fractured between the worlds into his eyes, momentarily blinding him.

$\approx$ ◆ $\approx$

The first spectral rays of the sun kissed the distant horizon off to

Grig's left. He had no idea how long he'd sat on the hard packed scrabble. His bones creaked and protested as he turned to watch the spectacular sunrise.

These brief morning displays proved to be one of the few good things he'd discovered in the last couple of days. The rest of this land could go suck a dragon egg for all he cared.

Grig never thought he'd long to see rain again, but the parched earth belched up great whirlwinds of fine sand as the early morning calm gave way to sporadic gusts of hot air. These dust storms gained speed as they raced unchecked across the flat land, only to die out as suddenly as they were born, the air taken from their whorls.

By the day's end, sand permeated everything. Even Malie emerged from the bottom of her sling covered in the blasted stuff. All of them had taken to wearing a makeshift bandana across their nose and mouth in order to breathe.

Early morning and late evening were the only times they could eat a meal without ingesting a mouthful of grit. The nights were cold and dry beyond belief. This was a true high desert where the temperature plummeted after dark. Grig hated being cold even more than having his feet tickled.

The first night he had near frozen to death before Dannel threw his own blanket on top of Grig's and crept beneath it to share their body heat. Once he'd gotten accustomed to the sleeping arrangements, it didn't seem so odd. The druid always had Lillith to sleep with, but Taznakie seemed to relish the chill. He even found it too warm when Malie snuggled closer, and sent her complaining to nap with Dannel and Grig.

Taznakie always rose first in the mornings. Quickly, he'd stoke the dwindling fire with the strange, flaky objects Raurk called cow pies. Grig assumed the makers of these cow pies were long dead. Just another victim of the Thousand Years War.

The pies gave off enough heat to satisfy Grig, even if it was a rather pungent warmth. So, once the fire roared, the elf poked his nose out and prayed he was snug in his own bed. Such a miracle would mean the last couple of weeks had been naught but a bad dream.

A deep sleeper, Dannel probably hadn't even missed him yet. He wondered how long before Raurk would discover his absence. If anyone could find him it would be Raurk.

As he watched, the sun separated company with the earth's horizon and the first eddies of swirling sand rose into the warming air. At times, three, four and five of these twisters marched in a row like drunken soldiers. In addition, they made the strangest sound as they ripped the oxygen from the surrounding sky. More than once, they'd reminded Grig of the screaming banshees they'd left behind so long ago.

Buzzards, great carrion eating birds, took to the skies along with the whirling dust. They circled endlessly waiting for one of the travelers to drop. Precious little in this wasteland existed to eat and nothing escaped the sharp eyes of the scavengers.

A stray groat slithered across the sand toward Grig. "Shoo, get away from me." He threw a pebble at the reptile. A huge beetle as large as Grig's head buzzed overhead and then left.

Grig stifled a scream at the sound of heat-lightning splitting the burning air. This place reminded him of Golgotha, except for the absence of tainted rain.

Three dust plumes painted against the green lightning drew his eyes. He shook his head in disbelief. "What the . . . ?"

These weren't the upright spinning columns of sand produced by the wind devils he'd grown accustomed to. In his mind, they resembled the flaring wakes of a giant reptile plowing through water.

As he watched, they converged into one large, dirty smudge on the skyline, but then parted again into separate columns. "Me and my stupid modesty. This can't be good. Maker, why did I walk away from camp?"

The sporadic dust devils zigzagged toward him. All he could do was wait to see what time would bring. He hoped the dirty smudges converging upon his isolated vigil would collapse into nothing or head in another direction. "It's just sand," he prayed.

He gave a bitter laugh. Three dragons, a three-headed troll and three whatever those things were. Raurk had said three was Urania's number. This made it very bad luck, and this new phenomenon didn't rest easy upon his senses.

He waited, trying to judge how far away the dust plumes were but nothing broke the smooth land to add perspective to their size or distance.

More importantly, he searched for refuge should the need arise. The tough little desert birds might dart in and out between the thorny branches of the cactus, but he wasn't a bird.

With ever mounting apprehension and an undeniable curiosity, Grig Dothrie stared unblinking as the phenomenon approached. "No, go somewhere else. Leave me be."

Before long, he realized his original assessment of the situation was inaccurate. There were four feathery plumes of dust, not three. The smallest, in the lead, blended against those in pursuit. Pursuit being the key word. Whichever direction the first entity veered, the other three followed.

Grig laughed with irrational relief. He still had no idea what he dealt with and didn't care as long as there were four of them headed in his direction, not three. "You fool!" he heard Theron Raurk's voice in his head.

Quicker than he believed possible, a four legged, bovine looking creature raced past. He remembered Captain Ardle calling them beefras. It sported gray and white stripes, and very long horns jutting from each side of its head. The animal bawled with fear, its chops lathered and eyes rolling wildly.

The three men thundering into view hot on the heels of the beefra sent Grig's empty stomach into his throat. Vinegary gall filled his mouth, fear gripped his guts. It didn't take a genius to know trouble stared him in the face.

☙ ◆ ❧

Whooping like banshees, lariats whistling about their heads, the three hostrich riders nearly passed Grig Dothrie before they knew he was there. Reining his mount sharply, Sheb Matthews, the lunatic in the lead, skidded to an abrupt and very dusty halt. The other men pulled in their mounts in the interest of self-preservation, ropes still in hand.

Sheb was one hell of a good-time guy, but he was insane as a rabid skunker as any of his cronies could testify. Passing him on a hostrich, regardless of the reason, put them at peril of immediate and violent retribution. So it was in the interest of self-preservation that they risked rolling their hostrichs asses over teakettles rather than riling Sheb's temper.

Sheb was not in the mood to overlook someone he could bully. Especially if the varmint appeared to shrink into the ground before his eyes. The beefra might have escaped him, but this kid out here in the middle of nowhere posed fair game.

"Hello," Grig said softly.

"Hello?" Sheb mimicked with malice. "That all you got to say for yourself, brat? What in hell you doin' out here? Where's your momma? And take that ridiculous hat offen your head when I speak to you. Let me see your ugly face. I'd see the whites of the eyes of those who insult my good reputation."

"Uh. Well. Uh . . ." Grig stammered.

"Speak up, boy!" Sheb roared, ripping the hat from Grig's head.

"Wall, lookie here, Jeeter," he sniggered to his cronies. It didn't matter which one since they both answered to their surname.

"That's an elf, by golly," Ezra Jeeter said.

"What makes you think you know so much, Jeeter?" Sheb snarled. "There ain't no elves in Throckmorton, Texas and you know it. We don't allow no such trash in our town. Never have. Never will. Me and Daddy seen to that. I reckon you ain't never seen no elf before, right, Jeeter?" He stepped close enough to blow sour whiskey breath in Ezra's face. "Have you?" His hand rested on the butt of his revolver jammed into the waist of his jeans.

"Nope, I ain't never seen no elf before." Ezra dropped into Sheb's drawling dialect in an effort to pacify the bully, "But I've done rea . . . seen pictures." He'd practically admitted he could read. Not something he wanted to disclose to Sheb.

Like his Daddy, Sheb viewed reading as a bizarre sort of voodoo or pagan rite. Better the Jeeter twins claim they could spit fire or walk on water than acknowledge they could read when it came to Sheb Matthews. He might not be stupid, but most the time he was playing with two partial decks and had gotten the joker from both.

Ezra and Zeke suspected Sheb and his daddy had torched the last remaining schoolhouse in Throckmorton. It didn't matter that Ms. Jeeter and her twins were asleep inside. As far as the Matthews clan was concerned, school teachers ranked right up there with gnomes, trolls, elves and all those other freaks of nature.

Being the runtiest, youngest, smallest, and smartest boys in town, and not wanting to suffer for their superior intellect, the Jeeter twins knew when to keep their mouths shut. They hid their fear behind silly grins, pushing, shoving, and lewd jokes.

Catching the faux pas, Zeke added to the lie. "Yeah, a guy at the saloon was showin' around pictographs a couple of days back. He'd run across a whole bunch of them freaks in a place called Mecca. You know the guy, tall, big potbelly, and a patch over one eye? The boys ran him off night before last."

Sheb whirled on the Jeeter twins with a menacing scowl and a drawn pistol. "How many times I gotta tell you boys I ain't no moron?" His tone stayed soft, but Zeke and Ezra knew they'd hit a sore point. Problem was, they couldn't figure out *which* point they'd hit. Instead of throwing Sheb off, they'd accidentally triggered his rage. When he got in one of his moods, it took little to throw Sheb into a snit.

Grig grasped a slender thread of hope for a stay of execution. While Sheb was haranguing his cronies, escape might be possible. Silent as a ghost in a thick fog, he sidled one step at a time toward the large cactus to his right. Ears tuned to the verbal barrage so proficiently delivered by the hot-blooded Sheb, the elf wracked his brain. Even if he ran, Sheb would ride him down like the terrorized beefra.

With only half his mind Grig heard one of the Jeeter twins whine, "Come on Sheb, we didn't mean nuttin." More interesting though, the beefra snuffled back toward the arguing men. With the immediate danger past, the animal's natural curiosity and stupidity drew it toward the screaming, spitting Sheb.

Grig watched from the corner of his eyes. If they could ride the hostrichs, why couldn't he ride the four-legged, striped beefra? He knew very little about such things, but it was worth a try.

Sprinting toward the unwary animal, Grig leapt onto the creature's back and hung on for dear life. He tried to reach the giant horns without success, so instead, he cast a healing web to anchor himself to the terrified bovine hybrid, and none too soon.

"Yee, ha! Lookie thar, Sheb," Zeke yelled. "Crazy son-of-a-bitch. I ain't never seen nobody ride a beefra before."

Legs stiff as a post, the beefra bounced like a spring into the air three or four times to dislodge the elf. When this didn't work, it whirled, wild-eyed in pursuit of its own silky tail, randomly punctuated with one of the stiff-legged, hiccupping leaps into the air.

Sheb Matthews found himself lewdly aroused at such chaos. He inched closer to enjoy the elf's predicament. "Yahoo!" He slapped at the beefra with his rope. "Ridem, jerk-wad."

"How in hell is that boy hangin' on?" Ezra yelled.

"Beats the crap outta me," Zeke answered.

Spittle ran down Sheb's chin and his eyes glazed over. "He ain't nuttin but a scrawny little feller. I tried to ride one of them crazy critters once when I was little . . ." He clamped his mouth shut and looked at the twins to see if they'd heard.

Half-digested food flooded Grig's throat and erupted past his lips.

Sheb received a face full of bile. "You stinkin', pointy eared little freak. I'll kill you for that."

Ezra and Zeke hid their grins behind grubby hands. Not sure what to do, they rushed forward in unison to aid the bully. "Get away from me, you idiots!" he roared. "You did that on purpose. I'll get even if it's the last thing I do."

"We—we didn't do nuttin," Ezra stammered.

Zeke averted his face, still grinning. "Gawd, that stinks. I got a rag in my saddlebag, and a little water. Let me go get it and we'll have you cleaned up in no time."

"Don't touch me." Sheb fired wildly into the air with a large, long-barreled, Colt .45. "Get that varmint off that beefra so I can rip his head off. Then I'm gonna stuff your twin heads up your twin butts while I whistle *Dixie*." He punctuated every third or fourth word with another bullet fired into the faultless, blue sky.

The Jeeter twins stared at Sheb. "You sure about that, Sheb?" Zeke inched away.

"Yeah," Ezra said. "We don't want to go off and leave you all alone lessen you're sure. You might need us."

Sheb grabbed him by the collar and shook. "You see that beefra headed to China? Them gunshots spooked him real bad. I don't see any way you can go after that ol' boy while you stand here with your thumbs up your butts. Do you?"

Zeke and Ezra glanced at each other, at Sheb, the dwindling elf, and back to Sheb.

"Morons!" Sheb bellowed. "If I have to go after that devil's frog-spawn myself, I'll stick this pea shooter up your left nostril and blow the snot outta both your pimple butts before I set my boot in the stirrup. Now get the hell outta here."

Ezra and Zeke hurtled for the two hostrichs grazing placidly on the short prairie stubble. In a flash, they streaked across the flat plain in hot pursuit of the beefra again.

Goliath, Sheb's hostrich, often shied at his own shadow, balked at loud sounds, and bolted at the most inopportune times. So far, he'd held his ground at the raucous yelling, the strange antics of the beefra, and the thundering crashes of the Colt .45, but when the other hostrichs flew from his side, Goliath followed suit. Neck stretched as far as it would go, nostrils flaring and ears pinned to his head, he sprinted after his companions.

Sheb screamed, "I hope you fall offen the nearest cliff!" He pounded his fist on the closest cactus and danced around in pain. "You no good, two-legged pile of crap. Don't ever show your sorry ass around me again. If I weren't hurtin' so bad, I'd use this here six-shooter on you."

≫ ◆ ≪

Grig wondered if he'd made the right decision in mounting the beefra. It appeared what the beast lacked in brains, they made up for in the ability to run. "Look out," Grig screamed. The animal plowed straight through another obstacle in its path. Then it paused to lurch stiff-legged into the air.

Grig felt like he was getting his brains beat out. The healing web binding him to the animal's back worked too well. He couldn't have fallen off if he'd tried. "Ar–va–do . . ." but he couldn't finish the release spell. Of necessity, he clung to the strange creature's back with all his might.

Zeke and Ezra chased the beefra across the plain. They were the closest thing to a knight in shining armor that would come along. Finally, they gained on the flagging, bovine retard.

Fear of their leader swayed them more than any misplaced idea of being do-gooders, but this poor chap had done nothing to deserve Sheb's wrath.

Like many twins before them, they needed few spoken words to communicate their thoughts. Maybe if they could get to the elf before Sheb, they might be able to spirit him away to safety. They knew this land much better than Sheb ever hoped to and there were plenty of places to hide a fella if you knew where to look.

Grig bit his tongue with rattling teeth. Bloody drool and dirt caked the corner of his mouth. He was beyond caring whether the two cowboys ever caught up to him. "Break a leg, damn you," he mumbled with his face pressed into the run-amuck creature's pumping shoulders. Convinced things couldn't possibly get worse, he closed his eyes and prayed.

In the lead, Ezra drew bead on the beefra and let fly with an expertly aimed toss of his lariat, catching the hysterical beast by the back foot.

A split second later, Zeke leaped off his hostrich and threw the beefra to the ground with a mighty thud. The cowboy grabbed three feet and wrapped them tightly with a rawhide thong and threw both hands in the air. "Six seconds, brother. Bet you can't beat that time."

Ezra took a second to scan the horizon behind them before dismounting. The sight of Goliath with an empty saddle a hundred yards in the rear caused him a sharp intake of breath. Sheb Matthews was nowhere in sight.

"Ezra, get down here and help me get this thing off this fella," Zeke called. "He's still alive. I think this imbecile beefra broke a couple ribs when it fell on him. Give me your knife. I don't know what this is holding him on, but it's tougher than dried snot."

Ezra flipped his prized Bowie knife hilt first and handed it to his brother. "Don't you go losing that, Jeeter." His mind was still occupied with the black hostrich staring at them with huge, rolling eyes. "One thing about Goliath, he ain't mean." He reached to stroke the hostrich's neck.

"What are you talking about?" Zeke asked.

Ezra surveyed the landscape. "I don't rightly know. This is spooky. I can't imagine Goliath throwing Sheb. So where in hell is that bastard?"

"I don't fancy a bullet in my back when we ain't looking." Zeke glanced around nervously.

"Damned if I do, either," Ezra answered.

Zeke threw the knife on the ground and stood. "I can't cut that thing. We gotta figure some other way to get this ol' boy loose."

Ezra knelt on his knees and tested the strands of the healing web. "Where you think Sheb's gotten to?"

"I reckon he's waiting for us to bring this bloke back." Zeke stared the way they'd just come. "You think he's somewhere out there with a broken neck? Goliath's awful worked up."

Ezra shook his head. "It'd serve him right, but my guess is he's laying low, just waiting to ambush us. We'd better get this elf-fella loose before the beefra gets its wind back . . ."

"And good old Sheb sneaks up on us." Zeke glanced over his shoulder.

"Damned if I know how we're gonna cut it off him," Ezra said. "Since it didn't come apart in all that knockin' about, I'm thinking it has to be magic of his doing."

"Gimme the canteen," Zeke said. "Maybe a swig of water will bring him around. I don't want to kill the beefra if it rousts awake too soon. That'd piss Sheb off, for sure."

"More likely he'll get tired of waiting and come looking to shoot us," Ezra added.

"Come on fella," Zeke coaxed, dribbling a bit more warm water between Grig's bruised lips. "Wake up. We gotta get you outta here."

At this moment, a pack of screaming banshees would have been more inviting to Grig than opening his eyes on the parched land called East Texas. Clawing at the canteen, he did his best to push it away. "Nnn . . . Nnn . . ." he moaned.

"Don't do that." Surprisingly gentle, Zeke cradled the elf in his arms as he poured warm water down his throat. "You gotta wake up before Sheb catches us. Come on fella. Please?" It was a plaintive entreaty.

The winded beefra bawled again and did its best to clamber to its feet. Grig was suddenly wide awake. "Avardo oria." He released the bonds of the healing web with the wave of his hand, but he could do little else. Ezra shoved the exhausted animal from Grig's legs allowing his twin brother to pull the elf to safety.

"Can you walk?" Zeke patted Grig's shoulder. "Sheb's gonna show up madder than a wet groat, and I don't want to be here when he does. He's awful tetchy today."

Grig barely moved his head from side to side. It hurt too much to say anything. But a longing gaze at the canteen brought it to his lips again. After a racking gulp, he wheezed, "My legs are broken."

"I'm surprised your neck ain't busted." Ezra snorted. "The way that critter hit the ground, it's a wonder you both ain't dead. What kept you from fallin' off is a puzzle to me. Problem is how we gonna get you out of sight before Sheb takes a hankering to show his ugly face?"

"I don't suppose you could ride even if we put you up on Goliath?" Zeke didn't sound hopeful.

Another long drag on the canteen was followed by a bunch of nonsense sounding words neither twin understood. Color returned to Grig's face one shade at a time.

"You just did magic, right?" Ezra stared with his mouth open.

Grig nodded.

Zeke's face contorted in terror. "Well, don't be doing that in front of Sheb." He cast a furtive glance over his shoulder. "He'd string you up faster than the KKK could."

"I'll be sure to remember that." Still shaky, Grig stood on his own, amused when Ezra and Zeke dropped their hands from him and backed away.

"How'd you do that?" Zeke looked like he was about to run. "I'd a sworn your legs was busted along with them ribs."

"Magic. Remember?" Grig scoffed.

The twins looked askance at Grig. "Don't hurt us mister. We don't mean you no harm," Ezra pleaded.

"I won't use magic to injure you unless you force me."

Zeke blew a sigh of relief.

"Since we've settled that issue," Grig said. "Do you plan to fulfill your idiot leader's orders, or am I momentarily safe?"

"Whoa, fella," Ezra, raised both hands in defense. "We're on your side."

"My name is Grig." The elf bristled.

"Okay, Mister Grig. I'm Ezra and my brother here's Zeke. But we'd be better off putting as much distance between us and Sheb as possible. He ain't exactly the sociable type."

"So where is this paragon of humanity at this very moment?" Grig's ire threatened to get the better of him.

The twins stared at each other. "You talking about Sheb Mathews, Mister Grig?" Zeke scratched his head an extracted a squirming lout. "Damn critters"

"Is Sheb the madman you were with?"

"Yeah, that's him all right," Ezra said. "Last we seen him, he was blasting away at everything in sight with that blunderbuss of his. I'm guessing that's when Goliath took it into his pea brain to run off."

"Sheb will be plenty mad about that." Ezra grinned with what appeared to be a bit of malice. "I wish I could've seen the look on his face when his hostrich done run off. According to good old Sheb Matthews, nobody takes a shat without his permission."

"I don't understand half of what you say," Grig complained.

Zeke laughed. "I suppose that makes us even, cause half what you say goes right over my head."

"Can we go back?" The elf waved vaguely over his shoulder. "I'm tired and dirty and hungry . . ."

"That's the best idea I heard so far." Zeke scratched absently at his crotch. "Big brother, what do you think?"

Ezra shrugged. "Let's put him up on Goliath and find out."

Grig pointed at the huge, black hostrich. "You want *me* to get on *that*?" His voice shook with fear. "If I couldn't ride the shorter beefra, what makes you think I can ride a hostrich?"

"Simple as pie," Ezra answered.

"No, I can't ride that beast," Grig wheezed. "That other one fair massacred me. This Goliath creature stands at least half again as tall. No. No, way. I'd sooner try to fly."

Zeke smiled. "Mister Grig, that old beefra weren't never meant to be ridden. I never seen anyone stay on one as long as you did."

"Yeah, me neither," Ezra agreed. "But Goliath was trained to ride ever since he was a little bitty colt. He won't give you no trouble. Especially if you don't yell at him like Sheb does."

"No."

"Then, I guess you'd better start walking," Ezra said. "I figure you should catch up with us 'bout noon tomorrow. Just keep your eye on those two big yuccas to the right of that hill. That's where we picked you up."

"Either that," Zeke said. "Or sprout them wings you was jawing about."

"Where?" Grig demanded. To him all the ugly, stunted trees looked the same and there wasn't a single hill in sight.

"Right there." Ezra pointed.

"Come on you guys," Zeke said. "I don't like sitting out here in the open. We don't know where Sheb is, but I'd rather be on my hostrich and moving when we meet up with him again."

Ezra nodded. "You coming or staying, Mister Grig?"

Grig's shoulders slumped. "It appears I don't have a choice. How do you get up on that *thing*?"

Zeke lifted Grig from his feet, nearly hoisting the elf over the mammoth hostrich's back. "Fella, you don't weigh nuttin'." He guided Grig's leg over the saddle. "That's more like it. Here, take the reins in your left hand. Press your knees into his sides to hold on. Goliath will follow Blue and Buddy so all you have to do is stay in the saddle." He clucked at the hostrichs, setting them in motion.

"This isn't working." Grig swallowed the bile rising in his throat. He hadn't realized just how tall Goliath was until he sat in the saddle and looked down. "Uh . . . I think I'm going to be ill." His previous motion sickness threatened to rear its ugly head again.

"Don't watch the ground," Ezra or Zeke said.

Grig swiped at the cold sweat running into his eyes. "Where am I supposed to look? How will Goliath know where to put his feet?"

"Quit being such a pansy, Mister Grig," Ezra said. "Goliath knows better than you where to plant his feet. Just concentrate on the horizon and you'll be fine."

Grig soon found the gentle rocking of the hostrich no longer bothered him. He allowed himself the luxury of hope. "Did you see my friends when you came upon me?"

"Not a soul but you, fella." Ezra shook his head.

"Which one are you?" Grig shaded his eyes for a better look.

"I'm Ezra. I got the gray hat. Zeke here wears a brown one."

Grig inspected their dusty headgear. It was difficult to tell the difference, but decided not to comment. These strange look-alike men were his only hope. "I was traveling with my friends and got separated during the night. I hoped you'd seen them." Grig didn't hold as much hope as his words.

Ezra shrugged. "We need to pick up the pace a little, Mister Grig if you think you can hang on."

Grig hung tighter to the pommel of the saddle. "You didn't see anyone at all?" he asked again.

"Not a soul," the twins denied in unison.

❧ 51 ❧

Sheb Matthews stood before the tall, slender man, brandishing his pistol threateningly and screaming profanities at the top of his lungs.

The sight of the man calmly peering at him only served to make Sheb Matthews angrier. "Who in hell are you?" He pointed the pistol at the druid's face.

"I'm Theron Raurk of the Druid Council."

Sheb growled. "You're one of them magic men, ain't ya?"

Raurk nodded. "I suppose you could say that."

"What'd you do with my hostrich? And don't make excuses, 'cause I ain't in no mood to listen to a pack of your lies."

Raurk cleared his throat and motioned for his companions to stay where they were. Although he'd never seen a gun before, the thing reeked of death. The smell of gunpowder did nothing to allay his anxiety. "My good man, I have no idea what you're referring to. I was simply sitting here waiting the return of my fellow traveler."

"A sawed off little pimple butt with pointy ears?" Sheb glanced over his shoulder. "If you're with *that* guy, I should kill ya just for lookin' at me."

Raurk held his hands in front of him, palms up. "I can't imagine what Master Grig might have done to garner your rage."

"What'd he do?" Sheb squawked. "That freak stole my beefra . . . And my hostrich. Then he chased off my two best friends. He probably killed 'em for all I know." Growing more agitated, spittle tracked through the dirt on his chin as he tried to keep a bead on the druid and watch the boy, woman, and other man at the same time.

"Dirty little scoundrel pushed me into a cactus and damned near crippled my shootin' hand. I think it must have been poisonous and I'm imaginatin you. One minute I was all alone, then you're standing there threatening my life. My head's all abuzz, and I'm seeing things."

"What makes you think you're hallucinating?"

Sheb emitted a shrill wolf whistle. "Cause that there's the purtiest woman I've ever laid eyes on and no way would someone like *her* be out here with an ugly cuss like *you*."

"I say, Raurk, what's all the commotion?" Magried Whittlebottom said. He clanked toward Sheb. "All this shooting woke me up. I guess I sleep like the dead." He chuckled at his own joke.

Sheb's revolver shook in his hand. "That there's a walkin', talkin' skeleton. Keep it away from me!"

"Nay, guv'nor, I'm an air-pirate. Pleased to meet you." Whittlebottom bowed. "Taznakie raised me and me crew from the grave. I've been having such a wonderful time. We visited a dragon, and she laid a clutch of eggs while we were there. Her daughter, Rilieann, will replace her when the time comes."

Sheb gawked. "I ain't hearin' this." He clapped his hands over his eyes. "There ain't no such thing as air-pirates. And my idea of a dragon is a white-lightning' hangover."

"Oh, I say." Whittlebottom advanced toward Sheb. "This is real, isn't it?" He poked the man in the chest then chucked him under the nose.

Sheb backed up and wiped his hand across his face, nearly ripping his nose off with the revolver. "Son-of-a-bitch, get away from me!" He aimed the gun toward the pirate.

"Stop." Raurk raised his hand slowly to calm Sheb. "Take it easy, mister. I assure you, you aren't hallucina—"

He was cut off by the thunder of the Colt .45. "Lord almighty, deliver me!" Sheb screamed, dancing in a circle. "Snakes. I hate snakes. Help." He whirled to run and tripped over his own feet. He landed in the sand, face down, whimpering.

Three giant snakes slithered toward Sheb's prone body. The fourth, Grig's guardian, Tsunami, coiled about his neck and down his back.

"Call them off," Raurk said. "This man's more threat to himself than anyone else." He turned his back and walked away in disgust.

❧ 52 ❧

Urania stroked the gilt edge of the dais where the Light of Ishram lay. The warding spell flared and the book opened of its own accord. She jerked away, as if burned. With the thrill of the forbidden, she searched the small room. Was someone there? For a moment, she thought she saw a strange gerrub, but that couldn't be. She shook her head, wondering what was behind this sudden change.

The door remained half-closed, just as she'd left it. Urania approached and pulled it toward her. The Eunuch Watcher, Lorca, sat at the writing desk, exactly where she'd left him. While she watched, he bent his head closer to the parchment, better to see the words in front of him.

"Lorca?"

"Yes," he answered, not looking up.

"Nothing." She pushed the door closed with a barely audible click. The Light beckoned. Did she dare read it? She ran her hands through her hair, noticing that her ears were tender to the touch. "Do you finally grant me access to your secrets?"

Her breath came in short gasps. Her heart raced, and she placed her hand over it to feel the solid beat. The power of the Light beckoned to her. She'd waited so long for this moment. Had the time finally come? She searched the room again, confirming she was alone.

Urania approached one hesitant step, then backed away. The warding spell sparked blue and then green. She couldn't take her eyes from the book she longed to own. "Sweet Maker, is this an invitation?"

She paced back and forth, wondering what to do. "I've waited a lifetime for this. Will I rule chaos again?" She felt faint with anticipation.

Gathering her resolve around her like a mantle, Urania approached. Bending over the book, she read:

Nancy K. Harmon

And the Lord God commanded the man, "You are free to eat from any tree in the garden; but you must not eat from the tree of the knowledge of good and evil, for when you eat of it you will surely die."

Mesmerized, she leaned closer, barely brushing the Light. Thunder rolled through the small room, lightning flashed. Jagged ice crystals plunged from the ceiling. Wind ripped the air from her lungs. Urania screamed and fell to the floor.

❧ 53 ❧

Raurk gauged the sun and sighed. The noon hour fast approached with no sign of Grig Dothrie or the Jeeter twins. He found it difficult to believe Sheb's accusations of murder. "Where are you, my friend? We shall fail without you." He raised his hand to shade his eyes.

Taznakie had bound the raving Sheb, and then deposited the smelly lout next to the fire. Much to Raurk's relief, he'd fallen silent when Tsunami wound around his knees. The other guardians returned to their walking stick appearance, but without Grig's presence, Tsunami must remain as a serpent.

Every time the cowboy glanced toward Whittlebottom, he hung his head and shivered. "You ain't natural, bugger," Sheb yelled, spraying spit down the front of his dirt-caked shirt.

Raurk squatted next to the fire. When Sheb refused to look at him, the druid yanked a tuft of greasy hair upward to get his attention. "Are you sure you don't know where they are?"

Sheb spit, barely missing the druid. "I wouldn't tell you nuttin' even if I did know. You'll probably eat my soul for dinner anyway, so don't go 'specting me to spill my guts." He gave a lascivious glance toward Lillith. "Lessen that purty lady over there was to ask real nice." He gave a vulgar wink and hawked another giant goober into the sand.

"Mind your manners, Sheb Matthews, lest I do something we both regret." Raurk wrenched the cowboy's head to the side. "That woman is my wife and I don't take kindly to your insinuations. Do you understand?"

Sheb squawked. "What'd you go and do that for? I was just funnin' ya. Can't ya take a joke?"

"No." Raurk stood and turned away.

"I've heard all about you druids," Sheb called. "Daddy and me run a fella out of town once 'cause he was casting the evil eye at my momma. I'll do the same to you and those other freaks when I get loose from here."

Raurk sighed. "Happy as a groat wallowing in pig shit," he muttered.

"What?" Lillith asked.

"Nothing, my love. Our visitor has no idea how to find Grig." He eyed the cup in her hand. "Where are you going with that?"

Lillith gave him a one-armed hug. "The man may be our prisoner. And he may be dumb as a troll, but we still need to provide for his needs. I'm surprised he hasn't demanded to be released to take care of . . . personal needs."

Raurk looked back to the grungy cowboy. "From the smell of him, I don't think that's a problem. Just give him the water. I'm tired of his hysterics."

"Excuse, me, guv'nor," Whittlebottom said. "I believe there's something going on just over there." He pointed toward the mass of boiling, bruised clouds bearing down on their camp.

"Lillith," Raurk bellowed. "Gather whatever you can and join me. Taznakie, release Sheb."

"Rarumph?" Taznakie pointed toward the bound Sheb.

"No, don't knock him cold. I'll restrain him until we're clear."

"What about me," Dannel yelled over the rising wind.

"Help Lillith. We don't have much time."

᠂ ◆ ᠂

"Sweet Maker, what *is* that?" Grig pointed to the churning clouds. Rain ran down his face in rivulets. Wind whipped around him.

"Tornado!" Zeke screamed. He ran for the hostrichs and tossed a set of reins to Ezra. "Mister Grig, we gotta get out of here." He whipped his mount into a frenzied gallop followed by his brother—and Goliath.

Grig couldn't take his gaze from the approaching disaster. Howling wind ripped the ten-gallon hat from his head. For a moment he thought it would tear his clothes from his back. Rain blurred his sight, still he made no move.

Lightning assaulted him from all directions. The earth moved beneath his feet, and Grig knew he was going to die.

⪼ **54** ⪻

Light . . . confusion . . . and there was that damned gerrub again. The sound of someone pounding on the door battered at Urania Braith. Her brain recoiled at the sight of the Light of Ishram hanging above her.

"Urania, are you all right? What's going on?" Lorca called.

She heard the words, but couldn't put meaning to them. She levered herself upward on one hand. "My head." She wiped a trickle of blood from her mouth with the back of her hand.

"Urania, answer me."

"Stop that infernal racket, Lorca, before I . . ." Her mind wandered before she finished the sentence.

What was that banging? She searched the room, her eyes coming to rest on the Light. Then she remembered. She'd leaned closer to read. Then what?

Urania struggled to her knees, grasping the chair leg to steady herself. "I had no idea." The pounding at the door ceased. At last, she could think. Her ears hurt and she was having trouble focusing, something was wrong with her eyes. She swallowed the acid taste rising in her throat and shook her head to clear the haze.

She had to read more. Greed and longing consumed her. Power . . . the Light would give her power to wreck havoc again. With trepidation, she approached. "You've failed, Raurk. You're too late." A harsh laugh escaped her lips. "The Light of Ishram bends to my will."

The words on the page blurred. She blinked several times. "Don't touch it" she whispered. After a moment, she could make out the writing.

> *"Now the serpent was more crafty than any of the wild animals the Lord God had made. He said to the woman, "Did God really say, 'You must not eat from any tree in the garden.'?"*

The woman said to the serpent, "We may eat fruit from the trees in the garden, but God did say, 'You must not eat fruit from the tree that is in the middle of the garden, and you must not touch it, or you will die.'"

"You will not surely die," the serpent said to the woman. "For God knows that when you eat of it your eyes will be opened, and you will be like God, knowing good and evil."

Urania had no idea how long she stood there. "What does it mean?" Her tongue felt foreign in her mouth. "What's happening to me?"

"Urania, open the door. They're here," Lorca said.

"Yes, I must open the door." She stumbled, not sure where she was going.

"Do you hear me? Raurk is coming."

She pulled the door toward her. "Bring me an apple from the garden." She smiled vacantly at Lorca. "The Light of Ishram is mine."

Lorca backed away. "Didn't you hear me? Raurk is almost here. He's about to enter the Garden of Eden. And you want an apple?"

She licked her lips and smiled. "I heard you. Now—bring me my apple. I would have knowledge."

"Urania . . ."

"What is it, you fool?"

Lorca's eyes grew large. "Have you . . . have you looked in the mirror?"

❧ **55** ❧

"**Raurk**, I can't hold on," Dannel screamed. Wind ripped at the travelers.

"Just a little longer. The storm is almost past. Already the rain lessens." The druid hoped he was right. None of them could survive this onslaught if it didn't abate soon.

"Yargo." Taznakie pointed skyward.

A patch of blue flickered against the dark and then spread across the horizon like blood dripping into a barrel of water. The howling wind subsided to a gentle breeze. A lone, bedraggled figure staggered toward them.

"Grig Dothrie!" Dannel pelted toward him. He threw himself into the elf's arms and sobbed. "We thought you were lost. Raurk said we couldn't go on without you. We've waited ever so long and then a huge storm came up and Whittlebottom was nearly swept away."

"Young man, compose yourself," Grig said. But he hugged the lad to his chest. "I never thought I'd see any of you again."

Taznakie hit the pair with full force. He tossed Grig into the air, then laughed and cried at the same time. "Geres orble."

"I'm sure Master Grig is glad to see you as well," Raurk said. He waited with Lillith to welcome the straggler back into their fold.

"Look out," Grig said. "That man's insane. He tried to kill me." He pointed to the dazed Sheb Matthews staggering toward them.

Sheb drew his gun, glanced at the travelers and bolted. "Don't try to follow me, any of you," he yelled over his shoulder, blasting into the air with the .45. The desert swallowed him without a trace.

The worlds shifted again as they watched. A verdant forest stretched to the horizon. Towering mountains wreathed in snow lay ahead. In the distance, a castle brooded in a deep valley. "The Garden of Eden," Raurk said.

∂⊱ ◆ ⊰∾

The travelers huddled in a burned-out mill. The giant grinding stones lay about in broken pieces. Centuries of dust, turned to mortar with the daily rains, had settled in a thick blanket across everything. Abandoned bird nests clogged the gears of the waterwheel and rodents scurried away in fright.

Grig watched another flock of brightly colored birds lift into the air and fly from Urania's castle. "Where are they going?" The rumble of falling stone from the castle's south turret drew his attention. "The witch's warding spells grow weak. I can taste the rot of them."

"I feel it, too," Raurk said. "But don't let that deceive you. It could be another of Urania's schemes."

"That doesn't make any sense." Lillith followed the flock with her gaze.

Raurk shrugged. "The garden is dying. The animals flee while they can."

"Would Urania destroy her own home?" Grig watched a herd of small, four-legged creatures bound through the garden.

"I don't know," Raurk said. "She's capable of anything."

"Wow, look at the buzzards." Dannel pointed toward a dilapidated structure across the valley. "Is that where they keep the dragons?"

Raurk nodded. "Judging by the size of it, I'd say yes."

The wind shifted and brought the stench of rotted flesh to their hiding place. Lillith blanched at the smell. "That explains the scavengers. Do you think someone killed the dragons?"

"Where will the birds go?" Dannel asked. "Can they cross between worlds as we did?"

"Let's hope so." Raurk started as a knot of noisy birds darted through the rafters overhead. "Anywhere away from Urania and her valley has to be an improvement."

Grig watched as if in deep thought. "If the garden is dying, how far will the destruction spread? Can the birds fly far enough to escape?"

"I hadn't given it any thought," Raurk pondered. "Urania destroys what she can't control. I don't know what her game is, but we daren't underestimate her."

"Look." Lillith pointed to a darkly dressed figure emerging from the castle. "Is that Urania?"

"No." Raurk shook his head. "It's difficult to tell from this distance, but I'd say it's Lorca, her Eunuch Watcher. I feel sorry for the poor man. He's at her beck and call and she's proved to be a cruel mistress."

"Why doesn't he just leave?" Lillith gasped as Lorca looked directly toward their shelter. "Does he know we're here? Will he tell her?"

"I don't have an answer to your questions." Raurk sighed and turned away.

"What's he doing?" Dannel pointed toward the Watcher.

Lillith stared in disbelief. "He's picking sapples."

Raurk turned back to watch in fascination. "No, my love. Those are true apples from the Garden of Eden. Probably the only ones left in all the known worlds."

Grig clutched at the druid's sleeve. "Is that Whittlebottom? What's he doing? He'll give us away. You should never have trusted him."

"Damn him!" Raurk spied the pirate sneaking up behind Lorca. "When did he leave?"

They watched the air-pirate casually stroll up to Lorca from behind and tap him on the shoulder. The Watcher dropped his basket in surprise and faced Whittlebottom. An animated conversation with much gesturing ensued. At last, the pirate nodded toward the mill. Lorca backed away into the arms of Taznakie.

"I think you've lost control, Raurk," Lillith said.

"It was never mine to lose." The druid watched, as spellbound as the others.

Taznakie twisted Lorca's arm behind his back and half-dragged, half-marched the Watcher toward the ramshackle mill.

"What do we do now?" Grig asked.

Raurk sighed. "Unless you have a better suggestion, we wait."

❧ 56 ❧

Her head ached and Urania felt like her body burned from within. She staggered from her bedroom, glad to see Lorca was nowhere about. The Light of Ishram had transformed her, but did she really want to witness those changes?

"I say, luv, you look like hell." A strange voice said from behind her. "What *have* you done to yourself? I'd sue my hairdresser if I were you."

Urania whirled to locate the intruder. "Who are you?" She shook her head, attempting to clear the fog from her thoughts. "How did you get in?"

"Oh, that." Whittlebottom waved a dismissive hand. "That nice chap, Lorca, pointed out the most expedient way to enter undetected. The lad was a bit persnickety, but we persuaded him it was in his best interest to cooperate."

Indecision flooded Urania's mind. "Lorca betrayed me?"

"Aye, that he did, luv."

"I don't believe you. He's always been my most loyal servant." She staggered to the hallway door and yanked it open. "Lorca, show your-self before I . . ."

"Lorca's flown the coup, luv. Hmm, I believe that's how the saying goes."

"You lie. Lorca would never desert me." She stalked with uneven steps toward the pirate, but he easily avoided her grasp.

"You repeat yourself, Urania. Now, about Lorca. He spilled his guts. He can't wait to get the hell out of your clutches. His words, not mine." Whittlebottom raised a glass of wine to the light. "I really do miss little things like this." He held the goblet under where his nose should have been. "Ah, a wonderful vintage. Did your vineyards do the bottling?""

Urania slapped the glass from his hand. "You insane fool! I should blast you to hell."

"But you won't," Whittlebottom said, half turning his back to the witch.

"You dare turn your back on me?" She seized the skeleton by the shoulder to turn him about.

"That's not a wise move, luv. I've beheaded men for lesser offences."

Urania gave a ruthless laugh. "You can't hurt me, pirate. *I* command the Light of Ishram."

"Who commands whom?" He eyed her skeptically.

"I'll show you," she hissed.

"Save your energy, luv." He cupped Urania's elbow in his bony grip. "You have more to worry about than a derelict air-pirate. Come look in the mirror. Lorca told us your . . . uh . . . appearance had altered." Whittlebottom guided her toward the fireplace. "I didn't believe him at first, but I *do* think you frightened him."

"Nonsense." She jerked her arm away and backed toward the bedchamber. "I haven't changed. Nothing's changed. I still own the Light of Ishram. Raurk is powerless to take it from me."

"Oh, my. Your poor mother." Whittlebottom followed her. "To have birthed such an abomination must have been very traumatic." He picked imaginary lint from her collar.

"I'm as normal as you—or anyone else."

"You mean to tell me you've always had eyes like a serpent's?"

"You lie!" She tried to push him away, but lost her balance.

The pirate steadied her. "Time to get a grip, Urania. Look in the mirror if you don't believe me. Oh my, what's this? Lorca didn't mention the scales around your temples before. Or . . . maybe those are new . . ."

"Out of my way, pirate!" She rushed to the mirror. "No, no, no!"

Whittlebottom eased through the French doors onto the balcony. "She's all yours, Raurk. Please exercise caution, her confusion won't last forever."

☙ ◆ ❧

Urania lay on the floor, her body curled around the dais, heaving dry tears. "What have you done to me?" she wailed, and pulled at her hair. The mirror had revealed more than she wanted to know.

The yellow, diamond-shaped irises of a viper had stared back at her. Her beautiful lavender eyes were gone. Her perfect, shell-like ears had vanished, replaced by small holes at each side of her head. But the most disturbing transformation was the beginning of a forked tongue.

The warding spell crackled and showered her with acid green sparks. "What have you done to me?" she repeated, rising to her feet on wobbly legs. "I've waited four thousand years to unlock your secrets. You can't destroy me."

Urania lunged at the Light and missed. The dais teetered precariously and righted itself. "Stop! Stop!" she screamed, clapping her hands over her ear holes. She staggered and nearly fell. "The pain—it's too much!"

❧ 57 ❧

Raurk rested in an oversized chair, one of a pair flanking the fireplace. He cradled the ancient book of poetry in his hands, open to the familiar lines of *Dreamscapes*. "At last, I understand." He ran his fingers over the page.

Across the room, Lorca sat at his desk. "This is insane, waiting for Urania in her own chambers. She's been closed in with the Light for days. How do you know she hasn't harnessed its power?"

Raurk looked up as the rumble of falling stones shook the floor. "Did you make sure all the servants have left? The castle crumbles around our ears. I don't want anyone else to get hurt."

"Yes, of course. I spoke to the dragon master before you arrived and he refused to leave before destroying the last female and her eggs."

"I take it that's what drew the scavengers."

"Yes, their loyalty belonged to Urania and he didn't want them loosed upon the world." Lorca stood up and paced. "How can she not know we're here? When is she coming out?"

"I have no idea."

"What kind of siege is this? Why did you bring so many if all you're going to do is sit here and wait?" He stopped to glare out the window. "What if she doesn't come out?" His words barely carried to Raurk. "What will you do then?"

"Then we'll find a way to lure her out. But I don't think that'll be necessary."

Lorca turned to glare at the druid. "How can you be so calm? Urania will see all of us dead before she gives up the Light of Ishram, and you just sit there reading a book."

"If you fear for your life, leave now. We'll manage without you." Raurk closed the book and stood. "There's nothing here to hold you."

The Watcher sighed, running a hand over his eyes. "I'd be crazy not to fear for my life. I've spent years wondering when she'd grow tired of me, and strike the final blow." He fingered the cut below his right ear. "She'll slaughter me before you can move. I know her too well."

Raurk nodded and waited for Lorca to continue.

"What do you want from me?" The Watcher sank into his chair.

"A commitment. Nothing more."

❧ ◆ ❧

Urania burned with fever. Sick and disoriented, she pulled open the door to her bedchamber. The rumble of voices from the outer chamber confused her. "Who's there?" she croaked. "Lorca, where are you? Bring me chilled wine."

Lorca froze. "What should I do?" he mouthed.

"Whatever you please, but lure her to you," Raurk answered.

"Blast her to hell while you can," Grig muttered. He stood just out of sight behind the window tapestries.

"Quiet," Raurk hissed. Silently, he beckoned to Lorca. "Don't delay."

Lorca swallowed bile and took a deep breath. "What do you want, Urania? I'm leaving. The castle is falling into ruins."

"Don't leave me," she whined. "I'm burning up. I need wine. Bring it in here." She blundered into the dressing table and nearly fell. "Hurry, you fool, I feel like I'm on fire."

"Get it yourself." Lorca's voice quivered, but he stood his ground. "I *said* I was leaving."

Urania crashed against the door, splintering the rotting wood. "You sniveling jackanapes, I told you to bring me wine!" She staggered into the room, raised a hand to cast a spell at the Watcher.

"I wouldn't do that if I were you," Raurk said.

"You . . . . What are you doing here?" She glared at the druid and then turned on Lorca. "Why didn't you warn me?"

Grig stepped from his hiding place. "I'd listen to Raurk if I were you."

Urania shook her head. "What . . . ?" Confused, she clawed at her hair, coming away with handfuls of her ebony locks. For long moments she simply stared. "This is your fault, Lorca. Get them out of here." She turned toward her bedchamber.

"Stop where you are," Grig spat.

She turned back in slow motion and pinned her snake-like gaze on the elf. "You have no power over me." Urania suddenly lunged toward Lorca.

"Stop her! Stop her!" Lorca screamed.

Grig's arms flew into the air. "Raldux rendalix servitious german cleetus." The healing web covered Urania in ironclad cords.

She tore at the snare searing her flesh. "Get it off me," she whimpered. Blisters festered and burst on her arms. A wisp of bitter smoke tainted the air.

"In a moment," Raurk said. He opened the book in his lap. "I want you to listen to something first. Do you remember the poem, *Dreamscapes*? It appears to have undergone a transformation in the past couple of hours. I always wondered why it was so important even though neither of us understood its meaning."

Her head jerked up. "No . . ." A mewl escaped her lips.

"Let me see," Raurk flipped through the pages. "Yes, here it is. I'll give you the short version. There's much more.

'But Jesus called the children to him and said, "Let the little children come to me, and do not hinder them, for the kingdom of God belongs to such as these."'

Urania Braith screamed and slumped to the floor, writing in agony. "No more," she sobbed. "You're killing me."

"'Tis about time someone gave her what for," Whittlebottom said. "Sorry I'm late. I was convincing some silly wench to get out while she could. I found her hiding in one of the ground floor apartments." He glanced at Urania. "Oh, I say, have I missed all the fun?"

"It's about over." Grig answered. He turned to Lorca. "Shall we put an end to the witch?"

The Eunuch Watcher shook his head, striding to his former tormentor. He lifted his foot and placed it across her neck, but didn't lower his weight. He stood motionless weighing his options. "No," he said. "Leave her be." Giving a violent shudder, he turned away. "She's not worth it."

"That's it?" Grig glanced from Lorca to Raurk. "I thought we'd have a huge battle on our hands."

Raurk shrugged. "The Light of Ishram has done most of the work for us."

"So, we just waltz in, take the book and then leave?" Grig searched the room with his gaze. "This is too easy."

"Our work here isn't done," Raurk rose to his feet. "Taznakie, bring Dannel and Lillith."

⤳ ◆ ⤶

Dannel entered the room on tiptoe. "Is she dead? I've never seen a dead person before." He stopped to gawk at the prone figure of Urania Braith.

Raurk shook his head. "She's not dead."

"What's wrong with her? She looks like a snake."

"I'll explain later. For now, I'd like you to set Sprite to guard her. Then we'll finish here and be gone."

"Yes, sir." Dannel's natural exuberance deserted him. He placed the walking stick on the floor and imagined the giant serpent it would become.

"Are you sure this is a good idea?" Lillith eyed her brother. "He's just a child."

"That's the point." Raurk hugged her quickly and then turned to Dannel.

"Let one of the others retrieve the Light of Ishram," she said. "I'll stay here with Dannel."

"Sorry, my love. That won't work. Dannel and Taznakie must enter the chamber and bring the book to us. Then, I should be able to handle it."

He gave the boy an encouraging smile. "Are you up to the task, young man?"

"Yes, sir." Dannel nodded. "Come on, Taznakie." He took the big man's hand. "Promise you'll wait for us right outside the door."

"We all promise," Grig said. He delivered a resounding hug and then turned away, wiping his eyes. "I guess my part's done for now."

Dannel took tentative steps into the secret chamber. His eyes rested upon the Light of Ishram and a wide smile spread across his boyish face. He didn't notice Tanus crouched in the corner. "I've come for you," he whispered.

A golden glow flooded the small chamber the moment Dannel crossed the threshold. The warm scent of summer suffused the air.

"I think it likes you," Taznakie said.

Dannel stopped and drew back to look at his companion in surprise. "I understood you."

"I . . . Uh . . . It's about time." Taznakie breathed a sigh of relief. "Let's get this over with." He motioned toward the Light.

"All right. Will it hurt?"

"I don't think so," Taznakie answered. "Go on. I'm right here with you."

Dannel reached with a cautious finger toward the Light of Ishram. Birdsong and the scent of flowers filled the room. Dannel's face lit with an angelic light. "Yes," he said. "I'll take you home."

The book's pages closed as if blown by a gentle breeze and the warding spell pulsed golden. Dannel placed both hands on the cover. "Taznakie it's too heavy, help me."

"Are you all right, in there?" Lillith's voce edged on panic.

Dannel appeared in the doorway with Taznakie helping to support the Light. "Take it, Raurk. I want to go home."

"This will protect it." The druid placed the book into a large silk bag embroidered with runes. "The sooner we deal with Urania Braith, the better."

☙ ◆ ❧

"She's gone," Lillith shrieked. "Where's Sprite? He was supposed to watch her."

"There," Raurk said, pointing at the still form of the guardian.

"Sprite!" Dannel cried. "What'd she do to him?" He held the inert serpent for Raurk to examine. "I think he's dead."

"Find the witch," Raurk bellowed. "We've got to stop her."

Grig poked the empty gown ensnared in his healing web with his staff. An asp slithered toward him at lightning speed. "Get away," he shrieked.

"Kill it!" Dannel shouted. "That's Urania."

Taznakie lurched at the snake but was too late to stop it from dropping to the garden below.

Grig bolted to the balcony. "I don't see her." He turned to the druid. "Look, Tanus is following her. Should I go too? Maybe I could . . ."

"No, you'd be in her element." Raurk said. "You don't stand a chance."

"Are you sure? Let Taznakie go with me."

"My stupidity has further endangered the known worlds," Raurk said with a sigh. "I'll go after Urania Braith, but not today. We must return the Light of Ishram to its proper place."

-Epilogue-

Grig zapped the last poisonous Nemrak vine from his tree house and brushed his hands together. "That'll do it." It'd taken him a month, but at last he could occupy his former home in safety.

"Look what I found." Taznakie pushed open the door. In his arms, he carried Was-he and Was-nt, Grig's male gerrubs. Close upon his heels, the spectral Tanus, nipped and hissed at the boys.

"Where did you find them?" He nuzzled his old friends with a sad smile while Tanus watched half-in, half-out the door.

"They came in last night with the washerwoman. It was so late she didn't want to disturb you. Another family from down the road returned this morning. Word has spread that the village returns to normal. I cleared the well this morning. We have pure water again."

"I'm glad." Grig placed two large slabs of butter on a leaf for the gerrubs. "This is the first time I've seen Tanus since we got home."

Taznakie nodded his head. "I think she stayed behind with Malie until now. I'm glad she showed up. I think she'll be around a long time."

"Maybe . . ." Grig surveyed his home.

"What is it?" Taznakie followed the elf's gaze.

Grig shrugged. "Have you wondered why it didn't take as long to get home as it should have? Did Raurk lead us on a wild goose chase initially?"

Taznakie hand-fed another slice of butter to each of the gerrubs. "I don't think so."

"Then what?" Grig slammed his fist on the table. "Our lives will never be the same."

"Aye, 'tis true." Taznakie imitated the druid. "Raurk said we each had our part to play, but we had to be prepared to play them. Perhaps it was the journey that made us ready."

"Aye," Grig slumped into a chair. "Will you accompany Raurk when he goes after Urania again?"

Taznakie sighed. "Probably. What about you?"

"If I know Raurk, he'll leave us no choice." He looked up to Taznakie and smiled. "At least I'll have one companion I can trust."

The End

About the Author

Nancy K.
Harmon

At the age of eight, Nancy discovered the school library and became an avid reader. Science Fiction and Fantasy became her favorite genres as a young adult, but she still reads nearly everything she gets her hands on, including the labels on cereal boxes.

The Light of Ishram came about as a result of her son, Jason's, fourth grade English assignment. He had to write a short story with the aid of a parent, and the characters of Grig Dothrie and Theron Raurk were born.

Twenty-plus years later, after many modifications, hair pulling, and a huge learning curve, the short story has become an epic tale. Nancy's second book, "The Tower of Babel" is under construction.

Nancy devotes her time to reading, writing, and crafts. She lives with her husband and the current feline princess of the household, Marble.

Jason, 4th Grade

Also from Pen-L Publishing

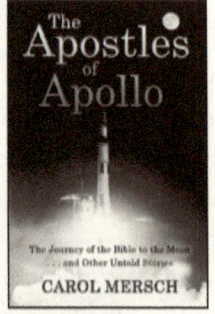

Visit Pen-L.com for more great books!